War of the Wolf

BOOKS BY BERNARD CORNWELL

1356

THE FORT

AGINCOURT

Nonfiction

WATERLOO

The Saxon Tales

THE LAST KINGDOM

THE PALE HORSEMAN

THE LORDS OF THE NORTH

SWORD SONG

THE BURNING LAND

DEATH OF KINGS

THE PAGAN LORD

THE EMPTY THRONE

WARRIORS OF THE STORM

THE FLAME BEARER

The Sharpe Novels (in chronological order)

SHARPE'S GOLD
Richard Sharpe and the
Destruction of Almeida,
August 1810

SHARPE'S ESCAPE
Richard Sharpe and the
Bussaco Campaign,
1810

SHARPE'S FURY
Richard Sharpe and
the Battle of Barrosa,
March 1811

SHARPE'S BATTLE
Richard Sharpe
and the Battle of
Fuentes de Onoro,
May 1811

SHARPE'S COMPANY
Richard Sharpe and
the Siege of Badajoz,
January to April 1812

SHARPE'S SWORD
Richard Sharpe and the
Salamanca Campaign,
June and July 1812

SHARPE'S ENEMY
Richard Sharpe and the
Defense of Portugal,
Christmas 1812

SHARPE'S HONOR
Richard Sharpe and
the Vitoria Campaign,
February to June 1813

SHARPE'S REGIMENT
Richard Sharpe and the
Invasion of France,
June to November 1813

SHARPE'S SIEGE
Richard Sharpe and the
Winter Campaign, 1814

SHARPE'S REVENGE
Richard Sharpe and the
Peace of 1814

SHARPE'S WATERLOO
Richard Sharpe and the
Waterloo Campaign,
15 June to 18 June 1815

SHARPE'S DEVIL
Richard Sharpe and the
Emperor, 1820–1821

War of the Wolf

A Novel

Bernard Cornwell

An Imprint of HarperCollins*Publishers*

Originally published in Great Britain in 2018 by HarperCollins Publishers.

Map © John Gilkes 2018

FIRST HARPERLUXE EDITION

ISBN: 978-0-06-286442-0

HarperLuxe™ is a trademark of HarperCollins Publishers.

Library of Congress Cataloging-in-Publication Data is available upon request.

18 19 20 21 22 ID/LSC 10 9 8 7 6 5 4 3 2 1

War of the Wolf
is dedicated to the memory of
Toby Eady,
my agent and dear friend.
1941–2017

Contents

Place Names

The spelling of place names in ninth- and tenth-century Britain was an uncertain business, with no consistency and no agreement even about the name itself. Thus London was variously rendered as Lundonia, Lundenberg, Lundenne, Lundene, Lundenwic, Lundenceaster, and Lundres. Doubtless some readers will prefer other versions of the names listed below, but I have usually employed whichever spelling is cited in either the *Oxford Dictionary of English Place-Names* or the *Cambridge Dictionary of English Place-Names* for the years nearest or contained within Alfred's reign, AD 871–899, but even that solution is not foolproof. Hayling Island, in 956, was written as both Heilincigae and Hæglingaiggæ. Nor have I been consistent myself; I have preferred the modern form Northumbria to Norðhymbralond to avoid the suggestion that the boundaries of the ancient kingdom coincide with those of the modern county. So this list, like the spellings themselves, is capricious.

Bebbanburg	Bamburgh, Northumberland
Berewic	Berwick on Tweed, Northumberland
Brunanburh	Bromborough, Cheshire
Cair Ligualid	Carlisle, Cumbria
Ceaster	Chester, Cheshire
Cent	Kent
Contwaraburg	Canterbury, Kent
Dunholm	Durham, County Durham
Dyflin	Dublin, Eire
Eoferwic	York, Yorkshire (Saxon name)
Fagranforda	Fairford, Gloucestershire
Farnea Islands	Farne Islands, Northumberland
Gleawecestre	Gloucester, Gloucestershire
Heagostealdes	Hexham, Northumberland
Heahburh (fictional name)	Whitley Castle, Alston, Cumbria
Hedene	River Eden, Cumbria
Huntandun	Huntingdon, Cambridgeshire
Hwite	Whitchurch, Shropshire
Irthinam	River Irthing
Jorvik	York, Yorkshire (Danish/Norse name)

Lindcolne	Lincoln, Lincolnshire
Lindisfarena	Lindisfarne (Holy Island), Northumberland
Lundene	London
Mædlak	River Medlock, Lancashire
Mærse	River Mersey
Mameceaster	Manchester
Monez	Anglesey, Wales
Ribbel	River Ribble, Lancashire
Ribelcastre	Ribchester, Lancashire
Snæland	Iceland
Spura (fictional name)	Birdoswald Roman fort, Cumbria
Sumorsæte	Somerset
Tamweorthin	Tamworth, Staffordshire
Temes	River Thames
Tine	River Tyne
Usa	River Ouse, Yorkshire
Wevere	River Weaver, Cheshire
Wiltunscir	Wiltshire
Wintanceaster	Winchester, Hampshire
Wirhealum	The Wirral, Cheshire

PART ONE

The Wild Lands

One

I did not go to Æthelflaed's funeral.

    She was buried in Gleawecestre in the same vault as her husband, whom she had hated.

Her brother, King Edward of Wessex, was chief mourner and, when the rites were done and Æthelflaed's corpse had been walled up, he stayed in Gleawecestre. His sister's strange banner of the holy goose was lowered over the palace, and the dragon of Wessex was hoisted in its place. The message could not have been plainer. Mercia no longer existed. In all the British lands south of Northumbria and east of Wales there was only one kingdom and one king. Edward sent me a summons, demanding I travel to Gleawecestre and swear fealty to him for the lands I owned in what had been Mercia, and the summons bore his name followed by the words

Anglorum Saxonum Rex. King of the Angles and the Saxons. I ignored the document.

Within a year a second document reached me, this one signed and sealed in Wintanceaster. By the grace of God, it told me, the lands granted to me by Æthelflaed of Mercia were now forfeited to the bishopric of Hereford, which, the parchment assured me, would employ said lands to the furtherance of God's glory. "Meaning Bishop Wulfheard will have more silver to spend on his whores," I told Eadith.

"Maybe you should have gone to Gleawecestre?" she suggested.

"And swear loyalty to Edward?" I spat the name. "Never. I don't need Wessex and Wessex doesn't need me."

"So what will you do about the estates?" she asked.

"Nothing," I said. What could I do? Go to war against Wessex? It annoyed me that Bishop Wulfheard, an old enemy, had taken the land, but I had no need of Mercian lands. I owned Bebbanburg. I was a Northumbrian lord, and owned all that I wanted. "Why should I do anything?" I growled at Eadith. "I'm old and I don't need trouble."

"You're not old," she said loyally.

"I'm old," I insisted. I was over sixty, I was ancient.

"You don't look old."

"So Wulfheard can plow his whores and let me die in peace. I don't care if I never see Wessex or Mercia ever again."

Yet a year later I was in Mercia, mounted on Tintreg, my fiercest stallion, and wearing a helmet and mail, with Serpent-Breath, my sword, slung at my left hip. Rorik, my servant, carried my heavy iron-rimmed shield, and behind us were ninety men, all armed, and all mounted on war horses.

"Sweet Jesus," Finan said beside me. He was gazing at the enemy in the valley beneath us. "Four hundred of the bastards?" He paused. "At least four hundred. Maybe five?"

I said nothing.

It was late on a winter's afternoon, and bitterly cold. The horses' breath misted among the leafless trees that crowned the gentle ridge from where we watched our enemy. The sun was sinking and hidden by clouds, which meant no betraying sparks of light could be reflected from our mail or weapons. Away to my right, to the west, the River Dee lay flat and gray as it widened toward the sea. On the lower ground in front of us was the enemy and, beyond them, Ceaster.

"Five hundred," Finan decided.

"I never thought I'd see this place again," I said. "Never wanted to see it again."

"They broke the bridge," Finan said, peering far to the south.

"Wouldn't you, in their place?"

The place was Ceaster, and our enemy was besieging the city. Most of that enemy was to the east of the city, but smoking campfires betrayed plenty to the city's north. The River Dee flowed just south of the city walls, then turned north toward its widening estuary, and by breaking the central span of the ancient Roman bridge, the enemy had ensured that no relief force could come from the south. If the city's small garrison was to fight its way out of the trap they would need to come north or east where the enemy was strongest. And that garrison was small. I had been told, though it was nothing more than a guess, that fewer than a hundred men held the city.

Finan must have been thinking the same thing. "And five hundred men couldn't take the city?" he said derisively.

"Nearer six hundred?" I suggested mildly. It was hard to estimate the enemy because many of the folk in the besiegers' encampment were women and children, but I thought Finan's guess was low. Tintreg lowered his head and snorted. I patted his neck, then touched Serpent-Breath's hilt for luck. "I wouldn't want to assault those walls," I said. Ceaster's stone walls had been built by the Romans, and the Romans had built well. And the city's small garrison, I thought, had been well led. They had repelled the early assaults, and so the enemy had settled down to starve them out.

"So, what do we do?" Finan asked.

"Well, we've come a long way," I said.

"So?"

"So it seems a pity not to fight." I gazed at the city. "If what we were told is true, then the poor bastards in the city will be eating rats by now. And that lot?" I nodded down to the campfires. "They're cold, they're bored, and they've been here too long. They got bloodied when they attacked the walls, so now they're just waiting."

I could see the thick barricades that the besiegers had made outside Ceaster's northern and eastern gates. Those barricades would be guarded by the enemy's best troops, posted there to stop the garrison sallying out or trying to escape. "They're cold," I said again, "they're bored, and they're useless."

Finan smiled. "Useless?"

"They're mostly from the fyrd," I said. The fyrd is an army raised from field laborers, shepherds, common men. They might be brave, but a trained house-warrior, like the ninety who followed me, was far more lethal. "Useless," I said again, "and stupid."

"Stupid?" Berg, mounted on his stallion behind me, asked.

"No sentries out here! They should never have let us get this close. They have no idea we're here. And stupidity gets you killed."

"I like that they're stupid," Berg said. He was a Norseman, young and savage, frightened of nothing except the disapproval of his young Saxon wife.

"Three hours to sunset?" Finan suggested.

"Let's not waste them."

I turned Tintreg, going back through the trees to the road that led to Ceaster from the ford of the Mærse. The road brought back memories of riding to face Ragnall, and of Haesten's death, and now the road was leading me toward another fight.

Though we looked anything but threatening as we rode down the long, gentle slope. We did not hurry. We came like men who were finishing a long journey, which was true, and we kept our swords in their scabbards and our spears bundled on the packhorses led by our servants. The enemy must have seen us almost as soon as we emerged from the wooded ridge, but we were few and they were many, and our ambling approach suggested we came in peace. The high stone wall of the city was in shadow, but I could make out the banners hanging from the ramparts. They showed

Christian crosses, and I remembered Bishop Leofstan, a holy fool and a good man, who had been chosen as Ceaster's bishop by Æthelflaed. She had strengthened and garrisoned the city-fort as a bulwark against the Norse and Danes who crossed the Irish Sea to hunt for slaves in the Saxon lands.

Æthelflaed, Alfred's daughter, and ruler of Mercia. Dead now. Her corpse was decaying in a cold stone vault. I imagined her dead hands clutching a crucifix in the grave's foul darkness, and remembered those same hands clawing my spine as she writhed beneath me. "God forgive me," she would say, "don't stop!"

And now she had brought me back to Ceaster.

And Serpent-Breath was about to kill again.

Æthelflaed's brother ruled Wessex. He had been content to let his sister rule Mercia, but on her death he had marched West Saxon troops north across the Temes. They came, he said, to honor his sister at her funeral, but they stayed to impose Edward's rule on his sister's realm. Edward, *Anglorum Saxonum Rex*.

Those Mercian lords who bent their knee were rewarded, but some, a few, resented the West Saxons. Mercia was a proud land. There had been a time when the King of Mercia was the most powerful ruler of Britain, when the kings of Wessex and of East Anglia and the chieftains of Wales had sent tribute, when Mercia was the largest of all the British kingdoms. Then the Danes had come, and Mercia had fallen, and it had been Æthelflaed who had fought back, who had driven the pagans northward and built the burhs that protected her frontier. And she was dead, moldering, and her brother's troops now guarded the burh walls, and the King of Wessex called himself king of all the Saxons, and he demanded silver to pay for the garrisons, and he took land from the resentful lords and gave it to his own men, or to the church. Always to the church, because it was the priests who preached to the Mercian folk that it was their nailed god's will that Edward of Wessex be king in their land, and that to oppose the king was to oppose their god.

Yet fear of the nailed god did not prevent a revolt, and so the fighting had begun. Saxon against Saxon, Christian against Christian, Mercian against Mercian, and Mercian against West Saxon. The rebels fought under Æthelflaed's flag, declaring that it had been her will that her daughter, Ælfwynn, succeed her. Ælfwynn, Queen of Mercia! I liked Ælfwynn, but she could no more have ruled a kingdom than she could have speared a charging boar. She was flighty, frivolous, pretty, and petty. Edward, knowing his niece had been named to the throne, took care to have her shut away in a convent, along with his discarded wife, but still the rebels flaunted her mother's flag and fought in her name.

They were led by Cynlæf Haraldson, a West Saxon warrior whom Æthelflaed had wanted as a husband for Ælfwynn. The truth, of course, was that Cynlæf wanted to be King of Mercia himself. He was young, he was handsome, he was brave in battle, and, to my mind, stupid. His ambition was to defeat the West Saxons, rescue his bride from her convent, and be crowned.

But first he must capture Ceaster. And he had failed.

"It feels like snow," Finan said as we rode south toward the city.

"It's too late in the year for snow," I said confidently.

"I can feel it in my bones," he said, shivering. "It'll come by nightfall."

I scoffed at that. "Two shillings says it won't."

He laughed. "God send me more fools with silver! My bones are never wrong." Finan was Irish, my second-in-command, and my dearest friend. His face, framed by the steel of his helmet, looked lined and old, his beard was gray. Mine was too, I suppose. I watched as he loosened Soul-Stealer in her scabbard and as his eyes flicked across the smoke of the campfires ahead. "So what are we doing?" he asked.

"Scouring the bastards off the eastern side of the city," I said.

"They're thick there."

I guessed that almost two thirds of the enemy were camped on Ceaster's eastern flank. The campfires were dense there, burning between low shelters made of branches and turf. To the south of the crude shelters were a dozen lavish tents, placed close to the ruins of the old Roman arena, which, even though it had been used as a convenient quarry, still rose higher than the tents above which two flags hung motionless in the still air. "If Cynlæf's still here," I said, "he'll be in one of those tents."

"Let's hope the bastard's drunk."

"Or else he's in the arena," I said. The arena was built just outside the city and was a vast hulk of stone. Beneath its banked stone seating were cave-like rooms that, when I had last explored them, were home to wild dogs. "If he had any sense," I went on, "he'd have abandoned this siege. Left men to keep the garrison starving, and gone south. That's where the rebellion will be won or lost, not here."

"Does he have sense?"

"Daft as a turnip," I said, and then started laughing. A group of women burdened with firewood had stepped off the road to kneel as we passed, and they looked up at me in astonishment. I waved at them. "We're about to make some of them widows," I said, still laughing.

"And that's funny?"

I spurred Tintreg into a trot. "What's funny," I said, "is that we're two old men riding to war."

"You, maybe," Finan said pointedly.

"You're my age!"

"I'm not a grandfather!"

"You might be. You don't know."

"Bastards don't count."

"They do," I insisted.

"Then you're probably a great-grandfather by now."

I gave him a harsh look. "Bastards don't count," I snarled, making him laugh, then he made the sign of the cross because we had reached the Roman cemetery that stretched either side of the road. There were ghosts here, ghosts wandering between the lichen-covered stones with their fading inscriptions that only Christian priests who understood Latin could read. Years before, in a fit of zeal, a priest had started throwing down the stones, declaring they were pagan abominations. That very same day he was struck down dead and ever since the Christians had tolerated the graves, which, I thought, must be protected by the Roman gods. Bishop Leofstan had laughed when I told him that story, and had assured me that the Romans were good Christians. "It was our god, the one true god, who slew the priest," he had told me. Then Leofstan himself had died, struck down just as suddenly as the grave-hating priest. Wyrd bið ful āræd.

My men were strung out now, not quite in single file, but close. None wanted to ride too near the road's verges because that was where the ghosts gathered. The long, straggling line of horsemen made us vulnerable, but the enemy seemed oblivious to our threat. We passed more women, all bent beneath great burdens of firewood they had cut from spinneys north of the graves. The nearest campfires were close now. The afternoon's light was fading, though dusk was still an hour or more away. I could see men on the northern city wall, see their spears, and knew they must be watching us. They would think we were reinforcements come to help the besiegers.

I curbed Tintreg just beyond the old Roman cemetery to let my men catch up. The sight of the graves and thinking of Bishop Leofstan had brought back memories. "Remember Mus?" I asked Finan.

"Christ! How could anyone forget her?" He grinned. "Did you . . ." he began.

"Never. You?"

He shook his head. "Your son gave her a few good rides."

I had left my son in command of the troops garrisoning Bebbanburg. "He's a lucky boy," I said. Mus, her real name was Sunngifu, was small like a mouse, and had been married to Bishop Leofstan. "I wonder where Mus is now?" I asked. I was still gazing at Ceaster's northern wall, trying to estimate how many men stood guard on the ramparts. "More than I expected," I said.

"More?"

"Men on the wall," I explained. I could see at least forty men on the ramparts, and knew there must be just as many on the eastern wall, which faced the bulk of the enemy.

"Maybe they were reinforced?" Finan suggested.

"Or the monk was wrong, which wouldn't surprise me."

A monk had come to Bebbanburg with news of Ceaster's siege. We already knew of the Mercian rebellion, of course, and we had welcomed it. It was no secret that Edward, who now styled himself King of the Angles and Saxons, wanted to invade Northumbria and so make that arrogant title come true. Sigtryggr, my son-in-law and King of Northumbria, had been preparing for that invasion, fearing it too, and then came the news that Mercia was tearing itself apart, and that Edward, far from invading us, was fighting

to hold onto his new lands. Our response was obvious;
do nothing! Let Edward's realm tear itself into shreds,
because every Saxon warrior who died in Mercia was
one less man to bring a sword into Northumbria.

Yet here I was, on a late winter's afternoon beneath
a darkening sky, coming to fight in Mercia. Sigtryggr
had not been happy, and his wife, my daughter, even
unhappier. "Why?" she had demanded.

"I took an oath," I had told them both, and that had
stilled their protests.

Oaths are sacred. To break an oath is to invite the
anger of the gods, and Sigtryggr had reluctantly agreed
to let me relieve the siege of Ceaster. Not that he could
have done much to stop me; I was his most powerful
lord, his father-in-law, and the Lord of Bebbanburg,
indeed he owed me his kingdom, but he insisted I take
fewer than a hundred warriors. "Take more," he had
said, "and the damned Scots will come over the frontier." I had agreed. I led just ninety men, and with those
ninety I intended to save King Edward's new kingdom.

"You think Edward will be grateful?" my daughter
had asked, trying to find some good news in my per-
verse decision. She was thinking that Edward's gratitude might persuade him to abandon his plans to invade
Northumbria.

"Edward will think I'm a fool."

"You are!" Stiorra had said.

"Besides, I hear he's sick."

"Good," she had said vengefully. "Maybe his new wife has worn him out?"

Edward would not be grateful, I thought, whatever happened here. Our horses' hooves were loud on the Roman road. We still rode slowly, showing no threat. We passed the old worn stone pillar that said it was one mile to Deva, the name the Romans had given Ceaster. By now we were among the hovels and camp-fires of the encampment, and folk watched us pass. They showed no alarm, there were no sentries, and no one challenged us. "What's wrong with them?" Finan growled at me.

"They think that if relief comes," I said, "it'll come from the east, not the north. So they think we're on their side."

"Then they're idiots," he said. He was right, of course. Cynlæf, if he still commanded here, should have sentries posted on every approach to the besiegers' camp, but the long cold weeks of the siege had made them lazy and careless. Cynlæf just wanted to capture Ceaster, and had forgotten to watch his back.

Finan, who had the eyes of a hawk, was gazing at the city wall. "That monk was full of shit," he said scornfully. "I can see fifty-eight men on the north wall!"

The monk who had brought me the news of the siege had been certain that the garrison was perilously small. "How small?" I had asked him.

"No more than a hundred men, lord."

I had looked at him skeptically. "How do you know?"

"The priest told me, lord," he said nervously. The monk, who was called Brother Osric, claimed to be from a monastery in Hwite, a place I had never heard of, but which the monk said was a few hours' walking south of Ceaster. Brother Osric had told us how a priest had come to his monastery. "He was dying, lord! He had gripe in his guts."

"And that was Father Swithred?"

"Yes, lord."

I knew Swithred. He was an older man, a fierce and sour priest who disliked me. "And the garrison sent him to get help?"

"Yes, lord."

"They didn't send a warrior?"

"A priest can go where warriors cannot, lord," Brother Osric had explained. "Father Swithred said he left the city at nightfall and walked through the be-siegers' camp. No one challenged him, lord. Then he walked south to Hwite."

"Where he was taken ill?"

"Where he was dying as I left, lord," Brother Osric had made the sign of the cross. "It is God's will."

"Your god has a strange will," I had snarled.

"And Father Swithred begged my abbot to send one of us to reach you, lord," Brother Osric had continued, "and that was me," he finished lamely. He had been kneeling in supplication, and I saw a savage red scar crossing his tonsure.

"Father Swithred doesn't like me," I said, "and he hates all pagans. Yet he sent for me?"

The question had made Brother Osric uncomfortable. He had blushed, then stammered, "He . . . he . . ."

"He insulted me," I suggested.

"He did, lord, he did." He sounded relieved that I had anticipated an answer he had been reluctant to say aloud. "But he also said you would answer the garrison's plea."

"And Father Swithred didn't carry a letter?" I asked, "a plea for help?"

"He did, lord, but he vomited on it." He had grimaced. "But it was nasty, lord, all blood and bile."

"How did you get the scar?" I had asked him.

"My sister hit me, lord." He had sounded surprised at my question. "With a reaping hook, lord."

"And how many men in the besieging force?"

"Father Swithred said there were hundreds, lord."
I remember how nervous Brother Osric had been, but
I put that down to his fear at meeting me, a famous
pagan. Did he think I had horns and a forked tail? "By
God's grace, lord," he went on, "the garrison fought off
one assault, and I pray to God that the city hasn't fallen
by now. They beseech your help, lord."

"Why hasn't Edward helped?"

"He has other enemies, lord. He's fighting them in
southern Mercia." The monk had looked up beseech-
ingly. "Please, lord! The garrison can't last long!"

Yet they had lasted, and we had come. We had left
the road by now, and our horses walked slowly through
the besiegers' encampment. The luckiest folk had found
shelter in the farm buildings that had been made by
the Romans. They were good stone buildings, though
the long years had destroyed their roofs, which were
now untidy heaps of thatch on beams, but most people
were in crude shelters. Women were feeding the fires
with newly gathered wood, readying to cook an evening meal. They seemed incurious about us. They saw
my mail coat and silver-crested helmet, saw the silver
ornaments on Tintreg's bridle, and so realized I was a
lord and dutifully knelt as I passed, but none dared ask
who we were.

I halted in an open space to the northeast of the city.

I gazed around, puzzled because I could see few horses. The besiegers must have horses. I had planned to drive those horses away to prevent men using them to escape, as well as to capture the beasts to defray the costs of this winter journey, but I could see no more than a dozen. If there were no horses then we had the advantage, and so I turned Tintreg and walked him back through my men until I reached the packhorses. "Unbundle the spears," I ordered the boys. There were eight heavy bundles tied with leather ropes. Each spear was about seven feet long with an ash shaft and a sharpened steel blade. I waited as the bundles were untied and as each of my men took one of the weapons. Most also carried a shield, but a few preferred to ride without the heavy willow boards. The enemy had let us come into the center of their encampment and they must have seen my men taking their spears, yet still they did nothing except watch us dully. I waited for the boys to coil the leather ropes, then climb back into their saddles. "You boys," I called to the servants, "ride east, wait out in the fields till we send for you. Not you, Rorik."

Rorik was my servant, a good boy. He was Norse. I had killed his father, captured the boy and now treated him like a son, just as Ragnar the Dane had treated me as a son after his forces had cut my father down in battle.

"Not me, lord?" he asked.

"You follow me," I told him, "and have the horn ready. Stay behind me! And you don't need that spear."

He pulled the spear out of my reach. "It's a spare one for you, lord," he said. He was lying, of course, he could not wait to use the weapon.

"Don't get yourself killed, you idiot," I growled at him, then waited to see that the boys and the pack-horses were safe beyond the encampment's edge. "You know what to do," I called to my men, "so do it!"

And it began.

We spread into a line, we spurred forward.

Smoke from the campfires was acrid. A dog barked, a child cried. Three ravens flew eastward, wings dark against gray clouds, and I wondered if they were an omen. I touched spurs to Tintreg's flanks and he leaped forward. Finan was on my right, Berg on my left. I knew they were both protecting me, and I resented that. Old I might be, but weak no. I lowered the spear-point, nudged Tintreg with a knee, then leaned from the saddle and let the spear-point slide into a man's shoulder. I felt the blade jar on bone, relaxed the thrust, and he turned with eyes full of pain and astonishment. I had not tried to kill him, just terrify. I rode past him, felt the blade jerk loose, swung the spear back, raised the blade, and watched the panic begin.

Imagine you are cold, bored, and hungry. Maybe weak with sickness too, because the encampment stank of shit. Your leaders are telling you nothing but lies. If they have any idea how to end the siege, short of waiting, they have not revealed it. And the cold goes on, day after day, a bone-biting chill, and there is never enough firewood, despite the women going every day to forage. You are told that the enemy is starving, but you are just as hungry. It rains. Some men slip away, trying to reach home with their wives and children, but the real warriors, the household troops who man the great barricades outside the city gates, patrol the eastward road. If they find a fugitive he is dragged back, and, if he is lucky, whipped bloody. His wife, if she is young, vanishes to the tents where the trained warriors live. All you can think of is home, and even though home is poor and your work in the fields is hard, it is better than this endless hunger and cold. You were promised victory and have been given misery.

Then, on a late afternoon of lowering clouds, as the sun sinks in the west, the horsemen come. You see big horses carrying mail-clad men with long spears and sharp swords, helmeted men with wolf heads on their shields. The men are screaming at you, the thump of the big hooves is loud in the muck of the encampment, your children are screaming and your women cowering, and the brightest thing in the winter afternoon is not the shine of the blades, not even the silver that crests the helmets nor the gold hanging at the attackers' necks, but blood. Bright blood, sudden blood.

No wonder they panicked.

We drove them like sheep. I had told my men to spare the women and children, even most of the men too, because I did not want my horsemen to stop. I wanted to see the enemy running and to keep them running. If we paused to kill then we gave that enemy time to find their weapons, snatch up shields, and make a defense. It was better to gallop through the hovels and drive the enemy away from their piled shields, away from their spears, away from their reaping hooks and axes. The order was to strike and ride, strike and ride. We came to bring chaos, not death, not yet. Death would come.

And so we wheeled those big horses through the encampment, our hooves hurling up clods of mud, our spears sharp. If a man resisted, he died, if he ran, we made him run faster. I saw Folcbald, a huge Frisian, spear a flaming log from a campfire and toss it onto a shelter, and others of my men copied him. "Lord!" Finan shouted to me. "Lord!" I turned to see he was pointing south to where men were running from the tents toward the clumsy barricade that faced the city's eastern gate. Those were the real warriors, the household troops.

"Rorik!" I bellowed. "Rorik!"

"Lord!" He was twenty paces away, turning his horse ready to pursue three men wearing leather jerkins and carrying axes.

"Sound the horn!"

He spurred toward me, curbing his horse as he fumbled with the long spear and tried to retrieve the horn that was slung on his back by a long cord. One of the three men, seeing Rorik's back turned, ran toward him with a raised ax. I opened my mouth to shout a warning, but Finan had seen the man, twisted his horse, spurred, and the man tried to run away, Soul-Stealer flashed, her blade reflecting the flames of a fire, and the axman's head rolled off. The body slewed along the ground, but the head bounced once, then landed in the fire where the grease that the man had rubbed into his hair while cleaning his hands flared into sudden and bright flame.

"Not bad for a grandfather," I said.

"Bastards don't count, lord," Finan called back.

Rorik blew the horn, blew it again, and kept blowing it, and the sound, so mournful, insistent, and loud, drew my horsemen back together. "Now! Follow me!" I shouted.

We had wounded the beast, now we had to behead it.

Most of the folk fleeing our rampage had gone south toward the big tents, which evidently housed Cynlæf's trained warriors, and it was there that we rode, together now, knee to knee, spears lowered. Our line of horsemen only split to avoid the fires that spewed their sparks into the coming darkness, then, as we spurred into a wide open space between the miserable shelters and the tents, we quickened. More men appeared among the tents, one carrying a standard that stretched out as he ran toward the barricade that was supposed to deter the defenders from sallying out of the city's eastern gate. The barricade was a crude thing of overturned carts, even a plow, but it was still a formidable obstacle. I saw that the standard-bearer was holding Æthelflaed's banner, the daft goose holding a cross and a sword.

I must have laughed, because Finan called to me over the sound of hooves on turf, "What's funny?"

"This is madness!" I meant fighting against men who fought under a banner I had protected all my grown life.

"It is mad! Fighting for King Edward!"

"Fate is strange," I said.

"Will he be grateful?" Finan asked the same question my daughter had asked.

"That family never was grateful," I said, "except for Æthelflaed."

"Maybe Edward will take you to his bed then," Finan said happily, and then there was no more time to talk because I saw the standard-bearer suddenly turn away. Instead of running to the barricade, he was hurrying south toward the arena, followed by most of the household warriors, and that struck me as strange. They numbered as many as we did, or almost as many. They could have formed a shield wall, using the barricade to protect their backs, and we would have been hard put to defeat them. Horses would not charge an obstacle like a well-formed shield wall. Our stallions would veer away rather than crash into the boards, so we would have been forced to dismount, make our own wall, and fight shield to shield. And the besiegers north of the fort, the men we had not yet attacked, could have come to assault our rear. But instead, the enemy ran, led by their standard-bearer.

And then I understood.

It was the Roman arena.

I had been puzzled by the lack of horses, and now realized that the besiegers' beasts must have been placed

in the arena rather than in one of the thin-hedged pad-
docks to the east. The vast building lay outside the city's
southeastern corner, close to the river, and was a great
circle of stone inside which banks of seats surrounded
an open space where the Romans had enjoyed savage
displays featuring warriors and fearsome animals. The
arena's central space, ringed by a stone wall, made it a
safe, even an ideal, place for horses. We had been riding toward the tents, thinking to trap the rebel leaders,
but now I shouted at my men to spur toward the great
stone arena instead.

The Romans had puzzled me when I was a child.
Father Beocca, who was my tutor and was supposed
to turn me into a good little Christian, praised Rome
for being the home of the Holy Father, the Pope. The
Romans, he said, had brought the gospel to Britain,
and Constantine, the first Christian to rule Rome, had
declared himself emperor in our own Northumbria.
None of that inclined me to like Rome or the Romans,
but that changed when I was seven or eight years old
and Beocca walked me into the arena at Eoferwic. I
had stared amazed at the tiers of stone seats climbing
all around me to the outer wall where men were using
hammers and crowbars to loosen masonry blocks that
would be used to make new buildings in the growing
city. Ivy crawled up the seats, saplings sprang from

cracks in the stone, while the arena itself was thick with grass. "This space," Father Beocca told me in a hushed voice, "is sacred."

"Because Jesus was here?" I remember asking.

Father Beocca hit me around the head. "Don't be stupid, boy. Our lord never left the holy land."

"I thought you told me he went to Egypt once?"

He hit me again to cover his embarrassment at being corrected. He was not an unkind man, indeed I loved Beocca even though I took a delight in mocking him, and he was easy to mock because he was ugly and crippled. That was unkind, but I was a child, and children are cruel beasts. In time I came to recognize Beocca's honesty and strength, while King Alfred, who was no one's fool, valued the man highly. "No, boy," Beocca went on that day in Eoferwic, "this place is sacred because Christians suffered for their faith here."

I smelled a good story. "Suffered, father?" I had asked earnestly.

"They were put to death in horrible ways, horrible!"

"How, father?" I had asked, hiding my eagerness.

"Some were fed to wild beasts, some were crucified like our Lord, others were burned to death. Women, men, even children. Their screams sanctify this space." He had made the sign of the cross. "The Romans were cruel until they saw the light of Christ."

"And then they stopped being cruel, father?"

"They became Christians," he had answered evasively.

"Is that why they lost their lands?"

He had hit me again, though not forcefully nor angrily, yet he had sown a seed in me. The Romans! As a child it was their force that impressed me. They were from so far away, yet they had conquered our land. It was not ours then, of course, but it was still a far land. They were winners and fighters, they were heroes to a child, and Beocca's disdain made them only more heroic to me. At that time, before my father's death and before Ragnar the Dane adopted me, I thought I was a Christian, but I never had a fantasy of becoming a Christian hero by facing a wild beast in Eoferwic's decaying arena. Instead, I dreamed of fighting in that arena, and saw myself placing a foot on the bloodied chest of a fallen warrior as thousands cheered me. I was a child.

Now, old and gray-bearded, I still admire the Romans. How could I not? We could not build an arena, nor make ramparts like those that surrounded Ceaster. Our roads were muddy tracks, theirs were stone-edged and spear-straight. They built temples of marble, we made churches of timber. Our floors were beaten earth and rushes, theirs were marvels of intricate tilework. They had laced the land with wonders, and we, who had taken the land, could only watch the wonders decay, or patch them with wattle and thatch. True, they were a cruel people, but so are we. Life is cruel.

I was suddenly aware of shrieks coming from the city's ramparts. I looked to my right and saw helmeted warriors running on the wall's top. They were keeping pace with us as best they could, and cheering us on. The shrieks sounded like women, but I could only see men there, one of them waving a spear over his head as if encouraging us to kill. I lifted my spear to him, and the man responded by jumping up and down. He had ribbons, white and red, attached to the crown of his helmet. He screeched something at me, but he was too far away, and I could not catch his words, only sense that he was celebrating.

No wonder the garrison was happy. Their enemy had crumpled, and the siege was lifted, even if most of Cynlæf's troops were still in their encampment. But those troops had shown no lust to fight. They had run or hidden in their shelters. Only the household troops opposed us, and they were now fleeing toward the dubious safety of the old arena. We caught a few laggards, spearing them in the back as they stumbled southward, while others, more sensible, threw down their weapons and knelt in abject surrender. The light

was fading now. The reddish stone of the arena reflected the flames of the nearest campfires, giving the
masonry the appearance of being washed in blood. I
curbed Tintreg by the arena's entrance as my men,
grinning and elated, reined in around me.

"There's only this one way in?" Finan asked me.

"As I remember, yes, but send a half-dozen men
around the back to make sure."

The one way in was an arched tunnel that led beneath the tiered seats into the arena itself, and in the
fading light I could see men pushing a cart to make a
barricade at the tunnel's far end. They watched us fearfully, but I made no move to attack them. They were
fools, and, like fools, they were doomed.

Doomed because they had trapped themselves. It
was true there were other entrances to the arena, but
those entrances, which were evenly spaced about the
whole building, only led to the tiered seating, not to
the fighting space at the arena's center. Cynlæf's men
had kept their horses in the arena, and that made sense,
but in their desperation to escape they had fled to the
horses, and so found themselves ringed by stone with
just one way to escape, and my men guarded that one
tunnel.

Vidarr Leifson, one of my Norse warriors, had led
horsemen around the whole arena and returned to con-

firm that there was just the one entrance to the fighting level. "So what do we do, lord?" he asked, twisting in his saddle to peer into the tunnel. His breath clouded in the cold evening air.

"We let them rot."

"Can they climb up to the seats?" Berg asked.

"Probably." There was a wall a little higher than a tall man that prevented wild beasts from leaping up to maul the spectators, so our enemy could scramble up to the seats and try to escape through one of the stairways, but that meant abandoning their precious horses, and, once out of the building, they would still have to fight past my men. "So block every entrance," I ordered, "and light fires just outside every stairway." The barricades would slow any attempt by Cynlæf's men to escape, and the fires would warm my sentries.

"Where do we get firewood?" Godric asked. He was young, a Saxon, and had once been my servant.

"The barricade, you fool," Finan said, pointing to the besiegers' makeshift wall that guarded the road leading from the eastern gate.

And just then, as the day's last light drained in the west, I saw that men were coming from the city. The eastern gate had been opened, and a dozen horsemen now threaded their way through the narrow gap between the city's ditch and the abandoned barricade.

"Get those barriers built!" I commanded my men, then turned a tired Tintreg and spurred him to meet the men we had rescued.

We met them beside the city's deep ditch. I waited there and watched as the horsemen approached. They were led by a tall young man, clad in mail and with a fine helmet decorated with gold that glinted red from the distant fires. The cheek-pieces of his helmet were open to reveal that he had grown a beard since I had last seen him, and the beard, black and clipped short, made him look older. He was, I knew, twenty-five or twenty-six, I could not remember just when he had been born, but now he was a man in his prime, handsome and confident. He was also a fervent Christian, despite all my efforts to persuade him otherwise, and a big gold cross hung at his chest, swinging against the shining links of mail. There was more gold on his scabbard's throat and on his horse's bridle, and ringing the brooch that held his dark cloak in place, while a thin circlet of gold ringed his helmet. He reined in close enough to reach out and pat Tintreg's neck, and I saw he wore two gold rings over the fine black leather of his gloves. He smiled. "You are the very last person I expected, lord," he said.

And I swore at him. It was a good oath, brief and brutal.

"Is that the proper way," he asked mildly, "to greet a prince?"

"I owe Finan two shillings," I explained.

Because it had just begun to snow.

It is one of the privileges of age to be in a hall, warmed by a fire, while in the night the snow falls and the sentries shiver as they watch for enemies trying to escape from a trap they have made for themselves. Except now I was not sure who was trapped, or by whom.

"I never sent Father Swithred to fetch help," Æthelstan said. "Your monk lied. And Father Swithred is in good health, God be thanked."

Prince Æthelstan was King Edward's eldest son. He had been born to a pretty Centish girl, the daughter of a bishop, and the poor girl had died whelping him and his twin sister, Eadgyth. After the pretty girl's death Edward had married a West Saxon girl, and had fathered another son, which made Æthelstan an inconvenience. He was the king's eldest son, the ætheling, but he had a younger half-brother whose vengeful mother wanted Æthelstan dead because he stood between her son and the throne of Wessex, and so she and her supporters spread the rumor that Æthelstan was a bastard because Edward had never married the pretty Centish girl. He had indeed married her, but in secret because his father had not given permission, and over the years the rumor was embellished so that now Æthelstan's mother was said to be the daughter of a shepherd, a low-born whore, and no prince would ever marry such a girl, and the rumor was believed because truth is ever feeble against passionate falsehood.

"Truly!" Æthelstan now told me. "We didn't need relief, I asked for none."

For a moment I just stared at him. I loved Æthelstan like a son. For years I had protected him, fought for him, taught him the ways of the warrior, and when I had heard from Brother Osric that Æthelstan was under siege and hard-pressed, I had ridden to rescue him. It did not matter that saving Æthelstan was against the interests of Northumbria, I had sworn an oath to protect him, and here I was, in the Roman great hall where he had just told me that he had never sought my help. "You didn't send Father Swithred?" I asked. A log cracked in the fire and spat a bright spark onto the rushes. I ground the spark beneath my foot.

"Of course not! He's here." Æthelstan gestured across the hall to where the tall, stern-faced priest watched me suspiciously. "I have asked Archbishop Athelm to appoint him Bishop of Ceaster."

"And you didn't send him out of the city?"

"Of course not! I had no need."

I looked at Finan, who shrugged. The wind had picked up, driving the smoke back into the great hall, which had been a part of the Roman commandant's house. The roof was made of sturdy timbers covered with tiles, many of which remained, though at some time a Saxon had hacked a hole in the tiles to let the smoke out. Now the freshening wind gusted the smoke back, swirling it around the blackened rafters. Snowflakes came through the roof-hole, a few even lasting long enough to die on the table where we ate. "So you never sought my help?" I asked Æthelstan yet again.

"How often do I have to tell you?" he asked, pushing the jug of wine toward me. "And besides, if I'd needed help, why send for you when my father's forces are closer? You wouldn't have helped me anyway!"

I growled at that. "Why would I not help you? I swore an oath to protect you."

"But trouble in Mercia," he said, "is good for Northumbria, yes?"

I nodded grudgingly. "It is."

"Because if we Mercians fight each other," Æthelstan went on, "we can't be fighting you."

"Do you want to fight us, lord Prince?" Finan asked.

Æthelstan smiled. "Of course I do. Northumbria is ruled by a pagan, by a Norseman—"

"By my son-in-law," I interrupted him harshly.

"—and it is the fate of the Saxons," Æthelstan ignored my words, "to be one people, under one king and one God."

"Your god," I snarled.

"There is no other," he said gently.

Everything he said made sense, except for his nonsense about one god, and that good sense meant I had been lured across Britain for no good purpose. "I should have left you here to rot," I growled.

"But you didn't."

"Your grandfather always said I was a fool."

"My grandfather was right about so many things," Æthelstan said with a smile. His grandfather was King Alfred.

I stood and walked to the hall door. I pulled it open and just stared at the glow of fire above the eastern ramparts. Much of that glow came from the encampment where Cynlæf's men sheltered from the snow that was slanting fast from the north. Braziers burned on the ramparts, where cloaked spearmen kept a watch on the cowed enemy. The brighter light of two flaming torches just outside the hall's great doors showed the new snow piling against the house walls.

So Brother Osric had lied. We had brought the monk south with us, but I had gotten tired of his endless complaining about the cold and about his saddle sores, and we had let him leave us at Mameceaster, where, he claimed, the church would shelter him. I should have killed the bastard instead. I shivered, suddenly feeling the night's cold. "Rorik," I shouted back into the hall, "bring my cloak!"

Brother Osric had lied. The monk had told me that Æthelstan had fewer than a hundred warriors, but in truth he had twice as many, which was still a very small garrison for a place the size of Ceaster, but enough to stave off the feeble assaults Cynlæf had made. Brother Osric had told me the garrison was starving, but in truth they had storehouses still half-full with last year's harvest. A lie had brought me to Ceaster, but why?

"Your cloak, lord," a mocking voice said, and I turned to see it was Prince Æthelstan himself who had brought me the heavy fur garment. He was cloaked himself. He nodded to one of the sentries to close the hall door behind us, then stood beside me to watch the snow fall soft and relentless. "I didn't send for you," he said, draping the thick fur across my shoulders, "but thank you for coming."

"So who did send the monk?" I asked.

"Maybe no one."

"No one?"

Æthelstan shrugged. "Perhaps the monk knew of the siege, wanted to summon help, but knew you'd mistrust him, so he invented the tale of Father Swithred."

I shook my head. "He wasn't that clever. And he was frightened."

"You frighten many Christians," Æthelstan said drily.

I stared at the snow whirling around the corner of the house opposite. "I should go to Hwite," I said.

"Hwite? Why?"

"Because the monk came from the monastery there."

"There's no monastery at Hwite," Æthelstan said. "I'd like to build one, but . . ." his voice trailed away.

"The bastard lied," I said vengefully. "I should have known!"

"Known? How?"

"He said Father Swithred walked south from here. How could he? The bridge was broken. And why send Swithred? You'd have sent a younger man."

Æthelstan shivered. "Why would the monk lie? Maybe he just wanted to summon help."

"Summon help," I said scornfully. "No, the bastard wanted to get me away from Bebbanburg."

"So someone can attack it?"

"No. Bebbanburg won't fall." I had left my son in command, and he had twice as many warriors as he needed to hold that gaunt and forbidding fortress.

"So someone wants you away from Bebbanburg," Æthelstan said firmly, "because so long as you're in Bebbanburg they can't reach you, but now? Now they can reach you."

"Then why let me come here?" I asked. "If they wanted to kill me, then why wait till I'm among friends?"

"I don't know," he said, and neither did I. The monk had lied, but for what reason I could not tell. It was a trap, plainly it was a trap, but who had set it, and why, were mysteries. Æthelstan stamped his feet, then beckoned me to accompany him across the street, where our footsteps made the first marks in the fresh snow. "Still," he went on, "I'm glad you did come."

"I didn't need to."

"We were in no real danger," he agreed, "and my father would have sent relief in the spring."

"Would he?"

He ignored the savage disbelief in my voice. "Everything has changed in Wessex," he said mildly.

"The new woman?" I asked caustically, meaning King Edward's new wife.

"Who is my mother's niece."

That I had not known. What I did know was that King Edward had discarded his second wife and married a younger girl from Cent. The older wife was now in a convent. Edward claimed to be a good Christian, and Christians say that marriage is for life, but a hefty payment of gold or royal land would doubtless persuade the church that their doctrine was wrong, and the king could discard one woman and marry another. "So you're now in favor, lord Prince?" I asked. "You're the heir again?"

He shook his head. Our footsteps squeaked in the new snow. He was leading me down an alley that would take us to the eastern gate. Two of his guards followed us, but not close enough to hear our conversation. "My father is still fond of Ælfweard, I'm told."

"Your rival," I said bitterly. I despised Ælfweard, Edward's second son, who was a petulant piece of weasel shit.

"My half-brother," Æthelstan said reprovingly, "whom I love."

"You do?" For a moment he did not answer me. We were climbing the Roman steps to the eastern wall, where braziers warmed the sentries. We paused at the top, staring at the encampment of the defeated enemy. "You really love that little turd?" I asked.

"We are commanded to love one another."

"Ælfweard is despicable," I said.

"He might make a good king," Æthelstan said quietly.

"And I'll be the next Archbishop of Contwaraburg."

"That would be interesting," he said, amused. I knew he despised Ælfweard as much as I did, but he was saying what it was his familial duty to say. "Ælfweard's mother," he went on, "is out of favor, but her family is still wealthy, still strong, and they've sworn loyalty to the new woman."

"They have?"

"Ælfweard's uncle is the new ealdorman. He took Edward's side, and did nothing to help his sister."

"Ælfweard's uncle," I said savagely, "would whore his own mother to make Ælfweard king."

"Probably," Æthelstan agreed mildly.

I shivered, and it was not the cold. I shivered because in those words I sensed the trap. I still did not know why I had been lured across Britain, but I suspected I knew who had baited the trap. "I'm an old fool," I said.

"And the sun will rise tomorrow."

"Lord Prince! Lord Prince!" an excited voice interrupted us. A small warrior was running along the ramparts to greet us; a warrior small as a child, but dressed in mail, carrying a spear, and wearing a helmet decorated with red and white ribbons.

"Sister Sunngifu," Æthelstan said fondly as the small figure dropped to her knees in front of him. He touched a gloved hand to her helmet and she smiled up at him adoringly. "This is the Lord Uhtred of Bebbanburg," he introduced me, "and Sister Sunngifu," he was talking to me now, "raised a band of fifty women who stand guard on the ramparts to give my warriors a chance to rest and to deceive the enemy of our numbers. The deception worked well!"

Sunngifu moved her gaze to me, offering a dazzling smile. "I know the Lord Uhtred, lord Prince," she said.

"Of course you do," Æthelstan said, "I remember now, you told me."

Sunngifu was smiling as if she had waited half her life to greet me. I saw she was wearing a nun's gray habit beneath the mail coat and thick cloak. I reached down and gently lifted the ribbon-decked helmet just enough to see her forehead, and there was the small reddish birthmark, shaped like an apple, the only disfigurement on one of the most beautiful women I have ever known. She was looking up at me with amusement. "It's good to see you again, lord," she said humbly.

"Hello, Mus," I said.

The little warrior was Mus, Sunngifu, Sister Gomer, bishop's widow, whore, and troublemaker.

And damn the trap, I was suddenly happy to be in Ceaster.

Two

"So, you remember Sister Sunngifu?" Æthelstan asked me. We had left the ramparts and were leaving the city through the eastern gate, going to inspect the sentries who guarded the enemy trapped in the arena. It was cold, snow made the ground treacherous, and Æthelstan must have been tempted to stay in the great hall's warmth, but he was doing what he knew should be done; sharing his men's discomfort.

"Sunngifu is difficult to forget," I said. A dozen of Æthelstan's guards now followed us. Within a quarter mile there were hundreds of defeated enemy, though I expected no trouble from them. They had been cowed, and now sheltered in their makeshift hovels waiting to see what the morning brought. "I'm surprised she became a nun," I added.

"She's not a nun," Æthelstan said, "she's a novice when she's not pretending to be a soldier."

"I always thought she'd marry again," I went on.

"Not if she's called to God's service."

I laughed at that. "Her beauty is wasted on your god."

"Beauty," he said stiffly, "is the devil's snare."

The fires we had placed around the arena lit his face. It was tight, almost angry. He had asked me about Sunngifu, but now it was plain he was uncomfortable talking of her. "And how," I asked mischievously, "is Frigga?" Frigga was a young girl I had captured near Ceaster some years before and had given to Æthelstan. "She's a beauty, I remember," I went on, "I almost kept her for myself."

"You're married," he said censoriously.

"You're not," I retorted, "and it's time you were."

"There will be a time for marriage," he said dismissively. "And Frigga married one of my men. She's a Christian now."

Poor girl, I thought. "But you should be married," I said. "You can practice with Sunngifu," I teased him, "she plainly adores you."

He stopped and glared at me. "That is unseemly!" He made the sign of the cross. "With Sister Sunngifu?

With Bishop Leofstan's widow? Never! She's a most pious woman."

God in his dull heaven, I thought as we walked on, and Æthelstan didn't know her real story?

I will never understand Christians. I can understand their insistence that their nailed god rose from the dead, that he walked on water and cured diseases, because all gods can do those things. No, it's their other beliefs that astonish me. Sunngifu had been married to Bishop Leofstan, a good man. I liked him. He was a fool, of course, but a holy fool, and I remember him telling me that one of his god's prophets had married a whore called Gomer. I forget now why this prophet married a whore, it's all explained in the Christian holy book. I do recall that it wasn't just because he wanted to bounce her, it was something to do with his religion, and Bishop Leofstan, who at times had the brain of a mayfly, decided to do the same, and had plucked Sunngifu from some Mercian brothel and made her his wife. He solemnly assured me that his Gomer, as he insisted on calling her, had reformed, had been baptized, and was indeed a living saint, but when he wasn't looking, Sunngifu was humping my men like a demented squirrel. I had never told Leofstan, but I had tried to expel Sunngifu from Ceaster to stop the frequent injuries caused by men fighting for her favors. I had failed, and here she still was, and, for all I knew, still merrily bouncing.

We were walking toward the firelit arena with snow whirling about us. "You do know that before Sunngifu married the bishop she was—" I began.

"Enough!" Æthelstan interrupted me. He had stopped again and now looked at me fiercely. "If you're about to tell me that Sister Sunngifu was a harlot before she married, I know! What you don't understand is that she saw the sinfulness of her life and repented! She is living proof of redemption. A witness of the forgiveness that only Christ can offer! Are you telling me that is falsehood?"

I hesitated, then decided it was best to let him believe whatever he chose. "Of course not, lord Prince."

"I have suffered from malicious gossip my whole life," he said angrily, beckoning me onward, "and I detest it. I have known women raised in the faith, pious women, women full of good works, who are less saintly than Sunngifu! She is a good woman, an inspiration to us all! And she deserves a heavenly reward for what she has achieved here. She tends the wounded, and comforts the afflicted."

I almost asked how she administered that comfort, but managed to bite my tongue. There was no way to argue with Æthelstan's piety, and I had watched him grow ever more pious over the years. I had done my best to convince him that the older gods were better, but I had failed, and now he was becoming more and more like his grandfather, King Alfred. He had inherited Alfred's intelligence and his love of the church, but to those he added the skills of a warrior. He was, in short, formidable, and I had the sudden realization that if I had just met him for the first time, instead of having known him since he was a child, I would probably dislike him. And if this young man became king, I thought, then Alfred's dream of one Saxon country under the rule of one Christian king could well come true, indeed was likely to come true, which meant that this young man, whom I thought of as a son, was the enemy of Northumbria. My enemy. "Why do I always end up fighting for the wrong side?" I asked.

Æthelstan laughed, then surprised me by clapping my shoulder, maybe regretting the angry tone he had used just a moment before. "Because at heart you're a Saxon," he said, "and because, as we've already agreed, you're a fool. But you're a fool who'll never be my enemy."

"I won't?" I asked threateningly.

"Not by my choice!" He strode ahead, making for the arena's entrance, where a dozen of my men stood close to the great fire that burned in the archway. "Is Cynlæf still inside?" he called out.

Berg was the closest of the sentries, and he glanced at me as if wondering whether he should answer. I nodded. "No one's left the arena, lord," Berg said.

"Are we sure Cynlæf's here?" I asked.

"We saw him two days ago," Æthelstan said. He smiled at Berg. "I fear you're suffering a cold night."

"I'm Norse, lord, the cold doesn't worry me."

Æthelstan laughed at that. "Nevertheless I'll send men to relieve you. And tomorrow?" He paused, distracted by Berg, who was gazing past him.

"Tomorrow we kill them, lord?" Berg asked, still staring northward over Æthelstan's shoulder.

"Oh, we kill them," Æthelstan said softly, "we certainly kill them." Then he turned to see what had attracted Berg's attention. "And perhaps we begin the killing now," he added in a sharp tone.

I also turned to see a dozen men approaching. Eleven were warriors, all in mail, all cloaked, all bearded, all wearing helmets, and three carrying shields painted with creatures I supposed to be dragons. Their swords were sheathed. The firelight reflected from gold at one man's neck and shone silver from a cross that was worn by the one priest who accompanied them. The warriors stopped some twenty yards away, but the priest kept walking until he was a couple of paces from Æthelstan, where he dropped to his knees. "Lord Prince," he said.

"Stand, stand! I don't expect priests to kneel to me! You represent God. I should kneel to you."

"Earsling," I said, but too softly for Æthelstan to hear.

The priest stood. Two crusts of snow clung to his black robe where he had knelt. He was shivering, and, to my surprise, and even more to the priest's astonishment, Æthelstan strode forward and draped his own thick cloak about the man's shoulders. "What brings you here, father?" he asked. "And who are you?"

"Father Bledod," the priest answered. He was a skinny man with lank black hair, no hat, a straggly beard, and frightened eyes. He fidgeted with the silver cross. "Thank you for the cloak, lord."

"You're Welsh?"

"Yes, lord." Father Bledod gave an awkward gesture toward his companions. "That is Gruffudd of Gwent. He would speak with you, lord."

"With me?"

"You are the Prince Æthelstan, lord?"

Æthelstan smiled. "I am."

"Gruffudd of Gwent, lord, would return to his home," the priest said.

"I am surprised," Æthelstan said mildly, "that Gruffudd of Gwent thought to leave his home in the first place. Or did he come to Mercia to enjoy the weather?"

The priest, who seemed to be the only Welshman capable of speaking the Saxon tongue, had no reply. He just frowned, while the eleven warriors stared at us in mute belligerence.

"Why did he come?" Æthelstan asked.

The priest made a helpless gesture with his left hand, then looked embarrassed. "We were paid to come, lord Prince," he admitted.

I could see that answer made Æthelstan angry. To the Welshmen he doubtless looked calm, but I could sense his fury that Cynlæf's rebellion had hired Welsh troops. There had ever been enmity between Mercia and the Welsh. Each raided the other, but Mercia, with its rich fields and plump orchards, had more to lose. Indeed the first warrior I ever killed in a shield wall was a Welshman who had come to Mercia to steal cattle or women. I killed four men that day. I had no mail, no helmet, just a borrowed shield and my two swords, and that was the day I first experienced the battle-joy. Our small force of Mercians had been led by Tatwine, a monstrous beast of a warrior, and when the battle was done, when the bridge where we had fought was slippery with blood, he had complimented me. "God love me," I remembered him saying in awe, "but you're a savage one." I was a youngster, raw and half-trained, and thought that was praise.

Æthelstan controlled his anger. "You tell me that Gruffudd comes from Gwent," he said, looking at the man who showed the glint of gold at his neck. "But tell me, father, is not Arthfael King of Gwent?"

"He is, lord Prince."

"And King Arthfael thought it good to send men to fight against my father, King Edward?"

Father Bledod still looked embarrassed. "The gold, lord, was paid to Gruffudd."

That answer was evasive and Æthelstan knew it. He paused, looking at the warriors standing in the snow. "And who," he asked, "is Gruffudd of Gwent?"

"He is kin to Arthfael," the priest admitted.

"Kin?"

"His mother's brother, lord Prince."

Æthelstan thought for a moment. It could hardly have been a surprise that Welsh troops were at the siege. The Welsh and the Mercians were enemies and had always been enemies. King Offa, who had ruled Mercia in the days of its greatness, had built a wall and ditch to mark the frontier and had sworn to kill any Welshman who dared cross the wall, but of course they dared, indeed they seemed to regard the barrier as a challenge. The Mercian rebellion was an opportunity for the Welsh to weaken their traditional enemy. They would have been fools not to take advantage of the Saxon troubles, and the kingdom of Gwent, which lay on the other side of Offa's ditch, must have hoped to gain land if Cynlæf's rebellion had succeeded. A few dead warriors was a small price to pay if the Welsh gained some prime Saxon farmland, and it was plain that King Arthfael had made that bargain with Cynlæf. Father Bledod had done his best to absolve the Gwentish king of blame, and Æthelstan did not press him. "Tell me," he said instead, "how many men did Gruffudd of Gwent bring to Ceaster?"

"Seventy-four, lord."

"Then tell Gruffudd of Gwent," Æthelstan said, and each time he repeated the name he invested it with more scorn, "that he and his seventy-four men are free to cross the river and go home. I will not stop them." And that, I thought, was the right decision. There was no point in picking a quarrel with a defeated force. If Æthelstan had chosen to kill Gruffudd and his Welshmen, which he was surely entitled to do, the news of the massacre would spread through the Welsh kingdoms and provoke retaliation. It was better to provoke gratitude by allowing Gruffudd and his men to crawl back to their hovels. "But they may travel with nothing more than they brought with them," Æthelstan added.

"If they steal so much as one goat I will slaughter all of them!"

Father Bledod showed no concern at the threat. He must have expected it, and he knew as well as Æthelstan that the threat was a formality. Æthelstan just wanted the foreigners gone from Mercia. "Your goats are safe, lord," the priest said with sly humor, "but Gruffudd's son is not."

"What of his son?"

The priest gestured toward the arena. "He is in there, lord."

Æthelstan turned and stared at the arena, its blood-red walls lit by fire and half obscured by snow. "It is my intention," he said, "to kill every man inside."

The priest made the sign of the cross. "Cadwallon ap Gruffudd is a hostage, lord."

"A hostage!" Æthelstan could not hide his surprise. "Are you telling me that Cynlæf doesn't trust Gruffudd of Gwent?" Æthelstan asked, but the priest did not answer, nor did he need to. Gruffudd's son had clearly been taken hostage as a surety that the Welsh warriors would not desert Cynlæf's cause. And that, I thought, meant that Gruffudd must have given Cynlæf cause to doubt the Welshmen's loyalty.

"How many of your seventy-four men still live, priest?" I asked.

Æthelstan looked annoyed at my intervention, but said nothing. "Sixty-three, lord," the priest answered.

"You lost eleven men assaulting the walls?" I asked.

"Yes, lord." Father Bledod paused for a heartbeat. "We put ladders against the northern gate, lord, we took the tower." He meant one of the two bastions that flanked the Roman gate. "We drove the *sais* from the rampart, lord." He was proud of what Gruffudd's men had achieved, and he had every right to be proud.

"And you were driven from the gate," Æthelstan remarked quietly.

"By you, lord Prince," the priest said. "We took the tower, but could not keep it."

"And how many *sais*," I used Bledod's word for the Saxons, "died with you on the gate?"

"We counted ten bodies, lord."

"No," I said, "I want to know how many of Cynlæf's men died with you."

"None, lord," Father Bledod could not hide his scorn, "not one."

Æthelstan understood my questions now. Cynlæf had let the Welshmen lead the assault and had done nothing to support them. The Welsh had done the fighting and the Saxons had let them die, and that experience had soured Gruffudd and his men. They could have resisted our arrival the previous day, but had chosen not to fight because they had lost faith in Cynlæf and his cause. Æthelstan looked at the warriors lined behind the priest. "What can Gruffudd," he asked, "give me in return for his son's life?"

The priest turned and spoke with the short, broad-chested man who wore the gold chain about his neck. Gruffudd of Gwent had a scowling face, a gray tangled beard, and one blind eye, his right eye, which was white as the falling snow. A scar on his cheek showed where a blade had taken the sight from that eye. He spoke in his own language, of course, but I could hear the bitterness in the words. Father Bledod finally turned back to Æthelstan. "What does the lord Prince wish from Gruffudd?"

"I want to hear what he will offer," Æthelstan said. "What is his son worth? Silver? Gold? Horses?"

There was another brief exchange in the Welsh language. "He will not offer gold, lord," the priest said, "but he will pay you with the name of the man who hired him."

Æthelstan laughed. "Cynlæf hired him!" he said. "I already know that! You waste my time, father."

"It is not Cynlæf," it was Gruffudd himself who spoke in halting English.

"Of course it was not Cynlæf," Æthelstan said scornfully, "he would have sent someone else to bribe you. The devil has evil men to do his work."

"It is not Cynlæf," Gruffudd said again, then added something in his own language.

"It was not Cynlæf," Father Bledod translated. "Cynlæf knew nothing of our coming till we arrived here."

Æthelstan said nothing for a few heartbeats, then reached out and gently took his cloak from Father Bledod's shoulders. "Tell Gruffudd of Gwent that I will spare his son's life and he may leave at midday tomorrow. In exchange for his son he will give me the name of my enemy and he will also give me the gold chain about his neck."

Father Bledod translated the demand, and Gruffudd gave a reluctant nod. "It is agreed, lord Prince," Bledod said.

"And the chain," Æthelstan said, "will be given to the church."

"Earsling," I said again, still too low for Æthelstan's ears.

"And Gruffudd of Gwent," Æthelstan went on, "will agree to keep his men from raiding Mercia for one whole year." That too was agreed, though I suspected it was a meaningless demand. Æthelstan might as well have demanded that it did not rain for a whole year as expect that the Welsh would end their thieving. "We will meet again tomorrow," Æthelstan finished.

"Tomorrow, *edling*," Gruffudd said, "tomorrow." He walked away, followed by his men and by Father Bledod. The snow was falling harder, the flakes whirling in the light of the campfires.

"I sometimes find it difficult," Æthelstan said as he watched them walk away, "to remember that the Welsh are Christians."

I smiled at that. "There's a king in Dyfed called Hywel. You'd like him."

"I've heard of him."

"He's a good man," I said warmly, and rather surprised myself by saying it.

"And a Christian!" Æthelstan was mocking me.

"I said he was good, not perfect."

Æthelstan crossed himself. "Tomorrow we must all be good," he said, "and spare the life of a Welshman."

And discover the name of an enemy. I was fairly sure I already knew that name, though I could not be certain of it, though I was certain that one day I would have to kill the man. So a Welshman must live so that a Saxon could die.

Edling, a Welsh title, the same as our ætheling, meaning the son of the king who would be the next king.

Gruffudd of Gwent, who I assumed was a chieftain of some kind, even maybe a minor king himself, had used the title to flatter Æthelstan, because no one knew who would succeed King Edward. Æthelstan was the oldest son, but malicious rumor, spread by the church, insisted he was a bastard, and almost all the ealdormen of Wessex supported Ælfweard, Edward's second son, who was indubitably legitimate. "They should make me King of Wessex," I told Æthelstan next morning.

He looked shocked. Perhaps he was not fully awake and thought he had misheard. "You!"

"Me."

"For God's sake, why?"

"I just think the best-looking man in the kingdom should be king."

He understood I was joking then, but he was in no mood for laughter. He just grunted and urged his horse on. He led sixty of his warriors, while I led all of mine who were not already guarding the arena where Father Bledod was waiting for us. I had told the Welsh priest to join us. "How else will we know who Gruffudd's boy is?" I had explained. Away to our left, many of Cynlæf's defeated men were already walking eastward with their wives and children. I had sent Finan with twenty men to spread the news that they should leave or else face my warriors, and Finan's small force had met no opposition. The rebellion, at least in this part of Mercia, had collapsed without a fight.

"Father Swithred," Æthelstan said as he watched the beaten men walk away, "thought we should kill one man in ten. He said it was the Roman way."

"Why don't you?"

"You think I should?" he asked.

"No," I said firmly, "I think you should let them go. Most of them aren't warriors. They're the folk who tend the fields, raise the cattle, dig ditches, and plant the orchards. They're carpenters and fullers, leather-workers and plowmen. They came here because they were ordered to come, but once home they'll go back to work. Your father needs them. Mercia is no use to him if it's hungry and poor."

"It's little use to him if it's rebellious."

"You've won," I said, "and most of those men wouldn't know a rebellion from a wet fart. They were led here. So let them go home."

"My father might disagree."

I scoffed at that statement. "So why didn't your father send a relief force?"

"He's ill," Æthelstan said, and made the sign of the cross.

I let Tintreg walk around an unburied corpse, one of Cynlæf's house-warriors we had killed the previous day. Snow had settled on the body to make a soft shroud. "What's wrong with the king?" I asked.

"Tribulations," Æthelstan said curtly.

"And how do you cure that?"

He rode in silence for a few paces. "No one knows what ails him," he finally said, "he's grown fat, and short of breath. But he has days when he seems to recover, thank God. He can still ride, he likes to hunt, he can still rule."

"The problem," I said, "sounds like an old sword in a new scabbard."

"What does that mean?"

"It sounds as if his new bride is wearing him out."

Æthelstan bridled at that, but did not argue. Instead he looked up at the sky that had cleared overnight. A bright sun glinted from the snow. It would melt quickly, I thought, as quickly as the siege had ended. "I suppose he's waiting for the weather to improve," Æthelstan went on, "which means he might be coming soon. And he won't be happy that the rebels are leaving unpunished."

"So punish their leaders," I said. The leaders of the rebellion, at least in northern Mercia, had trapped themselves in the arena.

"I intend to."

"Then your father will be happy," I said, and urged

Tintreg on to the arena entrance where Finan waited. "Any trouble?" I called out to him. Finan had relieved Berg in the middle of the night, taking fresh troops to guard the arena. Æthelstan had also sent a score of men, and, like Finan, they all looked cold and tired.

Finan spat, evidently a gesture of scorn for the men trapped in the arena. "They made one feeble effort to get out. Didn't even get past their own barricade. Now they want to surrender."

"On what terms?" Æthelstan asked. He had heard Finan, and had spurred his horse forward.

"Exile," Finan said laconically.

"Exile?" Æthelstan asked sharply.

Finan shrugged, knowing what Æthelstan's answer would be. "They're willing to surrender their lands and go into exile, lord Prince."

"Exile!" Æthelstan exclaimed. "Tell them my answer is no. They can surrender to my justice, or else they fight."

"Exile them to Northumbria," I said mischievously. "We need warriors." I meant we needed warriors to resist the inevitable invasion that would engulf Northumbria when the Mercian troubles were over.

Æthelstan ignored me. "How are you talking to them?" he asked Finan. "Are you just shouting through the entrance?"

"No, you can go inside, lord Prince," Finan said, pointing to the closest staircase leading up to the tiered seating. It seemed that at first light Finan had ordered the barricade removed from that entrance and had led a score of men up to the arena's seats from where they could look down on the trapped enemy.

"How many are there?" Æthelstan asked.

"I counted eighty-two, lord Prince," Finan said, stepping forward to hold Æthelstan's bridle. "There may be some we haven't seen inside the building. And some of those we saw are servants, of course. Some women too."

"They're all rebels," Æthelstan snarled. He dismounted and strode toward the staircase, followed by his men.

Finan looked up at me. "What does he want to do?"

"Kill the lot."

"But he's letting the Welsh live?"

"One enemy at a time."

Finan turned to watch as Æthelstan and all his warriors filed into the nearest staircase. "He's changed, hasn't he?"

"Changed?"

"Become stern. He used to laugh a lot, remember?"

"He was a boy then," I said, "and I tried to teach him how to be a king."

"You taught him well, lord."

"Too well," I said softly, because Æthelstan had come to resemble his grandfather, and Alfred had never been my friend. I thought of Æthelstan as a son. I had protected him through boyhood, I had trained him in the skills of a warrior, but he had hardened in the last few years, and now believed his destiny led to a throne despite all the obstacles that ambitious men would place in his way. And when he was king, I thought, he would lead swords and spears into Northumbria, he would be our conqueror, he would demand my homage, and he would require my obedience. "If I had any sense," I said to Finan as I dismounted, "I would side with Cynlæf."

He laughed. "It's not too late."

"Wyrd bið ful āræd," I said, and that is true. Fate is inexorable. Destiny is all. We make oaths, we make choices, but fate makes our decisions.

Æthelstan was mȳ enemy, but I had sworn to protect him.

So I told Finan that he should stay outside the arena, told him what he was to do there, then followed my enemy up the stairs.

"You will throw down your weapons," Æthelstan called to the men in the arena, "and you will kneel!" He had taken off his helmet so that the trapped men would have no trouble recognizing him. He usually wore his dark hair cropped very short, but it had grown during the siege and the cold morning wind lifted it and swirled his dark blue cloak around his mailed figure. He stood in the center of a line of warriors, all implacable in mail and helmets, all with shields painted with Æthelstan's symbol of a dragon holding a lightning bolt. Behind them, standing on one of the snow-covered stone tiers, Father Swithred was holding a wooden cross high above his head.

"What is our fate?" a man called up from the arena floor.

Æthelstan made no answer. He just stared at the man.

A second man stepped forward and knelt. "What is our fate, lord Prince?" he asked.

"My justice." That answer was said in a voice as cold as the snow-shrouded corpses we had passed on our way to the arena.

Silence. There had to be a hundred horses in the arena. A score of them had been saddled, perhaps readied for a desperate dash through the entrance tunnel, and in front of them, huddled like the horses, were Cynlæf's men. I looked for Cynlæf himself and finally saw him at the back of the crowd, close to the saddled stallions. He was a tall, good-looking man. Æthelflaed had been fond of him and had chosen him as her daughter's husband, but if there was such a place as the Christian heaven and she was looking down now she would approve of Æthelstan's grim resolve to kill Cynlæf.

"Your justice, lord Prince?" the kneeling man, who had the sense to use Æthelstan's title, asked humbly.

"Which is the same as my father's justice," Æthelstan said harshly.

"Lord Prince," I said softly. I was standing barely two paces behind him, but he ignored me. "Lord Prince," I said again, louder.

"Silence, Lord Uhtred," Æthelstan said without turning. He also spoke softly, but with a trace of anger that I had dared to intervene.

I wanted to tell him that he should offer mercy. Not to all of them, of course, and certainly not to Cynlæf. They were, after all, rebels, but tell close to a hundred men that they will face grim justice and you have close to a hundred desperate men who would rather fight than surrender. But if some thought they would live, then those men would subdue the others, and none of our men need die. Yet it seemed Æthelstan had no use for mercy. This was a rebellion, and rebellions destroy kingdoms, so rebellions must be utterly destroyed.

Father Bledod had joined me and now tugged nervously at my mail sleeve. "Gruffudd's son, Cadwallon, lord," he said, "he's the tall beardless boy. The one in the dun cloak." He pointed.

"Quiet!" Æthelstan growled.

I took the Welsh priest away from Æthelstan, leading him around the lowest tier until we were out of earshot. "Half of them have dun cloaks," I said.

"The boy with reddish hair, lord."

He pointed, and I saw a tall young man with long dark red hair tied at the nape of his neck. He wore mail, but had no sword, suggesting that he was indeed a hostage, though any value he possessed as a hostage had long since vanished.

Only one man in Cynlæf's band had knelt, and he only because he had understood that Æthelstan would not talk unless he was shown respect. That man glanced around uncertainly and, seeing his companions still standing, began to rise.

"I said kneel!" Æthelstan called sharply.

The answer came from a tall man standing close to Cynlæf. He pushed men aside, bellowed a challenge, and hurled a spear at Æthelstan. It was a good throw. The spear flew straight and fast, but Æthelstan had time to judge its flight and he simply stepped one pace to his left and the spear crashed harmlessly into the stones at Father Swithred's feet. And then Cynlæf and his immediate companions were hauling them-

selves into saddles. More spears were thrown, but now
Æthelstan and his men were crouching behind their
shields. I had brought just two men with me, Oswi and
Folcbald, the first a Saxon, lithe and serpent-quick,
the second a Frisian built like an ox. They put up their
shields, and Father Bledod and I crouched with them. I
heard a blade thump into a willow board, another spear
flew over my head, then I peered between the shields to
see Cynlæf and a dozen men spurring into the entrance
tunnel. The makeshift barricade had been pulled aside,
and the way out looked clear because I had told Finan
to hide his men at either side of the outer entrance to let
Cynlæf believe he had a way to escape.

The rest of Cynlæf's men started to follow their
leader into the tunnel, but suddenly stopped, and I
knew that Finan had made his shield wall across the
arena's entrance the moment he heard the commotion.
It would be two shields high, bristling with spears,
and no horse would charge it. Some of Cynlæf's men
were retreating back into the arena's open space, where
a few knelt in surrender while a handful of stubborn
men threw their last spears at Æthelstan and his men.
"Down!" Æthelstan shouted to his warriors, and he
and his men jumped into the arena.

"Fetch the Welshman," I told Oswi and Folcbald,
and they also leaped down. Folcbald landed awkwardly

and limped as he followed Oswi. It was a good long way down, and I was content to stay high and watch the fight that promised to be as brief as it would be brutal. The floor of the arena had once been fine sand, now it was a slushy mix of sand, horse dung, mud, and snow, and I wondered how much blood had soaked it over the years. There was more blood now. Æthelstan's sixty men had made a shield wall, two ranks deep, that advanced on the panicking rebels. Æthelstan himself, still without a helmet, was in the front rank that kicked the kneeling men out of their way, sparing their lives for the moment, then hammered into the panicked mass crowding at the entrance. Those rebels had no time to make a shield wall of their own and there are few slaughters as one-sided as a combat between a shield wall and a rabble. I saw the spears lunge forward, heard men screaming, saw men fall. There were women among the mob, and two of them were crouching by the wall, covering their heads with their arms. Another woman clutched a child to her breast. Riderless horses panicked and galloped into the arena's empty space where Oswi was darting forward. He had thrown his shield aside and carried a drawn sword in his right hand. He used his left to snatch Cadwallon's arm to tug him backward. A man tried to stop him, lunging a sword at Oswi's belly, but there were few men as quick as Oswi. He let go of the Welshman, leaned to one side so that the sword slid a finger's breadth from his waist, then struck up with his own sword. He hit the man's wrist and sawed the blade back. The enemy's sword dropped, Oswi stooped, picked up the fallen blade, and held it to Cadwallon, then lunged his own sword to tear open his opponent's cheek. That man reeled away, hand half severed and face pulsing blood as Oswi again tugged Cadwallon backward. Folcbald was with them now, his huge size and the threat of his heavy war ax sufficient to deter any other foe.

That enemy was beaten. They were being driven back out of the entrance tunnel, which meant Finan and his men were advancing. More and more of Cynlæf's men were kneeling, or else being kicked aside and told to wait, weaponless, in the arena's center. There were enough corpses heaped on the arena floor to check Æthelstan's advance, and his shield wall had stopped by the tangled bodies, and one of the horsemen, coming from the entrance, turned his stallion and spurred it at Æthelstan himself. The horse stumbled on a body, slewed sideways, and the rider struck down with a long-handled ax that crashed onto a shield, then two spears were savaged into the stallion's chest and the beast screamed, reared, and the rider fell backward to be slaughtered by swords and spears. The horse fell and went on screaming, hooves thrashing until a man stepped forward and silenced it with a quick ax blow to the head.

"You must be happy, father," I said to the priest, Bledod, who had stayed with me.

"That Cadwallon is safe, lord? Yes."

"No, that Saxons are killing Saxons."

He looked at me in surprise, then gave a sly grin. "I'm grateful for that too, lord," he said.

"The first man I killed in battle was a Welshman," I told him, taking the grin off his face. "And the second. And the third. And the fourth."

"Yet you've killed more Saxons than Welshmen, lord," he said, "or so I hear?"

"You hear right." I sat on the stone seats. Cadwallon, safe with Oswi and Folcbald, was beneath us, sheltering beside the arena's inner wall, while Cynlæf's men were surrendering meekly, letting Æthelstan's warriors take their weapons. Cynlæf himself was still mounted and still carrying a sword and shield. His horse stood in the entrance, trapped between Finan's shield wall and Æthelstan's men. The sun broke through the leaden clouds, casting a long shadow on the bloodied ground. "I'm told Christians died here," I said to Bledod.

"Killed by the Romans, lord?"

"That's what I was told."

"But in the end the Romans became Christians, lord, God be thanked."

I grunted at that. I was trying to imagine the arena as it had been before Ceaster's masons broke down the high stone seating for useful building blocks. The upper rim of the arena was jagged, like a mountain range. "We destroy, don't we?" I said.

"Destroy, lord?" Bledod asked nervously.

"I burned half this city once," I said. I remembered the flames leaping from roof to roof, the smoke thick. To this day the masonry walls of the streets were streaked with black. "Imagine what this city was like when the Romans were here."

Father Bledod said nothing. He was watching Cynlæf, who had been driven to the arena's center, where he was now surrounded by a ring of spearmen, some of them Finan's men and some Æthelstan's. He turned his horse as if seeking a way out. The horse's rump showed a brand, a C and an H. Cynlæf Haraldson.

"White-walled buildings," I said, "with red roofs. Statues and marble. I wish I could have seen it."

"Rome must have been a wonder too," Bledod said.

"I hear it's in ruins now."

"Everything passes, lord."

Cynlæf spurred his horse toward one side of the ring, but the long spears came up, the shields clashed as they were braced together, and Cynlæf swerved away. He carried a drawn sword. The scabbard at his left hip was bound in red leather and studded with small gold plaques. The scabbard and sword had been a gift from Æthelflaed, last ruler of independent Mercia, and soon, I thought, they would belong to Æthelstan, who would doubtless give them to the church.

"Everything passes," I agreed. "Look at the city now. Nothing but thatch and wattle, dirt and dung. I doubt it stank like a cesspit when the Romans were here."

A word of command from Æthelstan caused the ring of men to take a pace forward. The ring shrank. Cynlæf still turned his horse, still looking for an escape that did not exist.

"The Romans, lord . . ." Bledod began, then faltered.

"The Romans what?" I asked.

Another word of command and the ring shrank again. Spears were leveled at the man and his branded horse. A score of Æthelstan's warriors were now guarding the prisoners, herding them to one side of the arena while the dead made a tideline of bloody corpses by the entrance.

"The Romans should have stayed in Britain, lord," Father Bledod said.

"Because?" I asked.

He hesitated, then gave me his sly grin again. "Because when they left, lord, the *sais* came."

"We did," I said, "we did." We were the *sais*, we Saxons. Britain had never been our home any more than it was home to the Romans. They took it, they left, and we came and we took it. "And you hate us," I said.

"We do indeed, lord." Bledod was still smiling and I decided I liked him.

"But you fought against the Romans, didn't you? Didn't you hate them?"

"We hate everyone who steals our land, lord, but the Romans gave us Christianity."

"And that was a good exchange?"

He laughed. "They left! They gave us back our land, so thanks to the Romans we had our land and we had the true faith."

"Then we came."

"Then you came," he agreed. "But maybe you'll leave too?"

It was my turn to laugh. "I think not, father. Sorry."

Cynlæf was turning his horse continually, plainly fearing an assault from behind. His shield was lime-washed white without any symbol. His helmet was chased with silver that glinted in the wintry sun. He wore his hair long like the Danes so that it flowed down his back. Æthelstan called out again, and once again the ring of spearmen contracted, men leaving the front rank as the weapons and shields tightened on Cynlæf.

"So what will happen now, lord?" Bledod asked.

"Happen?"

"To us, lord. To King Gruffudd's men."

"King Gruffudd?" I asked, amused. His kingdom was probably the size of a village, a patch of scrubby land with goats, sheep, and dung heaps. There were as many kings in Wales as fleas on a dog, though Hywel of Dyfed, whom I had met and liked, was swallowing those petty kingdoms to make one great one. Just as Wessex was swallowing Mercia, and, one day, would swallow Northumbria. "So he's a king?"

"His father was before him," Bledod said, as if that justified the title.

"I thought Arthfael was King of Gwent?"

"So he is, lord. Gruffudd is king beneath Arthfael."

"How many kings does Gwent have?" I asked, amused.

"It's a mystery, lord, like the trinity."

Cynlæf suddenly spurred his horse forward and slashed down with his sword. He had little room to move, but doubtless he hoped he could cut his way through the circle of men, though he must have known the hope was desperate, and so it was. The sword crashed into a shield and suddenly men were all around him, reaching for him. Cynlæf tried to draw the sword back, but one of Æthelstan's warriors leaped up and seized his sword arm. Another snatched the horse's bridle, while a third seized Cynlæf's long hair and dragged him backward. He fell, the horse reared and neighed, then the men backed away, and I saw Cynlæf being pulled to his feet. He was alive. For now.

"Your King Gruffudd can leave with his son," I told Bledod, "but only after he tells us who bribed you. Not that he needs to tell us. I already know."

"You still think it was Cynlæf?" he asked.

"It was Æthelhelm the Younger," I said, "Ealdorman Æthelhelm."

Who hated me and hated Æthelstan.

Æthelhelm the Elder was dead. He had died a prisoner in Bebbanburg. That had been inconvenient because his release had depended on his family paying me a ransom. The first part of that ransom, all in gold coins, had arrived, but Æthelhelm contracted a fever and died before the second payment was delivered.

His family had accused me of killing him, which was nonsense. Why kill a man who would bring me gold?

I would have been happy to kill him after the ransom was paid, but not before.

Æthelhelm had been the richest man in the kingdom of Wessex, richer even than King Edward to whom Æthelhelm had married his daughter. That marriage had made Æthelhelm as influential as he was wealthy, and it also meant that his grandson, Ælfweard, might become king after Edward. Ælfweard's rival, of course, was Æthelstan, so it was no surprise that Æthelhelm had done all he could to destroy his grandson's rival. And because I was Æthelstan's protector I had also become Æthelhelm's enemy. He had fought against me, he had lost, he had become my prisoner, and then he had died. We had sent his body home in a coffin, and I was told that by the time it reached Wiltunscir the corpse had swollen with gas, was leaking filthy liquid, and smelled vile.

I had liked Æthelhelm once. He had been genial and even generous, and we had been friends until his oldest daughter married a king and whelped a son. Now Æthelhelm's eldest son, also called Æthelhelm, was also my enemy. He had succeeded his father as Ealdorman of Wiltunscir, and believed, wrongly, that I had murdered his father. I had taken gold from his family, and that was cause enough to hate me. I also protected Æthelstan. Even though King Edward had put aside his second wife and taken a younger woman, Æthelhelm the Younger still supported Edward because he hoped to see his nephew become the next king, but that support was given only so long as Ælfweard, Æthelhelm's nephew, remained the crown prince. If Ælfweard became king, then Æthelhelm the Younger would remain the most powerful noble in Wessex, but if Æthelstan became king, then Æthelhelm and his family could look forward to royal revenge, to a loss of their estates, and even to enforced exile. And that prospect was more than enough reason to bribe a Welsh chieftain to take his famously savage warriors to Ceaster. If Æthelstan were to die, then Ælfweard would have no rival, and Æthelhelm's family would rule in Wessex.

So Æthelhelm the Younger had cause to want Æthelstan dead, but, if it were possible, he hated me even more than he detested Æthelstan, and I did not doubt he sought my death just as eagerly as he wished for Æthelstan's. And it was not just the death of his father that had prompted his hatred, but the fate of his youngest sister, Ælswyth.

Ælswyth had been captured alongside her father, and, after his death, she chose to stay at Bebbanburg rather than return to her family in Wessex. "You can't," I had told her.

"Why not, lord?" she had asked. I had summoned

her and she had stood in front of me, so young, so pale, so vulnerable, so enchantingly beautiful.

"You can't stay," I had spoken harshly, "because I have an agreement with your family. You will be returned to them when the ransom is paid."

"But the ransom isn't paid, lord."

"Your father is dead," I had insisted, and wondered why she showed so little grief, "so there can be no more ransom. You must go home, as agreed."

"And your grandchild must go too, lord?" she had asked innocently.

I had frowned, not understanding. My only grandchildren, my daughter's two children, were in Eoferwic. Then I did understand, and I had just stared at her. "You're pregnant?" I finally said.

And Ælswyth had smiled so very sweetly. "Yes, lord."

"Tell my son I'll kill him."

"Yes, lord."

"But marry him first."

"Yes, lord."

So they did marry, and in time a child was born, a boy, and as is the custom in our family he was named Uhtred. Æthelhelm the Younger immediately spread a new rumor, that we had raped Ælswyth and then forced her into the marriage. He called me Uhtred the Abductor, and no doubt he was believed in Wessex where men were ever ready to believe lies about Uhtred the Pagan. It was my belief that the summons from Edward that had required me to travel to Gleawecestre to pay homage for my Mercian lands had been an attempt to bring me within sword's length of Æthelhelm's revenge, but why lure me across Britain to Ceaster? He would have known I would bring warriors, and all he would have achieved was to combine my forces with Æthelstan's men, making the task of slaughtering either of us that much harder.

I had no doubt that Æthelhelm the Younger had committed treason by hiring Welsh troops to kill his nephew's rival. But it made no sense that he would have persuaded the monk to tell me the lies that had brought me across Britain to Ceaster.

Beneath us, on the arena's floor, the first prisoner died. A stroke of a sword, a severed head, and blood. So much blood. Æthelstan's revenge had started.

Not every prisoner died, Æthelstan showed more sense than that. He killed those men he judged to be close to Cynlæf, but spared the youngest. Thirty-three men died, all put to the sword, and I remembered a day when I had handed Æthelstan my sword and told him to kill a man.

Æthelstan had been a boy with an unbroken voice,

but I was training him to be a king. I had captured Eardwulf, also a rebel. It had happened not far from Ceaster, beside a ditch, and I had beaten Eardwulf down so that he lay half stunned in the scummy water. "Make it quick, boy," I had told Æthelstan. He had not killed before, but a boy must learn these skills, and a boy who would be king must learn to take life.

I thought about that day as I watched Cynlæf's men die. All had been stripped of their mail, stripped of anything of value. They shivered as, one by one, they were led to their deaths. Æthelstan must have remembered that distant day too because he used his youngest warriors as his executioners, doubtless wanting them to learn the lesson he had learned beside that ditch, that killing a man is hard. Killing a helpless man with a sword takes resolve. You look into their eyes, see their fear, smell it too. And a man's neck is tough. Few of the thirty-three died cleanly. Some were hacked to death, and the old arena smelled as it must have smelled when the Romans filled the tiered seats and cheered the men fighting on the sand below; a stink of blood, shit, and piss.

Æthelstan had killed Eardwulf quickly enough. He had not tried to hack off the rebel's head, but had instead used Serpent-Breath to cut Eardwulf's throat, and I had watched the ditch turn red. And Eardwulf had been Eadith's brother, and Eadith was now my wife.

Cynlæf died last. I thought Æthelstan might kill the rebel leader himself, but instead he summoned his servant, a boy who would grow to be a warrior, and gave him the sword. Cynlæf's hands were bound, and he had been forced to his knees. "Do it, boy," Æthelstan ordered, and I saw the youngster close his eyes as he swung the sword. He slammed the edge into Cynlæf's skull, knocking him sideways and drawing blood, but Cynlæf had hardly been hurt. His left ear was sliced open, but the boy's blow had lacked force. A priest, there were always priests with Æthelstan, raised his voice as he chanted a prayer. "Swing again, lad," Æthelstan said.

"And keep your eyes open!" I shouted.

It took seven blows to kill Cynlæf. Those of his men whom Æthelstan had spared would swear new oaths to a new lord, they would be Æthelstan's men.

So the rebellion was defeated, at least in this part of Mercia. The fyrd, dragged from their fields and flocks, had gone to their homes leaving only melting snow, the ashes of campfires, and Gruffudd's Welshmen who waited beside Cynlæf's tents.

"He calls himself a king," I told Æthelstan as we walked toward the tents.

"Kingship comes from God," Æthelstan said. I was surprised by that response. I had merely been trying to amuse him, but Æthelstan was in a grim mood after the killings. "He should have told us he was a king last night," he said disapprovingly.

"He was in a humble mood," I said, "and wanted a favor. Besides, he's probably king of three dung heaps, a ditch, and a midden. Nothing more."

"I still owe him respect. He's a Christian king."

"He's a mucky Welsh chieftain," I said, "who calls himself a king until someone who owns two more dung heaps than he does comes and slices his head off. And he'd slice your head off too if he could. You can't trust the Welsh."

"I didn't say I trusted him, merely that I respect him. God endows men with kingship, even in Wales." And, to my horror, Æthelstan stopped a few paces from Gruffudd and bowed his head. "Lord King," he said.

Gruffudd liked the gesture and grinned. He also saw his son who was still guarded by Folcbald and Oswi. He said something in Welsh that none of us understood.

"Gruffudd of Gwent begs you to release his son, lord Prince," Father Bledod translated.

"He agreed to give us a name first," Æthelstan said, "and his chain, and a pledge that he will keep the peace for a year."

Gruffudd must have understood Æthelstan's words because he immediately took the gold links from around his neck, handed them to Bledod, who, in turn, gave them to Æthelstan, who immediately handed the chain to Father Swithred. Then Gruffudd began telling a tale that Father Bledod did his best to interpret even as it was being told. It was a long tale, but the gist of it was that a priest had come from Mercia to talk with King Arthfael of Gwent, and an agreement had been made, gold had been given, and Arthfael had summoned his kinsman, Gruffudd, and ordered him to take his best warriors north to Ceaster.

"The king," Æthelstan interrupted at one point, "says the priest came from Mercia?"

That provoked a hurried discussion in Welsh. "The priest offered us gold," Father Bledod told Æthelstan, "good gold! Enough gold to fill a helmet, lord Prince, and to earn it we simply had to come here to fight."

"I asked if the priest was from Mercia," Æthelstan insisted.

"He was from the *sais*," Bledod said.

"So he could have been a West Saxon?" I asked.

"He could, lord," Bledod said unhelpfully.

"And the name of the priest?" Æthelstan demanded.

"Stigand, lord."

Æthelstan turned and looked at me, but I shook my

head. I had never heard of a priest named Stigand. "But I doubt the priest used his own name," I said.

"So, we'll never know," Æthelstan said bleakly.

Gruffudd was still speaking, indignant now. Father Bledod listened, then looked embarrassed. "Father Stigand is dead, lord Prince."

"Dead!" Æthelstan exclaimed.

"On his way home from Gwent, lord Prince, he was waylaid. King Gruffudd says he is not to blame. Why would he kill a man who might bring him more *sais* gold?"

"Why indeed?" Æthelstan asked. Had he expected to hear his enemy's name? That was naive. He knew as well as I did that Æthelhelm the Younger was the likely culprit, but Æthelhelm was no fool, and would have taken care to conceal the treachery of hiring men to fight against his own king. So the man who had negotiated with Arthfael of Gwent was dead, and the dead take their secrets to the grave.

"Lord Prince," Bledod asked nervously, "the king's son?"

"Tell King Gruffudd of Gwent," Æthelstan said, "that he may have his son."

"Thank you—" Bledod began.

"And tell him," Æthelstan interrupted, "that if he fights again for men who rebel against my father's throne then I will lead an army into Gwent and I will lay Gwent waste and turn it into a land of death."

"I will tell him, lord Prince," Bledod said, though none of us who were listening believed for one heartbeat that the threat would be translated.

"Then go," Æthelstan commanded.

The Welshmen left. The sun was higher now, melting the snow, though it was still cold. A blustery wind came from the east to lift the banners hanging from Ceaster's walls. I had crossed Britain to rescue a man who did not need rescuing. I had been tricked. But by whom? And why?

I had another enemy, a secret enemy, and I had danced to his drumbeat. Wyrd bið ful āræd.

Three

The next day dawned bright and cold, the pale sky only discolored by smoke from the fires as Æthelstan's men burned the remnants of Cynlæf's encampment. Finan and I, mounted on horses captured from the rebels, rode slowly through the destruction. "When do we leave?" Finan asked.

"As soon as we can."

"The horses could do with a rest."

"Maybe tomorrow, then."

"That soon?"

"I'm worried about Bebbanburg," I confessed. "Why else would someone drag me across Britain?"

"Bebbanburg's safe," Finan insisted. "I still think it was Æthelhelm who tricked you."

"Hoping I'd be killed here?"

"What else? He can't kill you while you're inside Bebbanburg, so he has to get you outside the walls somehow."

"I spend enough time with Stiorra and her children," I pointed out. My daughter, Queen of Northumbria, lived in Eoferwic's rambling palace, which was a mix of Roman grandeur and solid timber halls.

"He can't reach you in Eoferwic either. He wanted you out of Northumbria."

"Maybe you're right," I said, unconvinced.

"I'm always right. I'm from Ireland. I was right about the snow, wasn't I? And I'm still waiting for the two shillings."

"You're a Christian. Patience is one of your virtues."

"I must be a living saint then." He looked past me. "And talking of saints."

I twisted in the saddle to see Father Swithred approaching. The priest was mounted on a fine gray stallion that he rode well, calming the beast when it shied sideways as a man threw an armful of dirty thatch onto a fire. Smoke billowed and sparks flew. Father Swithred rode through the smoke and curbed the stallion near us. "The prince," he said brusquely, "requests your company today."

"Requests or requires?" I asked.

"It's the same thing," Swithred said, and turned his horse, beckoning us to follow him.

I stayed where I was and held out a hand to check Finan. "Tell me," I called after Swithred, "you're a West Saxon?"

"You know I am," he said, turning back suspiciously.

"Do you give orders to West Saxon ealdormen?"

He looked angry, but had the sense to suppress the fury. "The prince requests your company," he paused, "lord."

"Back in the city?"

"He's waiting at the north gate," Swithred said curtly. "We're riding to Brunanburh."

I spurred my horse alongside the priest's gray. "I remember the day I first met you, priest," I said, "and Prince Æthelstan told me he didn't trust you."

He looked shocked at that. "I cannot believe—" he began to protest.

"Why would I lie?" I interrupted him.

"I am devoted to the prince," he said forcefully.

"You were his father's choice, not his."

"And does that matter?" he asked. I deliberately did not answer, but just waited until, reluctantly, he added, "lord."

"The priests," I said, "write letters and read letters.

Prince Æthelstan believed you were imposed on him to report back to his father."

"And so I was," Swithred admitted, "and I will tell you precisely what I report to the king. I tell him his eldest son is no bastard, that he is a good servant of Christ, that he is devoted to his father, and that he prays for his father. Why do you think his father trusts him with the command of Ceaster?" He spoke passionately.

"Do you know a monk called Brother Osric?" I asked suddenly.

Swithred gave me a pitying look. He knew I had tried to trap him. "No, lord," he said, giving the last word a sour taste.

I tried another question. "So Æthelstan should be the next King of Wessex?"

"That is not my decision. God appoints kings."

"And is your god helped in his choice by wealthy ealdormen?"

He knew I meant Æthelhelm the Younger. It had occurred to me that Swithred might be sending messages to Æthelhelm. I had no doubt that the ealdorman sought news of Æthelstan and probably had at least one sworn follower somewhere in Ceaster, and I was tempted to think it must be Swithred because the stern, bald priest disliked me so much, but his next words surprised me.

"It's my belief," he said, "that Lord Æthelhelm persuaded the king to give this command to the prince."

"Why?"

"So he would fail, of course. The prince has three
burhs to command, Ceaster, Brunanburh, and Mameceaster, and not sufficient men to garrison even one
of them properly. He has rebels to contend with, and
thousands of Norse settlers north of here. Dear God!
He even has Norsemen settled on this peninsula!"

I could not hide my astonishment. "Here? On
Wirhealum?"

Swithred shrugged. "You know what's been happening on this coast? The Irish defeated the Norse settlers,
drove many of them out, and so they came here." He
gestured northward. "Out beyond Brunanburh? There
might be five hundred Norse settlers there, and even
more north of the Mærse! And thousands more north of
the Ribbel."

"Thousands?" I asked. Of course I had heard stories of the Norse fleeing Ireland, but thought most
had found refuge in the islands off the Scottish coast
or in the wild valleys of Cumbraland. "The prince is
letting his enemies settle on Mercian land? Pagan enemies?"

"We have small choice," Swithred said calmly.
"King Edward conquered East Anglia, now he's King

of Mercia, and he needs all his troops to put down unrest and to garrison the new burhs he's making. He
doesn't have the men to fight every enemy, and these
Norsemen are too numerous to fight. Besides, they're
beaten men. They were defeated by the Irish, they lost
much of their wealth and many of their warriors in
those defeats, and they crave peace. That's why they've
submitted to us."

"For now," I said sourly. "Did any of them join
Cynlæf?"

"Not one. Ingilmundr could have led his men against
us or he could have attacked Brunanburh. He did neither. Instead he kept his men at home."

"Ingilmundr?" I asked.

"A Norseman," Swithred said dismissively. "He's
the chieftain who holds land beyond Brunanburh."

I found it difficult to believe that Norse invaders
had been allowed to settle so close to Brunanburh and
Ceaster. King Edward's ambition, which was the same
as his father King Alfred's, was to drive the pagan foreigners out of Saxon territory, yet here they were on
Ceaster's doorstep. I supposed that ever since Æthelflaed's death there had been no stable government in
Mercia, Cynlæf's rebellion was proof of that, and the
Northmen were ever ready to take advantage of Saxon
weakness. "Ingilmundr," I said forcefully, "whoever he

is, might not have marched against you, but he could have come to your relief."

"The prince sent word that he was to do no such thing. We had no need of help, and we certainly had no need of pagan help."

"Even my help?"

The priest turned to me with a ferocious expression. "If a pagan wins our battles," he said vehemently, "then it suggests the pagan gods must have power! We must have faith! We must fight in the belief that Christ is sufficient!"

I had nothing to say to that. The men who fought for me worshipped a dozen gods and goddesses, the Christian god among them, but if a man believes the nonsense that there is only one god then there's no point in arguing because it would be like discussing a rainbow with a blind man.

We had ridden to the north of the city where Æthelstan and a score of armed riders waited for us. Æthelstan greeted me cheerfully. "The sun's shining, the rebels are gone, and God is good!"

"And the rebels didn't attack Brunanburh?"

"So far as we know. That's what we're going to find out."

For almost as long as I could remember, Ceaster had been the most northerly burh in Mercia, but Æthelflaed had built Brunanburh just a few miles north and west to guard the River Mærse. Brunanburh was a timber-walled fort, close enough to the river to protect a wooden wharf where warships could be kept. The purpose of the fort was to prevent Norsemen rowing up the Mærse, but if Swithred was right then all the land beyond Brunanburh between the Dee and the Mærse was now settled by pagan Norse. "Tell me about Ingilmundr," I demanded of Æthelstan as we rode.

I had asked the question in a truculent tone, but Æthelstan answered enthusiastically. "I like him!"

"A pagan?"

He laughed at that. "I like you too, lord," he said, "sometimes." He spurred his horse off the road and onto a track that skirted the Roman cemetery. He glanced at the weather-worn graves and made the sign of the cross. "Ingilmundr's father held land in Ireland. He and his men got beaten and driven to the sea. The father died, but Ingilmundr managed to bring off half his army with their families. I sent a message early this morning asking that he should meet us at Brunanburh because I want you to meet him. You'll like him too!"

"I probably will," I said. "He's a Norseman and a pagan. But that makes him your enemy, and he's an enemy living on your land."

"And he pays us tribute. And tribute weakens the payer and acknowledges his subservience."

"Cheaper in the long run," I said, "just to kill the bastards."

"Ingilmundr swore on his gods to live peaceably with us," Æthelstan continued, ignoring my comment.

I leaped on his words. "So you trust his gods? You accept they are real?"

"They're real to Ingilmundr, I suppose," Æthelstan said calmly. "Why make him take an oath on a god he doesn't believe in? That just begs for the oath to be broken."

I grunted at that. He was right, of course. "But no doubt part of the agreement," I said scathingly, "was that Ingilmundr accepts your damned missionaries."

"The damned missionaries are indeed part of the agreement," he said patiently. "We insist on that with every Norseman who settles south of the Ribbel. That's why my father put a burh at Mameceaster."

"To protect missionaries?" I asked, astonished.

"To protect anyone who accepts Mercian rule," he said, still patient, "and punish anyone who breaks our law. The warriors protect our land, and the monks and priests teach folk about God and about God's law. I'm building a convent there now."

"That will terrify the Northmen," I said sourly.

"It will help bring Christian charity to a troubled land," Æthelstan retorted. His aunt, the Lady Æthelflaed, had always claimed the River Ribbel as Mercia's northern frontier, though in truth the land between the Mærse and the Ribbel was wild and mostly ungoverned, its coast long settled by Danes who had often raided the rich farmlands around Ceaster. I had led plenty of war-bands north in revenge for those raids, once leading my men as far as Mameceaster, an old Roman fort on a sandstone hill beside the River Mædlak. King Edward had strengthened those old walls and put a garrison into Mameceaster's fort. And thus, I reflected, the frontier of Mercia crept ever northward. Ceaster had been the northernmost burh, then Brunanburh, and now it was Mameceaster, and that new burh on its sandstone hill was perilously close to my homeland, Northumbria. "Have you ever been to Mameceaster?" Æthelstan asked me.

"I was there less than a week ago," I said ruefully. "The damned monk who lied to me left us at Mameceaster."

"You came that way?"

"Because I thought the garrison would have news of you, but the bastards wouldn't talk to me, wouldn't even let us through the gate. They let the damned monk in, but not us."

Æthelstan laughed. "That was Treddian."

"Treddian?"

"A West Saxon. He commands there. Did he know it was you?"

"Of course he did."

Æthelstan shrugged. "You're a pagan and a Northumbrian and that makes you an enemy. Treddian probably thought you were planning to slaughter his garrison. He's a cautious man, Treddian. Too cautious, which is why I'm replacing him."

"Too cautious?"

"You don't defend a burh by staying on the walls. Everything to the north of Mameceaster is pagan country, and they raid constantly. Treddian just watches them! He does nothing! I want a man who'll punish the pagans."

"By invading Northumbria?" I asked sourly.

"Sigtryggr is king of that land in name only," Æthelstan replied forcefully. He saw me flinch at the uncomfortable truth, and pressed his argument. "Does he have any burhs west of the hills?"

"No," I admitted.

"Does he send men to punish evildoers?"

"When he can."

"Which is never," Æthelstan said scornfully. "If the pagans of Northumbria raid Mercia," he went on, "then we should punish them. Englaland will be a country ruled by law. By Christian law."

"Does Ingilmundr accept your law?" I asked dubiously.

"He does," Æthelstan said. "He has submitted himself and his folk to my justice." He ducked beneath the splintered branch of an alder. We were riding through a narrow belt of woodland that had been pillaged by the besiegers for firewood and the trees bore the scars of their axes. Beyond the wood I could see the reed beds that edged the flat gray Mærse. "He has also welcomed our missionaries," Æthelstan added.

"Of course he has," I responded.

Æthelstan laughed, his good humor restored. "We don't fight the Norsemen because they're newcomers," he said. "We were newcomers ourselves once! We don't even fight them because they're pagans."

"We were all pagans once."

"We were indeed. No, we fight to bring them into our law. One country, one king, one law! If they break the law, we must impose it, but if they keep it? Then we must live with them in peace."

"Even if they're pagans?"

"By obeying the law they will see the truth of Christ's commandments."

I wondered if this was why Æthelstan had demanded my company; to preach the virtues of Christian justice to me? Or was it to meet Ingilmundr, with whom he was so plainly impressed? For a time, as we rode along the Mærse's southern bank, he talked of his plans to strengthen Mameceaster, and then, impatient, he spurred his horse into a canter, leaving me behind. Mudflats and reed beds stretched to my right, the water beyond almost still, just occasionally ruffled by a breath of wind. As we drew closer to the burh I saw that Æthelstan's flag still flew there, and two low lean ships were safely tied at the wharf. It seemed Cynlæf's men had made no attempt to capture Brunanburh, which, as it turned out, had been garrisoned by a mere thirty men, who opened the gates to welcome us.

As I rode through the gate I saw that Æthelstan had dismounted and was striding toward a tall young man who went to his knees as Æthelstan came close. Æthelstan raised him up, clasped the man's right arm with both hands, and turned to me. "You must meet Ingilmundr," he exclaimed happily.

So this, I thought, was the Norse chieftain who had been allowed to settle so close to Ceaster. He was young, startlingly young, and strikingly handsome, with a straight blade of a nose and long hair that he wore tied in a leather lace so that it hung almost to his waist. "I asked Ingilmundr to meet us here," Æthelstan told me, "so we could thank him."

"Thank him for what?" I asked once I had dismounted.

"For not joining the rebellion, of course!" Æthelstan said.

Ingilmundr waited as one of Æthelstan's men translated the words, then took a simple wooden box from one of his companions. "It is a gift," he said, "to celebrate your victory. It is not much, lord Prince, but it is much of all that we possess." He knelt again and laid the box at Æthelstan's feet. "We are glad, lord Prince," he went on, "that your enemies are defeated."

"Without your help," I could not resist saying as Æthelstan listened to the translation.

"The strong do not need the help of the weak," Ingilmundr retorted. He looked up at me as he spoke, and I was struck by the intensity of his blue eyes. He was smiling, he was humble, but his eyes were guarded. He had come with just four companions, and, like them, he wore plain breeches, a woolen shirt, and a coat of sheepskin. No armor, no weapons. His only decorations were two amulets hanging at his neck. One, carved from bone, was Thor's hammer, while the other was a silver cross studded with jet. I had never seen any man display both tokens at once.

Æthelstan raised the Norseman again. "You must forgive the Lord Uhtred," he said. "He sees enemies everywhere."

"You are Lord Uhtred!" Ingilmundr said, and there was a flattering surprise and even awe in his voice. He bowed to me. "I am honored, lord."

Æthelstan gestured, and a servant came forward and opened the wooden box, which, I saw, was filled with hacksilver. The glittering scraps had been cut from torques and brooches, buckles and rings, most of them ax-hacked into shards that were used instead of coins. A merchant would weigh hacksilver to find its value, and Ingilmundr's gift, I thought grudgingly, was not paltry. "You are generous," Æthelstan said.

"We are poor, lord Prince," Ingilmundr said, "but our gratitude demands we offer you a gift, however small."

And in his steadings, I thought, he was doubtless hoarding gold and silver. Why did Æthelstan not see that? Perhaps he did, but his pious hopes of converting the pagans exceeded his suspicions. "In an hour," he said to Ingilmundr, "we will have a service of thanksgiving in the hall. I hope you can attend and I hope you will listen to the words Father Swithred will preach. In those words is eternal life!"

"We shall listen closely, lord Prince," Ingilmundr

said earnestly, and I wanted to laugh aloud. He was saying everything Æthelstan wanted to hear, and though
it was plain Æthelstan liked the young Norseman, it
was equally plain he did not see the slyness behind Ingilmundr's handsome face. He saw meekness, which
the Christians ridiculously count as a virtue.

The meek Ingilmundr sought me out after Swithred's interminable sermon, which I had not attended. I
was on Brunanburh's wharf, idly gazing into the belly
of a ship and dreaming of being at sea with the wind in
my sail and a sword at my side when I heard footsteps
on the wooden planks and turned to see the Norseman.
He was alone. He stood beside me and for a moment
said nothing. He was as tall as I was. We both gazed
into the moored ship and, after a long moment, Ingilmundr broke our silence. "Saxon ships are too heavy."

"Too heavy and too slow."

"My father had a Frisian ship once," he said, "and it
was a beauty."

"You should persuade your friend Æthelstan to give
you ships," I said, "then you can sail home."

He smiled, despite my harsh tone. "I have ships,
lord, but where is home? I thought Ireland was my
home."

"Then go back there."

He gave me a long look, as if weighing the depth of

my hostility. "You think I don't want to go back?" he asked. "I would, lord, tomorrow, but Ireland is cursed. They're not men, they're fiends."

"They killed your father?"

He nodded. "They broke his shield wall."

"But you brought men away from the battle?"

"One hundred and sixty-three men and their families. Nine ships." He sounded proud of that, and so he should have been. Retreating from a defeat is one of the hardest things to do in war, yet Ingilmundr, if he spoke truth, had fought his way back to the Irish shore. I could imagine the horror of that day; a broken shield wall, the shrieks of maddened warriors slaughtering their enemies, and the horsemen with their sharp spears racing in pursuit.

"You did well," I said, and looked down at his two amulets. "Which god did you pray to?"

He laughed at that. "To Thor, of course."

"Yet you wear a cross."

He fingered the heavy silver ornament. "It was a gift from my friend Æthelstan. It would be churlish to hide it away."

"Your friend Æthelstan," I said, mocking the word "friend" with my tone, "would like you to be baptized."

"He would, I know."

"And you keep his hopes alive?"

"Do I?" he asked. He seemed amused by my questions. "Perhaps his god is more powerful than ours? Do you care which god I worship, Lord Uhtred?"

"I like to know my enemies," I said.

He smiled at that. "I am not your enemy, Lord Uhtred."

"Then what are you? A loyal oath-follower of Prince Æthelstan? A settler pretending to be interested in the Saxon god?"

"We are humble farmers now," he said, "farmers and shepherds and fishermen."

"And I'm a humble goatherd," I said.

He laughed again. "A goatherd who wins his battles."

"I do," I said.

"Then let us make sure we are always on the same side," he said quietly. He looked at the cross that crowned the prow of the nearest ship. "I was not the only man driven out of Ireland," he said, and something in his tone made me pay attention. "Anluf is still there, but for how long?"

"Anluf?"

"He is the greatest chieftain of the Irish Norse and he has strong fortresses. Even fiends find those walls deadly. Anluf saw my father as a rival, and refused to help us, but that is not why we lost. My father lost the battle," he gazed across the placid Mærse as he spoke, "because his brother and his men retreated before the fight. I suspect he was bribed with Irish gold."

"Your uncle."

"He is called Sköll," he went on, "Sköll Grimmarson. Have you heard of him?"

"No."

"You will. He is ambitious. And he has a feared sorcerer," he paused to touch the bone-hammer, "and he and his magician are in your country."

"In Northumbria?"

"Northumbria, yes. He landed north of here, far north. Beyond the next river, what is it called?"

"The Ribbel."

"Beyond the Ribbel where he has gathered men. Sköll, you see, craves to be called King Sköll."

"King of what?" I asked scornfully.

"Northumbria, of course. And that would be fitting, would it not? Northumbria, a northern kingdom for a Norse king." He looked at me with his ice-blue eyes and I remember thinking that Ingilmundr was one of the most dangerous men I had ever met. "To become king, of course," he went on in a conversational tone, "he must first defeat Sigtryggr, yes?"

"Yes."

"And he knows, who does not, that King Sigtryggr's

father-in-law is the renowned Lord Uhtred. If I were Sköll Grimmarson I would want Lord Uhtred far from his home if I planned to cross the hills."

So this was why he had sought me out. He knew I had been lured across Britain, and he was telling me that his uncle, whom he plainly hated, had arranged the deception. "And how," I asked, "would Sköll do that?"

He turned to stare again at the river. "My uncle has recruited men who settled south of the Ribbel, and that, I am told, is Mercian land."

"It is."

"And my friend Æthelstan insists that all such settlers must pay tribute and must accept his missionaries."

I realized he was talking about the monk. Brother Osric. The man who had led me on a wild dance across the hills. The man who had lied to me. And Ingilmundr was telling me that his uncle, Sköll Grimmarson, had sent the monk on his treacherous errand. "How do you know all this?" I asked.

"Even we simple farmers like to know what is happening in the world."

"And even a simple farmer would like me to take revenge for his father's betrayal?"

"My Christian teachers tell me revenge is an unworthy thing."

"Your Christian teachers are full of shit," I said savagely.

He just smiled. "I almost forgot to tell you," he went on calmly, "that Prince Æthelstan asked that you should join him. I offered to carry the message. Shall we stroll back, lord?"

That was the first time I saw Ingilmundr. In time I would meet him again, though in those later encounters he shone in mail, was hung with gold, and carried a sword called Bone-Carver that was feared through all northern Britain. But on that day by the Mærse he did me a favor. The favor, of course, was in his interest. He wanted revenge on his uncle and was not yet strong enough to take that revenge himself, but the day would come when he would be strong. Strong, deadly, and clever. Æthelstan had said I would like him, and I did, but I also feared him.

Æthelstan had requested that I accompany him to Brunanburh and I had thought it was simply an opportunity for him to tell me about his hopes for Mercia and Englaland, or perhaps to meet Ingilmundr, but it seemed there was another reason. He was waiting for me at the fort's gate, and, when we joined him, he beckoned for me to walk a small way eastward. Ingilmundr left us alone. Four guards followed us, but stayed well out of earshot. I sensed that Æthelstan was nervous. He commented on the weather, on his plans to rebuild Ceaster's bridge, on his hopes for a good spring planting, on anything, it seemed, rather than the purpose of our meeting. "What did you think of Ingilmundr?" he asked when we had exhausted the prospects of harvest.

"He's clever," I said.

"Just clever?"

"Vain," I said, "untrustworthy and dangerous."

Æthelstan seemed shocked by that answer. "I count him as a friend," he said stiffly, "and I hoped you would too."

"Why?"

"He's proof we can live together in peace."

"He still wears Thor's hammer."

"So do you! But he is learning better! He's eager for the truth. And he has enemies among the other Norse, and that could make him a friend to us, a good friend."

"You sent him missionaries?" I asked.

"Two priests, yes. They tell me he is earnest in his search for truth."

"I want to know about your other missionaries," I went on, "those you sent to the Norse who settled south of the Ribbel."

He shrugged. "We sent six, I believe. They are brothers."

"You mean monks? Black monks?"

"They are Benedictines, yes."

"And did one of them have a scar across his tonsure?"

"Yes!" Æthelstan stopped and looked at me, puzzled, but I offered him no explanation for my question. "Brother Beadwulf has that scar," he told me. "He tells me he had an argument with his sister when he was a child and he likes to say she gave him his first tonsure."

"She should have slit his throat," I said, "because I'm going to tear his belly open from his crotch to his breastbone."

"God forgive you!" Æthelstan sounded horrified. "They already call you the priest-killer!"

"Then they can call me monk-killer too," I said, "because your Brother Beadwulf is my Brother Osric."

Æthelstan flinched. "You can't be sure," he said uncertainly.

I ignored his words. "Where did you send Brother Beadwulf or whatever he's called?"

"To a man called Arnborg."

"Arnborg?"

"A Norse chieftain who once held land on Monez. He was driven out by the Welsh, and settled on the coast north of here. He leads maybe a hundred men? I doubt he has more than a hundred."

"How far north?"

"He came to the Ribbel with three ships and found land on the southern bank of the river. He swore to keep the peace and pay us tribute." Æthelstan looked troubled. "The monk is a tall man, yes? Dark hair?"

"And with a scar that looked as if someone had opened up his head from one ear to the other. I wish they had."

"It sounds like Brother Beadwulf," Æthelstan admitted unhappily.

"And I'm going to find him," I said.

"If it is Brother Beadwulf," Æthelstan said, recovering his poise, "then perhaps he just wanted to help? Wanted the siege lifted?"

"So he lies to me about his name? Lies about where he's from?"

Æthelstan frowned. "If Brother Beadwulf has transgressed then he must suffer Mercian justice."

"Transgressed!" I mocked the word.

"He is a Mercian," Æthelstan insisted, "and while he is on Mercian soil I forbid you to harm him. He may be in error, but he is a man of God, and therefore under my protection."

"Then protect him," I said savagely, "from me."

Æthelstan bridled at that, but held his temper. "You may deliver him to me for judgment," he said.

"I am capable, lord Prince," I said, still savage, "of dispensing my own justice."

"Not," he said sharply, "inside Mercia! Here you are under my father's authority." He hesitated, then added, "and mine."

"My authority," I snarled, "is this!" I slapped Serpent-Breath's hilt. "And on that authority, lord Prince, I am riding to find Jarl Arnborg."

"And Brother Beadwulf?"

"Of course."

He stood straighter, confronting me. "And if you kill another man of God," he said, "you become my enemy."

For a moment I had no idea what to say, and for the same moment I was tempted to tell him to stop being a pompous little earsling. I had known him and protected him since he was a child, he had been like a son to me, but in the last few years the priests had got to him. Yet the boy I had nurtured was still there, I thought, and so I suppressed my anger. "You forget," I said, "that I swore an oath to the Lady Æthelflaed to protect you, and I will keep that oath."

"What else did you swear to her?" he asked.

"To serve her, and I did."

"You did," he agreed. "You served her well, and she loved you." He turned away, staring at the bare low branches of bog myrtle that grew in a damp patch beside a ditch. "You remember how the Lady Æthelflaed liked bog myrtle? She believed the leaves kept fleas away." He smiled at the memory. "And you remember this ditch, lord?"

"I remember it. You killed Eardwulf here."

"I did. I was just a boy. I had bad dreams for weeks afterward. So much blood! To this day when I smell bog myrtle I think of blood in a ditch. Why did you make me kill him?"

"Because a king must learn the cost of life and death."

"And you want me to be king after my father?"

"No, lord Prince," I said, surprising him. "I want Ælfweard to be king because he's a useless piece of weasel shit, and if he invades Northumbria I'll gut him. But if you ask me who ought to be king? You, of course."

"And you once took an oath to protect me," he said quietly.

"I did, to the Lady Æthelflaed, and I kept that oath."

"You did keep it," he agreed. He was staring into the ditch where some skims of ice still lingered. "I want your oath, Lord Uhtred," he said.

So that was why he had summoned me! No wonder he had been nervous. He turned his head to look at me, and I saw the determination in his face. He had grown up. He was no longer a boy or even a youth. He had become as stern and unbending as Alfred, his grandfather. "My oath?" I asked, because I was not sure what else to say.

"I want the same oath you gave to the Lady Æthelflaed," he said calmly.

"I swore to serve her," I said.

"I know."

I owed Æthelstan. He had been beside me when we recaptured Bebbanburg, and he had fought well there even though he had had no need to be in that fight. So yes, I owed him, but did he know he was asking the impossible? We live by oaths and we can die by them. To give an oath is to harness a life to a promise, and to break an oath is to tempt the punishment of the gods. "I swore loyalty to King Sigtryggr," I said, "and I cannot break that oath. How can I serve both you and him?"

"You can swear an oath," he said, "that you will never oppose me, never thwart me."

"And if you invade Northumbria?"

"Then you will not fight me."

"And my oath to my son-in-law?" I asked. "If," I paused, "when you invade Northumbria my oath to Sigtryggr means I must oppose you. You would want me to break that oath?"

"It is a pagan oath," he said, "and therefore mean-ingless."

"Like the oath you took from Ingilmundr?" I asked, and he had no reply to that. "My oath to Sigtryggr rules my life, lord Prince," I spoke his title with conde-scension. "I swore to the Lady Æthelflaed that I would protect you, and I will. And if you fight Sigtryggr I will keep that oath by doing my best to capture you in battle and not kill you." I shook my head. "No, lord Prince, I will not swear to serve you."

"I am sorry," he said.

"And now, lord Prince," I went on, "I am riding to find Brother Osric. Unless, of course, you choose to stop me."

He shook his head. "I will not stop you."

I watched him walk away. I was angry that he had asked for my oath. He should have known me better, but then I told myself he was growing into his author-ity, that he was testing it.

And I was pursuing Arnborg. Ingilmundr had told me that his uncle, Sköll Grimmarson, had received the allegiance of Norsemen settled south of the Ribbel, and I assumed Arnborg was one of those men. And Arnborg had sheltered Brother Osric, Brother Beadwulf, who had lied to me. I wanted to know why, and I suspected that Brother Beadwulf, after leaving us at Mameceaster, would have gone back to Arnborg's steading. So to find the monk I needed to go north.

I needed to go into the wild lands.

We did not leave at once. We could not. Our horses needed more rest, a half-dozen of the beasts were lame, and even more required reshoeing. So we waited three days, then left to go north, though the first part of our journey took us east toward the brine pits that soured the land around the River Wevere. Great fires burned where men boiled the brine in iron vats and where salt made heaps like snowdrifts. The Romans, of course, had made the saltworks, or at least had expanded them so they could supply all Britain with salt, and to make that easy they had embanked a road across the water meadows, raising it on a great causeway of gravel.

I had scouts ranging ahead, though there was small need of them on the wide flat plain across which the road ran like a spear. I expected no trouble, though only a fool traveled Britain's roads without taking precautions. In places we passed through thick woodland and it was possible that stragglers from Cynlæf's forces might be looking for unarmed travelers, but no hungry or desperate men would dare attack my men, who wore mail and helmets and were armed with swords.

But hungry, desperate men might have attacked our

companions, who were eighteen women on their way to establish the convent that Æthelstan wanted in Mameceaster and a dozen merchants who had been stranded in Ceaster by the siege. The merchants, in turn, had servants who led packhorses laden with valuable goods; tanned hides, silverware from Gleawecestre, and fine spearheads forged in Lundene. One packhorse carried the corpse of a man who had followed Cynlæf. The head was separately wrapped in canvas, and both head and body would be nailed to Mameceaster's main gate as a warning to others tempted to rebel against King Edward's rule. Æthelstan, his manner cold and distant after I had refused to give him my oath, had asked me to protect the merchants, packhorses, nuns, and corpse all the way to Mameceaster. "I'm not going that far," I told him.

"You're going to the Ribbel," he had pointed out, "going by Mameceaster is your easiest route."

"I don't want the settlers on the Ribbel to know I'm coming," I said, "which means I can't use the roads." Roman roads would lead us to Mameceaster and another road left that fortress and went north to Ribelcastre, a Roman fort on the Ribbel. Following such roads made travel easy; there was little chance of getting lost in endless tracts of wooded hills, and, at least in the larger settlements, there were barns to sleep in, smithies to shoe horses, and taverns accustomed to feeding travelers. But Arnborg, who I suspected might have occupied the old Roman fort at Ribelcastre, would have men watching the road. So I planned to approach him from the west, through land settled by Norsemen.

"The nuns need protection," Æthelstan had protested.

"So protect them," I had said, and so twenty-two of Æthelstan's spearmen rode to guard the travelers on the last part of their journey.

Sunngifu was one of the women. "What I don't understand," I said to her, "is why you need a convent in Mameceaster."

"Nuns are needed everywhere, Lord Uhtred," she said.

"Mameceaster," I said, "is a frontier burh. All the land around it is pagan, nasty and dangerous."

"Like you?"

I looked down at her. I had offered her one of my spare horses, but she had refused, claiming that Jesus's disciples had walked everywhere, so she and the sisters should do the same. "I'm nasty?" I asked. She just smiled. She was so breathtakingly beautiful even in a dark gray habit with a cowl covering her startling fair hair. "You'd better hope I am nasty," I told her, "because that will keep you safe."

"Jesus keeps me safe, lord."

"Jesus will be no damned use to you if a Danish war-band comes out of that wood." I nodded toward a stretch of leafless trees to the east, and thought of Abbess Hild, my friend now in far-off Wintanceaster, who had been raped repeatedly by Guthrum's Danes. "It's a cruel world, Mus," I said, using her old nickname, "and you have to hope the warriors defending you are just as cruel as your enemies."

"Are you cruel, lord?"

"I'm good at war," I told her, "and war is cruel."

She looked ahead to where Æthelstan's horsemen rode. "Will they be enough to protect us?"

"How many other travelers have you seen on this road?" I asked. We were going north, entering low hills and leaving the wide flat plain with its lazy rivers behind us.

"Not many," she said.

"Just three today," I said, "and why? Because this is dangerous country. It's mostly Danish with just a few Saxons. Until Edward made his burh at Mameceaster it was ruled by a Dane, and that was only two years ago. Now that country is being settled by Norsemen. I think it's madness sending you to Mameceaster."

"Then why won't you protect us all the way?"

"Because twenty-two warriors are enough to keep

you safe," I said confidently, "and because I have urgent business somewhere else and it will be quicker for me to cut across country." I was tempted to escort the nuns all the way to Mameceaster, but the temptation was solely because of Mus. I wondered about her. When she had been married to Bishop Leofstan she had whored enthusiastically, but Æthelstan had been certain she was a reformed sinner. Maybe she was, but I did not like to ask her. "What will you do in Mameceaster?" I asked instead.

"Maybe I'll take my vows."

"Why haven't you taken them yet?"

"I don't feel worthy, lord."

I gave her a skeptical look. "Prince Æthelstan believes you're the holiest woman he knows."

"And the prince is a good man, lord, a very good man," she said, smiling, "but he doesn't know women very well."

Something in her tone made me look at her again, but her face was all innocence, so I ignored her remark. "So what will you do in Mameceaster?" I asked instead.

"Pray," she said, and I made a scornful sound. "And heal the sick, lord." She gave me her dazzling smile. "And what's your business, lord, that makes you abandon me?"

"I have to kill a monk," I told her, and, to my surprise, she laughed.

We left them next morning, striking west into wooded hills. I had not been truthful with Mus, our quickest route was to follow the convenient Roman roads, but I needed to approach Arnborg's settlement without being discovered, and that meant cutting across the country, finding our way by instinct and by the sun. I doubled my scouts. We were entering land where the Danish had been reinforced by Norse settlers, where few Saxons survived, land that had been claimed by Mercia, but never occupied by Mercian troops. Mameceaster, the nearest burh, had been made deep in this land, a defiant gesture by Edward that claimed that he was king of all the country south of the burh, but many of the people here had not even heard of Edward.

The land was rich, but sparsely settled. There were no villages. In southern Mercia and in Wessex, which was now supposedly all one kingdom, there were settlements of cottages, usually built around a church and with no defensive palisade, but here what dwellings existed were almost all behind strong timber walls. We avoided them. We ate hard cheese, stale bread, and smoked herrings that Æthelstan's steward had given us from his storehouses. We carried forage bags for the horses because the spring grass was still weeks away. We slept in the woods, warmed by fires. Folk would see those fires and wonder who had set them, but we were still far south of the Ribbel, and I doubted that Arnborg would hear of us. Men must have seen us, even if we did not see them, but all they saw were some ninety armed riders with their servants and spare horses. We flew no banner, and the wolf heads on our shields were faded. If any folk did see us they would avoid us because in a dangerous land we were the danger.

Next day, late in a cold afternoon, we saw the Ribbel. It was a sullen day with a gray sky and a gray sea, and ahead of us stretched the wide estuary where gray mudbanks were edged with endless marshes. Smoke rose into the windless air from a dozen settlements on the estuary's shores. No ships disturbed the river's channels that threaded the mud, though I could see a score of fishing boats hauled above the high-tide mark. It was close to low tide now and some of the withies marking the channels were out of the water, which swirled fast and flat. The tide was big there, and the river was draining to the sea. "Good living," Finan murmured, and he was right. I could see the fish traps in the tangled channels, and both the mudbanks and the water were bright with birds; seabirds and shorebirds, swans and waders, godwits and plovers, geese and sanderlings. "Dear God," Finan said, "but look at those fowl! You'd never go hungry here!"

"There's good salmon too," I said. Dudda, a ship-master who had once guided us across the Irish Sea, had told me the Ribbel was a marvelous river for salmon. Dudda was a drunkard, but a drunkard who knew this coast, and he had often told me his dream of settling beside the Ribbel's estuary, and I could see why.

The settlers were Norsemen now. I doubted they had seen us. We had approached the river slowly, leading our horses, only moving when our scouts gave a signal. Most of my men and all our horses were now in a swale of icy puddles and brittle reeds, hidden from the river lands by a low rise crowned with trees and brush where I had posted a dozen men. I joined them, climbing the shallow slope quietly and slowly, not wanting to explode birds from their nests, and once on the crest I could see far across the estuary, and see rich steadings, too many steadings. As soon as we rode out of the icy swale we would be seen, and the news of armed strangers would spread across the river lands, and Arnborg, wherever he was, would be warned of our coming.

I was gazing at the closest steading, a substantial hall and barn surrounded by a freshly repaired palisade. The thatch on one of the lower buildings was new, while smoke rose from a hole in the highest roof. A boy and a dog were driving sheep toward the steading's open gates where one man slouched. The man was far away, but Finan, who had the keenest eyesight of any man I knew, reckoned he wore no mail and carried no weapon.

"We go there tonight," I told Finan. "You, me, Berg, and Kettil."

I had no need to explain what I planned. Finan nodded. "And the second group?"

"Eadric can pick a dozen men."

Finan looked up at the clouded sky. "There'll be no moon," he warned, meaning that we would be shrouded in utter darkness, liable to lose our way and blunder helplessly in the night.

"Then we go slowly and carefully," I said. I watched the last sheep disappear into the steading and saw the gates closed. The raw wood where the palisade had been patched suggested that whoever owned the steading had gone to expense and trouble to keep his home safe, yet the man guarding the gate had looked anything but alert. My father had always said that ramparts don't make you safe, it's the men guarding the ramparts who keep your women from rape, your children from slavery, and your livestock from slaughter. I guessed that whoever was in the steading wished nothing more than to stay warm. It was a freezing winter afternoon, the sheep were safely home, and sensible folk would want to stay close to their hearth, confident that the wolves were locked out.

We waited deep into that dark night. It was cold, and we dared not set any fires. We shivered. The only lights were glimmers of firelight showing in a handful of the homesteads. The closest one showed no light except, at first, a faint fire-glow in the hole of the hall's roof, and even that faded. And still we waited, too cold to sleep. "We'll be warm soon," I murmured to the men close to me.

I had memorized the look of the land. I knew we must walk across rough pasture to find a ditch and then follow the ditch north and west until we came to a straggling hedge that would take us east to the track where we had seen the sheep being herded, and that track would lead us to the closest steading. And we must become sceadugengan, the shadow-walkers, creatures of the night.

It is no wonder that the gates are closed and the hall doors barred at night, because the darkness is when the sceadugengan walk. They are shape-shifters; goblins, elves, sprites, and dwarves. They might choose to appear as beasts, as wolves or bulls, they come from Midgard to haunt the land, and they are neither alive nor dead, they are horrors from the shadows. And as at last we crossed the pasture, treading carefully in the absolute darkness, I thought of the old poem, the lay of Beowulf, which had been chanted in my father's hall and was still chanted in the same hall, now mine. "Com on wanre niht. Scriðan sceadugenga; sceotend scoldon," the harpist declaimed, and we would shudder at the thought of ghouls slithering from the darkness. "Then out of the night slides the shadow-walker; stealthy warrior." And we were the stealthy warriors.

I chanted the phrase over and over in my head as we left the woodland and walked toward the ditch. "Scriðan sceadugenga; sceotend scoldon, scriðan sceadugenga; sceotend scoldon." Over and over I said it silently, a mindless chant to keep the demons away. The approach to the steading seemed to take much longer than I had anticipated, so that I began to fear we had lost our way, but at last I smelled woodsmoke, and Finan must have seen some faint glow off to our left because he plucked my cloak. "This way," he whispered.

We followed the track. No grass beneath our feet now, only frost-hardened mud, sheep droppings, and horse dung, but there was the smallest glimmer of flame-light showing through a shutter of the hall that revealed a chink between the palisade's logs. No dog barked, no one shouted a challenge as at last we reached the steading. The gate was edged by two high trunks into which iron hinges were secured. We heard nothing except our footfalls, the sigh of a small night wind, the distant howl of a vixen, and an owl calling. "Ready?" I murmured to Berg and Kettil.

"Ready," Berg answered.

I stood with my back to the gate, linked my hands to make a step, and Berg, who was young and strong, put his hands on my shoulder, one foot on my hands, and heaved himself upward. I pushed him as he went. He made a scrabbling noise as he straddled the gate's top, and I waited for the howl of dogs as Kettil took his place. "I'm over!" Berg called softly. He had jumped down on the gate's far side, and I heaved Kettil up. He followed Berg over the gate, and I thought the noise they made must wake the dead, especially when the two lifted the great locking bar that scraped in its brackets. Still no barking. The hinges squealed as Berg and Kettil pushed the gate open.

"Call Eadric," I said, and Finan gave a short, sharp whistle. Eadric's men had followed us, and now they spread around the whole steading, their task to make certain no one left by a gate we had not seen or by climbing as Berg and Kettil had done. Eadric himself, with two men, joined us as Berg and Kettil pushed the great gate fully open. "Easy work, lord," Kettil said.

"So far."

The dogs woke at that moment. There were two of them that began barking somewhere to my left, but they had to be tethered because neither came close. The sheep began bleating, which only made the dogs even noisier. Finan and I had gone to the hall door and I heard movement on the far side, then a woman's voice shouted at the dogs to stop their noise. I drew Serpent-Breath as Finan slid Soul-Stealer from her long scabbard. I had expected to break the hall door down, but it seemed the folk inside would open it for us because I heard the bar being lifted and a wooden bolt shot.

The door was pushed open, immediately throwing light into the yard. Inside the hall a servant was feeding the hearth, and flames leaped up, and in that brighter light I saw two men, both bare-headed and neither wearing mail, standing with long spears a couple of paces beyond the door. A woman, swathed in a blanket, stood between them.

And what did they see?

They saw a nightmare. They saw warriors with drawn swords, warriors in mail, warriors with decorated helmets and closed cheek-pieces, cloaked warriors, night warriors, shadow-walkers with naked blades. One of the two men raised his spear and I smacked it aside with Serpent-Breath. The man's move had been tentative, he was too scared to attack with any force, maybe he had hardly meant to threaten me, but had just raised his blade without thinking. He gasped as my heavier blade drove the spear out of his hand. It clattered to the floor as Finan and I stalked into the hall. Eadric and his men followed us closely. "Drop that spear!" I snarled at the second man, and, when he did not obey, Finan just took the weapon from him.

"Who are you?" the woman asked. She showed more defiance than the two men, who backed away from us. Her gray hair was tied in a knot at the nape of her neck beneath a white woolen cap. She was tall, stoutly built, with a commanding face and indignant eyes. She clutched the heavy blanket around her shoulders and stared at me belligerently. "Who are you?" she demanded again.

"Your guests," I said, and walked past her to the hearth where the servant who had been reviving the fire now cowered. "Eadric!"

"Lord?" Eadric ran to me, grateful for what small warmth the hearth gave.

"Saxons!" the woman spat at me.

I ignored her. "Search the steading," I told Eadric, "then light a fire in the yard and try not to burn down the palisade."

The fire's glow would be a signal to our men still

waiting in the swale where the puddles were thick ice. Eadric, an older man and utterly reliable, was probably the best of my scouts. He twisted some dry floor rushes around a piece of wood, stooped to light it, and then carried the makeshift torch into the darkness, followed by two of his men. "Kettil, Berg! Search the hall," I ordered. There was a high platform in the hall, and beneath it a separate chamber. "Look in there," I told Berg, pointing to the chamber's door, then sheathed Serpent-Breath and walked back to the woman. "Your name," I asked in Danish, a language most of the Norse understood.

"My name is not for Saxon scum," she said.

I looked at the two disarmed men. "Your servants?" She did not answer, but did not need to. She was plainly in command of this household, and the two men looked as frightened of her as they were of me. "I'll blind both," I said, "one eyeball at a time, till you tell me your name."

She wanted to defy me, but relented when I drew a knife from my belt and one of the servants whimpered. "Fritha," she said reluctantly.

"Widow? Wife? What?"

"I am married to Hallbjorn," she said proudly, "and he will come soon, come with all his men."

"I'm terrified," I answered. Eadric's men were

carrying firewood from the hall into the yard. There was some small danger of alerting the nearer steadings if we lit a great fire in the open air, but it was a risk I was willing to take. Even if someone saw the flames I doubted they would investigate on this dark, freezing night, and I needed to bring my men and horses out of the cold and into warmth and shelter.

Berg, grinning happily, pushed two maidservants into the hall. "No one else here, lord," he said, "and there's just one door at the back."

"Barred?"

"Yes, lord."

"Keep it barred," I said, then pointed at the maids. "You two. Find food and ale, bring it. All of it!" One of the girls glanced at Fritha as if seeking her permission and I just growled, took one pace toward her, and she ran.

Fritha had noticed the hammer amulet that hung over my mail. She saw the same symbol around Berg's neck, then glanced at Finan, who wore a cross. She was confused, and I saw that she was about to speak when there was a sudden shout from outside the hall, a yelp, then a moment of silence before men laughed. Fritha clutched her hands together.

Eadric came in from the yard where the fire was now burning. "More women and children in the small hall, lord," he said, "two slaves in the barn, pair of dogs, a flock of mangy sheep, and just one horse."

"Bring all the people in here," I ordered him. "And what was that noise we just heard?"

Eadric shrugged. "It was outside, lord."

The answer to my question proved to be a boy, no more than eleven or twelve, who was dragged in by a grinning Folcbald, the big Frisian. "The little bugger jumped the palisade, lord," Folcbald explained, "and was running away."

"Don't hurt him!" Fritha called. "Lord, please!"

I walked to her, stared her in the eye. "So I'm no longer scum?"

"Please, lord," she said.

"Your son?" I guessed, and she nodded. "Your only son?" She nodded again. "His name," I demanded.

"Jogrimmr," she said the name in a whisper. There were tears in her eyes.

"Where were you going, Jogrimmr?" I asked the boy, though I still looked into his mother's eyes.

"To get help," the boy answered, and I could hear the defiance in his unbroken voice. I turned to see him glaring at me. Folcbald loomed above him, grinning.

I looked back to his mother, but still talked to the boy. "And tell me, Jogrimmr, where your father is."

"Coming to kill you."

"Many have tried, boy. I've filled the benches of Valhalla with men who thought I could be killed. Now tell me what I want to know."

The boy was stubbornly silent, and it was his mother who answered. "He has gone to join his lord."

"Arnborg?" I guessed.

"Arnborg," she said.

"Arnborg is a great lord!" the boy called behind me.

"Arnborg," I said, "is a piece of toad shit. And where is he?"

I still gazed into Fritha's eyes and saw a flicker of fear there. "I won't tell you!" Jogrimmr called boldly.

"Folcbald," I said, still looking at Fritha, "how do we kill small boys these days?"

Folcbald must have looked bemused because he said nothing, but Kettil, who was searching the hall's high platform, was quick-witted. "We killed the last one by nailing his head to a wall, lord."

"I remember," I said, and smiled at Fritha. "Where is Arnborg?"

"They went east, lord!" she said.

"The nail went in quickly, am I right, Kettil?"

"Much too fast, lord," he called down to me, "he died before he could tell us anything! You said the next time we must drive the nail slowly."

"And how did we kill the boy before that?"

"Oh, that one screamed, lord!" Kettil said happily. "Wasn't he the one we burned to death?"

"No," Folcbald had at last understood what we were saying, "we skinned that little bastard alive. It was the youngster before him we burned. Remember? He was a fat little boy and he sizzled. Smelled like bacon on a hot rock."

"Arnborg went east!" Fritha said desperately, "I don't know where!"

I believed her. "When?" I asked.

"A fortnight ago."

I heard hoofbeats sounding in the firelit yard and knew the rest of my men had brought the horses safely to the steading that was now ours. The hall began to get crowded as my warriors came into the warmth, and as the men, women, and children we had captured were driven inside. "How many men rode with your husband?" I asked Fritha.

"Six, lord."

"And how many with Arnborg?"

She shrugged. "Many, lord?" She plainly did not know, but I pressed her anyway.

"Many? A hundred? Two hundred?"

"Many, lord!"

"To join Sköll?" I asked.

She nodded. "Yes, lord. To join Sköll."

"Sköll is a great king!" her son called defiantly. "He is a warrior of the wolf! He has a sorcerer who turns men into ice!"

I ignored him, dismissing his words as a child's boast. "And Sköll," I still talked to Fritha, "where did he go?"

"East, lord," she said helplessly.

"And Arnborg's hall," I asked, "how far is it?"

"Close, lord."

"And how many men has he left there?"

She hesitated, then saw me glance at her son. "Maybe twenty, lord?"

We shut the gates, put the horses in the smaller hall and the barns, fed the great hearth, ate Hallbjorn's food, and some of us slept, though only after we had questioned every captive and learned that Arnborg's hall truly was close, built beside the Ribbel where the river widened out to the great estuary. Fritha, scared for her son's life, was eager to talk now and reckoned it was less than an hour's walk. "You can see it from our roof, lord," she said.

"He'll have left men there," Finan said to me in the dawn.

"But where has he gone? Where has Sköll gone?"

"East," Finan said unhelpfully. "Maybe just a cattle raid? A big one?"

"In winter? There'll be few cattle outside." We slaughtered our herds as the autumn faded and winter's grip chilled the land, keeping alive just enough beasts to breed for the following year, and most of those precious animals would be behind palisades. I had the dread feeling that I had made the wrong decision, that I should not be seeking the treacherous monk, but hurrying back to Bebbanburg. But Fritha had said her menfolk had left two weeks before, which meant that whatever they had left to do had probably been done already. And we had come this far, so we might as well find the monk with the scarred tonsure. If, indeed, he had returned here.

Which meant we must capture Arnborg's hall.

Nothing in war is simple, though fate had been kind to us on the night we took Hallbjorn's steading. We lost one horse that broke a leg when he stumbled into a ditch, but otherwise the worst we suffered was cold.

Assaulting Arnborg's hall would not be so easy. But at least the capture of Hallbjorn's steading had taken us close to the hall, and better still we had been undiscovered. We were on Arnborg's land, and none of his men knew we were there. Yet the moment we left the steading we could no longer hide, we must race across the winter ground to reach the palisade before any news of our coming alerted the men left to guard the hall. We had questioned Fritha and her people and had learned that the hall was built beside a creek of the Ribbel, that it was surrounded by barns and huts, that it had a strong palisade, and that Arnborg had left a garrison to protect his home. One servant, who had carried eggs to the hall the day before, agreed with Fritha that there were perhaps twenty men, "Or maybe thirty, lord?"

"Maybe forty, perhaps fifty," Finan growled as we spurred the horses on frost-hardened ground.

"At least he's not in the Roman fort," I said. I had feared Arnborg might have occupied the old fort that lay well inland, but it seemed, from what we had heard, that Arnborg liked to be close to the Ribbel's estuary so that his ships could slip out to sea where rich cargoes could be captured.

Twenty men did not sound like a fearsome enemy, but their advantage was that they could shelter behind their palisade, and though that wooden fence might not be as formidable as Bebbanburg's great ramparts, it would still be a daunting obstacle, which is why we rode hard and fast. If the defenders knew we were coming they could prepare, but if we appeared suddenly and unexpectedly then half of them would be in the hall, warming themselves by the hearth. We followed a well-beaten track that curved around the Ribbel's numerous channels. We crossed salt marshes, threaded reed beds, and all around us the shorebirds called and flew away in great flocks. No one could miss the sight of those thousands of white wings filling the sky, so Arnborg's men would know someone was moving on the estuary's bank, but why would they suspect an enemy?

Our horses' hooves smashed the cat ice where the track forded a shallow creek. Serpent-Breath was bouncing at my hip, while the shield on my back thumped rhythmically against my spine. We climbed a long shallow slope topped by a thick windbreak of willow and alder, ducked under low branches, and cantered out into the thin sunlight again, and there was Arnborg's steading, just as Fritha's people had described it.

It was a shrewd place to make a hall. One of the many creeks of the Ribbel curved here, and the water protected two sides of the high palisade. Three ships were moored in that creek, tied to a timber wharf that lay on the northern side of Arnborg's steading, which stretched southward by at least sixty paces. Inside the wall were the roofs of a hall and a cluster of other buildings; barns, stables, and storehouses. The one gate I could see was on the southern side, and it was closed. A flag hung above the gate, but in that morning's windless air it was impossible to see any badge or symbol on the cloth. There had to be a fighting platform beside the gate because two spearmen stood there, both just gaping at us for the moment. I waved to them, hoping the gesture would convince them we were friends, but I saw one turn and shout back into the steading.

There were two ways to capture a walled steading. The first and easiest was to show the defenders by how many they were outnumbered and promise that they would live if they surrendered. It usually worked, but I knew I would probably have to fight for this hall. Arnborg was a warrior and a leader of warriors, and we knew he had left a garrison to defend his home, and that suggested they would rather fight than betray their lord's trust. So fight we would, but if we were to fight, I wanted it to be quick. "Berg!" I called. "You know what to do! So do it!"

I swerved off the track, going away from the palisade and forcing Tintreg onto a plowed field that slowed him. Finan and most of my men followed, but Berg led eleven of my youngest and most agile warriors straight toward the palisade's closest corner, which was protected, like the rest of the landward wall, by a flooded ditch. Reeds grew in the ditch and betrayed that it was not deep, indeed I suspected that the ditch dried out quickly on a falling tide. One of the slaves at Hallbjorn's farm had said the ditch was little more than knee-deep, and I could only hope he was right. The man who had shouted from the fighting platform was calling again, pointing to the corner where I saw Berg's horse scramble into the ditch and saw Berg steady himself with one hand on the palisade as he stood on the saddle, then I watched as he reached up and grasped the wall's top. For a heartbeat he was poised against the winter sky, then he scrambled over, and I saw there must be a platform at the corner because Berg was able to stand there, lean over, and help the next man. The other horses crowded into the ditch and it seemed to take a long time, but at last all twelve managed to climb from their horses' backs, clamber over the high wall, and jump from the fighting platform to the ground beyond.

"Remember when we could have done that?" Finan asked. He had reined in beside me.

I laughed. "If we had to, my friend, we still could."

"Two shillings says you'd have fallen off the horse," he said, and he was probably right.

The fighting platform did not extend along the whole length of the southern wall because the two spearmen at the gate had disappeared from sight rather than run to confront the invaders. I heard a shout, the clang of swords, and I nudged Tintreg toward the gate. The noise from within the steading was louder, the harsh clash and scrape of blade on blade, a bellow of anger. "I should have led them," I said.

"You'd still be halfway up the wall," Finan said. "That's a job for young fools, not old men like us."

And my young fools, proud warriors, did what we had demanded. I saw Godric appear on the gate's fighting platform, waving us forward, and then the gate was pushed open and I spurred Tintreg as I drew Serpent-Breath. We had surprised the garrison, and now we would punish them for being surprised. I kicked Tintreg out of the plowland back onto the track, his hooves thundered on the hard-packed earth of the brief causeway that crossed the shallow ditch, I ducked under the crossbar that crowned the gate, and saw a group of men running to my left, intent on attacking Berg's young warriors who had their backs to the palisade and were fighting off an equal number of sword-Norse. But most of the Norsemen were not in mail and wore no helmets. Then someone screamed a challenge to my right and I slewed Tintreg to face the sound and saw a spear coming toward me. I wrenched Tintreg back to the left, the spear slashed close beside me, so close that the leaf blade sliced my right boot. I spurred toward the warrior who had thrown it, then she screamed again and I saw it was a woman. She was dressed in a thick wool gown covered by a heavy cloak of dark fur and had a silver-chased helmet crammed over black hair. She was shouting for someone to bring her another spear, but it was too late. My horsemen were crowding through the gate, they lowered their spears and rode at Berg's assailants. I saw a blade slice into a spine, saw the man arch back like a bow under tension, then the Norsemen were dropping their swords and kneeling in surrender. At least two bodies lay in blood, while a wounded man crawled toward the huts with his guts trailing in the mud. A dog howled. The woman still screamed for another spear, so I rode to her and slapped Serpent-Breath across her helmet, and she seized my leg and tried to haul me from the saddle. I hit her again, much harder, still using the flat of the blade, and this time she staggered back, her helmet askew and a tangle of black hair shrouding her angry face.

"Shut the gates!" I called to Berg.

"Did you lose anyone?" Finan called.

"None!" Berg was hauling the gates closed.

"You did well!" I shouted, and it had been well done. The young men had crossed a palisade and they had fought off defenders who, though they had been surprised, had been more numerous and had reacted faster than we had expected. I touched the hammer at my breast and silently thanked the gods for our success, and it was at that moment that I was struck.

I was struck by a thought. That when the gods favor you one moment they will punish you the next.

And in that moment of small victory, beneath a clearing sky, the darkness came. The sudden thought was as sharp as Gungnir, Odin's dreadful spear, and it told me that I was cursed. I cannot tell how I knew I was cursed, but know it I did. I knew that the gods were laughing at me while the three Norns, those heartless spinners at the foot of Yggdrasil, were amusing themselves with my life threads. The sun was shining, but I felt as though storm-dark clouds were shrouding the world, and I just sat in the saddle, not moving, gazing blindly toward the huts where a crowd of Arnborg's people were watching us nervously.

"Lord?" Finan edged his horse close to mine. "Lord!" he said again, louder.

I looked up for a sign, for any omen that I was not cursed. A bird in flight would reveal the will of the gods, I thought, but no birds showed. In that place of birds, beside an estuary of birds, there was just the burning winter sun, the pale sky, and the high rippled clouds. "There's a curse on me," I said.

"No, lord," Finan said, touching the cross at his breast.

"It's a curse," I said. "We should have gone to Bebbanburg, not here."

"No, lord," Finan said again.

"Just find the monk," I said.

"If he's here."

"Find him!"

Though what good would it do to find Brother Beadwulf if I were cursed? I could fight Arnborg, I could fight Sköll, I could fight Æthelhelm, but I could not fight the gods. I was cursed.

Wyrd bið ful āræd.

Four

The gods are not kind to us, any more than children are kind to their toys. We are here to amuse the gods, and at times it amuses them to be unkind. The Christians, of course, claim that any misfortune is caused by our own sin, that ill fate is their nailed god's way of punishing us, and if you point out that the wicked thrive they simply say that their god is unknowable. Meaning they have no explanation. I had done nothing I could think of to earn the displeasure of the gods, but I did not need to have offended them. They were simply amusing themselves, playing with me like a child plays with a toy, and so I clutched the hammer amulet in my gloved hand and prayed I was wrong. Perhaps my conviction that I was cursed was false, but there were no birds in the winter sky, and that omen told me I was the plaything of cruel gods. Cruel? Yes, of course, just as children are cruel. I remember Father Beocca crowing with delight when I had once said that our gods are like children. "How can a god be like a child?" he had demanded.

"Don't you Christians say we must be like Christ?"

He had frowned, suspecting a trap, then had nodded reluctantly. "We must indeed be Christ-like, yes."

"And when I was a child," I had pressed him, "didn't you tell me that your nailed god said we must all be like little children?"

He had just stared at me, spluttered for a moment, then had remarked that the weather was getting colder. I miss Father Beocca. He would have dismissed my fears of being cursed, but I could not dismiss the certainty that my fate was suddenly dire. All I could do now was survive, and the beginning of that survival was to discover whether the monk Beadwulf was still in Arnborg's fort.

"Eerika," Finan said behind me. I turned, puzzled, to see him gripping the arm of the angry woman who had tried to kill me with her thrown spear. "She's called Eerika," Finan explained, "and she's Arnborg's wife."

"Where is Arnborg?" I asked her.

"Hunting you," she said.

"Hunting me where?"

"Wherever he is."

"I can make her talk, lord," Eadric said. He spoke in English so that Eerika did not understand him, but she understood the vicious look on his face.

"No," I said, then swung down from Tintreg's saddle and called for Rorik to take the stallion. "Lady," I spoke to Eerika, "last night we took Hallbjorn's farm. His wife defied me too. Where do you think she is now?" Eerika did not answer. She was a fine-looking woman, maybe thirty years old, with dark eyes and a high-boned face. "Hallbjorn's wife," I told her, "lives. As does her son. We hurt neither of them and I left her silver to pay for the food we ate. Do you understand me?" She still just stared at me silently. "I've no wish to hurt you," I went on, "but I do need answers and I promise I will get them one way or the other. It would be easier, I think, if you just talked to me. So, where is Arnborg?"

"Gone east," she said curtly.

"Where?"

"East," she said stubbornly.

"With Sköll?"

"With Jarl Sköll, yes! And pray you never meet him or his sorcerer!" She spat toward me, but her spittle fell short. The mention of Sköll's famous sorcerer made me shudder. Had he cursed me?

I walked toward her, Serpent-Breath still naked in my hand. I saw her eye the blade nervously. "The missionary monk, Beadwulf. Is he here?"

She sneered at that question. "Is that why you came?"

"Is the monk here?" I repeated patiently.

"You can have him," she said in derision, then jerked her head toward the buildings beyond the great hall. "In his hut, of course."

"Which hut?"

"The dirtiest hut. The smallest one."

"We'll be gone soon enough," I said as I sheathed Serpent-Breath, sliding her into her scabbard very slowly so that Eerika would take note and, sure enough, she looked at the blade as I pushed it home. "And my sword," I went on, "is unblooded. But if any of your men lifts a hand against us, her blade will be drenched in their blood. And if you lift your hand against us, the blood will be yours." I nodded to Finan. "Let her go."

And so Finan, Berg, and I walked past the great hall, past two barns, and past a reeking blacksmith's forge to where smaller huts were the homes of Arnborg's warriors. Most of those warriors had ridden with their lord, gone eastward, but their women were still here, and they watched as we walked toward the last hut, a small thatched hovel with smoke trickling from its roof-hole. Newly woven willow fish traps were piled by the doorway. A sullen woman confirmed that it was the monk's home. "They had a bigger one," she said, "but when the other monk died . . ." she shrugged.

"And the monk is here?" I asked her.

"He's there," she said.

The hut was nothing but reed thatch, wattle, and sunbaked clay. The entrance was so low that we would have had to crawl inside, so instead I drew Serpent-Breath again and rammed her blade into the moss-covered thatch. A woman screamed from inside, then screamed again as I tore the reeds apart, opening up a gaping hole in the roof, then hacked again to widen the hole down to the low doorway. Finan and Berg helped, pulling away timber, withies, and thatch, and then at last we could look down into the hut's interior.

Where there were two people sitting on the far side of a hearth where a small fire burned. One, a girl, was clutching a robe to her breasts and staring up at us with wide, frightened eyes, while next to her, looking equally terrified and with an arm around the girl's thin shoulders, was a man I did not at first recognize. Indeed, I feared I had broken into the wrong hut because the man sheltering the girl had no tonsure, instead he had a full head of dark hair. Then he looked up at me, and I did recognize him. "Brother Beadwulf," I said.

"No," he shook his head wildly, "no!"

"Or is it Brother Osric?" I asked.

"No," he whimpered, "no!"

"Yes," I said, then stepped into the ruined hut, bent down, and seized Brother Beadwulf by his black robe. He yelped, the girl gasped, then I dragged him out, pulling his unresisting body across the burning hearth so that he screamed in pain and his woolen robe started to smolder. I threw him down among the wreckage of the thatch and watched him beat out the small flames. "Brother Beadwulf," I said, "we need to talk." And so we did.

It was the girl, of course. Her name was Wynflæd, she might have been thirteen or fourteen. She was a Saxon slave, and as skinny as a peeled willow wand. She had large and timid eyes, a pointed nose, reddish hair, and prominent upper teeth. She looked like a half-starved squirrel, and Brother Beadwulf was in love with her. He had taken an oath of celibacy, which is one of the more stupid things that Christians demand of their monks, but squirrel-faced Wynflæd had proven far stronger than Beadwulf's solemn promises to his nailed god. "I married her, lord," he confessed as he crouched at my feet.

"So you're no longer a monk?"

"I'm not, lord."

"But you're dressed as a monk," I said, nodding at his scorched habit with its grubby black cowl and rope belt.

He shivered, whether out of fear or cold I could not tell. Probably both. "I have no other clothes, lord."

The squirrel crept out of the hut's ruins to kneel beside her lover. She lowered her head, then put out a small pale hand and Beadwulf took it. Both of them were shaking in fear. "Look at me, girl," I ordered her, and the timid eyes, pale blue, gazed at me fearfully. "You're Saxon?" I asked.

"Mercian, lord." Her voice was scarce above a whisper.

"A slave?"

"Yes, lord."

She had been scaring birds away from a newly sown field when the Norse raiders had found her. She said it had happened a year before. I asked where she came from, and she seemed confused by the question. "Home, lord," was all she could say. She started crying, and Beadwulf put an arm around her shoulders.

"Give me one good reason," I said to him, "why I should not take your head from your shoulders."

"They were going to kill her, lord," Beadwulf said.

"Wynflæd?"

"Arnborg said he would kill her if I didn't do what he wanted." He lowered his head and waited. I said nothing. "They said they would drown her, lord," Beadwulf muttered, "just as they drowned Brother Edwin."

"He was the other missionary?"

"Yes, lord."

"You say they drowned him?"

"You can see him, lord," Beadwulf said with a sudden pleading energy. He pointed northward. "He's still there, lord!"

"Where?"

"Out there, lord."

He had pointed toward a smaller gate that led, I assumed, to the long wharf where the ships were moored. I was curious. "Show me," I said.

Berg pushed the gate open and we went onto the timber wharf. The tide was low and the three ships were canted on the mud, their mooring lines slack. "There, lord," Beadwulf said, and pointed across the nearest ship's deck, and I saw a thick stake had been driven into the mudbank on the creek's further side. A skeleton hung there, held in place by twisted ropes. The skull had fallen off, the ribs were mangled, and the flesh had long been torn away by beaks.

"What happened?" I asked.

"Jarl Arnborg tied him there at low tide, lord."

"Why?"

"The jarl said we had no need to pay tribute to Mercia, lord, and he had no need of driveling missionaries. That's what he said, lord."

That made some sense. The Mercian rebellion would have persuaded Arnborg that the Saxons were weakened and he must have reckoned he no longer needed to pay tribute, nor keep Christian missionaries, and so Brother Edwin had been lashed to the stake, and I imagined the strong tide swirling up the creek, flooding the mudbank, and rising slowly for the amusement of the watching Norse. The monk would have cried out, praying to either his god or the Norse to spare him, to save him. And still that great tide rose, and he would have strained upward, gasping for every last breath, and in his ears would have been the laughter of his enemies. "Why didn't Jarl Arnborg kill you too?" I asked Beadwulf.

He gave me no answer so I seized his robe and pushed him to the wharf's edge where I made him gaze down into the rippled water that just covered the creek's muddy bed. "Why," I snarled, "did Jarl Arnborg not kill you too?"

He made a sound, half whimper, half moan, and I nudged him as though I was about to let him fall. "Tell me," I said.

"He thought I could be useful, lord," he whispered.

"By telling me lies."

"Yes, lord," he said. "I'm sorry, lord. Please, lord."

I held him above the shallow water for a few heart-beats, then pulled him back. "Why?" I asked. He was shaking so much that he seemed incapable of answering, and so I threw him hard against the palisade that edged the landward side of the wharf. He slid down to the planks. Wynflæd started toward him, then stopped when I drew Serpent-Breath.

"No!" she cried aloud.

I ignored her. Instead I pushed the sword's tip against Beadwulf's throat. "Why," I asked, "did Arnborg want me at Ceaster?"

"So you would not be at Jorvik, lord."

He had spoken so softly that I thought I had misheard. "So I would not be where?" I demanded.

"At Jorvik, lord. Eoferwic."

Jorvik? That was the name that the Danes and Norse used for Eoferwic. I stared at Beadwulf, puzzled. "Why would I be at Eoferwic?" I asked, more to myself than to the miserable excuse of a man who groveled at my feet.

"You were there at Christmas, lord," he answered, "and it's known that you're . . ." his voice dribbled away to silence.

"What is known?" I asked, lifting the sword-blade to touch the stubble on his chin.

"That you are often at Jorvik, lord."

"Where my son-in-law rules and where my daughter lives," I said, "so of course I visit Eoferwic." And suddenly I understood. Maybe the cold had dulled my wits, because I had been gaping at Beadwulf like an idiot, his answers making no sense. But now it all made sense, too much sense. "Are you telling me," I asked him, "that Sköll has gone to Jorvik?"

"Yes, lord," his voice was so faint I could scarcely hear him.

"Sweet Jesus," Finan said.

"Lord, please?" Wynflæd was crying.

"Quiet, girl!" I snapped. I pulled the sword back. "How many men does he lead?"

"Jarl Arnborg took sixty-three, lord."

"Not Arnborg. You fool! Sköll!"

"I don't know, lord," Beadwulf said.

I rammed the sword forward, checking it as the tip pressed on his throat. "How many men did Sköll lead to Jorvik?" I asked. Beadwulf had pissed himself, and a yellow stain showed on the frost-covered planks of the wharf. "How many?" I asked again, keeping the blade at his gullet.

"They all went, lord!" Beadwulf said, gesturing across the cold estuary.

"All?"

"The Norse, the Danes, all of them, lord." He gestured northward again. "All, lord! From here to the Hedene!"

The land north of the Ribbel was called Cumbraland, a wild land. It was supposedly a part of Northumbria, but Æthelstan had been right when he claimed that Cumbraland was lawless. Sigtryggr claimed it, but he did not control it. Cumbraland was a savage region of mountains and lakes where the strongest ruled and the weakest were enslaved. The River Hedene was the frontier with Scottish land, and between that border and the Ribbel were scores of Danish and Norse settlements. "How many rode to Eoferwic?" I asked.

"Hundreds, lord!"

"How many hundreds?"

"Three? Four?" It was plain Beadwulf did not know. "They all rode, lord, all of them! They believed no one would be ready for an assault in the winter."

And that was true, I thought. The fighting season began in the spring, because the winter was when folk crouched by the fire and endured the cold. "So why," I asked, "has Sköll gone to Eoferwic?" I knew the answer, but wanted Beadwulf to confirm it.

Beadwulf crossed himself, plainly terrified. "He would be King of Northumbria, lord." He dared look up at me, desperation on his face. "And he is terrible, lord!"

"Terrible?"

"Lord, he has a powerful sorcerer, and Sköll is an *úlfheðinn*."

Until that moment the curse had been a vague fear, as formless as the serpent-breath whorls on my sword's blade, but now the fear congealed into something as hard, cold, and terrifying as the blade itself.

Because my enemy was a wolf-warrior, and he would be King of all Northumbria.

I was cursed.

Eerika, Arnborg's wife, was laughing at us. "Sköll's men are the *úlfhéðnar*," she said, "and they will slaughter you. You are sheep, they are wolves. Your blood will soak the hillsides, your skin will make saddles, your flesh will feed pigs! They are the *úlfhéðnar*! You hear me, Saxon? They are the *úlfhéðnar*!"

We had gone to Arnborg's hall, where a dozen of my men raked through the bedding and the wooden chests in search of plunder. I had taken nothing but food and ale from Hallbjorn's steading, and even that I had paid for with hacksilver, but Eerika was determined to defy me, insult me, and frighten me, so I allowed my men to ransack her goods. I let her rant for the moment, stooping instead to one of the hearthstones and picking up an oatcake. I took a bite. "Good!" I said.

"May it choke you," Eerika snarled.

"Lord! Look!" Rorik, my servant, had dragged down the flag from above the gate. It was a pale gray banner on which was embroidered a black ax. He spread it wide and I saw that it was a careful piece of work, lovingly sewn through the long winter evenings, a fine flag edged with a border of black linen. "Shall I burn it, lord?"

"No! Keep it!"

"Take one thing from me," Eerika spat, "and your death will be slow. Your screams will echo in the underworld, your soul will go to the death-worm and writhe in timeless agony."

I took another bite from the oatcake. "Your husband is *úlfheðinn*?" I asked.

"He is a wolf-warrior, Saxon. He feeds on Saxon livers."

"And was thrown out of Ireland," I sneered. "Finan!"

"Lord?"

I smiled at Eerika. "Finan is from Ireland," I told her, then turned to him. "Tell me, Finan, what do the Irish do to the *úlfheðnar*?"

He smiled too. "We kill them, lord, but only after we've blocked our ears with wool."

"And why do you do that?" I asked, still looking at Eerika.

"Because their screams are like the crying of babies," Finan said.

"And no one likes that sound."

"So we dull our ears, lord," Finan went on, "and when the baby *úlfhéðnar* are all dead we enslave their women."

"What do you think of this one?" I asked, gesturing with the oatcake toward Eerika. "Too old for slavery?"

"She can cook," he said grudgingly.

Eerika turned on him. "May you die like a rat," she began, then stopped suddenly because I had rammed the rest of the oatcake onto her mouth.

I held it there, crumbling it against her stubbornly closed lips. "There is a slave market two days south of here," I told her, "and if I hear one more word from you I shall carry you there and sell you to some hungry Mercian. And it will not be your food he hungers for. So be quiet, woman."

She stayed quiet. In truth I rather admired her. She was a proud woman, her eyes were full of defiance, and she had the courage to confront us, but I had seen that her words were scaring some of my men. "Berg!" I shouted.

"Lord?" Berg was on one of the high sleeping platforms, searching through piles of fleeces.

"You told me once your brother is an *úlfheðinn?*"

"Both my brothers, lord." Berg was a Norseman, one of the many who followed me. I had saved him from execution on a Welsh beach, and he had been loyal to me ever since. "I have been an *úlfheðinn* too, lord," Berg said proudly. He touched a finger to his cheek where he had inked a wolf's head. That wolf mask was my symbol, painted on my men's shields, though the inked heads on Berg's cheeks looked more like a pair of half-decayed pigs.

"So tell us," I said, "what an *úlfheðinn* is."

"A wolf-warrior, lord!"

"We're all wolf-warriors," I said. "We carry the wolf head on our shields!"

"A wolf-warrior, lord, is given the spirit of the wolf before battle."

"He becomes a wolf?"

"Yes, lord! A wolf-warrior fights with the savagery of a wolf because he becomes a wolf in his spirit. He howls like a wolf, runs like a wolf, and kills like a wolf."

"But we men kill wolves," I said. I could see my Saxons, the few in the hall, were listening carefully.

"We don't kill Fenrir, lord," Berg said, "and Fenrir

is the wolf who will slaughter Odin in the final chaos of Ragnarok."

I saw Eadric cross himself. "So the wolf-warrior," I asked, "is given the spirit of a great wolf?"

"The greatest wolf, lord! Which means that an *úlf-heðinn* fights with the anger of the gods in his heart!"

"So how do we, mere men, defeat the *úlfhéðnar?*" I asked, hoping that Berg would be clever enough to understand why I was asking him these questions.

He was. He laughed and tossed a wolf pelt down from the platform. "We become *úlfhéðnar* ourselves, lord! And you have already killed the *úlfhéðnar* in battle after battle! You are a wolf-warrior, lord, maybe the greatest of all the wolf-warriors, and we are your pack."

I had killed *úlfhéðnar*. They were men who often howled like wolves, while other warriors called out insults. They liked to wear wolf skins. They fought like madmen, but madmen do not fight well. They have savagery and seem careless of danger, but the skill of war starts with the hours and days and weeks and months and years of practice; it is sword-skill, shield-craft, and spear-skill, the endless learning of the crafts of slaughter. I have seen enemies screaming like wild beasts, spitting as they charge with glazed eyes, but they died like other men, and they were often the first to die, yet still the *úlfhéðnar* scared many warriors. Some men claimed that the *úlfhéðnar* fought drunk, but so did other warriors, while Ragnar, who had adopted me, said that the wolf-warriors drank the piss of horses that had been fed the mushrooms that give a man strange dreams, and maybe he was right. Berg, sensibly, had mentioned none of that. Ragnar had feared the *úlfhéðnar*, saying they were stronger, quicker, and more savage than other fighters, and even the Christians, who claimed they did not believe in Odin or Fenrir or Ragnarok, were frightened by the madness of the *úlfhéðnar*.

"But we are better than the *úlfhéðnar*," I insisted. "We are the wolves of Bebbanburg, and the *úlfhéðnar* fear us! You hear me?" I called out to the whole hall. "They fear us! Why else send the monk to lie to us? The *úlfhéðnar* fear us!"

We had been lured across Britain. There was a compliment in that, though I was in no mood to appreciate it. Sköll Grimmarson had led an army east to Eoferwic, and the only reason for that journey was to take the throne of Northumbria from Sigtryggr, my son-in-law, and Sköll had taken care to make certain I was nowhere near that throne. Evidently the *úlfhéðnar* feared the wolves of Bebbanburg.

And, despite all I had tried to tell my men, I feared the *úlfhéðnar*.

And now we must ride east to meet them.

Beadwulf and his squirrel rode with us. I had thought to kill him in revenge for his treachery, but the squirrel had pleaded with me, and Beadwulf, on his knees, had promised to show me a great treasure if I spared him. "What's to stop me killing you after I take the treasure?" I had asked him.

"Nothing, lord," he had said.

"So show me."

He had led me to what I had thought was a small granary, a wooden hut raised on four stone pillars that were meant to keep rodents from entering. Beadwulf unbolted the door and climbed inside. I had followed to see dim shelves on which were stored pots, each about the size of a man's head. He took one down, placed it on a table, and used a small knife to cut through the wax that sealed the wooden lid. "This is the only one left, lord," he had said as he pulled the lid free and handed me the pot.

The pot held the chopped roots of some plant mixed with a host of small brown seeds. I had looked at Beadwulf in the hut's gloom. "Seeds and roots?"

"It's the secret of the *úlfhéðnar*, lord," he had said.

I took out a handful and sniffed. It stank. "What are they?"

"Henbane, lord."

I had let the seeds and roots fall back. Henbane was a weed, and we feared it because it could poison pigs, and pigs were valuable. "The *úlfhéðnar* eat this?" I had asked, dubiously.

Beadwulf shook his head. "I pound the mixture, lord," he showed me a pestle and mortar on the shelf, "then make an ointment of wool grease and the crushed plant."

"And Arnborg trusted you?"

"I was a herbalist in the monastery, lord. I know things that Arnborg's folk never discovered. When his wife was sick I cured her with celandine. You use the roots and you must say the *Pater Noster* ten times as you mix—"

"I don't care about celandine," I had snarled, "tell me about the henbane."

"I made the ointment for Jarl Arnborg, lord, and it was better than the paste Snorri made."

"Snorri?"

"Sköll's sorcerer, lord. He is a powerful sorcerer, lord," Beadwulf had made the sign of the cross when he said that, "but he used the leaves and petals of the plant to make his ointment. The seeds and roots have more power."

"So you make an ointment?"

"And the warriors smear it on their skin, lord."

"And what does that do?"

"The men think they can fly, lord. They stagger, they howl. Sometimes they just fall asleep, but in battle it turns them into madmen."

I sniffed the pot again and almost retched. "Have you tried it?"

"Yes, lord."

"And?"

"I thought I saw God, lord. He glowed and had wings."

"You saw God? Not Wynflæd?"

He had blushed. "I am a sinner, lord."

I gave him back the pot. "So Arnborg took seeds with him?"

"He took four jars of the prepared ointment, lord."

"You have the grease?"

"Yes, lord."

"Make me a pot," I had ordered him.

"Lord?" he had pleaded, and waited till I nodded. "If I stay here, lord," he went on, "Eerika will kill me. She will think I brought you here."

"You did bring me here," I had said, "but if you're so scared, just go. Walk south. Take your girl."

"They'll follow me, lord. Take us with you. I can treat the sick. Please, lord."

I had scowled at him. "How can I trust you?"

"Do I look like a man who would offend you again, lord?"

And that, I confess, had made me smile. Beadwulf was thoroughly cowed. It would have been easy to kill him, even satisfying, but Wynflæd was so pathetic, so wan and childlike, that I relented. "Make me the wolf ointment," I had told him, "and then you can ride with us."

We plundered the hall for warm clothing, took all eight horses that were still in Arnborg's stables, burned the three ships at the wharf, and, under a pale afternoon sun, went eastward.

Finan spurred his horse alongside mine. "You're such a weakling, lord," he said.

"I am?"

He grinned, turned, and nodded toward Beadwulf and Wynflæd who were mounted on the same horse, a big, placid gray gelding we had taken from Arnborg's stables. The squirrel sat in front, enfolded by the monk's arms. "I felt sorry for her," I said.

"That's what I meant."

"Killing him would be too easy."

"So what will you do with him?"

I shrugged. "Let them both go, I suppose. I don't care what happens to them. I care about Stiorra and my grandchildren."

Stiorra was my daughter, and sometimes I thought she should have been my son because she was the strongest of my children. My eldest boy shared her strength, but he had become a Christian, a priest no less, and that made him no son of mine. My second son, named Uhtred like me, was a good warrior and a good man, but he had none of Stiorra's strength of will. She had married Sigtryggr, who had once been my enemy, but was now my son-in-law and King of Northumbria, and they lived with their two children in the old Roman palace in Eoferwic. "Eoferwic's walls are strong," Finan said, reading my thoughts.

"But to Sigtryggr and Stiorra," I said, "the enemy are the Mercians. Not the pagans. If Sköll comes to their gate they'll likely invite him into the city."

"Not if he has an army with him," Finan retorted. He glanced toward the setting sun. "If I know Sigtryggr," he said, "then Sköll Grimmarson and his men are slaughtered by now." He saw he had not convinced me. "If two or three hundred warriors turned up at the Skull Gate at Bebbanburg, would you let them in?"

"Of course not."

"And you think Sigtryggr would?"

I touched the hammer hanging at my neck and prayed he was right.

We spent that night in the remnants of the Roman fort at Ribelcastre, a fort that had guarded the ford where the road that led north to Cair Ligualid crossed the Ribbel. I had thought that some of the Danes or Norse who had fled to this wild country would have taken the fort for themselves, but it was deserted, nothing but weather-worn turf walls and the rotted stumps of an ancient palisade. "They fear the place, lord," Beadwulf told me. "They believe it is a haunt of ghosts." He crossed himself.

"So you're still a Christian?" I asked sourly.

"Of course, lord!" He frowned uncertainly. "It's just that the monastic life . . ." he shrugged, evidently lost for words.

"Only lets you hump other monks?" I finished for him.

"Please, lord!" he protested, blushing.

"So what will your abbot do when he finds you've broken your vows?"

"If he finds me, lord? He'll beat me."

"I just hope Wynflæd is worth the beating," I said.

"Oh she is, lord! She is!"

We had ridden from Arnborg's home through good farm country, but we had seen few people, and those we did see were old, children, or women, which was hardly surprising if most of the men of fighting age had followed Sköll Grimmarson eastward. The first few steadings we had passed all belonged to Arnborg's men, who I assumed were now somewhere close to Eoferwic. I touched the hammer again, praying they were not in the city that lay some three or four days' journey across the high moors.

It was a cold night. We cut wood, mostly alder and birch, and used it for fires, confident that the fighting men of the district were far away. We had stripped Arnborg's hall of pelts, fleeces, even woolen rags, anything that might keep us warm. I placed sentries who gazed into the frost-bright night beneath a star-filled sky. The few high clouds were drifting southward and the next day promised to be dry, cold, and hard.

We had two ways to reach Eoferwic. The easiest route, and the longest, was to follow the good Roman road south to Mameceaster, then take another Roman road that went northeast and led straight to Sigtryggr's city. The shorter route also followed Roman roads, but one of Arnborg's slaves, a sullen Saxon who had driven cattle across the moors, told us the road was decayed. "You can get lost up there, lord," he had warned me.

"There are places the road is washed out. It's hard to follow."

Nevertheless I was determined to use the shorter route. I needed to reach Eoferwic swiftly, needed to discover what had happened in eastern Northumbria. Perhaps Sköll Grimmarson had not ridden to Eoferwic, but had gone to Bebbanburg instead? I only had Beadwulf's word for where Arnborg had gone. "Wasn't he worried you'd betray him?" I asked Beadwulf in the heart of that freezing night.

"He was holding Wynflæd as a hostage, lord."

I grimaced. "The power of women."

"Besides, lord," he went on, "I only discovered what they planned when I returned. When I came to you I still believed what Arnborg had told me, that Prince Æthelstan was under siege."

"And Arnborg paid Prince Æthelstan tribute," I said.

"He did once, lord."

But the Danes and the Norse who lived in the western wilds of Cumbraland had seen Mercia weakened by rebellion, and they, like Sigtryggr, had been living under the fear of a Saxon invasion. The Mercian rebellion had encouraged them to break free. "Why didn't they just ally with Sigtryggr?" I asked. "He fears the Saxons as much as they do."

"They believe he is weak, lord."

I laughed at that. "Sigtryggr? He's not weak."

"They call him a client king, lord."

"Client to who?"

"To the Christians."

"Christians! He's a pagan like me!"

"But Eoferwic is filled with Christians, lord, and the archbishop is there, and he's a Saxon."

"Hrothweard is a good man," I said grudgingly.

"Snorri says that the archbishop has ensorceled Sigtryggr, lord."

"Ensorceled?"

"Used magic spells to make Sigtryggr obedient, lord. And Jarl Arnborg says there are too many Saxon Christians in Northumbria, lord. He fears they would fight for Mercia if it came to war, and King Sigtryggr is blinded to the danger."

I shook my head. "Eoferwic is a Christian city, and Sigtryggr rules there. He needs the Christians, he tolerates them, and he tries hard not to make enemies of them." I turned and looked back into the firelit fort. "Most of my men are Christians. What am I supposed to do, slaughter them?"

"Sköll Grimmarson believes Northumbria needs a stronger king, lord," Beadwulf had finished.

So once again I was fighting for the Christians! I

would have laughed if I had not been so fearful for Eoferwic's fate. Everything Beadwulf told me that night
made sense. The Danes in Mercia had succumbed
to the Saxons, many of them becoming Christians,
just as the conquered Danes in East Anglia had converted. Mercia might be troubled by rebellion, but it
was plain to anyone that the Saxons wanted to invade
Northumbria when the rebels were defeated. They
were making King Alfred's dream come true. When I
was a child the land that would become Englaland had
been divided into four kingdoms; Northumbria, East
Anglia, Mercia, and Wessex. Four kingdoms and four
kings. The Danes had invaded, they had taken Northumbria, taken East Anglia, taken all of northern Mercia, and very nearly subjugated Wessex, but the Saxons
had fought back. I had fought back, at times reluctantly,
fighting to make Alfred's dream of one Saxon kingdom
come true, and the realization of that dream was so
close now! The West Saxons had already invaded East
Anglia and made it part of their kingdom, and now Edward, *Anglorum Saxonum Rex*, was binding Mercia to
the West Saxon throne. Only Northumbria was left. It
was the last pagan kingdom in Englaland.

And the Norse, the fierce Norse, were making Cumbraland their new home. No man fights the Norse will-
ingly, but their weakness is that they rarely unite. They

follow their chieftains and, when those chieftains quarrel, they fight each other. And those divisions had led to defeat in Ireland and to savage combats along the western coast of Scotland, and so the losers sailed in their dragon-boats to Cumbraland, the last refuge in Britain. And now a new leader had appeared, Sköll Grimmarson, who had performed the miracle of uniting the Norse war-bands, and was seeking his own kingdom, my kingdom, Northumbria.

"I should have taken the throne of Northumbria," I grumbled to Finan next morning.

"Yes, lord, you should. Why didn't you?"

"I never wanted to be a king."

"And if you had been king," he asked, "what would you have done?"

"I'd have hammered these Norsemen into obedience for a start," I said, though in truth I was talking nonsense. If Sigtryggr had taken men west into Cumbraland then either the Mercians or the Scots would have attacked Eoferwic in the east, and so long as he defended the east, so long would the western part of his kingdom stay lawless. "You don't win wars by defending," I said, "and if Northumbria is to stay free then it needs to attack."

But that was a notion as wispy as the high thin clouds that were being driven away by a brisk wind, and behind those wispy clouds was a wall of dark, tumultuous cloud that promised snow. It was still bitterly cold. The horses' hooves shattered ice at the river's edge when we took them to the ford to drink, while the turf on which we had tried to sleep was frost hard. Soon after dawn we loaded the packhorses, saddled the stallions, and left the smoking ashes of our campfires behind. I wanted to hurry, but dared not because we had few spare horses and could not risk losing any to a broken leg, and the Roman road was now little more than a trace of half-buried stones in the frost-paled turf of the hills. Our breath misted, and the small streams were frozen. The scouts, mounted on our swiftest stallions, rode ahead, and it was those scouts who first saw the approaching horsemen.

It was midafternoon. The sky was covered in dark cloud, and every few minutes there were spatters of sleet, though the threatened hard fall of snow had not yet arrived. The road, laid arrogantly straight across the flank of a hill, ignoring spurs and streams, had climbed all day, and we were now in bare, bleak moorland, still climbing, but I saw that our furthest scouts, maybe a mile ahead, had dismounted and were keeping below the skyline of a high spur. That told me there were other men even farther ahead, men who would have seen our scouts outlined against the gray winter sky if those scouts had not been so cautious. Then one of those far scouts hauled himself into his saddle, turned his horse, and spurred back toward us. "Trouble," Finan grunted.

There were no steadings this high on the moors. In summer sheep and goats might be brought here to graze, but in winter the land was empty, and so it was unlikely that any merchants would be traveling this broken road across the moors. "It must be men coming back from Eoferwic." I suggested.

"Defeated men, I hope," Finan said. He and I had hurried ahead to meet the scout, Kettil, curbing our horses where some yards of the road had long ago been washed away by a sudden flood. Kettil slowed as he neared us, and let his horse pick its way across the slope.

"Men, lord," he said, "maybe two hundred? Some on the road, some are driving cattle in the valley." The valley was a wide, boggy swale to our left.

"How far away?"

"A good mile beyond that crest, lord. And they're coming slow because of the cattle."

Any cattle captured at this time of year would have been taken from byres or barns, not from the fields. The herds had been slaughtered at the beginning of winter, with just enough beasts left safe behind walls to breed for the new year, so the approaching men must have raided Sigtryggr's land, maybe my land too, and had doubtless stolen cattle, silver, and slaves, and were now bringing their spoils home. The presence of the cattle, indeed of the men themselves, suggested they had failed to capture Eoferwic. Why else would they be coming west across the hills instead of staying in the city?

"Just two hundred men?" Finan asked.

"So far," Kettil said, "but more were still coming when I left."

"Scouts?" I asked.

"None, lord." Kettil spat. "Reckon they feel safe without them. There's enough of the bastards."

"We'll go south," I said bleakly. "We'll let them pass, but I want to capture some of the bastards too." I would have preferred to go north because the land there was more rugged, promising more hiding places, but the valley immediately to our north was wide, and I reckoned it would take too much time to reach the far crest, time in which the approaching enemy might see us, while the southern skyline was much closer. I stood in my stirrups, pointed south, and the far scouts, who had already started back toward us, saw my gesture and changed direction. Then I led my men over the hill, and, once hidden from the road, dismounted.

I lay on the crest, waiting, watching, and shivering. A hard fall of rain swept the valley. It was no longer sleet, so perhaps it was warmer, though I felt chilled to the marrow. The wind gusted, died, and gusted again, billowing the great veils of rain. The hard rain stopped, and for a while there was nothing to see except a pair of curlews above the empty valley and a buzzard drifting south on the uncertain wind. Was that an omen? During the night I had woken, cold and shivering, with the memory of a dream fresh in my mind. I had been steering a ship along a strange shore, looking for a safe harbor and finding none, and I had tried to see the message in that dream, but I could find nothing ominous in the dream-ship or the placid shore. The gods do talk to us in our dreams, just as the flight of birds can reveal their wishes, but it seemed the gods were not talking to me. The buzzard flew out of sight. I wanted a reassurance from the gods, and I was finding none.

"There," Finan said beside me, and I saw the first horsemen appear on the eastern crest.

And so they came, horseman after horseman, and in the wide valley to their north were straggling lines of cattle herded by boys. "Christ," Finan said, "there's more than two hundred of the bastards!"

Some men were on foot, while others guarded the women and children who had been captured. Those women would mostly be sold as slaves, though doubtless some would find new husbands among the Norse. I had gestured Beadwulf to join us, snarling at him to crawl the last few paces so his head did not show above the skyline. "Tell me if you see Sköll," I ordered him.

"I've never seen him, lord." He saw the anger on my face. "But they say he is a big man and that he wears a cloak of white fur."

For a time we lay in silence, just watching the folk trudge along the road. I counted over three hundred men before Beadwulf made a nervous sound. "There, lord," he said, his eyes widening as he watched a knot of horsemen, perhaps forty or fifty strong, appear beneath us.

"There what?"

"That must be Sköll Grimmarson," he said, speaking softly as though he feared the far horsemen could hear us. "The man in the white bear fur, lord," he added, and there, riding alone at the center of the horsemen, was a big man on a big horse wearing a big cloak of pure white fur.

I had heard of the white bears, though I had never seen one. But travelers said that in the far north where the snow never melts and where even in summer the sea is ice-locked there are massive bears with thick white pelts. I would never have believed such stories had I not once seen such a pelt for sale in Lundene, though at a price that only a king could afford. Most of the men riding with Sköll wore gray cloaks. Wolf pelts? Were those men, I wondered, the feared *úlfhéðnar*?

"And that's his sorcerer, lord," Beadwulf was whispering, "Snorri." He did not need to point out the sorcerer, who had long white hair and wore a long white robe beneath a cloak of dark fur. I instinctively touched my hammer amulet. "He's blind, lord," Beadwulf said.

"The sorcerer?"

"They say Sköll blinded him with a red-hot sword tip, lord."

"Jesus," Finan muttered in disgust. But it made sense to me. We know that Odin's great wisdom came at the price of an eye, so Sköll had made his sorcerer pay double the price to endow him with even more knowledge.

"Men fear Snorri," Beadwulf said, "because he sees the future and he can kill with a curse." He watched the riders beneath us. "And I think that's Arnborg," Beadwulf went on, "the man on the roan horse, lord. I think that's him. It looks like his horse."

The roan horse was some twenty paces behind Sköll and his sorcerer, but the rider was too far away for me to make out his face. He wore a helmet, a sword hung by his side, and a great dark cloak covered his horse's rump. Like most of the passing riders he slumped in his saddle, plainly weary, and I was tempted to tell my men to mount, then charge across the crest and wreak havoc on the horsemen below. Kill the leaders, I thought, and the rest of the Norsemen would be discouraged. It was a risk, I might lose some horses to broken legs, and perhaps the Norsemen were not as tired as they appeared, and I was still weighing the dangers of such an attack when even more riders appeared. "God in his heaven," Finan said, "but how many are there?"

There must have been at least sixty horsemen following Sköll's group. They were not quite the last, because a quarter mile or so behind came a straggling bunch of women and children, guarded by nine horsemen. Some of the women limped, others were carrying small children, while the riders were using spears to goad the captured slaves, who numbered some thirty or forty. "I want prisoners," I said, and looked at Finan. "Tell the Christians to hide their crosses."

Finan hesitated, as if tempted to warn me against trying something rash, then abruptly nodded and wriggled back downhill. "What will you do, lord?" Beadwulf asked me nervously.

"I need prisoners," I said. "I need to know what happened at Eoferwic." Did I really need to know? The appearance of the Norsemen suggested they had failed, and that was surely news enough, yet I wanted to know more. I wanted to know the full story of their failure. So I would take prisoners.

I looked westward. The road crossed a lower spur some half a mile away, and then dropped out of sight. If I timed my approach right, then Sköll and his men would not see what was happening behind them. And if they did? It would take them time to return and fight us, time enough for us to retreat, and I doubted they would want to pursue us far into the waning afternoon.

Behind me my men were mounting their horses. I went back and joined them, pulling myself into Tintreg's saddle. "Rorik!" I called. "You have that flag we took from Arnborg's hall?"

"Of course, lord."

"Put it on our staff!" One of our packhorses carried my wolf's head banner on a pole, and Rorik now untied that flag and laced on the captured banner. I did not want to charge recklessly down the hill and so risk breaking a horse's leg, but if we went slowly then the few men guarding the prisoners might send a warning to the warriors ahead. A familiar banner would reassure them that they had no need to raise the alarm. Or so I hoped. And, I thought, if I took just a handful of men, then the ruse would be even more convincing.

"Berg," I called, "choose eight men."

"Eight?"

"Just eight. All of them Norsemen or Danes! Rorik! Bring the flag."

"What about me?" Finan asked, reluctant to be left out of any fighting.

"I need you up here. Wait till we've captured the bastards, then show yourself if you need to." Finan was the only man I trusted to understand what I planned. If it all went wrong, if Sköll Grimmarson turned around and threatened us, then the sight of almost a hundred warriors on a hill crest might give him pause. It seemed he had failed to capture Eoferwic, so why would he want to lose more men? Warriors were valuable, even more valuable than the cattle and slaves he was driving westward.

"We go slowly," I told Berg. "No shields. I want them to think we're scouts returning to the road."

"They didn't have scouts, lord," Berg pointed out.

"Maybe these men at the rear don't know that," I said, then nudged Tintreg up the slope and saw that the larger mass of horsemen had disappeared across the western crest, while the small group of prisoners, guarded by the nine horsemen, were alone on the road. "Let's go," I said.

And so we walked the horses up the slope and then along the skyline. The wind blew harder, but our captured flag was heavy with rainwater and did not unfurl, and so I ordered Rorik to wave the staff. One of the horsemen below looked up. I watched the man, but he showed no alarm. Scouts normally carry no flags because they do not want to be noticed, but the horseman who stared up at us appeared to see nothing strange. He did not spur his horse ahead, but just looked away and kept the same slow pace, and so we angled down the hill. "You and I get ahead of them," I told Berg, knowing the other eight men, four of them Norsemen and four Danes, were listening. "The rest of you follow the captives. Don't alarm their guards! We're all friends."

Henkil Herethson laughed. He was a Danish Christian, a rarity in Northumbria, who had served in my cousin's garrison at Bebbanburg. He had fought us there, but had sworn allegiance to me and had proved himself loyal. He liked to fight with a double-bladed ax that now hung at his saddle. I noted that his cross was hidden.

"Don't draw swords," I went on, "till I beckon you. Then ride alongside them and watch to see when I draw Serpent-Breath. That's when you attack. And I want prisoners. Two prisoners at least. And Rorik!"

The boy grinned, knowing what I was about to say. "I'm to stay out of the fight, lord?"

"You're to stay out of the fight."

The enemy plainly suspected nothing because they had paused, waiting for us. We reached the road and spurred toward them as the prisoners collapsed at the road's edge. I could hear a child crying and saw one of the mounted men smack the infant's mother across the head with his spear shaft. "It is a horrible noise," Berg remarked to me.

"You'll hear it often enough," I said. "Is Hanna pregnant yet?"

"She might be, lord. We try hard enough."

I laughed, then held up a hand to check the men following us. They curbed their horses just a few paces from the rearmost enemy, while Berg and I went on. I nodded companionably to the nearest spearman and spurred Tintreg on past the prisoners to where a glum-looking man with drooping gray mustaches slumped in his saddle. His cloak, mail, and helmet looked better than the rest, and I assumed he was the leader. "It's cold!" I called.

"Almost lambing time," he said. "It should be warmer than this." He frowned, perhaps realizing that he had never seen me before. Water beaded the rim of his helmet. "You're one of Jarl Arnborg's men?"

"I'm his uncle," I said, "his father's brother."

"You were at Jorvik?"

"We were too late," I said. "We just came from Ireland. Folkmar," I introduced myself.

"Enar Erikson." he responded.

"We should keep going," I said. "There are Saxons over that hill." I nodded south.

Enar looked alarmed. "Following us?"

"Just searching. They were far off and didn't see us. But keep going anyway."

He waved his men on. Some of the women cried as they were prodded with the long spears, but they stood and shambled on reluctantly. "We should just kill them," Enar said, looking sourly at the prisoners. "We have enough slaves," he grumbled, "these ones are sick and slow."

"They'll still fetch silver," I said.

"Where? Dyflin has more than enough slaves already."

Dyflin, I knew, was the largest Norse settlement in Ireland, and the largest slaving town in the west. Most slaves were carried to Frankia or else sold in Lundene, but those markets were far away and difficult to reach from Cumbraland. "Slaves are slaves," I said vaguely, "they're all valuable."

"Then we should just kill the damned children," Enar said. "We can always give the women more." He chuckled at that.

"Why don't you?" I asked. He looked startled at that suggestion. "If they're slowing you down," I went on, "why not just kill the little bastards?"

He grimaced. "Young ones are valuable."

"They do make a horrible noise though," I said, then paused because four horsemen had appeared on the skyline ahead; four horsemen who were spurring back toward us. "Who are they?" I asked.

Enar muttered a curse, then twisted in his saddle. "Hurry them!" he shouted at his men, who responded by thumping their spear staves on the women's backs.

I wanted to curse too. I had deliberately brought a small number down the hill, relying on surprise to give us an advantage in the fight I knew lay ahead, but now the ten of us would face thirteen. I saw that all four of the approaching horsemen wore the gray wolf-pelt cloaks. Were they the *úlfhéðnar*? They rode fine horses, wore bright mail beneath the pelts, and had helmets crested with wolf tails. Their leader, or at least the man at their head, rode a tall black stallion, had a long fair beard, and his helmet was chased with silver. He looked young, but he had an arrogant confidence that spoke either of noble birth or early achievement. "If you can't keep up," he called to Enar as he came closer, "we'll abandon you. Make the bitches move faster!"

"We're trying, lord," Enar answered.

"Then try harder. Kill the ugliest bitch as an example." He reined in and frowned at me. "Who are you?"

"Folkmar, lord," I answered humbly.

He must have noted the quality of my bridle, mail, and helmet. "Where are you from? I haven't seen you before."

"The Ribbel, lord."

"He's Arnborg's uncle, lord," Enar put in helpfully.

"Arnborg's uncle was killed at—" the young man began, then snatched at his sword. I had already begun to draw Serpent-Breath and she was quicker from the scabbard than his blade, but he was fast. I swept the sword back-handed, but the young man ducked and spurred, and Serpent-Breath cut uselessly into his wolf-tail crest. He back-handed too, his blade striking my back, but without enough force to cut the mail beneath my cloak. He was on my right, but on my left one of his companions tried to ram his horse into Tintreg. The man's sword was half drawn as I cut Serpent-Breath across his face, starting blood. I spurred forward, turned back to my right to see the young man in the silvered helmet was close behind. He was fast, he was good. I began a second back-swing as he lunged his sword at my side, and that lunge should have pierced my mail and driven deep into my belly, and the only thing that saved me was his horse stepping on one of the big stones that edged the road. The horse staggered sideways, the young man's lunge went wide, and Serpent-Breath struck the back of his helmet hard. The blade split the metal and cracked into bone. I had a glimpse of blood and white bone, then the young man toppled from his rich saddle.

I turned Tintreg back. Another of the wolf-pelt warriors was spurring at me, sword raised to strike, and I roweled Tintreg hard, and felt the battle-rage. The stallion leaped forward, the man's sword came down savagely, but I had closed on him too fast and his sword arm struck my shoulder just as Serpent-Breath skewered into his belly, breaking mail. I turned away, twisting the blade as I let Tintreg's strength tug the sword free. Enar was in front of me now. He had drawn his sword, but seemed frozen by fear or indecision, and while he dithered I slammed Serpent-Breath down on his forearm with enough force to make him drop the sword, then, as I passed him I hammered the back of his helmet. I used the flat of the blade, knocking him forward onto his horse's mane. I was not sure he was stunned, so I slammed the hilt down onto his head, then snatched his horse's bridle and dragged it off the road. Berg, on the road's far side, had thrust his sword into the belly of one horseman and sliced off the sword

hand of another. One of the riders who had been prod-
ding the women with his spear stave rode at me, his
spear leveled, but I could see the fear in his eyes. The
violence had started so quickly, none of the Norsemen
had been ready for a fight, while my men were hungry. I spurred Tintreg again, slammed the spear aside
with Serpent-Breath and then, because he was now
too close, punched Serpent-Breath's heavy hilt into the
man's face. I felt his nose break, saw the blood splatter,
then he whimpered as Rathulf, one of my Danes, slid
a sword into the small of his back. The man toppled
sideways, his spear falling with a clatter onto the road-
side stones. "Take his horse!" I told Rathulf.

The women were shrieking, the children bawling,
and an unhorsed man was screaming as Henkil's ax
loomed above him. "Take prisoners!" I bellowed over
the cacophony. Henkil must have heard me, but still
slammed his heavy blade down, and a child shrieked in
terror as the fallen man's head was split in two. "Prisoners!" I shouted again, then saw that Enar had somehow recovered and was urging his horse westward. I
dug my heels into Tintreg's flanks, galloped alongside,
and hit the back of Enar's helmet again, harder still,
but again using the flat of my sword. This time he fell
from the saddle, and I seized his horse's bridle. Berg
came to help, dismounting and stripping away the un-

conscious man's sword belt. "What about the women, lord?" he asked.

"We can't help them," I said. I regretted that, but we were a small band of warriors in a wide land infested by the enemy. We had to move swiftly or die. I looked back to see that my men had beaten down all the remaining enemy. The suddenness of their attack had won the small fight, but three of the enemy had still escaped and were spurring their horses westward.

We had two prisoners. Enar was one. I dismounted and went to look at the young man whose sword had so nearly wounded me. He was either dead or unconscious. Serpent-Breath had opened the back of his helmet as if it were an eggshell, and there was a mess of bone and blood in the ragged gap. I kicked the fallen man in the chest to turn him over, but he showed no sign of feeling the blow. I stooped and ripped off a golden chain that hung at his neck, then took his sword, which had a hilt ringed with gold. I undid his sword belt, tugged it free, and the violence of the tug forced a groan from him. I sheathed the precious weapon and threw it to Rorik. "Look after it! It's valuable." I pulled myself back into the saddle and shouted at Berg to hurry. He had managed to drape Enar over a saddle and was tying his hands and feet to the girth strap. Rathulf was securing the second prisoner, a much younger man, while the women were begging us to take them away. One woman held her baby up to me. "Take her, lord! Take her!"

"We can't take any of you!" I hated telling her that. The best we could do for the women was to give them food we had found in sacks tied to the captured saddles. Three of the women were searching the corpses, looking for coins or food.

"Lord, we must hurry!" Berg said to me. He was right. The three horsemen who had escaped our attack were almost at the western crest of the road. It would not be long before Sköll sent men back to punish us.

"Are the prisoners secure?"

"Yes, lord."

"Then we go."

"Lord!" a woman called. "Please, lord!"

It hurt to leave them, but I dared not take them. We kicked our horses off the road and up the slope, leading five captured stallions and the two prisoners. Once over the crest I planned to go south until I was sure any pursuit had been left behind, then we would return to the road and hurry back east to Eoferwic.

We so nearly reached the crest. Our horses were laboring up the heather-thick hillside with only yards to go when Kettil looked back. "Lord!" he called. "Lord!"

I looked behind. Sköll's men had turned back, and now there was a line of horsemen on the western spur, and even as I watched more men joined that line. There were at least a hundred men, and, at their center, was the big man in the white fur cloak.

I turned again as we reached the crest and saw the enemy had started in pursuit.

We were being hunted.

Five

My plan had been to ride south, and, once out of sight of the road, turn east toward distant Eoferwic. I assumed the women we had left on the road would have told Sköll's men they had seen us heading south, and I had hoped that misdirection would be sufficient to send our pursuers toward Mercia while we rode eastward, but that hope was gone now because Sköll's scouts were already spurring up the slope and they would soon be close enough to see which way we headed. I had wanted time to escape and I was being given none.

I decided we would go east anyway. "That way!" I shouted at Finan, pointing. I spurred Tintreg to Finan's side. "The bastards are coming after us."

Finan instinctively looked around, but no pursuing horsemen were in sight yet. "What do we do?"

"We'll ride east and hope we can get back to the road." I looked up at the still empty skyline. "They can't pursue us forever."

"We hope," Finan said drily.

It was my fault. Discovering what had happened in Eoferwic could have waited, nothing I learned here would make the slightest difference to Sigtryggr. Either he was alive or he was dead, but I had given way to my impatience, and now I had a small army of vengeful Norsemen pursuing me. The curse was working, I thought grimly. I should never have sought out Beadwulf, but should have ridden straight for home, and now, by attacking Sköll's men and taking prisoners, I had made myself the hunted instead of being the hunter. My best hope was that Sköll would think I was in the vanguard of a Northumbrian pursuit and that an army was not far behind me. So far they had only seen a handful of my men, but soon the scouts would see we were over ninety strong. Why pick a fight with us? Sköll Grimmarson would just lose more men. It was a slender hope.

I swerved to reach the crest again. I was planning to slant down the hillside to rejoin the road, but when I reached the skyline I saw Norsemen racing east along the valley. There had to be fifty or sixty of them, and when I turned in the saddle I saw that even more Norsemen had reached the crest and were now following us. Two bands of pursuers, and the ones below had plainly been sent to get ahead of us. Sköll Grimmarson wanted to trap us.

So I turned south to escape his trap. I was fleeing.

My men outnumbered the smaller war-band racing east along the road, but I had nothing to gain by fighting it. We could have turned back, galloped downhill, and overwhelmed that smaller group, but I would lose men and horses in the fight. Some of my men would be wounded, and I must either abandon them to Sköll's mercy or try to carry them with us as we escaped. If we escaped, because the Norsemen in the larger war-band were sure to follow and help their comrades. So our only hope was to flee south and pray for nightfall, which was still two or three hours away.

At least the sight of our numbers made the nearest pursuers pause. They outnumbered us, but they had as little to gain from a fight as we did until they were reinforced and thus certain of defeating us easily. We crossed another crest and found a cattle track beaten through the heather and we followed that, going faster now. Ahead of us the land dropped away, leading to fields, and I could see smoke rising from settlements.

Somewhere ahead, a good long way ahead, we would pass into Mercia, but we could expect little help there. Any settler in these farmlands would be Danish, and the Danes who lived in southern Northumbria and northern Mercia had learned to be cautious.

"Lord!" Finan called.

I turned to see a small group of Norsemen coming fast behind us. They were galloping recklessly, each holding a spear. There were only eight of them, and what could eight men do against ninety?

They could frustrate us, and they did. They hung back for much of the time, then would gallop forward threateningly, and each time they approached we were forced to turn men around, and as soon as we did, they swerved away to avoid a fight. And each time we stopped and turned we were slowed down. Again and again they charged then turned away, and again and again we were forced to face them, and I knew the larger war-bands were not far behind and were getting closer. We needed to go faster, and so I put twenty men under Finan's command and had them ride to the right of the road, and another twenty under Berg's leadership who rode to the left. They took it in turns to face the annoying pursuers while the rest of us kept moving, and that checked the frustrating threats.

I rode beside Enar Erikson, who had recovered his

wits. I had taken a moment to sit him properly in his saddle, though with his hands tied at his back and his ankles lashed to the stirrup leathers. "So what happened at Eoferwic?" I asked him.

"Eoferwic?" He was puzzled because I had used the Saxon name instead of the name the Norse used.

"At Jorvik."

Rain dripped from his helmet and his mustache. "Will I live if I tell you?" he asked.

"You'll die if you don't."

"We lost," he said curtly. He ducked beneath a branch and almost lost his balance. We had left the moorland, and the road led through a spinney of stunted willow. As we climbed the gentle pastureland beyond the trees I looked behind and saw our enemy's large war-band was a mile away, but it was getting dark and they were being cautious despite outnumbering us. The two pursuing groups had joined, and together they had almost double my numbers, but they still seemed reluctant to fight. I could not see Sköll's white cloak among the distant pursuers, so I guessed he had sent another man to lead the warriors and he had doubtless told that man to be careful. If Enar was right then Sköll must have lost men at Eoferwic, and he doubtless did not want to lose more, and though he could overwhelm us in a fight he would pay dearly for our defeat. He had declared war on Sigtryggr, he had lost the opening fight, and I reckoned he needed every warrior to face my son-in-law's revenge. Or so I hoped.

The sun was low now and hidden by darkly heaped clouds. The wind gusted rain that had begun to fall steadily. We passed a steading that had smoke coming from the hall roof and was surrounded by a stout palisade. I knew my tired men must hope that I would attack the small farmstead and so give them a refuge with a hearth, but to stop now would be to invite our pursuers to besiege the place, and so we kept going into the wet dusk.

"So you lost," I said to Enar. "How?"

He told me the tale as we rode into the darkness. The young warriors who had annoyed us abandoned their pursuit and turned back to join the larger warband that seemed content to have chased us far away from the road across the moors. In the dying light and through the veil of hard rain I saw they had stopped. I suspected they would demand shelter in the steading we had passed.

Enar grudgingly told me that Sköll's best hope of capturing Eoferwic had been to move quickly, to cross the wide plain about the city as fast as possible and so take the garrison by surprise, but he had paused before he left the hills. "Where?" I asked.

Enar shrugged. "Just a settlement," he said. "There was a cave there."

"Why did he stop?"

"Weather. It was cold. It wasn't so cold when we left home, we thought spring had come, but winter came back. It closed in fast."

"You took shelter?"

"We had to! You could hardly see through the blizzard."

"How long did you wait there?"

"Just a day." A day was not long, but the pause must have been fatal to Sköll's hopes. "They knew we were coming," Enar continued bitterly, "so someone must have warned them. And the sorcerer told Sköll not to attack the city. At least that's what men said afterward."

"Doesn't Sköll take his sorcerer's advice?" I asked.

"Usually," Enar spoke abruptly, as if talking about Sköll's famed sorcerer troubled him.

"So why did Sköll attack?" I asked.

"We'd come so far," Enar said, "and Snorri . . ." his voice faded away.

"Snorri is the sorcerer?" I asked.

"He is."

"And he told Sköll not to attack?"

"Men said so," Enar spoke hesitantly, evidently reluctant to discuss the sorcerer. "But you can't always understand what Snorri says. Sometimes he speaks in riddles."

"But men fear him?" I pressed.

"Snorri is terrible," Enar said in a low voice. "When he looks at you—"

"I thought Sköll blinded him?"

"He did, but Snorri still sees you! He sees the future. And in battle . . ." his voice trailed away again.

"In battle?" I asked.

"He gazes at the enemy," Enar's voice was touched with awe, "and they die!"

"That didn't work in Jorvik," I said scornfully.

"Snorri didn't go into the city. Some days he's too weak to summon the gods, but when Snorri is strong then Sköll always wins. Always! The blind man stares and the living men die."

A blind sorcerer who could see the future and kill with a glance? So had Snorri seen me in his dreams? And had he cursed me? I touched the hammer and felt the emptiness that suggested the gods had abandoned me, and I could find no omen in the darkness to give me hope. Most of us had dismounted by now and were leading our horses. The night was thick, wet, and miserable. There was no chance of a pursuit in this foul darkness, even if the men behind us had a mind to keep going, yet still we stumbled on, finally stopping where some winter-bare trees offered an illusion of shelter. I was tempted to light a fire, but dared not. We would just have to suffer through the wet cold darkness.

We tied the two prisoners to a tree. "So what happened when you reached Jorvik?" I asked them.

"They invited us into the city," the second captive, a young man called Njall, answered from the dark.

"Invited you?"

He explained that Sköll had sent a small party ahead, just thirty men, none of them dressed for war, but pretending to be travelers. "They were to say they were looking for a ship to buy," Enar added. "The rest of us waited a couple of miles west of the place."

It was not a bad plan. A handful of men, none in mail, would have hardly looked like a threat to Sigtryggr's garrison. Enar said the thirty men had ridden through the village that spread on the Usa's western bank and crossed the Roman bridge. Then they must have reached the southwestern gate with its massive stone towers and high fighting platform. "We know the thirty men captured the gate," Enar said, "because they flew Sköll's wolf flag from one of the towers, and that was the signal for us to follow. Sköll sent his best men first."

"The *úlfhéðnar?*"

"The *úlfhéðnar,*" Enar confirmed, then continued

his story. "Sköll led them, but it was a trap. They'd let us capture the gate, but the streets beyond were barricaded, and behind the barricades was an army. And when a hundred or so were inside the city another band appeared at the river bank to cut them off. They made a shield wall to stop the rest of us crossing the bridge, so the men inside the city were trapped."

"And slaughtered," Finan put in with relish.

"Most of them, yes."

"Most of them," I repeated the words. "Didn't you say that Sköll was inside the city?"

A gust of wind brought rain spattering down from the branches. "Sköll," Enar said, "is an *úlfheðinn*. Ten men can't stand against Sköll." There was awe in his voice. "He came back through the gate with twenty of his wolf-warriors, and they attacked the shield wall barring the bridge. We attacked too, from the other side of the river, and we broke them. We ran the river red with their blood, but by then the city gates were closed."

So Sköll's lunge across Britain had failed. His sorcerer had been right, and the defenders of Eoferwic had thwarted him and so, as recompense for his followers, he had led them on a rampage through the wide farmlands around the city, taking slaves, plunder, and cattle, and had then started back across the hills to Cumbraland. "And Sigtryggr didn't pursue you?" I asked.

"He wasn't there."

"He'd gone south," Njall said sullenly.

"We captured a priest," Enar explained, "who said Sigtryggr had led men to Lindcolne." He said the unfamiliar name uncertainly.

"Mercians," Finan said sourly. He meant that there must have been some threat from Mercia on Northumbria's southern border, and Sigtryggr had led men to reinforce Lindcolne's garrison. I listened to the rain beating on the leafless trees and felt the frustration of ignorance. Had Edward of Wessex invaded Mercia? Was Lindcolne under siege? The only consolation I could find was that Eoferwic had survived and that the Norsemen had been defeated in the battle fought around the city's gate.

Whoever Sigtryggr had left in charge of Eoferwic's garrison had been clever, using the same tactics to defend the city that the Danes had used when my father had died. I had been a child then, forbidden to fight, and had watched as the Northumbrian army had charged through a great gap in Eoferwic's wall. The gap had been left on purpose, and once through the breach my father's forces were faced by a new wall, a barricade edging a killing ground, and the Danes had made great slaughter that day. Their poets had sung of it, their hard words chanted to a harpist's chords, and I still knew that song and sometimes chanted it myself, not out of bitterness because of my father's death, but out of gratitude because it was on that day of killing that Ragnar had captured me.

I was his Saxon slave and became like a son to him. I loved him like a father. I called myself Uhtred Ragnarson and took his religion, sloughing off Christianity like a snake shedding its skin. I grew up thinking I was a Dane, wanting to be a Dane, but fate had driven me back to the Saxons. Wyrd bið ful āræd.

"Sigtryggr will come for revenge," I told Enar.

He gave that threat a mocking laugh. "Jarl Sköll will want revenge too."

"For capturing you?" I asked in derision.

"For wounding his son," he said. "Or did you kill him?"

So the young man with the silver-chased helmet had been Sköll's son? I wished I had known because I would have dragged him with us as another prisoner. "I gave him a headache he won't lose quickly," I said. "What's the boy's name?"

"Boy?" Enar said. "He's a warrior, a man."

"Unker Sköllson," Njall said.

"Unker is a warrior, a man," Enar repeated, and then

added the words that told me the nature of the curse that the gods had wished on me, "and destroyer of queens."

"Destroyer of queens?" I asked.

"He and his father killed Sigtryggr's queen," Enar said.

And I could hear the gods laughing.

He and his father killed Sigtryggr's queen." For a bleak moment those words seemed unreal, almost as if I had dreamed rather than heard them.

In the dark, of course, Enar could not see me or else he might have kept quiet. Instead he continued his tale. "She led them. She was in mail and helmet, carrying a sword."

Finan's hand gripped my arm to keep me still and silent. "She fought?" he asked.

"Like a fiend. She was screaming insults at us, at Sköll and Unker."

"How do you know it was the queen?" Finan asked. He was still gripping my arm.

"She boasted of it!" Enar said. "She called out that her husband thought a mere woman could defeat Sköll."

"She must have had a bodyguard," Finan said, refusing to let go of me.

"No bodyguard could stand against Sköll!" Njall said proudly. "He and his son killed a dozen men."

"So he told us," Enar said, sounding amused, "the father and son fought through the wall, and Unker hooked the royal bitch out of the ranks with the beard of his ax and his father opened her royal belly with his sword, Grayfang."

One of the things they say about the *úlfhéðnar* is that they fight in a blind rage, like madmen. In battle, people say, the *úlfhéðnar* are possessed by the souls of wild beasts, of wolves who know no mercy and are hungry for flesh. They feel no pain and know no fear. Some, it is said, even fight naked to show they need no mail, no shield, no helmet, because no man can stand against them. The *úlfhéðnar* are beasts who fight like gods.

It was the word "bitch" that turned me into a beast. I stood up, ripped Serpent-Breath from her scabbard, and hacked at the two defenseless men tied to the tree. Finan tried to stop me, then must have backed away. He said I was howling like a soul in torment, that the prisoners were screaming, and then there was sudden warmth in the night as their blood sprayed onto my face and I was sobbing and still howling and hacking blindly in the darkness, hacking and hacking, driving the heavy sword into bark, wood, flesh, and bone. And when there was silence, when there were no more screams, when there were no more sounds of dying men moving or groaning, and when the blood no longer flew, I rammed the sword into the soil and howled at the gods.

Stiorra, my daughter, was dead.

Folk say parents have no favorites among their children, which is nonsense. Maybe we love them all, yet there is always one we love the most, and of my three children that one was Stiorra. She was tall, raven-haired like her mother, decisive, strong-willed, sensible, and shrewd. She loved the gods and had learned to divine their will, yet the gods had killed her in Eoferwic. Her blood was on the street and the gods were laughing. They have no pity.

We cling to shreds of hope. Maybe Stiorra had not died, but was wounded? Maybe Sköll's tale was merely the boast of a defeated man, a defiant lie to restore his reputation? Maybe it had been another woman? Yet it sounded so like Stiorra. If Sigtryggr was far away then she would have led his troops, but why lead them in person? Why not inspire them and let the warriors do the fighting? Yet Stiorra would have known that her presence in Eoferwic's main street would fire her warriors to greatness. And her death would have inspired them to a savage revenge, yet still Sköll had survived.

And Sköll's survival gave me one small consolation, that I would never rest until Sköll Grimmarson was at my feet and whimpering for mercy, and at that moment I would show him the same mercy that the gods had given me. That was small consolation, very small, but I clung to it through that night of misery. I wept, though no one saw my tears, and there were moments of despair, but there was always the knowledge that I would find Sköll and I would slaughter him. A curse must be followed by an oath, and I swore that oath in the rain-soaked darkness. Sköll Grimmarson must die.

When the first gray wolf-light touched the eastern hills I went back through the trees and found Serpent-Breath where I had left her. My men, those who were awake, watched me fearfully. The bodies of the two prisoners were still tied to the tree, their gaping wounds washed clean by the rain. I pulled Serpent-Breath from the leaf mold and tossed her to Rorik. "Clean her."

"Yes, lord."

"You should eat, lord," Finan told me.

"No," I said, not looking at him because I did not want him to see the tears that were blurring my eyes. "What I should do," I snarled, "is kill that damned monk."

"He's gone, lord," Finan said.

I turned, furious. "He's what?"

"He and his girl," Finan said calmly. "They stole two of the scouts' horses at first light."

"Didn't we set sentries?"

Finan shrugged. "They told Godric they were going for a shit."

"With horses?" Damn Godric. He had always been a fool. "Maybe I should kill Godric," I snarled. "Send him to me."

"Leave him to me," Finan said, fearing what I would do in my rage. "I'll give him a thumping," he promised.

Godric was enthusiastic enough, he could hold a shield and wield a sword, but had the brains of a slug. Brother Beadwulf, I thought, would have had small trouble convincing the fool that he meant no harm. I supposed the monk and his squirrel had fled back to Arnborg, presumably because he thought the Norse would catch and slaughter us, and Brother Beadwulf wanted to be certain he would survive the slaughter. I should have killed him, I thought sourly, yet the truth, of course, was that even if Beadwulf had not lured me across Britain I could still not have saved my daughter's life. I would have been in Bebbanburg, not in Eoferwic. "I should have killed him," I told Finan, "just to annoy Æthelstan."

"Add him to the list of men to be killed," Finan suggested, then offered me a lump of sodden bread. I shook my head, but did take his offer of a flask of ale. "That's the last of the ale," he said warningly.

I drank half, then gave him back the flask. "Food?"

"Ten loaves of rotting bread, some cheese."

"The gods love us," I said sourly.

"So where do we go, lord?" he asked.

"Send two scouts north," I said. "See if the bastards are still anywhere near."

"And if they are?"

I said nothing for a moment. One part of me, the savage part, wanted to ride recklessly north and plunge into the heart of Sköll's army, seek him out and have my revenge, but that was madness. "We go east," I finally said.

"To Eoferwic?"

I nodded. I needed to find Sigtryggr, and together we would avenge Stiorra.

"So we go back to the road?"

"No." The road might have been the quickest route to Eoferwic, but right now my men and our horses needed warmth, food, and rest. We would find none of those things on the moors, but our flight had brought us into a richer country, and I knew we would discover a steading that could provide what we needed. We had passed one such farmstead the night before, but it had been small and I suspected that by now Sköll's men would have stripped the place bare. I needed somewhere large and well stocked. "Do any of our men know this country?"

"Not one."

"So we're lost," I said.

Finan turned and nodded southward, "Mameceaster has to be somewhere down there."

"I need to go home," I said harshly, "so we'll ride east when the scouts get back, then find our own way."

"And those two?" Finan gestured at the dead captives.

"Leave them here, let the bastards rot."

Finan stared north through the persistent rain. "Sköll sounds like a mad bastard," he said, "and he'll want revenge for his son. He'll be coming for us."

"His son was alive when we left," I said.

"You still humiliated the boy. You took his sword."

I had thought I left Unker dying, but now I wondered if he had merely been stunned. He had bled enough, but head wounds always bled copiously. "He was fast," I said. "If his horse hadn't tripped you'd be singing a funeral song for me. For me and Stiorra."

"We'll make songs for her, lord," Finan said.

I just gazed north, saying nothing. A gray day with gray rain and gray cloud. I remembered my first impulse to ride after Sköll and wondered if Finan was right, and that Sköll, with the same impulse, was planning to ride south and wreak revenge for his son's wounding, but our two scouts returned to say that they had seen nothing. It seemed that Sköll's pursuit had been called off and that the Norsemen must now be riding for home, and so we set off in the opposite direction, riding slowly toward the gradually lightening horizon where the sun rose beyond the clouds. It still rained, only now it was a sullen drizzle. I sent more scouts ahead, telling them to look for a settlement as well as any sign of an enemy, and it was midmorning when Eadric rode back to say there was a plump valley to the south of us. We were following a winding stream through thick trees when Eadric brought his news. "It's just across the hills, lord," he said, gesturing to the south, "and there's at least three halls there. Big ones too."

We called in our other scouts, turned, and followed Eadric across the low hills and down a valley of rich pastureland where, as Eadric had said, there were three halls. All had palisades and all had smoke drifting from roof-holes toward the low, persistent clouds.

Berg turned his horse toward me. "Want us to leap the palisade again, lord?" he asked eagerly, gesturing to the nearest hall.

"No." I spurred Tintreg. I doubted we would need to fight. No men showed above the palisade, which was now little more than a long bowshot away, and that suggested there were few people in the hall. I wondered if the menfolk from this valley had ridden with Sköll, but that seemed doubtful. If they had, they would surely have returned by now, but no one watched from the steading's gate. The only sign of life was the smoke from the hearth. "They won't be happy," I told Berg, "but if they can't fight us they'll open their gate."

They did, and they were not happy. The family that lived in the hall was Danish, but only the womenfolk, their children, and three older men were there. The owner of the steading, we were told, had gone south with other men from the valley. "There's easy pickings in Mercia," Wiburgh, the mistress of the hall, told us. "Mercians are fighting each other, so we'll help ourselves." She watched as I looked around the hall. "And you'll help yourselves too," she added bitterly. "Who are you?"

"Travelers," I said. "So how many men rode south into Mercia?"

"Twelve? Maybe more. Depends if the folk across the hill decided to help."

"They rode to Mameceaster?"

"Is that the new Mercian fort?"

"It is."

"My husband's not a fool. He won't attack a fort, but there'll be pickings enough in the nearby country. They raid us, we raid them."

"For cattle?"

"For cattle, sheep, slaves, for anything we can eat or sell."

"And if you wanted to go to Jorvik," I asked, using the city's Danish name, "what road would you take?"

She laughed. "We have nothing to do with Jorvik! I don't know a man who's even been there. Why would we go? They're all strangers over there. Besides," she looked balefully at Finan's cross, "there are Christians there."

"You don't like Christians?"

"They eat babies," she said, touching a hammer necklace, "everyone knows that."

We ate no babies, but she did feed us a mutton stew with oatcakes, though it took a while for her servants to cook the meal. She grumbled, of course, that there were so many of us, but her storehouse was well stocked, and she was confident her husband would be bringing more food from Mercia. She was a plump and resourceful woman, resigned to our presence, and clever enough to know that if she treated us well we would return the favor. "You surprised us," she confessed to me after dark, "by coming from the hills. Not many come that way! If any come from the south we get warning."

"You live well here," I said.

"Few know we're here. We keep to ourselves."

"Except when you raid?"

"The brothers like to keep busy." She was spinning wool, her hands deft. "My husband's father, Fastulf, found the valley. There was a Saxon lord here then, but he died," she gave a brief laugh, "and Fastulf had three sons. So three sons and three farms. We call it the valley of the brothers."

I was gazing into the glowing embers beneath the burning logs, searching for an omen in the shimmering fire. "I had a brother," I said quietly, "but he died." She said nothing. "And I had a daughter too," I went on, "and she died."

She let the distaff drop and gave me a meaningful look. "You're a lord," she said, making it sound like an accusation. "Uhtred of Bebbanburg!"

"I am," I said. There had been no point in hiding who we were. We had stayed at the steading all day and my men must have told Wiburgh's servants who we were.

"I've heard of you," she said, then nodded at the chain I wore around my neck, "and you wear gold."

"I do."

"You wear gold," she said again, "and you don't even notice you're wearing it! A family could live for ten years on the metal you hang around your neck."

"So?"

"So the gods notice you! The more you become like the gods the more they're going to slap you down!" She wiped the wool grease from her fingers onto her robe. "When wolves attack the flock, which dog dies first?"

"The bravest," I said.

"The bravest, aye." She threw a billet of wood onto the fire. The two of us were sitting at one side of the hearth, slightly apart from the rest of the company. She watched the sparks settle into the smoldering ashes. "I had three sons too," she said wistfully, "and two died of the fever. But the eldest? He's called Immar and he's a good man. Sixteen now and fighting at his father's side." She looked at me. "So when did your daughter die?"

"A few days ago."

"She was ill?"

"Sköll Grimmarson killed her."

She made the sign to ward off evil. "Oh, he's a beast!"

"You know him?" I asked with quickening interest.

She shook her head. "We just hear things. But I don't believe half of what I hear." She picked up the distaff again.

"What do you hear?"

"He's a cruel man," she said, not looking at me. "He likes people to suffer. I hope . . ." her voice died away.

"From what I hear," I said, "my daughter died quickly. In battle."

"Thank the gods for that," she said fervently. "We've had runaway slaves come across the hills, and they tell us stories. He hunts people for pleasure, sets the dogs on them. He's said to have blinded two of his wives for daring to look at a young warrior, and the poor young man was gelded then sewn into a sheepskin and thrown to the hounds. And his sorcerer!" She made the two-fingered sign to ward off evil. "But as I said, I only believe half of what I hear."

"I'll kill him," I said.

"Maybe that's what the gods want."

"Maybe."

I slept that night. I had not expected to, but the gods gave me that small blessing. I had told Finan I would visit the sentinels we had put at the palisade, but he insisted I sleep. "I'll make sure they're awake," he said, and so he did. I dreamed, but none of what I dreamed revealed the wishes of the gods. I was on my own. They were watching me, waiting, wanting to see how their game ended.

With Sköll's death, I vowed. Or else my own.

The rain ended in the night and dawn brought a pale clear sky. The small wind was warmer, a promise of spring. I woke to the memory of Stiorra's death and the absurd hopes that she might yet live. I felt abandoned by the gods, and for a moment I was tempted to tear the hammer from around my neck and hurl it into the hearth's fire, but caution stopped me. I needed the help of the gods, not their enmity, and so I clutched the amulet instead.

"It would be sensible, lord," Finan came and crouched beside the revived fire, "to have a day of resting. The horses need it. We can dry out. It's a fine day dawning."

I nodded. "But I want to send out scouts."

"East?" he guessed.

I nodded. "To make sure Sköll's given up his pursuit. Then we continue east, back home." The word "home" was like ash in my mouth. I remembered Stiorra's joy when she had first seen Bebbanburg and how she had ridden a horse along the sand, her eyes bright, her laughter loud.

"We'll go back to the road?" Finan asked.

"It's probably the quickest way back."

"Sigtryggr must have learned the news by now," Finan said. "He could be on his way already."

"He'll probably be on the road we were using," I suggested, then frowned. "If he's coming."

"And why wouldn't he?"

"Maybe the Mercians are threatening?" I hated not knowing. I did not know where we were, I did not know what happened in Mercia, in Cumbraland, or in Eoferwic. I did not even know what happened at Bebbanburg. My son would have heard of his sister's fate by now, so was he leading men to avenge her?

"Have you thought about Æthelstan?" Finan asked.

"What about him?"

"We're probably closer to him than to Sigtryggr, and Æthelstan owes you."

I grimaced. "I like him, but he's getting to be like his grandfather, drunk on God. And the pompous little bastard wants my oath."

"He still owes you," Finan insisted, "and he's threatened by the Norse just as much as Sigtryggr."

I thought about that, except it was hard to think. All I could see in my mind was Stiorra dragged from a shield wall, screaming, a sword coming down, and her blood on the street. I prayed she had died fast. I tried

to summon a picture of her in my head, but it would
not come, any more than I could see her dead mother,
Gisela.

"Lord?" Finan said anxiously.

"I'm listening."

"Sköll threatens Mercia too," Finan insisted. "He
might have failed to capture Eoferwic, but Ceaster
would be a good consolation."

"If we invite Æthelstan into Northumbria," I said,
"it's a confession of weakness, that we can't control our
own kingdom. Besides, he has to help his father defeat
the Mercian rebels first. He might have ended Cynlæf's
hopes, but there were other rebels."

"Maybe they're already defeated?"

"Maybe. But if Æthelstan helps us defeat Sköll, what
happens to western Northumbria?"

Finan understood what I was suggesting. "Æthelstan
keeps hold of Cumbraland?"

"And makes it part of Mercia," I said, "part of Englaland. And Cumbraland belongs to Northumbria,
and my son-in-law is King of Northumbria." I paused.
"And if Æthelstan helps us," I went on, "then he'll
want my oath."

"Which he won't get."

"Not while I'm alive," I said grimly. "Damn the

Christians," I added, "and damn Edward's Englaland. I'm fighting for my own country."

"So we go east," Finan said.

"We go east."

"I'll lead a half-dozen scouts," he said.

"Just make sure we can reach the road," I said, "because that's probably the fastest way back to Eoferwic."

"And we leave tomorrow?"

"We leave tomorrow," I agreed.

But we left at midday because we were still being hunted.

Sköll Grimmarson wanted revenge. When I had first heard about Stiorra's slaughter my immediate thought had been to confront her killers, but sense had stopped me. Sköll, discovering his son's wounding, must have had the same impulse; to ride after the men who had dared insult his family and then to kill them in as imaginative a way as his foul mind could devise.

I had let sense rule me because I knew we were outnumbered, and that to attack Sköll was to invite our own defeat, but Sköll had no such restraints. He knew how many we were, he knew he had the advantage of numbers, so all he needed to do was find us, fight us, and kill us.

Except that in the fading twilight of the previous day, in the murk of the rainswept dusk, Sköll's scouts had seen our tracks going eastward, but they had not spotted the place where we had turned south. They must have spent a cold wet night under the bare trees, expecting to continue the pursuit at dawn, and, luckily for us, they had continued eastward until, somehow, they deduced that we had changed direction. Finan and his men had seen them as they retraced their steps. "I reckon they saw the smoke here and are coming to find out what causes it. And they'll be here soon, lord."

"How many?"

"I'm guessing three crews. It was hard to see them under the trees. But a lot. Too many. And Sköll was with them."

"I didn't see him yesterday."

"He's here, right enough. You can't miss that white cloak, lord. And he's got three crews at least."

Three crews would be around a hundred and twenty men, and we had seen far more than that on the road, which suggested Sköll had split his force, sending some men back home with the captured cattle and the slaves, and brought a fighting force to find us.

And now he was to the east of us, but coming toward us, which meant we could not return to the road, nor travel eastward, and so I had no choice but to go farther south. "I wonder how far Mameceaster is," I asked Finan as we left the steading.

"Your woman there reckoned two days."

"She didn't sound very sure."

"It can't be too far."

We would go south, looking for Mameceaster, and we would be safe if we could persuade the garrison to open its gates. I hated the thought of running for safety and begging for shelter, but I liked the idea of dying even less, so south we went. I had my usual scouts ahead, but this time I had six good men following us with orders to keep their eyes skinned for any pursuit. I tried to remember the name of the commander at Mameceaster, the man who had denied us entrance on our way to Ceaster. Treddian! Æthelstan had told me that Treddian was being replaced and I hoped the new man, if he had already been appointed, was more welcoming, because if Sköll continued his relentless pursuit I would need the shelter of Mameceaster's walls.

I took one precaution before we left the hall. I gave Wiburgh some hacksilver and told her to take all her people, all her valuables, and all the livestock up into the woods behind the steading. "Sköll Grimmarson will be coming," I said, "and he'll ask if you've seen me. You'd best not be here to answer him. And warn the other halls in the valley."

She had shuddered. "He'll like as not burn the place down."

"Then you'll rebuild," I said, "as we all do. And I'm sorry."

And I was sorry. Sorry for her, sorry for Northumbria, sorry for myself. My daughter was dead. The thought beat through me, a deep sorrow and a spur for revenge. But to take revenge I needed men. I needed Sigtryggr's troops, or more of my own men, who were at Bebbanburg, and when I had those men I vowed I would carry fire and slaughter through Cumbraland, and the prospect of that revenge was my only consolation.

We had ridden the length of the valley that headed south and west, and at its far end we followed a wider valley southward. Wiburgh had told me which way to ride. In the second valley, she said, we would find a drove road going south. "It's an old road, lord, Been there forever. Since long before we came," she had been talking to us at her steading's gate, "and if you meet Hergild and his brothers," she had continued, "warn him about Sköll." Hergild was her husband and I had promised I would warn him. I guessed that the road had been made by drovers herding their cattle and flocks south to feed the Roman settlements around Mameceaster. "You can't miss the road," Wiburgh had said, and she proved right. We made good progress.

The weather was kind, the ground was drying after the hard rain, and the scouts who followed us did not raise any alarm, and so I began to hope we had evaded Sköll's war-band. Maybe we would not need Mameceaster's shelter, maybe we could turn east again and ride to Bebbanburg.

Then one of the scouts ahead of us came racing back, his horse flinging up clods of damp turf. "God help us," Finan said quietly, watching the far figure.

"They've seen Wiburgh's husband," I suggested, "coming back home?" That seemed the obvious explanation. We knew that the Danes from the valley of the brothers had gone south to raid the country around Mameceaster, and I had been half expecting to meet them as they returned.

Eadric, the scout who was riding back with the news, reined in his horse. "Trouble, lord," he said, "horsemen a mile or so ahead. We don't know how many." There was no excitement in his voice, let alone enthusiasm. It was as if the trouble ahead was both inevitable and unavoidable.

"How many have you seen?" I asked.

"Only a dozen, lord. But I think there were more of them in the trees." He turned in his saddle to look north. "The road runs beside a big wood, lord, and those trees could hide an army."

"Were there any cattle?"

"None that I saw, lord. And the men all have shields and spears." He meant they were warriors. Men raiding for livestock rarely encumbered themselves with heavy shields; they preferred to travel swiftly, running from a fight rather than seeking one.

"Did they see you?" Finan asked.

"They saw us," Eadric said. "It's open land. They showed themselves when we crossed the crest." There was a slight rise in the road ahead, and Eadric said the woodland where the strangers had appeared lay a mile or so beyond it.

"Sköll?" I asked.

Eadric looked uncertain. "I didn't see any of those gray wolf cloaks, lord. But it could be his men. Could be anyone."

Damn it, but had Sköll somehow got ahead of us? If he had men who knew this country, then that was possible, but they must have ridden hard. I looked east and west, but on both sides of the valley were low, bare hills. If we tried to evade the men ahead we would be seen crossing the skyline. "Maybe they're friendly?" Eadric suggested.

"The only friend we have is Sigtryggr," I answered, "and it won't be him. Were they flying a banner?"

"None that I saw, lord," Eadric said.

"We can't avoid them," I said, "so let's confront them." If they were hostile, and they probably were, then perhaps our numbers alone would persuade them to let us pass. But only if we outnumbered the strangers. The alternative was to turn away, either retracing our steps, or riding eastward. The horsemen ahead might be Sköll's men, but instinct alone told me that was unlikely. I still felt certain that Sköll was behind us, so turning back offered no hope, while to turn east or west was simply to invite pursuit from new enemies. Sometimes all we have is instinct, and I was tired of running away. "We'll keep going," I said.

"And if there's too many of them?" Finan asked.

"We'll find out," I said grimly, and spurred Tintreg. I waved my men on. Perhaps the dozen men Eadric had seen were all that opposed us, in which case we would brush them aside and keep going. And perhaps my instinct was wrong and the mysterious warriors ahead were allies of Sköll and had numbers enough to trap us and slaughter us.

I crossed the low rise in the road. The valley widened ahead, the drove road leading straight southward between open pastureland. There were no settlements in sight. A mile or so ahead the road turned slightly eastward, staying beneath a wooded ridge, and it was there that the horsemen waited. "Still only a dozen," Finan said.

The horsemen stood motionless, just a dozen warriors barring the road. By now they must have seen how many we were, and if they numbered just a dozen then their best course was to turn and flee from us. They did not. "We need to get on the ridge," I told Finan. The ridge was high ground, and in any fight the higher ground is the best. "But not yet," I added. If there were more warriors waiting among the trees then I wanted them to think we would stay on the road. I would take the high ground at the last moment.

There were indeed more of them. As we drew closer they began to appear from the woods, and all of them were warriors. They wore gray mail and gray helmets, but none I saw had the gray cloak of an *úlfheðinn*. I tried to count the horsemen as they came from the thick undergrowth. Twenty, thirty, forty, and still they came. "What's on their shields?" I asked Finan, whose eyesight was much better than mine.

"Can't tell yet, lord. But they look Saxon to me."

And I felt a surge of relief. Why? As a Northumbrian, my enemies were the Saxons. It was the Saxons who were grinding down the Northmen, it was the Saxons whose ambition was to conquer every Dane and

Norseman and make a Christian Englaland, it was the Saxons who would impose their law on Northumbria, who would eradicate the older gods.

"They are Saxon!" Eadric said, and I could see that for myself now. The Northmen were more flamboyant, more colorful, while the men who barred our road looked drab. "Seventy-four," Finan had been counting, "and they have crosses on their shields."

"And priests," Eadric said, and I saw he was right. At least two black-robed men rode with the mail-clad warriors.

"But still no flag," Finan said, puzzled. I saw him touch the hilt of his sword. "You want us on the ridge, lord?" he asked.

I shook my head. I saw no reason why a Saxon war-band should pick a quarrel with me, indeed I had felt relief because the Saxons were the enemies of the Norse, and the enemy of my enemy is my friend. Yet I also felt disappointment. "We're still in Northumbria," I said.

"Are we?" Finan asked.

"I'm sure of it," I said. Yet here was a powerful war-band of Christians, with the cross on their shields and priests in their ranks, and they were deep inside Northumbria, deep inside a country they wanted to conquer, not just because it was ruled by Sigtryggr, a Norseman, but because they believed it was their holy duty to destroy paganism and replace it with the worship of their nailed God. I wanted a Britain where men could worship whatever god or goddess they chose, that allowed me to revere Thor and Odin, that was not subject to the whims and the greed of bishops and abbots, yet at that moment I also recognized that this priest-haunted war-band trespassing in my country was probably my salvation. Unless, of course, it was led by Æthelhelm the Younger. Yet I could see none of the red cloaks that Æthelhelm's men wore and, besides, we were far from Æthelhelm's native Wessex.

The enemy of my enemy should have been my ally, yet the Christians in front of us were readying for battle. The warriors had dismounted to make a shield wall, and the boys were leading the horses back to the trees. "They want to fight us?" Finan asked in surprise. We outnumbered them, unless they had yet more men we had not seen.

"They think we're Norse," I said. Like them we showed no flag, and this far north most warriors were pagans, so they had to assume we were enemies. Besides, like the Northmen, even my Saxons liked to wear crests and plumes on their helmets. Half of my men were Christians, yet they looked like pagans.

"If not us," Eadric said drily, "them," and he pointed behind us.

I turned and saw a scattering of horsemen on the low hills to the east. There were about twenty of them, still far away, but galloping southward on the crest, then there were suddenly more horsemen on the western skyline. "Sköll," Finan said flatly.

It could be no one else, and even as I watched them, I saw our scouts come hurrying along the drove road behind us. So Sköll had caught up with us. His scouts were coming south on either flank, while his main war-band would be advancing along the valley. We had a fearsome enemy behind us, while in front of us a shield wall began to clash sword-blades against willow-board shields. "They're probably thinking we're all Sköll's men," I said.

"If they think that," Finan said, "they should run like shit. They're outnumbered!"

Outnumbered or not the Christians seemed to be wanting a fight. They were still hammering their sword-blades against their cross-painted shields in a defiant invitation to come and test their wall.

Then the shield wall split, and two horsemen, both dressed in black, rode toward us. One was a priest, while the other, a black cloak draped over his gray mail, was a warrior. And I knew him.

It was Finan who spoke first. He was staring at the warrior with astonishment, then he made the sign of the cross because he believed he was seeing a ghost. "Lord," he said to me, his voice scarce above a whisper, "it's King Alfred!"

And he was almost right.

PART TWO

Eostre's Feast

Six

The warrior who approached us did look like King Alfred, though that King of Wessex had died years before the youngest of my warriors was even born. Yet this man had the same long, pale and stern face, the same disapproving eyes, the same short dark beard shot through with gray, the same air of containment that spoke of rigorous self-discipline, the same straight back, and the same reserve and calm.

His name was Osferth, and I knew him well. "Lord Prince," I greeted him, knowing he would reject the rank.

"I am no prince, Lord Uhtred," he said just as I had expected.

"You're welcome anyway," I said.

"Perhaps." He even sounded like King Alfred. He

had the same cold voice, precise and clear. A silver cross hanging from a chain studded with amber beads hung at his neck. It was the only decoration he allowed himself. His black cloak looked serviceable, but lacked a fur collar or embroidered hems. His mail was plain, his helmet plain, his boots plain, his horse's saddlery and bridle were leather and iron, his sword's hilt was wood and iron, his scabbard a plain sheath of wood. He looked past me, and I turned to see Sköll Grimmarson's men appearing on the road a mile or so behind me. "Is that Sköll Grimmarson?" he asked.

"It is; how did you know?"

"I didn't. I presumed. He's pursuing you?"

"I'd prefer to say he's following me. So you've heard of him?"

"I've heard of him," Osferth said, "and I've heard nothing good." He frowned, watching as Sköll's men stopped a half-mile away, checked by the sight of the shield wall. The scouts who had been riding the eastern ridge were coming down to join the larger group, but I noticed the horsemen on the western hills were staying on the high ground. They were scouts too, of course, all riding swift horses and none of them carrying a heavy shield that might slow them down. "They won't fight now," Osferth said confidently, "we outnumber them."

I was not so sure. A single horseman had left Sköll's ranks and was climbing the western hill. The man had a gray cloak and a long wolf tail flying from his helmet's crest. Sköll, meanwhile, seemed content to watch us. I looked back to Osferth. "You're far from home," I said accusingly.

"As are you, lord."

I gestured at the valley and the woodland. "Northumbria is my home."

"And Northumbrian Danes came to raid the farms around Mameceaster," he responded tartly, "and we killed them."

"Is that why you're here?"

"It's why we left Mameceaster," he said evasively.

"Was one of the raiders called Hergild?"

"He was." Osferth sounded slightly surprised, but did not ask how I knew that name. "My task is to discourage such raiders."

"Praise God," the priest who accompanied him said.

We both ignored the priest. "So you serve Treddian?" I asked Osferth.

"I replaced Treddian," Osferth said. "Prince Æthelstan put me in command of the burh at Mameceaster."

"I'm glad," I said, and I was.

"Glad, lord?"

"You deserve a command."

"I commanded at Brunanburh," he said with a trace of indignation.

"You did," I said. Æthelflaed had put Osferth, her half-brother, in command of the garrison, a decision that had annoyed King Edward, who disliked the fact that he was not his father's eldest son. Osferth was the eldest son, Alfred's bastard son, whelped on a servant girl before the young Alfred discovered he loved his god more than he loved women, a mistake I have never made. And the bastard Osferth, of all Alfred's children, most resembled his father. I had heard that Edward, the oldest legitimate son, had dismissed Osferth from Brunanburh after Æthelflaed's death, fearing perhaps that the bastard might prove a rival, and now Æthelstan had given him a bigger garrison to command. "Does your half-brother know you command Mameceaster?" I asked.

Osferth rewarded me with a cold gaze. "My half-brother?"

"King Edward."

He hated being reminded of his parentage, and had never tried to take advantage of it. "He surely will know if he doesn't already. We must wait to see if he approves." He frowned at Sköll's men, then cleared his throat. "I am sorry, lord," he spoke very awkwardly, "about your daughter. I am very sorry."

"So am I," I said. I looked up at Sköll's horsemen on the western ridge. "How did you hear about her?" I asked, still watching the horsemen, who were not moving. There had been twenty men there a moment ago, now there were only half that number, and none had come down into the valley.

"A man called Beadwulf told us," Osferth said, and that brought my eyes back to him.

"Brother Beadwulf?" I asked in surprise.

"Is he a monk? I think not. He travels with his wife."

"It's a nickname," I said dismissively. So Beadwulf and the squirrel, far from fleeing back to Arnborg, had ridden south to look for help. I owed them thanks, and revealing to the pious Osferth that Beadwulf was a monk in love would not be kind. And Beadwulf, I reasoned, had told Osferth about Sköll, which explained why Osferth had known who was pursuing me. "So you rode to rescue me?" I asked.

"Once we learned you were being pursued, yes."

I thought about what he had said as I gazed up at the western ridge. "You left Mameceaster," I said, "to pursue cattle-raiders. So how did you meet Beadwulf?"

"The poor man was captured by them," Osferth said, "he and his wife."

I flinched at that news. "I suppose they took turns with her?"

He looked pained. "I fear so."

Poor little squirrel, I thought. I had liked Wiburgh well enough, but if her husband raped captives then he deserved whatever death Osferth had given him. "I suppose you killed the raiders?" I asked.

"We captured six, the rest died."

"Where are the six?"

"I sent them back to Mameceaster."

"They raped a woman! Put them to death!"

"They must be tried when I return," he said stiffly. "If they are found guilty, they will die."

"Tried!" I said scornfully. "Just kill the bastards."

"There is law in Mameceaster," Osferth said, "the king's law."

A horn blared loud behind me, but I did not turn. "How many men, Finan?" I asked.

"Ninety-two," the Irishman said, "and coming closer. Then there are some on the—"

"I know about them," I interrupted him.

"Some men?" Osferth asked. "Where?"

"Scouts," I said, "on the hill."

He glanced at the western skyline where there were now just six men. He dismissed the half-dozen scouts as unimportant and looked back to Sköll's main force. The horn sounded again, louder now and more persistent. "He wants us to look at him," I said, meaning

Sköll wanted us to ignore the western crest, beyond which his real attack was forming. I still had my back to the Norse leader and his horsemen. "Can you see him, Finan?"

"Aye, the big bastard's right at the center of their line."

"The man with the white cloak?" Osferth asked.

"Skinned from a white bear," I said, "but he has the spirit of a wolf. He is an *úlfheðinn*."

"An *úlfheðinn*?" Osferth said. "I thought they were just rumors."

"The *úlfhéðnar* are not rumors, lord," the priest said, "though they are rare. They are warriors of the wolf. They anoint themselves with a sorcerous ointment that makes them behave like madmen. My people call it *berserkergang*."

"Your people, priest?" I asked.

"I am a Dane," he said calmly. He was young, stern-faced, and I had an impression of intelligence and severity.

"Father Oda," Osferth said, "was converted to the faith in East Anglia where his family had settled."

"God be praised," Oda said.

"And he is now my interpreter," Osferth went on, "and one of my chaplains."

"How many chaplains do you have?"

Osferth ignored the question. He knew me well enough to know that I would respond to his answer with mockery, and he did indeed know me. Years before, when he came into manhood, his father had sent him to be trained as a priest, but the young Osferth had yearned to be a warrior and he had pleaded with me to take him under my wing. In truth he should have been a priest; he had the piety, the dedication, the belief, even the passion, but his reading of the Christian scriptures had convinced him that his bastard birth made him unworthy of the priesthood. But nothing in the holy book said a bastard could not kill Danes, and so he had shrugged off the robe and put on mail. He was clever, like his father, and that cleverness had made him a useful warrior. He was brave too. His bravery, I knew, came from a deep fear, but he possessed the discipline to overcome the fear, and I admired him for that. I not only admired Osferth, I liked him, but I suspected that, like many Christians, he could never like a man who worshipped a different god. He looked past me as the horn sounded again. I was showing no alarm, and he must have thought that meant I believed the Norsemen posed no threat. We did, after all, outnumber them. "This meeting is fortuitous," Osferth said.

"You mean it's a chance to kill Sköll?" I asked.

"I mean," he said, sounding faintly annoyed, "that Prince Æthelstan said we might meet with you, and that if we did I was to give you a message."

"Before you tell me," I said, "can we line my horsemen beside your wall?"

He was startled by the question. He frowned. "Is that necessary?"

"Desirable," I said, "if Sköll decides to attack."

"He won't," Osferth said confidently.

"I'll do it anyway," I said, and told my men to form a line of horsemen on the right of Osferth's shield wall.

"Do you want shields, lord?" Rorik asked me. The boys and servants were looking after our spare mounts and the packhorses that carried our shields.

"You won't need shields," Osferth said, "because they won't fight."

"We need shields," I told Rorik.

"They won't fight!" Osferth insisted, even though Sköll's men were slowly advancing.

"You know that?" I asked.

"We outnumber them," Osferth said, though he sounded uncertain.

"We outnumber them," I agreed, "but they are the *úlfhéðnar.* They fight for pleasure."

"This is true," Father Oda put in. He made the sign

of the cross. "The *úlfhéðnar* have no fear. Some might even desire death because they believe they will be given a place of honor in Valhalla's feasting hall."

Osferth gazed at the enemy. Sköll was in the center of their line, looking huge in his great fur cloak, and next to him was a slim rider with long white hair and a long white beard wearing a pale robe that fell to his stirrups. It had to be Snorri, Sköll's feared sorcerer. He stared at us with his empty eye sockets and I felt the unease of that distant gaze, then he turned his gray horse and rode out of sight beyond the horsemen. Those horsemen carried bright-painted shields, their spear-points caught the winter light, and their horn defied us with its harsh notes. They had stopped some three or four spear-casts from us, but Sköll's younger men, the brave fools, cavorted on their horses nearer to us, calling out challenges and insults, daring us to face them in single combat.

"Finan?" I said softly, "choose thirty men."

"What are you doing?" Osferth demanded with some alarm.

"Lord Prince," I said, using the title to annoy him, "might I remind you that you are in Northumbria? That I am an ealdorman of Northumbria? And that if a lord of Northumbria wishes to hunt pigeons in his own country he does not need the permission of a West

Saxon bastard?" I smiled at him after the insult, and he said nothing.

"You are . . ." Father Oda began, then stopped as Osferth held up a hand to check the protest.

"Lord Uhtred only speaks the truth," Osferth said coldly, "if uncouthly."

"Finan!" I called, and he trotted his horse to me. "Dismount," I told him, "and lead your horses back to the wood. Do it slowly." Then I told him what he would discover in the wood and what he was to do, and Finan just grinned because he was eager for the fight to begin. And there would be a fight because to our left the leafless trees stretched to the crest of the western ridge, and halfway up that slope some pigeons had just clattered through the branches to fly in circles. There were men there. I could not see them because the underbrush was thick on the slope, but I knew they were there. Sköll had pulled his scouts off the eastern ridge, but had left men on the western hill, and those men were now coming slowly and cautiously down the long wooded slope. They believed we had not seen them, that we only had eyes for Sköll and his main force, but the startled pigeons had betrayed their presence.

Osferth was a clever man, as clever as his father King Alfred, but clever is not always cunning. He had formed a shield wall because his scouts had told him

I was approaching. He did not make the wall because he expected me to attack him, but because he wanted to look resolute and strong. He evidently had some message for me from Æthelstan, and it did not take cleverness on my part to know what that message was. Osferth had decided that this was not to be a meeting of old friends, but a harsh demand that I submit myself to Æthelstan's authority, and so the shield wall was meant to impress me.

Then Sköll's men had appeared, and Osferth had kept his shield wall in place because no one attacks a shield wall lightly. He expected Sköll to shout a challenge, to taunt us with insults, and then ride away rather than lose men in an assault on a shield wall. Osferth had faith in numbers, and we were the larger force, and clever as he was, Osferth could not imagine that Sköll would dare start a fight he was doomed to lose.

But Sköll had already lost face by failing to capture Eoferwic. He had led an army east and he had been defeated, and all he had to show for the effort was a few slaves and some skinny cattle. His men were not going to become rich from this expedition, and like all the Northmen, he had promised his followers wealth. That was why they were in Britain. Sköll had vowed to become King of Northumbria, and he would have promised his chieftains land, silver, women, cattle, and

slaves. Instead they were retreating back to their steadings on Cumbraland's western coast. A Norse chieftain
who failed to reward his men was a chieftain who would
lose his reputation.

But Sköll had seen the shield wall, and seen a chance
to win a victory that would yield horses, mail, saddlery, weapons, and captives. It would not even begin
to approach the plunder that he would have gained at
Eoferwic, but to retreat from the shield wall's challenge
would brand him as a coward and a failure. He had no
choice. He had to attack, and he had seen just how vulnerable Osferth was. And I had tried to think myself
into Sköll's place. How would I attack this shield wall?
How would I tear it into red ruin? And the answer was
obvious to me, though Osferth, clever as he was, had
not seen it.

A shield wall is a terrifying thing to assault, but
Sköll's men were mounted, and they could ride around
the wall and attack it from the rear, especially as Osferth's wall was straddling the road with its flanks in
the open pastureland. I did not doubt that Osferth
would take them back to the tree line before that could
happen, and Sköll's horsemen would have a hard time
with the tangling undergrowth and low branches,
and my horsemen would offer another challenge, but
Sköll, I knew, had no intention of letting Osferth fight

a messy battle at the edge of the wood. He planned to cut down Osferth's shield wall in the open country, and to make that happen he had sent a handful of horsemen to circle behind us, and those men were now moving quietly toward us, hidden by the trees on the western ridge, and when they saw Sköll's larger force was close enough, they would burst from the trees to charge the rear of Osferth's wall. Even a half-dozen spearmen, mounted on good horses, could tear a shield wall apart if they attacked from behind, and the result would be panic as Osferth's men turned to fight off the sudden assault, and during that panic Sköll's main force would charge. There would be a brief fight, a slaughter, then the horror of blood-slicked grass where the wall had once stood.

By now Finan had walked his men and their horses back to the trees. To Sköll, if he saw them go, it would have looked as though Finan was merely adding his horses to Osferth's stallions, which had been taken to the wood's edge and secured there, but Finan, as soon as he was among the trees, remounted. Sköll, I guessed, was taking more notice of my remaining men who were being given shields and spears. I touched Serpent-Breath's hilt and said a silent prayer before I leaned down and took a spear's thick ash shaft from one of the servant boys. Then I waited.

Sköll edged his men forward. The youngest of his warriors were shouting their challenges, riding within a spear's throw of Osferth's line, daring us to go forward and fight. I could see Sköll clearly now, a broad-faced, heavily bearded man wearing a helmet with silver cheek-pieces. He was shouting too, but I could not make out his voice among the others. He appeared to be gazing at Osferth, who sat his horse at the center of the wall.

Any moment now, I thought.

"Osferth!" I called.

"Lord?"

"March your men to the wood's edge! I want the trees protecting your left flank!"

"What—" he began.

"Do it!" I bellowed, and because in the past he had always accepted my command and perhaps because he still trusted me, he obeyed. "Be ready!" I called to the shield wall. "Keep your shields up as you go!"

And it began. But not as Sköll had planned.

He had thought to see his men burst from the trees to charge the rear of Osferth's shield wall. Instead they appeared much higher up the slope where they were being pursued by Finan's horsemen. I counted sixteen Norse horsemen, their stallions hurling up clods of earth as Finan spurred in pursuit. Not too far, not too far! I muttered it under my breath as Vidarr Leifson, a Norseman himself, back-handed his sword to unsaddle the rearmost fugitive. Beornoth, a Saxon, lunged down with a spear to gut the fallen man, then Finan was bellowing at his men to break off the pursuit and follow him down the slope. A half-dozen riderless horses came from the trees and followed Finan's men downhill. Osferth's men were almost at the wood as Finan galloped his horsemen along the face of the wall, scaring away two of Sköll's young warriors who had ridden close to jeer at us. "Now make some noise, damn you!" I shouted at the shield wall.

"We killed six of them," Finan said as he reined in close beside me.

"Now let's humble the bastards," I said.

Osferth's men had started banging their swords against their shields again. Finan and I rode along the face of the wall. "They're frightened of you," I called to Osferth's men, "so tell them what sons of miserable whores they are!"

Sköll had not moved, his line of horsemen stood still, their stallions' hooves pawing the damp earth. He had thought that his surprise attack would panic Osferth's men and make them easy meat for his blades, but instead they were unbroken and jeering him. His standard-bearer was holding a handsome triangular banner, which, as he waved it slowly from side to side, unfurled to reveal the badge of a snarling wolf. "Rorik!" I called.

"Lord?"

"Show them my banner." The wolf's head of Bebbanburg would challenge the snarling wolf of Sköll.

I waited till the banner was flying, then rode slowly toward Sköll. Finan came with me and, when we were halfway between the Norsemen and Osferth's troops I rammed my spear-blade into the turf and ostentatiously turned my shield so that the wolf's head was upside down. Then I waited.

I heard the hoofbeats behind me. "Is that Osferth?" I asked Finan. I did not want to look around, but kept my eyes on Sköll.

"It's Osferth," Finan confirmed, "with his priest."

Osferth reined in to my left. He said nothing, just looked at me resentfully. The priest stayed behind him.

"Sköll sent scouts along the western hill," I told Osferth, "and they were supposed to come down through the trees and attack you from the rear."

"You might have told me," he said.

"You mean you didn't see them?" I asked, pretending to be surprised.

He scowled, then shook his head ruefully. "Thank you, lord," he said. He looked at Sköll. "What's he doing?"

"Planning our deaths," I said.

"He surely won't fight?"

"Not now," I said, "and if your men were mounted I'd attack him."

"We could . . ." he began, then paused. He had either been about to suggest that we could advance anyway, but that would take his shield wall away from the wood that protected their left flank, or else he was going to say they could fetch their horses, but that would mean breaking the wall and giving Sköll a chance to charge. "I should have kept them mounted," he said.

"I would have done," I said mildly.

"My father . . ." he began, and again paused.

"Your father?" I asked.

"Always said you were a fool, lord, but a clever fool when it came to a fight."

I laughed at that, and just then Sköll spurred his horse forward. We numbered four men, and so he brought three of his own warriors, all riding slowly toward the inverted spear that, with my shield turned upside down, was a sign that we wanted a parley. "He's not going to fight now," Finan said.

"No?" I asked.

"He hasn't brought his sorcerer with him."

"What difference does that make?" Osferth asked.

"If he planned to fight," Finan said, "he'd want us to see his sorcerer and be frightened."

And that, I thought, was probably true. I remembered that the sorcerer had advised Sköll not to attack Eoferwic, and that forecast had turned out to be true, and I had just seen Snorri turn his back and ride away from us. "They haven't used their magic ointment either," Oda the priest said scornfully.

"How can you tell?" Osferth asked.

"They'd be screaming at us, even charging us."

We fell silent as Sköll and his companions drew nearer. I stared at him. This was the man who had killed Stiorra, and I felt the rage rise. Finan later said I was shuddering and that I was oblivious to the hand he laid on my arm. I do remember bile souring my gullet as I watched the Norseman approach. He was younger than I expected, perhaps around forty. He was broad shouldered and made even bigger by the heavy white cloak. Beneath it he wore glittering mail and a hammer of gold. There was gray in his beard, but the hair showing beneath the helmet's chased rim was blond. His face was deep-lined, his nose broad and broken, while his eyes were blue, narrow, and shrewd. He stopped a pace or so beyond the spear. For a moment he said nothing, but just looked at us with what seemed like amusement, and, when he spoke, his manner was surprisingly mild.

"So," he said, "we found Enar and Njall's bodies. Enar was an incompetent fool, but Njall had promise. Who killed them?"

"I did."

"While they were tied to a tree? You are brave, old man."

"What is he saying?" Osferth hissed.

"Nothing important," the priest said, "just insults."

"So who are you?" Sköll asked me.

"The man who killed Enar and Njall."

Sköll sighed, while his three companions scowled at me. All three wore gray wolf cloaks and had weather-tanned narrow faces. One had a black beard plaited into short stubs, a second had a scar that slashed clean across his swarthy face from the left jawbone to the right cheekbone, so that he appeared to have two nos-trils, one above the other, while the third smiled at me to show that he had filed his teeth into points.

Sköll sighed again and looked up into the sky as though seeking inspiration. A heavy ax hung on his right side, held from the saddle's pommel by a leather harness, while at his left hip was a huge sword, scab-barded in leather. The hilt was dull steel, the grips bound with wolf skin, and I knew that had to be Grayfang, the weapon that had killed my daughter. Sköll looked back to me. "You brought a sorcerer," he said, nodding toward Osferth's priest, "you fear me that much?"

"Why would I fear a failure like you?" I asked. "You ran from Ireland like a frightened child, and I hear that a woman chased you from Jorvik."

He nodded as if acknowledging the truth. "But the woman died," he said, "I killed her."

At that moment I just wanted to draw Serpent-Breath and slice him to red ribbons, but I was steeling myself to be calm. "You killed a woman," I said, "you are brave."

He shrugged. "She was brave, certainly, but she should not have fought us."

"She was a sorceress," I said, "who used the skull curse. Is your sorcerer good enough to avert that curse?"

Sköll gazed at me, judging my words. "If she was so powerful a sorceress," he said, "why did she die?"

"The Norns told her she must die," I said, "that it was her time, but that there was a purpose in her death."

"And how do you know that?" he asked. He still spoke calmly, but I noticed how he and his companions had all touched their hammers when I mentioned the skull curse. There was, so far as I knew, no such curse, but it was enough to unsettle Sköll. "How do you know she had a purpose?" he asked again.

"Because she spoke to me in dreams, of course."

"You invent stories like a child, old man."

"And the purpose of her death," I went on, "was to send you to Niflheim where the corpse-ripper will gnaw your flesh through the rest of time. You will writhe in agony, scream like a baby, and weep like a child. The sorceress told me the worm would gnaw the flesh from your bones, but you will never die, and as you suffer, as you whimper, you will hear the laughter of the heroes in Valhalla. All that she told me."

He was frightened by that. I saw his hand move toward the hammer again, but he checked the motion, dropping his hand to caress the big blade of the ax instead. "You talk bravely, old man. Do you fight bravely?" He waited for my answer, but I kept silent. "Do you want to fight me now?" he asked.

"I want to kill you."

He laughed at that. "Then fight me now, old man."

"Why would I sully my reputation by fighting a failure?" I taunted him.

"You have a reputation to sully?" he sneered.

"I am the old man who defeated your son in combat," I said. "Is that not reputation enough for you?"

And that, at last, roused him. He had been surprisingly restrained, but my words made him spur his horse forward and lean down to snatch my spear from the turf, but before he could level the unwieldy weapon, I had drawn Wasp-Sting, my short-sword, kicked Tintreg, and had lunged the sword's point into the tangle of his beard.

His three followers had all half drawn their swords. Finan was even faster, and his sword, Soul-Stealer, was already clear of her scabbard, but he froze just like the others when I rammed Wasp-Sting into Sköll's beard. Did I mean to kill him? Yes, but the horses moved slightly apart before the blade broke his skin and the stallion belonging to the man with the plaited beard was stopping Tintreg from moving further ahead. Sköll had his head back, held there by Wasp-Sting's sharp point.

"Enough!" Osferth snapped in English. "Put the sword down, lord," he added to me in a calm voice. "Please, lord, put it down."

Finan sheathed Soul-Stealer. He did it very slowly, very deliberately, then leaned over, and, still moving with extreme care, pushed my sword arm down. "This is a truce, lord," he chided me, "a truce."

"What are they saying?" Sköll asked me.

"That you have no honor," I snarled back.

"Who are you?" he asked.

"The man who will kill you," I answered, "and I swear on the gods that you will have no sword in your hand when you die."

He sneered at that. "You frighten me, old man."

"What is being said?" Osferth insisted.

"Childish insults," Father Oda said dismissively.

Sköll rammed the spear back into the turf and backed his horse away. I also backed Tintreg, who tossed his head and whinnied. Osferth put a gloved hand onto the horse's bridle as if to prevent me from attacking Sköll again. "You suggested the truce," he said to me, "why?"

"Because I want to see the man I'm going to kill," I answered, "and if your men were mounted we could finish the bastard off now."

"I came to find you," Osferth said, "not to start a war with Northumbria."

"The war has found you," I said, "so let's fight now."

"What are you saying?" Sköll demanded.

"Tell them to go home," Osferth insisted.

"You won't fight?"

Osferth frowned. He knew we outnumbered Sköll's men, he knew that in a fight we would eventually overwhelm the Norsemen, but he also knew that to start a fight was to lend his men to a purely Northumbrian quarrel, and if Æthelstan or King Edward were to discover that West Saxons and Mercians had died in a fight to settle a feud between two pagans they would not be happy. "I came to find you," he said stubbornly, "and I have no reason to fight this man."

"He attacked you!"

"The attack failed." He let go of Tintreg's bridle and half turned his horse away. "Tell him to go back home."

I leaned forward and took hold of the spear shaft. "My prince," I said to Sköll, "has decided to spare your rotten life. He advises you to go home unless you wish a shallow grave in this valley." I plucked the spear free and turned to follow Osferth.

"You're cowards!" Sköll shouted. "You run away like slaves!"

And so we did.

We outnumbered them and we ran away. Well, we rode away.

I had been tempted to attack. My hatred of Sköll tried to persuade me that my men would defeat his, but it would have been an expensive and incomplete victory. Men would die on both sides, and, because we were all on horseback, many would escape the slaughter. It is always the same with mounted battles, the moment one side looks as if it has gained the advantage, the other flees, and then it becomes a horse race. Good sense, and I retained just enough in the face of Stiorra's killer, told me that a fight on horseback between two equal forces would leave both sides weakened, and neither with an overwhelming victory. I wanted to face Sköll, and I wanted to kill Sköll, but I wanted to be certain that I faced him man-to-man, and that I disarmed him before slaughtering him to make sure that his vile face would not offend me in Valhalla's feasting hall.

If Osferth's men had joined mine, then our victory would have been certain, but Osferth had been right. He had no quarrel with Sköll, indeed Osferth had no business leading troops into Northumbria at all, so to return to Mameceaster with a report that he had lost a score of men in a fight that was none of his concern would almost certainly end with him losing command of Mameceaster's garrison.

"I am sorry, lord," he told me as we rode away.

"Sorry? Why?"

He looked embarrassed. "For your daughter. For your hopes of revenge."

"My daughter will be revenged," I said.

"I pray so."

"You do?"

"I pray for you," he said, still embarrassed, "I always have."

"You think your god wants Sköll dead?"

"I think my god weeps for Englaland," he said. "I think my god wants peace."

"And Northumbria?"

For a moment he was not sure what I meant, then he bridled. "God wants the Christians of Northumbria to be ruled by a Christian king. One religion, one language, one nation."

"So you'll invade us? Force us to our knees?"

He half smiled. "There might be another way, lord."

"What other way?" I demanded.

"By talking," he said, "by negotiation." He ignored my sneer. "You know the Easter Witan is to be held in Mercia?"

"I didn't know."

"It will be the first to combine the Witans of Mercia, East Anglia, and Wessex," he said, "and Prince Æthelstan thinks you should attend."

"Was that his message to me?"

"It was, it is."

I had expected another demand that I give Æthelstan my oath, though on reflection it seemed unlikely that Æthelstan would reveal that demand to anyone. Instead it seemed he wanted me to attend the Easter Witan so he could press me himself. At least I assumed as much. "And why should I go?" I asked truculently. "My lands in Wessex and Mercia were stripped from me."

"You must ask Prince Æthelstan, lord," Osferth said. "I was just charged with delivering the message."

"I need to find Sigtryggr," I said. "That's more important than any damned meeting of the Witan."

Two days later we rode into Mameceaster. The burh was new, built around a Roman fort that stood beside the River Mædlak on a low breast-shaped hill that had given the place its name. My men called it Titceaster. A wall of timber and earth surrounded the new streets with their small houses, but the real strength of the burh was the old fort. Our horses' hooves sounded loud on the stone-paved road that led through the twin arches of the fort's northern gate, which, like the walls of Ceaster, was built of stone, though Mameceaster's stone was darker. The lower courses were thick with moss, but the upper showed signs of repair where the long years had collapsed the ramparts. The body and separate head of one of Cynlæf's rebels stank on the old fort's gate. The two pieces had been nailed there and the birds feasted on the rotting flesh. "I always wondered," Osferth remarked as we rode past the macabre trophies, "why Sigtryggr didn't garrison the place first."

"Because it's in Northumbria?"

"No one knows! It certainly isn't in Northumbria now."

My son-in-law, or rather my once son-in-law, could

have fortified Mameceaster, but the truth was that he only had sufficient forces to garrison Eoferwic and Lindcolne. The other great fortresses of Northumbria were ruled by lords, as I ruled Bebbanburg, and as my journeying of the last weeks had proved we lords did not always do Sigtryggr's bidding. Edward of Wessex expected obedience from all his subjects, but Northumbria was ruled by Vikings who might or might not obey whoever called himself king in Eoferwic. "Northumbria was a great country once," I said to Osferth as we reached the center of the old Roman fort. "The Scots paid us tribute, the Mercians feared us, there was gold."

"Everything changed when the pagans invaded," he said. His men had vanished into the side streets where their families lived and where their horses were stabled. Mameceaster's fort reminded me of Ceaster because the Romans built their forts to a pattern. Their buildings had long collapsed, but the new houses, storerooms, and stables had been made where the old ones had stood. Ceaster still had a great hall, but here that hall was all timber and thatch, and close to it was a new church, even bigger than the hall. Everywhere the Saxons build they make a church.

"I will give you a house for your stay," Osferth said as he slid wearily from the saddle and let a servant take his horse's bridle.

A second servant took Tintreg in hand as I dismounted. "We won't stay long," I said, wincing at the aches in my back.

"Your horses need rest," Osferth insisted, "and you need rest." That was true. Even Tintreg, a hardy beast, had stumbled more than once as we approached the burh, and was sweating and panting.

"Two days," I said reluctantly, "then I need to join Sigtryggr."

Osferth hesitated, and I knew he wanted to mention the Witan again and encourage me to attend, but he seemed to acknowledge his words would be wasted. "Bettic will show you to your quarters," he said instead, nodding at his steward, a one-eyed man with a limp.

"And my men?"

"Will be fed and sheltered," Osferth said. He was already distracted by two young priests bringing him sheets of parchment. "We shall eat in the hall!" he called as he hurried away.

"He's like his father," I said to the steward.

"A pity he doesn't wear his father's crown, lord," Bettic said.

I made sure my men had food and somewhere to rest, gave them a pointless warning about picking fights in the taverns, then followed Bettic to a house on the southern side of the fort. It was one of the buildings that had kept their Roman walls, though the plaster had fallen away and the roof was thatch. There was a small outer room that I guessed had been a shop, and a larger inner chamber where there was a bed, a stool, a table, rushes on the floor, and a hearth. The weather had warmed and I refused Bettic's offer of a fire. Rorik, my servant, had followed us. "Fetch me something to eat," I ordered him, "and some ale. Some for yourself too."

"I'll show you where to find food, lad." Bettic had seen Rorik's confusion.

"Where did you lose the eye?" I asked the steward.

"East Anglia, lord. A nasty fight two years ago."

"I missed it," I said. I had been in Ceaster for most of the time that Edward had spent conquering East Anglia.

"And more's the pity," Bettic said. He went silent, but I looked at him quizzically and he shrugged. "The king lined us in front of a ditch, lord. The Danes pushed us back and we lost good men."

"In front of the ditch? Not behind it?"

"He reckoned it would stop us retreating."

"I had hopes of him once," I said bleakly.

"He beat the Danes in the end," Bettic said, but it was half-hearted praise. "I'll show your boy where to find food, lord."

Once he was gone I unbuckled my sword belt, pulled

my heavy mail with its greasy leather liner over my head, then lay on the bed and stared at the dirty thatch. I tried to summon Stiorra's face and could not. I remembered her vivacity, her quick smile, her sense. Where were her children now? I closed my eyes tight, reluctant to let the tears fall. I clutched the hammer tightly enough to hurt my fingers. The curse had struck, but was it finished? I had just wasted weeks of my life by crossing Britain to rescue a man who did not need rescuing, then pursuing an enemy halfway to Eoferwic, only to be stranded in this Mercian burh where a bell was ringing to summon the faithful to midday prayers. I thought of Bebbanburg, where the endless sea beat on the sand, where the wind blew about the hall, and where I should be at this moment.

"Greetings, lord," a voice said.

I had not heard anyone approach and I was startled. I sat up, looking for Serpent-Breath, then relaxed.

It was Mus. Also known as Sunngifu, Sister Gomer, bishop's widow, whore, and trouble-maker.

"Aren't you supposed to be at prayer?" I asked her sourly.

"We're always at prayer," she said, "life is prayer. Here, lord," she held out something wrapped in a scrap of linen, which I unwrapped to find a hunk of blood sausage. "And that's Lord Osferth's wine," she added, putting a flask at my feet.

"Lord Osferth?"

"He's a king's son, isn't he?"

"He's a bastard."

"Folk say that of Lord Æthelstan too."

"No, his parents were married. I know the priest who married them."

She had pulled the stool across the floor and sat opposite me. "Really?"

"Truly."

"So . . ." she began, then hesitated.

"So," I said, "Æthelstan is the rightful heir to his father's throne."

"But . . ." she said, and again hesitated.

"But," I went on, "that little shit Ælfweard has a powerful uncle."

"Æthelhelm?"

"Whose sister married Edward."

"But he put her aside," Mus said, "and he has another woman now."

"But Lord Æthelhelm," I pointed out, "leads four or five hundred warriors. The new woman just has nicer tits and no army." She giggled at that and I scowled at her. "You're not supposed to find that funny. You're a nun."

"Do I look like a nun?" She was dressed in a pale yellow linen shift, which, when I looked more closely, had hems embroidered with blue flowers. Expensive, I thought.

"You're not a nun?"

"I was only ever a postulant, lord."

"A postulant? That sounds like a boil."

"And I got squeezed," she said ruefully. "The abbess doesn't like me."

"So what," I began to ask, then decided the question did not need asking.

"I help in the hall," she answered anyway. "Lord Osferth likes me well enough." She saw my expression and laughed. "He'd like to, lord, but he's scared of his god."

I laughed too. "Men are fools. Women make them fools."

"It's our skill," she said, smiling.

"For some women, yes," I said, "but life isn't fair. Not all women are lovely."

"I'm told your daughter was beautiful."

I smiled. For some reason talking about Stiorra with Mus did not hurt. "She was. She was dark, not like you, and tall. She had a fierce beauty."

"I'm sorry, lord."

"It was fate, Mus, just fate." I drank from the flask

and found Osferth's wine was sour. "So you're a servant now?"

"I have charge of the maids in the hall and kitchen," she said, "and I came to ask a favor of you."

I nodded. "Ask it."

"There's a girl who joined us, I think you know her? Wynflæd. She has red hair."

"The squirrel," I said.

Mus laughed. "She looks like one, doesn't she? She and her husband are helping in the kitchens."

"He was a monk," I said, "and broke his vows."

"He was?" She sounded surprised.

"He preferred the squirrel's tits to a life of prayer."

"A lot of monks enjoy both," Mus said bleakly. "I want you to talk to Wynflæd, lord."

"Me?"

"You know what happened to her?"

"She was raped."

"Over and over," Mus said.

Rorik appeared at the inner door and looked confused by Mus's presence. "I have bread and cheese, lord," he stammered, "and ale."

"On the table," I told him, "then go and wash Tintreg." He looked at Mus and hesitated. "Go!" I said. He went. "Have some cheese," I told Mus.

She shook her head. "They hurt her, lord."

"She's not the first, she won't be the last."

"She cries at night."

"And Brother Beadwulf can't comfort her?"

"He's a weak man, lord."

I grunted at that. "So you want me to comfort her?" I asked scornfully.

"No." She spoke with a deal of force. She looked so beautiful and delicate, but there was a backbone of steel inside her small body.

"So what do you want?"

"Do you know what men say about you?"

I gave a snort of laughter. "That I'm old. They also call me Uhtredærwe," that meant Uhtred the Wicked, "they call me priest-killer and Ealdordeofol." The last meant chief of the devils.

"They also say that you're kind, that you're generous, and that you punish any man who rapes a woman."

I grunted. "The last thing you said is true."

"You won't even let your men beat their wives."

"I do sometimes." Rarely, though. I watched my father beat my stepmother, and it was not pretty. As for rape, I had seen what that had done to Ragnar's daughter, and to Hild, and few crimes angered me more. "So you're saying I'm soft," I challenged Mus.

"No, I'm saying Wynflæd needs to know that not all men are rapists or weaklings."

"And I can persuade her of that?" I asked dubiously.

"You're Uhtred of Bebbanburg. Everyone fears you."

I gave another snort. "You too, Mus?"

"I'm terrified of you, lord," she said with a smile. "Will you talk to her?"

"The last time I saw you, Mus," I said, "at least the last time before this year, I threatened to have the skin whipped off your back."

"I didn't believe you. Have you ever whipped a woman?"

"No."

"So I was right," she said. "Now will you talk to Wynflæd?"

I took a drink of the sour wine. "We're leaving in two days, Mus," I said, "and I'll be busy." The truth was that I had nothing particular to do before we left except give our horses time to recover, but I could not imagine anything I would say could help the squirrel, nor did I want to talk to her. What could I tell her? "She's a Christian, isn't she?" I asked. "So why doesn't she talk to a priest?" Mus responded to that with a scornful noise. "Or talk to you?" I suggested.

"She has talked to me; I think you'd be good for her."

It was my turn to make a scornful noise. "I'm going to Eoferwic, Mus. Eoferwic and Bebbanburg. I'm going home."

"I don't think you are, lord," Mus said quietly.

"You don't?" At first I thought I had misheard her, then shrugged. "It doesn't matter what you think, Mus, I must leave, I have to find Sigtryggr. I don't want to waste time, so believe me, we're going to Eoferwic."

"Then you won't find King Sigtryggr there, lord, because he's been summoned to Tamweorthin."

I just stared at her. "Summoned?"

"Invited, lord."

"Sigtryggr! To Tamweorthin?" Tamweorthin was a Mercian burh, a place that Æthelflaed had been fond of, and a place where there was a palace fit for a king. "How do you know?" I asked, still struggling to understand her news.

"I serve in the hall. You'd be surprised at the things we hear. Men think we don't exist except to serve them, and not just food and ale."

"Who invited him?" I asked, though I already knew the answer. Tamweorthin, like Gleawecestre or Wintanceaster or Lundene, was one of the few burhs where royalty could live in the luxury they loved.

"King Edward, of course," Mus said, "he wants King Sigtryggr to be at the Easter meeting of the Witan, so you won't have to leave for at least a week, lord, and that will give you time to talk to Wynflæd."

I stood and snarled. The impudence of Wessex! The only reason for Edward to invite Sigtryggr to a meeting of the Witan was to demand his fealty! To humiliate him publicly and make him a client king! "He won't go," I said angrily.

"Edward?"

"Sigtryggr. He won't go."

"But if he does, lord, will you speak to Wynflæd?" She hesitated. "Please, lord, for me?"

"For you, Mus," I growled, "yes. But I'm still leaving for Eoferwic in two days."

"Why?"

"Because Sigtryggr won't submit to Edward."

And at nightfall a messenger came to the hall from Æthelstan in Ceaster.

The message merely confirmed that Æthelstan was attending the Witan in Tamweorthin, and that, by the grace of God, King Sigtryggr of Northumbria had accepted King Edward's summons to attend. The message requested that the priests, monks, nuns, and laity of Mameceaster pray for the success of the Witan's deliberations.

So Sigtryggr was ready to grovel, and I had to talk to the squirrel.

There are two ways to hang a man, a quick way and a slow way, the first gives a merciful death, and the second provokes a dance of agony.

On the morning after our arrival, Osferth gave judgment in Mameceaster's great hall, a gaunt and dark building of oak and thatch built on a Roman floor of stone. There were few prisoners, most of whom were accused of thievery, and those were condemned to a whipping in the square that stood between the hall and the new church. Father Oda promised to pray for each man, though much good that does when the lash is ripping the flesh off the bones.

The last prisoners were the cattle-raiders, six of them, including Hergild, who proved to be a burly, red-faced man of middle age. They were accused of thievery and rape, they were asked if they denied the accusations, and the only response was from one man who spat on the floor. Father Oda served as translator, and, when Osferth pronounced all six guilty, the priest offered them a chance to be baptized, an offer they did not understand. "You will be washed," the Danish priest said, "and go before the judgment seat of Almighty God."

"You mean Thor?" Hergild asked.

Another man wanted to know whether being judged by the Christian god meant they would live. "Of course not," the priest said, "you must die first."

"And you want to wash us?"

"In the river," the priest said.

I had insisted that Wynflæd, the squirrel, watch the trial, all two or three minutes of it. She was shivering. I crouched beside her. "Did they all rape you?"

"All except that one, lord." She pointed a wavering finger at the youngest of the six men. I guessed he was about sixteen or seventeen, a broad-shouldered, straw-haired boy, who, like Wynflæd, looked close to tears.

"He didn't touch you?"

"He was kind."

"He tried to stop the rape?"

She shook her head. "But he gave me a coat afterward and said he was sorry and gave me something to drink."

Osferth was impatient. "Do they wish to convert?" he demanded of the priest.

"They do not, lord," Oda said severely.

"Then take them away. Hang them."

I stood. "Lord!" It seemed strange to call Osferth lord, even though he was the son of a king, but as the commander of the burh he deserved the title. "I have a favor to ask."

Osferth had also stood, but now paused, one hand on the arm of the chair he had been using. "Lord Uhtred?" He sounded suspicious.

"These men are Northumbrians. And I ask that they be put to death by Northumbrians."

"Why?" he demanded.

"My men need the practice," I said, which was entirely untrue.

"How?" Osferth asked.

"Just as you decreed," I said, "by hanging." I saw him hesitate. "You can send men to make sure we hang them all." I could see he was fearful that I would release them. "And their crime," I added, "was committed against a Northumbrian," I put my arm around the squirrel's thin shoulders. As far as I knew she was Mercian, but I doubted Osferth knew or cared where the squirrel came from. "So it is only fit," I finished, "to allow Northumbrians to punish Northumbrians for a crime committed in Northumbria."

"This is Mercia," he said stiffly, "and they must suffer Mercian justice."

"The rope will be Mercian," I promised, "and I ask you the favor of knotting it around their necks."

I had stressed the word "favor." Osferth might disapprove of me, but he knew full well that I had nurtured and protected him when he was younger. He paused, then nodded. "Hang them by midday, Lord Uhtred," he said, and, accompanied by two other priests who served as his clerks, he strode away, pausing at the door to point to Father Oda.

"Father! Go with Lord Uhtred. Bring me news of their deaths."

"I shall, lord." Father Oda bowed.

"You're also coming, girl," I told Wynflæd.

"Lord—" she began to protest.

"You're coming!"

Bettic the steward found me a half-dozen ropes made of twisted leather, we borrowed a dozen horses, then took the prisoners to their death. The six men already had their hands bound, and we just had to walk them out of the southern gate and through the shallow ford of the Mædlak. On the far bank there were some small houses, a barn, and a cattle shed, and beyond that were oak trees. I had put Wynflæd on a docile mare, which scared her anyway, and I led her by the bridle. "There are two ways," I told her, "to hang a man. A quick way and a slow way." She looked at me with wide eyes and was too scared to say anything.

"The quick way," I went on, "is the merciful way. They're dead before they know it." She was clutching the saddle's pommel with both hands. "Have you ever ridden a horse before?" I asked her.

"Only when we traveled with you," she said in a voice so frightened I could hardly hear her.

"This mare won't throw you," I said. "Relax, push your feet down. Now, as I was saying, there's a quick way and a slow way. To kill a man the quick way you have to find a long branch that's about two spears' length above the ground. Are you listening?"

"I am, lord."

"It has to be a long branch because you need to pull the end of the branch down. You loop a rope over the end and you haul it down till it's only a spear's length above the ground. What did I just say?"

"Haul the branch down until it's only a spear's length away, lord."

"Good girl. Now, once you've hauled it down you hold it down, then you tie another rope around the same branch and you tie the other end of that new rope around the prisoner's neck. It seems to work best if you have the knot under one of his ears. Do you understand me?"

"I do, lord." She was trying to push her feet down to reach the stirrups. Father Oda, riding behind us, was leaning forward to listen.

"So you have the branch bent down close to the ground," I went on, "and the man is tied by the neck to the same branch, and all you do is let go of the first rope. What do you think happens?"

She frowned at me, thinking. "The branch goes up, lord?"

"It flies up!" I said. "It springs up! Like the horn of a bow when you loose the string. And it breaks the bastard's neck, just like that!" I snapped the fingers of my right hand, causing my horse to flick his ears back. "Sometimes," I went on, "it rips the man's head clean off!"

The squirrel flinched, but she was listening.

"So the quick way is merciful, I said, "and usually messy. Then there's the slow way. That's much simpler and much more painful. You simply throw a rope over any branch that's high enough, tie one end around the prisoner's neck, and haul him up! He chokes to death. It takes a long time! He'll piss himself while he's dying, and his legs will jerk, and you hear him struggling for breath. Have you ever seen a man hanged?"

She shook her head. "No, lord."

"Now," I went on, "I have a decision to make." I nodded at the six prisoners who were trudging ahead of us. "Do I hang them quickly? Or slowly?" I looked at her expectantly, but she just gazed back wide-eyed. "What do you think we should do?" I asked.

For a moment I thought she would not answer. She was looking at the prisoners, then suddenly turned back to me. "The slow way, lord."

"Good girl."

"But not him," she pointed at the youngest man.

"Not him," I agreed, then turned in the saddle. "Do you agree, Father Oda?"

"They are pagans, why should I care how they die? Kill them how you please, lord."

"It's not what pleases me," I said, "it's what Wynflæd wants." I looked back to her. "You're sure now? The slow way?"

"The very slow way," she said vengefully.

And revenge is sweet. The Christians preach some utter nonsense about revenge. I have heard their priests solemnly advise folk to meekly accept a beating, to even offer the other cheek so the beating can continue, but that is merely to grovel. Why would I grovel to Sköll? I wanted revenge, and only revenge would satisfy Stiorra's spirit. Revenge is justice, and I gave Wynflæd justice.

Most of the men who had raped her were already dead, left to rot in whatever place Osferth's men had found them, and now the others died before her eyes. I stripped them naked, then made her watch as they danced on the ropes and pissed themselves and as their bowels loosened and as they choked, and by the time the second one died she was smiling, and the last noise the fifth one heard was her laughter. Good little squirrel.

That left the youngest. I waited till the last of the five was dead, then put a rope around the boy's neck. He was shivering, despite still being clothed. "What's your name, boy?"

"Immar Hergildson."

"You just watched your father die."

"Yes, lord."

"You know why he died?"

Immar glanced at Wynflæd. "Because of her, lord."

"You didn't protest when they raped her."

"I wanted to, lord, but my father . . ." He started to cry.

I hauled on the rope, making Wynflæd gasp. I hauled again, pulling Immar Hergildson a fingernail's breadth above the leaf mold. "Can you wield a sword, Immar?"

"Yes, lord," he choked.

"Father Oda!" I called.

"Lord?" the Danish priest seemed unmoved by anything he had seen beneath the oak trees.

"How many men have you seen hanged here today?"

"Six," he said calmly.

"Are you sure?"

"Lord Osferth will ask if I saw six men hanged. I shall say yes, but if you want that one to live," he nodded at Immar, "I should let his feet touch the ground, lord."

I dropped Immar to the ground and untied the rope from his neck. Father Oda deliberately looked away, and so far as I know he never did tell anyone that I had spared the boy's life. Not, I think, that Oda the Dane cared. In time he became a bishop, and long before that he had gained the reputation of being a stern and unbending leader of the church, but on that day in Mameceaster he let me use mercy.

"You are now one of my men," I told Immar, and we made him kneel, made him put his hands over mine that were clasped about Serpent-Breath's hilt, and then, still gasping for breath, he swore he would be my man to death.

"I talked to Wynflæd," I told Mus that night.

"I know," she said, "thank you."

And later we fell asleep.

Seven

Osferth was not invited to Tamweorthin. "King Edward," he had told me stiffly, "would prefer I did not attend."

"Or even exist?"

"That too," he admitted with a tight smile.

"Look after Mus," I told him the night before we left Mameceaster.

"Mus?"

"Sunngifu."

He grimaced. "She's a capable woman," he said distantly.

"And looking for a husband, I think."

That got no reaction except from Mus, who laughed when I told her. "Oh, I couldn't marry Lord Osferth," she said, "it would be like marrying a priest!"

"You were married to a priest," I reminded her.

"But Leofstan was a gentle and kind man. Lord Os-ferth is troubled. He doesn't think God loves him, poor man." Mus, I thought, was a gentle and kind woman. I gave her the last two of my gold coins.

"You can ride with us," I suggested.

"To where? Bebbanburg? I don't think your wife would approve."

"She wouldn't," I agreed.

"I'm happy here," she said, sounding anything but happy, "and I'll find a husband."

"I'm sure you will."

She stood on tiptoe to kiss me. "Kill Sköll, lord."

"I shall."

"I know."

Mus did not come with us, but Brother Beadwulf and Wynflæd rode with the boys and servants who led our spare horses and who herded the pack animals with their burdens of spears and shields. Wynflæd had gone on her knees to me, begging that she and her husband serve me. "I don't want to stay here, lord," she said, meaning Mameceaster.

"Too many sad memories?" I asked her.

"Yes, lord," she said, and so I agreed.

We left by the southern gate, and once across the river we passed the five bodies still hanging from the branches of a spreading oak. Their eyes were gone, their skin was blackening, and ravens had ripped the flesh down to bone. Immar Hergildson, equipped now with a mail coat, an old helmet, and a sword, forced himself to look at his father. "You have no father now," I told him. "This is your family," I gestured toward my men, "and when we have time," I went on, "we must let your mother know you're alive."

"Thank you, lord," he said, and I reflected that the valley of the three brothers had lost all three of them.

Then I forgot the dead brothers as we rode south through fields showing the first signs of the new year's crops, beside pastures where fresh-born lambs bleated, and by woods hazed with new leaves. A fat land, I thought, which is why men fought for it. The Romans had captured it, then we Saxons took it, and after us came the Danes, and now the Norse were strengthening their hold on the wilder lands of Cumbraland and casting greedy eyes on these plump fields. I touched Serpent-Breath's hilt. "They'll always need us," I said to Finan.

"They?"

"Whoever needs a sword."

He chuckled. "Who are we fighting for these days?"

"Sigtryggr, of course."

"And he's making peace."

I shrugged. "We'll find out," I said. At the Mercian town of Tamweorthin.

That the Easter meeting of the Witan was to be held at Tamweorthin was proof that the rebellion in Mercia was over. Osferth, before I left, had told me that every ealdorman, every bishop, and a good number of abbots had been summoned, and Edward, before issuing the invitations, must have been certain that the Mercian roads were safe for travel. And this meeting of the Witan was notable because it was the first where men from Wessex, Mercia, and East Anglia were to be brought together to hear the king's decrees, to make laws, and to seal Edward's claim that he was *Anglorum Saxonum Rex*. The only Angles or Saxons who were not part of Edward's kingdom were those who lived in Northumbria, and that, I reckoned, was why Sigtryggr had been summoned. He was to submit to Edward's authority, or at least I assumed that was why Edward had demanded his presence.

We did not ride all the way to Tamweorthin. If Osferth was right, and I was sure he was, then the burh would be crammed with ealdormen and churchmen, all with their retinues, and every tavern, barn, store, and house would be full. There would be tents in the fields, there would be fights in the streets, there would be stale bread, sour ale, and vomit, so we found a steading a half-day's ride north of the burh where my men could stay. I paid hacksilver for their keep, then rode south with just Finan, Rorik, and Berg for company. Finan looked alarmed at such a small group. "That bastard Æthelhelm will be there," he warned me.

"So will Sigtryggr," I said, "and he'll have men. Besides, we're not invited, so turning up with a war-band will look like a threat."

It was still two days before Easter, but already the pastures outside the burh were thick with tents. Wagons loaded with barrels of salted fish and smoked meat were lumbering toward the gates, other wagons were heaped with barrels of ale or wine. "If we're not invited," Finan asked, "why are we here?"

"Because Sigtryggr would want us here, and because Æthelstan asked me to come. I doubt Edward even knows I'm here."

He laughed. "Which means they won't be happy to see us."

Nor were they. The guards at the burh's northern gate let us through without a challenge, despite the hammer hanging from my neck, but when I found the steward in the gatehouse of the palace the welcome turned sour. He was a bald, middle-aged man with a red face and gray mustache, helped by three clerks who sat at a table heaped with lists. "Who are you, lord?" he asked. The "lord" was grudging, provoked by the gold chain around my neck. He saw the hammer too and grimaced.

"Ealdorman Uhtred," I said, "of Bebbanburg."

That, at least, drew a satisfying reaction. He stiffened, looked frightened, then flapped a hand at the clerks. "Find Lord Uhtred," he said, then bowed to me, "a moment, lord."

Two of the three clerks were priests, which was to be expected. King Alfred had started schools throughout Wessex and encouraged them in Mercia, hoping that folk would learn to read and write. Some had, but almost all the literate men became priests, and so they were the men who codified the laws, copied the charters, wrote the king's letters, and drew up the countless lists of royal property.

The youngest priest, a scrawny boy with a boil on his cheek and a dirty mark on his forehead, cleared his throat. "There's no Lord Uhtred on the lists," he said, frightened out of his wits. He held up a sheaf of papers with a quivering hand. "I know," he said weakly, "because I copied all the lists, and there's no . . ." his voice faded away.

"You have tents, lord?" the steward asked hopefully.

"I just need quarters for four men and four horses," I said.

"But you're not on the list," the steward complained, then looked alarmed as I drew a small knife from my belt. "Lord!" he protested, taking a step back.

I smiled at him, drew the knife across the ball of my thumb, then picked up a clean quill. I dipped the nib in my welling blood, pulled one of the lists toward me, and wrote my name. "There," I said, "I'm on the list." I sucked the shallow cut, then wiped it on my leggings. "Where are you quartering King Sigtryggr?"

The steward hesitated, glanced at the clerks, then looked back to me. "He's in the Bullock, lord."

"That's a tavern?"

"Yes, lord," the steward said.

"King Sigtryggr isn't being given quarters in the palace?" I asked, though the question was really an indignant protest.

"He's given the Bullock, lord. No one else will be there, just the king and his followers."

"So it's a big tavern?"

The steward hesitated again, and the three clerks stared down at their lists. "No, lord," the steward finally admitted. "King Sigtryggr is only bringing sixteen men, lord." I suspected he meant that Edward had insisted that Sigtryggr did not arrive with a small army.

"Sixteen men," I said, "so it's a small tavern with rancid ale and rotten food?"

"I wouldn't know, lord," the steward muttered.

"You put a king in a small shitty tavern because he's a pagan?" I asked, and the steward had no answer to that so I put him out of his misery. "It will do for us too," I said, then smiled at the scrawny young priest. "We'll all be pagans together, sacrificing virgins at midnight." The poor boy made the sign of the cross, and I pointed my bloody hand at him. "Make sure I'm on the list for the Witan too," I snarled, "otherwise we'll sacrifice you as well."

"Yes, lord," he said.

"You've got dirt on your forehead," I said, "so has he," I pointed to the other priest.

"Because it's Good Friday, lord. The day our Lord died."

"Is that why they call it good?"

They just stared at me, appalled, and we went to the Bullock.

And next day Sigtryggr arrived.

He was angry. What did I expect? And there was no one except me on whom to vent that anger. "You didn't kill him?" he demanded of me. "And you had your sword at his throat?"

I let him rage. He got drunk that night, and I saw

that a one-eyed man could weep like any other. Svart, the commander of his household troops, helped him to bed, then came back and poured himself a pot of ale. "Horse piss," he said in disgust, "Saxon horse piss." Svart was a huge man, a great beast of a warrior with broad shoulders and a thick black beard into which were woven two lower jawbones of wolves. "We were in Lindcolne," he said, "when Sköll attacked Eoferwic."

"Why Lindcolne?"

He shrugged. "King Edward sent men to talk. It was about this," he waved a huge hand around the room, meaning that the Saxon delegation had gone to Lindcolne to invite Sigtryggr to the Witan. "The queen said we shouldn't go. She said that if they wanted to talk that meant they weren't wanting to fight, so we should ignore them. Let them worry, she said. Then Hrothweard persuaded him." Hrothweard was the Archbishop of Eoferwic, a West Saxon and a good man. My son-in-law had ever tolerated Christians, offering them hospitality and protection, favors that the Christians never offered to pagans in their own lands.

"I was told the Mercians had invaded," I said, "and that was why you went south."

He shook his head. "No, it was just men talking. Ten crows and three lords." He meant ten priests.

"I should have been there. In Jorvik."

"We've all been saying that." He poured more ale. "She was a clever one."

He meant Stiorra. I nodded. "She was clever from a child."

"Now he doesn't know what to do."

"Kill Sköll."

"Besides that."

I took the jug and poured more horse piss. "His children?" I meant my grandchildren.

"Safe in Jorvik," Svart said.

"Stiorra's mother," I said, "cast the runesticks and said Stiorra would be the mother of kings." Svart said nothing. A draft flickered the rushlights on the table. "Another wise woman," I went on, "said I would lead armies. That there would be a great battle, and seven kings would die."

"My grandmother," Svart said, "cast the sticks when I was born. They said I'd be dead before I could walk."

"Seven kings," I poured him the last of the ale. "I'll settle for one Norseman."

Svart raised his pot. "To Sköll's death," he said.

"Sköll's death," I echoed.

Somewhere in the night a child cried and a hooded hawk screeched. I wished Mus had come with us. I prayed to the gods before I slept, begging them to show me the future in a dream, but if they did I could not remember it when I woke.

It was dawn on Eostre's feast day.

Ragnar, who became my father after he captured me, always sacrificed to Idunn in the spring. "She brings us flowers, lambs, and women," he had told me, "so she deserves a generous gift."

"She brings us women?"

He had ruffled my hair. "You'll understand one day."

His Saxon slaves were given a feast on Idunn's day, and they called it Eostre's feast because their goddess of the spring was called Eostre. There were songs, there was laughter, there was dancing in the pastures if the weather was good and then folk would go to the woods to finish the dance. The hall was hung with boughs bright with petals and new leaves. Idunn and Eostre, I suppose they are the same goddess, bring us new life, they give us bud and blossom, fledglings and lambs. The feast is joyous and the land is adorned with flowers, with primroses and cowslips, bluebells in the woods, lilac and lilies. The Christians, unable to stop folk welcoming the rebirth of the year, made it their own feast day, a feast to celebrate their nailed god's death and resurrection. Father Beocca liked to call the feast Pascha. "That's the proper name," he insisted to me, "Pascha," but insist as the priests liked, everyone still called it Easter, which was Eostre's day.

And that Eostre's day dawned chill and wet. The rain came in great swaths from the west, poured from the thatch, and ran like streams down the hill where the old fort stood at Tamweorthin's heart. It had not been a Roman fort, but a Saxon citadel of wood and earth, and all that remained of the old defenses was a ridge of turf above a steep, short slope that had once been the ramparts. A passage led through the ridge, beyond which lay the royal palace and Tamweorthin's largest church. Sigtryggr and I, cloaked against the malevolent rain, climbed the hill toward the palace. Svart, Berg, and two other warriors followed us. Finan had gone to church as he always did on Eostre's day, and Sigtryggr and I, bored with the Bullock's small rooms, were exploring the town. "I was supposed to go to the church," Sigtryggr told me.

"Supposed?"

He shrugged. "Hrothweard said it was expected of me."

"Is the archbishop here?"

Sigtryggr nodded. "He is, only he won't be quartered in a dirty tavern, will he? They'll give him space in the palace." He grimaced. "I was told I couldn't bring more than sixteen followers."

"Why come at all?"

"They promised safe conduct," he evaded my question.

I could hear singing coming from the church at the hill's top. King Edward was in the gaunt wooden building, as was Æthelstan and most of the nobility of Mercia, Wessex, and East Anglia. I had a sudden memory of the night Ragnar's hall burned. Kjartan the Cruel had set that fire and had reaped the screams of the trapped, the slaughter at the door, and the shriveled corpses in the ashes. The singing went on, a drone of monks, and we turned into the Mallard, a big tavern by the lane that led up the hill. It was almost empty because the law said that folk must go to church on Eostre's day and Tamweorthin's six churches were doubtless full, but a pair of servants were putting new rushes on the tavern floor and happily brought us ale. We sat by the hearth.

"Why did I come?" Sigtryggr asked, gazing at the flames.

"Stiorra would have told you to stay at home."

"She would, yes."

"They're humiliating you," I said.

Svart growled in protest at my words, but Sigtryggr just nodded agreement. "They are," he said, "and we'll find out how tomorrow." The Witan always began on Eostre's feast, but the first day, the Sunday, was given over to the priests, and the Witan's real business would wait till the morning. Sigtryggr stretched out a foot and pushed a log into the heart of the fire. "I sometimes wish you'd never made me King of Northumbria," he continued. "I could be in a good ship at sea with the whole world waiting to be robbed."

"So go back to sea," I said.

He smiled ruefully. "I'm a king!" For a moment his one eye glistened. "Stiorra would never forgive me," he went on. "She wants, wanted, our son to be king. You know what she called me? The last pagan king. And you can't be the last, she always said that. You can't be the last."

Stiorra had been right. I had never thought of it before, but Sigtryggr was the last pagan king in all Britain. The Saxon lands were all Christian. Alba, which some folk called Scotland, was Christian, though I suspected that some of their mountain savages, all hair and grunts, probably still worshipped sticks, stones, and stumps. The Welsh were Christian, though that never stopped them raiding Christian Mercia to steal cattle and slaves. There were a few pagans still clinging to their steadings in the hills of Cumbraland, but even there the Christians built churches and cut down the ancient groves where the old gods lived. Only Northumbria, my country, was ruled by a pagan. Yet when

I had been a young man, all fury and sword-skill, the last kingdom had been Wessex. My people, the Saxons, had been driven southward by the pagan Northmen until the only lands they could call their own were the sea marshes of Sumorsæte. Then we had fought back. We had killed the sword-Danes, slaughtered the spear-Danes, we had clawed our land back, and now Northumbria was the last kingdom, the last realm where folk could worship whatever god they chose.

Sigtryggr glanced up at the roof-hole as a gust of wind swirled the smoke and dashed in a shower of raindrops. "You want to know why I'm here," he said. "In Lindcolne I have forty-six household warriors, in Eoferwic I have a hundred and seventy-three. That's when they're not ill. I can count on the men of Dunholm, and I have your warriors. If it comes to war," he hesitated, "when it comes to war, I can lead maybe four hundred really good troops. The jarls will give me another three hundred. The host? Maybe a thousand who can half fight. Am I wrong?"

"The jarls will give you more than three hundred," I said.

"They won't! Remember that bastard Thurferth?"

"I do," I said grimly.

"A dozen jarls have followed him. Now they're under Edward's protection. They've been baptized." Thur-

ferth was a rich Dane who owned estates on the southern border of Northumbria and, threatened by Mercian
invasion, had chosen to become a Christian and bend
his knee to the Saxon king. "If I fight Thurferth and
his followers," Sigtryggr went on, "I'm fighting King
Edward. And I'll get no help from the west, will I?"
He meant Cumbraland, which was supposedly a part of
Northumbria.

"No help," I agreed.

"And meantime that bastard Constantin would love
to take Bebbanburg's land and make it Scottish. So,"
he struck his fingers one by one, counting his enemies,
"I have the Scots to the north, my fellow Norsemen
to the west, and Saxons to the south, and fewer than
two thousand men to fight them all. And that is why
I'm here." He drained his ale. "Being humiliated,"
he added bitterly, "is a price worth paying to ensure
peace with the biggest of my enemies." He fell silent
as a flurry of voices sounded outside the tavern door,
which was suddenly thrown open to let in a group of
rain-soaked men. They were warriors, judging by the
swords they wore, and with them was a priest.

"Christ on his cross," one of the warriors said, "I
thought that bastard would never stop preaching.
You!" the last word was shouted at one of the servants.
"We need ale. Mulled ale!"

"And food!" another man called.

They took off their cloaks and I put my hand on Serpent-Breath's hilt because all the rain-darkened cloaks were red, and I only knew one man who insisted that his followers wear the same color cloaks. "We'll have the fire too," the first man said with the easy arrogance of a lord who was accustomed to having his own way. He was clean-shaven and had a thin face unscarred by disease or war. There was gold at his neck and on his wrists. He strode toward us, then saw me and stopped. I saw the flicker of fear in his eyes, instantly gone as he counted us and realized he had twice the men we did. "I said we'd have the fire," he challenged us.

It was Æthelhelm the Younger, whose father, my enemy, had died a prisoner in Bebbanburg and whose sister was my son's wife. "I'm not finished with the fire," I answered.

Æthelhelm's men spread, hands on sword hilts. Svart, smiling, stood. He was a giant, so tall that he needed to bend his shaggy head beneath the tavern's smoke-blackened beams. "I haven't killed a Saxon in days," he growled, but as he spoke in the northern tongue none of Æthelhelm's men understood him. But they saw his massive size and not one of them seemed eager to face him.

"The king," I said, "finds your presence offensive. You smell like lizard shit."

"The king?" Æthelhelm was momentarily confused, thinking I meant Edward, then Sigtryggr stood beside Svart, and he too was frightening. He had a blade of a face, the one-eyed face of a man who has fought in too many battles and did not fear a mere tavern brawl.

"So sit on the room's far side," I said, "and try not to fart."

One of Æthelhelm's men, a brave one, took a pace forward, but the priest pulled him back. "There are to be no fights! The king has decreed it! No fights. On pain of your immortal souls!"

For a moment the room was still, then Æthelhelm spat toward us. "This room stinks of pagans. We'll drink elsewhere."

They picked up their cloaks and went back into the rain.

In my anger at Sköll I had almost forgotten I had other enemies. And the bitterest of those was now in Tamweorthin.

And, like me, he wanted revenge.

He has a hundred and twelve household warriors here," Finan told me.

I swore. "I have you and Berg."

"Æthelhelm is probably pissing himself in fear then."

I smiled dutifully. Would Æthelhelm attack me? Or rather would he direct his men to attack me? King Edward was adamant that there be no fighting in Tamweorthin while the Witan convened, but he might as well have ordered men to stop pissing against church walls. In fact he had ordered that, but they pissed just the same. And there were always fights. The town was full of Mercian and West Saxon warriors and, though Edward might be king of both kingdoms, there was small love between them. So yes, Æthelhelm would try to kill me, though he would make sure no one could accuse him of ordering the murder.

"It will be at night," Finan said. It was the evening of Eostre's feast, and we were sitting by the Bullock's fire. Rain still beat on the roof.

"We stay here then," Berg suggested.

Finan shrugged. "He'll burn the tavern down."

"And the whole town with it?" Sigtryggr asked.

"He won't give a rat's turd for the town, lord King," Finan said, "not if he can dance on Lord Uhtred's bones."

"In this rain," Berg said, "a fire would be hard to set."

And just then there was a hammering on the tavern's street door.

"Shit," the King of Northumbria said.

Finan moved to a window and edged back a shutter. He swore. "Too dark to see," he said. The hammering sounded again, and Finan moved to the left-hand side of the door while Svart went to the right. Both men drew their swords, while Berg and six of Sigtryggr's warriors made a line behind a heavy bench we had placed a couple of paces from the doorway. Sigtryggr and I went to stand with Svart. The owner of the tavern, a Saxon, hustled his two serving girls out through the back door. The hammering on the door sounded a third time, more urgently, and I nodded to Finan, who reached out, lifted the heavy locking bar, and let it fall.

The door burst open and eleven swords pointed at a sopping-wet priest who took two steps into the room and then fell to his knees. "God's mercy!" he called.

Svart stepped into the rain. "No one else here," he growled.

Eleven swords slid into eleven scabbards. Svart locked the door again. "Get up," I told the priest, "and who are you?"

"Father Lucus, lord." He looked fearfully at the mail-clad men who surrounded him, noticed Sigtryggr's thick gold chain, and bowed to him. "Lord King," he said.

"Why are you here?" I demanded.

"The king sent me, lord." Father Lucus bowed again,

this time to me. "He demands," he hesitated, "desires your attendance, lord." Rainwater dripped from his black robes and cloak.

"Just mine?" I asked.

"Yes, lord. And at once, lord. If you please, lord."

"How do we know you're the king's messenger?" Finan demanded.

Father Lucus's expression of sheer incredulity was answer enough. "I can assure you I am," he stammered.

"Does Ealdorman Æthelhelm know I'm summoned?" I asked.

Father Lucus's puzzlement at the question was obvious, but he answered anyway. "He was in the hall, lord," he said, "but I don't know if he knows, lord."

"He knows," Sigtryggr spoke enough of the Saxon tongue to follow what was being said. "The king was at supper?" he asked the priest.

"Yes, lord King."

"If a king summons a man, then news of it is whispered through the hall." Sigtryggr spoke from experience. "So Æthelhelm knows."

"The king desired your presence swiftly, lord," Father Lucus insisted nervously.

"Finan," I said, "Berg, you two come with me."

"We're coming too," Sigtryggr said eagerly. There was the prospect of a fight, and that always thrilled him. He might be King of Northumbria, but at heart he was still a Norse raider.

"But stay back from us," I told him, "well back."

He opened his mouth to argue, then saw what I meant. He grinned. "You won't even know we're there."

I put on a helmet, then a hooded cloak that hid the armor. We were already wearing our mail coats. I had insisted on that from the moment we returned from seeing Æthelhelm. "We're ready," I told Father Lucus, and the three of us followed the priest out into the pelting rain. A wash of lantern light from the tavern's open door showed a stream running down the street's center, then the door closed and we walked uphill, our way lit by the small leakage of fire or candlelight from the chinks of shutters. "Do you know what the king wants?" I shouted to Father Lucus. I had to shout because the wind and rain were so loud.

"He didn't say, lord."

The Bullock was built opposite the burh's outer wall that was a black shadow to our right, and suddenly another shadow moved in that darkness, and Berg's sword was halfway out of his scabbard when a voice spoke. "Alms, lord, alms?"

A beggar. "I thought all the beggars had been thrown out of the burh," I said to the priest.

"They creep back, lord. They're like rats."

We turned left down a street of metalworkers whose
fires burned bright. Dogs barked. The door of a small
church was open, casting dim rushlight into the street.
A priest, a white cape half covering his black robes, was
kneeling at the altar. Ahead of us, just beyond the big
Mallard tavern, the lane turned right to climb through
the turf ridge that was all that remained of the old fort,
and beyond that ridge lay the arched entrance to the
palace courtyard. Æthelflaed had loved this place, but
I had never liked it, and I liked it even less when we
came to the palace's torchlit archway. "Weapons, lord,"
Father Lucus muttered to me.

Guards had come from a shelter and were waiting for
us to surrender our swords. Only the royal guards were
allowed to carry weapons inside the king's hall and so
I dutifully unbuckled Wasp-Sting's belt, then Serpent-
Breath's. I felt naked, but the guard commander, an
older man with a scarred face and two fingers missing
from his left hand, reassured me. "I was with you at
Eads Byrig, lord. I promise your swords are safe." I
tried to remember his name, but could not place him.
He rescued me before I needed to ask. "Harald, lord. I
rode with Merewalh."

I smiled. Merewalh was a good man, a Mercian who
had often fought beside me. "How is Merewalh?"

"He does well, lord, he does well. He commands the Gleawecestre garrison now."

"And you lost your fingers at Eads Byrig?" I asked.

"That was a woman with a corn sickle, lord." Harald grinned. "You can't win every time, can you?"

I gave him a shilling as was expected of me, then followed Father Lucus across the courtyard, through a great door, and so into the bright light of the royal hall. Candles burned on two rows of tables, more were hanging in heavy iron brackets suspended from the roof beams, while a fire burned fierce in the central hearth and a smaller one, though just as fierce, in a brazier on the raised platform that was illuminated by a score of candles as thick as a man's arm. There must have been at least a hundred and fifty men on the hall's benches, while the tables were piled with the remnants of a feast. There were the carcasses of geese and ducks, pigs' heads flensed to the bone, ale jugs, bread, fish bones, oyster shells, and wine flasks; a feast, I thought sourly, to which neither I nor Sigtryggr had been invited. A harpist played close to the platform, but his music was drowned by talk and laughter, which died when men saw us come into the light. Even the harpist stopped playing for a few heartbeats. We must have looked grim, three men in mail and helmets, and the royal guards, arrayed along the hall's sides, started toward us until one recognized me and held up a hand to check his fellows. "Finan, Berg," I said to my companions, "find someone you know and get some food. And don't get into an argument."

The only woman in the hall was seated on the platform, where, at the long table, there were just three people. King Edward was in the center, to his left was his son Ælfweard, and on his right the queen. I had seen the queen some years before in the royal encampment outside Huntandun, and had been struck by her dark-eyed beauty and had thought then that she was just another of Edward's beautiful whores. And so she probably had been, but she had also been a nobly born whore, daughter of Sigehelm, Ealdorman of Cent. She must have been an excellent whore because she had replaced Ælflæd, the sister of Æthelhelm the Younger, who was now a discarded wife shut away in a Wessex convent. And so the well-born whore had become Queen Eadgifu of Mercia, but not of Wessex, because that kingdom, for whatever reason, still refused to give the king's wife the title of queen. Eadgifu was certainly more beautiful than the discarded Ælflæd. Her skin had the flawless bloom of youth, she had a high pale forehead, huge eyes, and hair as black as a raven's wing, crowned by a gold circlet that held a single large emerald. Her dress was as dark as her hair, heavily embroidered with colorful birds and swags of ivy. A white shawl of rare and costly silk was draped on her shoulders. She watched as I climbed the dais steps. "Welcome, Lord Uhtred," she said.

I took off my helmet and bowed to her. "The king summoned me, my lady," I explained my presence. I should have bowed to the king, of course, and waited for him to speak, but Edward was slumped on the table, apparently asleep and most likely drunk. "Maybe I should return in the morning, my lady?"

Eadgifu gave her husband a scornful glance. "Or talk to me instead, Lord Uhtred?" She beckoned me.

"A pleasure, my lady." It was no such thing. Talking to the queen when the king was drunk was a dangerous thing to do, and even more dangerous when the conversation was in full view of the assembled ealdormen of Wessex, Mercia, and East Anglia. They were indeed watching us. Prince Ælfweard, who hated me, looked both bored and drunk, but he was not yet asleep. He had frowned when he recognized me, but now pointedly ignored me and gestured to a servant to pour him more wine.

Eadgifu clapped her hands, and another servant scurried from the shadows. "A bench for Lord Uhtred," she commanded, "and wine. Have you eaten?"

"I have, my lady."

"Better than us, I expect. My husband did summon you, but seems to have forgotten." She smiled brightly. "So we have a chance to talk." She had spoken lightly, but I suspected Edward was far too drunk to have summoned me, which meant that Eadgifu had wanted to talk with me, and wanted to have that talk in front of her husband's nobility. Dangerous, indeed. I turned to look down into the firelit hall and saw Æthelstan sitting at the table to my left. He nodded gravely, then shrugged as if to tell me that he did not know why I had been summoned. I looked at the other long table and saw Æthelhelm the Younger. He was staring at me with a blank expression, then looked away as I caught his eye.

"Sit, Lord Uhtred," Queen Eadgifu commanded. The servant had brought me a stool. I sat.

Eadgifu leaned toward me, the white shawl parted and I could not help notice how low the dress was cut at her breasts. The candlelight cast a deep shadow in her cleavage as she briefly touched my hand. "I heard about your daughter. I am full of regret."

"Thank you, my lady."

"I shall pray for her soul."

"Thank you, my lady."

"I have two infant sons myself now," she said, "and I cannot imagine the sorrow of losing a child." I said nothing to that. "Prince Edmund," she went on, "is my firstborn." She smiled again, and then, to my surprise, laughed. It was forced laughter, as inappropriate as it was unnatural. She was still leaning close. She smelled of lavender. "You have a son, Lord Uhtred?" she asked.

"I do, my lady."

"Such precious things, sons," she said, still smiling. "My husband was surprised you were here in Tamworthin."

"He should be surprised, my lady," I said, "because he didn't invite me to the Witan."

"Why ever not?" She was speaking softly, so softly that even if Edward had been awake he would have found it difficult to hear her, and the low voice also made me lean close so that to the watching guests it must have appeared that we were conspiring together. She laughed again, though at what I could not tell.

"I'm told I no longer hold land in Wessex or Mercia, my lady," I explained.

She looked sympathetic and reached out a ringed hand to touch my arm. "That is so unjust, Lord Uhtred."

I was tempted to say I had no need of estates in Wessex or Mercia, that Bebbanburg was all I wanted, but instead I shrugged. "Bishop Wulfheard was granted my Mercian estates. I doubt I'll see those lands again. The church doesn't surrender property, my lady."

"Bishop Wulfheard! Such a horrid man!" she said brightly, still with that smile.

"Not my favorite bishop," I said drily.

She laughed. "Then you'll be pleased to know Wulfheard is not here. They say he's dying."

"I'm sorry," I said dutifully.

"No you're not. I'm told he has leprosy." She smiled at me. Her teeth were surprisingly white and even. "Are you really a pagan?"

"I am, my lady."

She laughed again, louder this time, and Edward muttered something, moved his head, but did not seem to wake. I could see his face more clearly now and was shocked. His skin was lined and blotched, his beard was gray, he looked ill. Ælfweard edged his chair closer, trying to overhear our conversation. I supposed he was eighteen or nineteen years old, about the same age as Eadgifu. He was a moonfaced, sullen boy with petulant eyes and a pathetic fringe of a beard. I saw him stare indignantly at his uncle, Æthelhelm, then look back to me. I caught his eye, smiled, and he scowled. "I think you're the first pagan I've met," Eadgifu said.

"You've met many, my lady."

"I have?"

"Among your husband's troops."

Again that bright laughter. "I assure you, lord," she said, "my husband's men are all good Christians."

"And in battle," I said, "many men who wear the cross take care to die with a sword in their hand."

She opened her eyes wide with surprise. "I don't understand."

"To make certain they go to Valhalla."

She laughed yet again, and even patted my arm. It was such an unnatural reaction that, for a moment, I wondered if she was as drunk as her husband and his son, yet though she smiled and laughed so unnaturally, her voice was sober. She kept her hand on my arm as she asked her next question. "How many men have you killed, Lord Uhtred?"

"Too many," I said sharply, and she twitched back at the vehemence of my tone.

She forced the smile back, then the scrape of benches on a stone floor made her look down into the hall, and, for an instant, I saw a look of pure venom on her pretty face. I turned too, and saw that Æthelhelm was leaving, striding toward the door followed by six of his men. Custom dictated that no man should leave a feast hall before the king rose from the table, but I suppose neither Æthelhelm nor Edward cared about that courtesy this evening. "Do you know Lord Æthelhelm?" Eadgifu asked, and now she was not smiling.

"Not well. I knew his father better."

"And your son married Lord Æthelhelm's sister?" She still watched Æthelhelm and his followers.

"He did."

"So you are bound to the family by treaty?" she asked, looking back into my eyes.

"You know we're not, my lady. We're bound by bonds of mutual hatred."

She laughed, and this time the laugh was genuine, and loud enough to attract glances from the hall. She lay her hand on my arm again. She wore a glove of fine kidskin, and over the pale leather were rings of gold, decorated with jet and rubies. "I am so glad we had this talk," she said.

"As am I, my lady," I replied politely and, understanding that I was being dismissed, stood and bowed to her. I walked to the steps, watched by the men at the long tables, and, as I went down to the hall floor, I saw Father Lucus standing by the wall where the guards slouched. I beckoned him. "Tell me," I said, "did the king summon me?"

"So I was told, lord," he answered nervously.

"Told by whom?"

"By the queen, lord."

"And the king was already asleep?"

"He was tired, lord," the priest answered carefully.

I left him. Finan and Berg joined me. "So what," Finan asked, "was that about?"

"That black-haired bitch," I said as we walked down the hall's length, "has just given Æthelhelm another reason to kill me."

"Why?" Berg asked.

"Because she has a son called Edmund."

"A son called—"

"I'll explain later. We need our swords first."

Eadgifu had said nothing important to me, but that was not why she had summoned me. All that mattered was what men saw, and what they had seen was a queen in close conversation with Uhtred of Bebbanburg, a queen smiling and laughing. And why was it important that men see that? Because she had a son called Edmund.

King Edward had a dozen children. I had lost count, but I had noticed that Æthelstan, his eldest son, had not been invited to the top table where Ælfweard was seated. So far as Wessex was concerned Æthelstan and his twin sister were bastards, by-blows of a youthful indiscretion, which meant that the ætheling, the eldest legitimate son, was Ælfweard, Æthelhelm's nephew, which in turn meant that Wessex expected Ælfweard to inherit his father's throne and with it the riches of southern Englaland. Æthelhelm's family would control the kingdom then, and Edward's other sons, the sons of different women, would be lucky to escape with their lives. Eadgifu had hinted, no, she had more than hinted, that I would be rewarded by the return of my southern lands if I supported her son's claim on the throne, but she had been too clever to seek a formal alliance with me. She must have known I would refuse to offer her an oath, so instead she had staged a dumb show of smiles, laughter, and intimacy that would convince the watching nobles and churchmen that Uhtred of Bebbanburg was her ally.

I turned to look back when I reached the hall door. Two servants were helping Edward to his feet. He was fading, I thought, and the men on the long benches were already taking sides. Many would support Æthelhelm because of his wealth and power, but others would follow Eadgifu in hopes that they could share the plunder of Æthelhelm's estates. And some of those men, the lesser nobles who had their own reasons for disliking Æthelhelm, would declare for Eadgifu if they believed I was her ally. I might be old, but I was still formidable. Edward, I thought, should have destroyed Æthelhelm at the same time that he cast off Æthelhelm's sister as his wife, but he must have known that would start a civil war in Wessex that would likely end in his own death and the possible destruction of his kingdom. So for the moment, Ælfweard was still the ætheling, and that kept Æthelhelm content.

But if Æthelhelm believed I was Eadgifu's champion then he would want to slide a blade into my belly, twist the blade, and dance on my guts. "We should go home to Northumbria," I grumbled, "and kill Sköll. This mess is none of our business."

Except Sigtryggr had been summoned to the Witan. So the mess was ours whether we liked it or not.

And we followed Æthelhelm into the rain-swept night.

Harald, the guard commander who had fought beside me at Eads Byrig, handed me my swords. "Have you seen Lord Æthelhelm?" I asked.

"He took his men into the royal chapel, lord." Harald nodded across the courtyard where an open door led into a chamber lit by candles. I could just hear the low chanting of monks beneath the insistent seethe of hard rain. So Æthelhelm would claim he was at his prayers while his men hunted me through Tamweorthin's dark streets.

I gave Harald another coin, then the three of us left the palace. For a moment we sheltered from the rain by lingering under the big arch where burning torches guttered in the wind. The town lay dark beneath us, stinking of sewage and smoke. "You think Æthelhelm's men have had time—" Berg began, then was interrupted by Finan.

"We were summoned over an hour ago," the Irishman said. "So the bastard has had plenty time enough to send his dogs into the town."

"But where?" I asked. The rain still pelted down. We were talking beneath the palace arch, and must have been visible to anyone in the lower town, so I moved into the rain and a deeper darkness where the old fort's turf ridge stood at the top of the steep slope. "He won't attack us close to the palace."

"He won't?" Berg asked.

"Too many royal guards within earshot."

"So his men are waiting in the town?"

"Sigtryggr's out there too," Finan said, crouching beside me.

"But he can't see us and we can't see him."

I was in a bitter mood. Brother Beadwulf had led me a dance across Britain, my daughter had died, Sköll had escaped my vengeance, and Eadgifu had toyed with me for her own ambitions. Now Æthelhelm was taking me for a fool, and I suspected his men were waiting for us. Or were they? The night was so foul and dark, perhaps he had decided to wait.

There had been a time when I was proud of my ability to stalk the night as a sceadugenga, a shadow-walker, but in this relentless downpour I would not stalk anyone, merely blunder. I cursed, then Finan touched my elbow. "Listen!" I listened and heard nothing but the beat of rain on the thatch below us. Finan must have had better hearing. "Who is it?" he called.

"Me, lord!" a voice called, and I dimly saw a shadowy figure scrambling up the slope. It was Rorik, my servant. He almost slipped back down the slick turf, but I grabbed his wrist and hauled him to the top. "King Sigtryggr sent me, lord."

"Where is he?"

"Down there, lord," Rorik said, and I suppose he pointed at the lower town, though much good that did us in the darkness. "He says there are seven men waiting in Saint Ælfthryth's church, lord."

"Do they have red cloaks?"

"I didn't see them, lord."

"And where's this church?"

"Right there, lord! The closest church."

"In the metalworkers' street?" Finan asked.

"Yes, lord."

"And Sigtryggr's where?" I asked.

"He just said to tell you that he's close by and waiting, lord."

I remembered passing the church. It had an open door and was lit by rushlights and candles, and it made sense for my enemies to wait there. In this darkness they would never see me, let alone recognize me, but the small light cast through the church door would be enough for them, and once in the street seven men would make short work of us.

"Back to the road," I said, "and we're drunk. Rorik? Stay out of trouble's way."

We went back to the fort's approach road and started singing. If Eadgifu could provide Tamweorthin with a dumb show, I could provide another kind of pretense. I bellowed the song of the butcher's wife, a favorite with drunken men, and staggered to hold Finan's arm. We came to the crossroads at the foot of the hill, and now the metalworkers' street with its smithies was to our left. I could see the wash of light from the small church through which the rain made silver streaks. We stopped for a moment and I sang louder, then dashed into a shadow and made the noise of a man vomiting. A dog howled and I howled back as Finan lurched toward me, keening a song in his native Irish. "I want a prisoner," I told him, then howled again, provoking a half-dozen dogs to bark frantically.

I pushed Rorik into the shadows on the uphill side of the street, told him to stay there, then Finan, Berg, and I staggered along the street's center. The dogs still barked, but men were shouting at them to be silent. The people who lived there must have been aware of men moving in the night, and sensible folk made sure their doors were barred as they prayed for the noises to move away. We three just sang louder, and I saw a man appear in the church doorway. He drew back, waiting for us to come into the dim wash of light. "I want to be sick," I said loudly.

"Not on my boots again," Finan answered just as loudly.

I put my hand on Serpent-Breath's hilt as Finan loosened Soul-Stealer. "Sing, you Irish bastard," I slurred at him as we staggered past the church, "sing!"

And they came. The church door darkened as they pushed through, seven men with seven swords, and we turned, and I was aware of other men coming from the shadows behind me. Sigtryggr led them. He was shouting a challenge in his native Norse, but the first of the attackers was closer. He leaped for me, still convinced he faced a drunkard. He lunged, trying to run me through with his blade, but I had drawn Serpent-Breath and she slid his blade aside, I stepped closer and punched my sword's hilt into his face and felt the crunch of breaking bone or teeth. A Norseman's spear came past me and buried its blade in the man's belly. I turned to avoid a second lunge and back-swung Serpent-Breath into a bearded face, dragging her edge back to cut into the man's eyes. He dropped his sword and screamed. Finan had driven Soul-Stealer into a man's throat while Berg, with Bone-Ripper, was standing over a fallen man. I saw Bone-Ripper's bright blade go down and the dark blood spurt, then Sigtryggr's Norsemen were past us, driving the survivors back toward the crossroads, but still more men appeared from the alley by the big tavern. They were the last of Sigtryggr's men, led by Svart, and the three surviving attackers were now trapped between their enemies. One hesitated, and Svart bellowed in fury as he drove his heavy sword down through the man's neck and into his rib cage. The remaining pair fled into the church.

"They didn't put up much of a fight," Sigtryggr grumbled.

The man I had blinded was moaning, crawling on his hands and knees, fumbling for his sword. Berg stepped to him, there was the sound of a blade in meat, and the man went still. "I need prisoners," I said, and went into the church.

Saint Ælfthryth's was a poor church, little more than a thatched barn with a rush-covered floor. The altar was a plain table on which hung a white cloth. Four candles, thick with wax, burned on the altar, which held a crucifix made of dull iron. The two sidewalls were decorated with leather hangings crudely painted with saints, beneath which rushlights burned in iron stands, while the edges of the small nave were heaped with sacks of charcoal, presumably because the church was the safest and driest place for the smiths to store their fuel. Loose charcoal crunched beneath my feet as I walked toward the simple altar where the priest, a thin pale man, stood facing us. "They have sanctuary!" he called.

"We claim sanctuary!" one of the men shouted desperately.

"What's sanctuary?" Berg asked. He still held BoneRipper, her blood diluted by the rain.

Sigtryggr came up beside me, his men crowding in behind. "Why are we just watching them?" he asked. "Why not kill them?"

"They have sanctuary."

Svart was holding a severed hand. I assumed he meant to boil the flesh off the bones and add them to his beard. "I'll kill them," he growled.

"I need prisoners," I said, then looked at the two men. "Put your swords down," I told them, and, when they hesitated, shouted the order. They dropped their swords.

The priest, a brave man considering he faced a group

of armed men in his nighttime church, held up a hand. "They have sanctuary," he said again.

"They have sanctuary, lord," I corrected him, then walked to the altar and used the edge of the white cloth to clean the blood and rain from Serpent-Breath's blade. "Sanctuary," I explained for the benefit of any of Sigtryggr's Norsemen unfamiliar with the idea, "is offered by the church to criminals. So long as they remain here we can't touch them without being criminals ourselves." I kicked the two men's swords toward Berg. "If we assault them here we'll be punished."

"They won't dare punish me," Sigtryggr said.

"You haven't experienced the fury of the priests," I said. "They preach peace and demand the death of their enemies. Besides, I want to release them."

"Release them?" Sigtryggr exclaimed.

"Someone has to give Lord Æthelhelm the good news," I explained, then I pushed Serpent-Breath into her scabbard and turned back to the two men. Both were young. One had a bruise on his cheek and was shaking with fear, the other was surly and had the courage to face me boldly. I had been using Danish to talk to Sigtryggr, but now used the Saxon tongue. "Who are you?" I asked the surly man.

He hesitated, tempted to defiance, then decided

sense was the better choice. "Helmstan," he muttered. I waited and saw the resentment in his eyes. "Lord," he added.

"Who do you serve?"

Again the hesitation, and it was the second man, younger and more frightened, who stammered the answer. "Grimbald, lord."

"Grimbald," I repeated the name, which was unfamiliar to me. "And who does Grimbald serve?" I asked. Helmstan was scowling at his companion and said nothing so I drew Wasp-Sting, my short-sword, and smiled at him. "This one hasn't drawn blood tonight, and she's thirsty."

The priest started a protest, but went silent when I turned Wasp-Sting's blade toward him. "Who does Grimbald serve?" I asked again.

"Grimbald serves Lord Æthelhelm, lord," Helmstan said reluctantly.

"Did Grimbald lead you tonight?"

"No, lord."

"Who did?"

"Torthred, lord."

It was not a name I knew, and I assumed whoever Torthred was he was now dead in the street. "Did Torthred serve Grimbald?" I asked.

"Yes, lord."

"And what were your orders tonight?" I asked. Neither man answered, so I took a pace toward them and lifted Wasp-Sting. "They call me the priest-killer," I said. "Do you think I care a rat's arse about sanctuary?"

"We were ordered to kill you, lord," the more frightened man whispered the words. He moaned when I placed Wasp-Sting's blade on his bruised cheek.

I left the blade there for a few heartbeats, then stepped back and sheathed the seax. "Tell Grimbald," I told both men, "that he has two new enemies. Uhtred of Bebbanburg and Sigtryggr of Northumbria. Now go."

They went.

Eight

"If we're to crush Sköll," Sigtryggr told me the next morning, "we must have peace with Edward. I can fight one or the other, not both."

"Edward's ill," I said, "he won't fight."

"You're certain of that?" Sigtryggr challenged me, and all I could do was shrug. "He might be ill," Sigtryggr went on, "but his armies aren't." He paused as Svart opened the tavern's shutters to let in sunlight. The rain had stopped. Sigtryggr leaned forward to blow out a rushlight. "If Edward can't lead his armies," he said gloomily, "his ealdormen can."

"They're fighting like starving dogs over who inherits the throne."

"And the sure way to unite them," Sigtryggr said, "is to give them a common enemy, me." He speared a slab of bacon with his knife and stared at it moodily. "Why does he want peace? Why doesn't he just invade?"

"Because his kingdom is a mess," I said. "The Mercians are still grumbling, the East Anglian Danes are restless, he's got a new wife with tits that smell of lavender, and he fears us."

"Fears us?"

"Suppose he invades," I suggested. "Suppose he marches an army north through Lindcolne and we beat his bones to powder?"

"Can we?" he asked gloomily. "They'll outnumber us."

"They're Saxons," Svart growled, "of course we can beat them."

"He'll outnumber us," I allowed, "but you know as well as I do that numbers aren't everything. He thinks he can beat us, but he isn't certain of it." I tore off a hunk of stale bread, decided I wasn't hungry, and threw it to one of the tavern's dogs. "And remember," I went on, "we're the dreaded Northmen. When I was a young man we reckoned a Danish warrior was worth three Saxons."

"Four," Svart put in.

"That didn't prove true," I said, earning a scowl from Svart, "but the fear lingers. The Saxons think we're pagan savages, and they'd rather talk us into submission than fight us. They will fight us if they have to, but Edward fears defeat, because if we break his armies then East Anglia revolts, the Mercians will demand their own king again, and the Wessex nobles will want a new king."

Sigtryggr smiled wanly. "Maybe we should just invade Mercia? Beat the bastards."

"We do that," I said, knowing he was not serious, "and Constantin of Scotland will stab us in the back."

Sigtryggr grunted. He was dressed for the Witan, wearing a robe of dark blue wool edged in cloth of gold. A simple crown, nothing more than a ring of gilt bronze, rested on a table beside his jug of ale. "This ale tastes like cow piss," he grumbled. "You don't think I should make peace with Edward?"

"It depends on the price."

"I want Sköll dead," he said vengefully. "Killing that bastard is worth any price."

"Worth submission to Edward?"

Sigtryggr looked at me mournfully. "I have little choice."

"Baptism?"

"I don't mind getting wet."

"Tribute?"

He grinned. "I'll equip a pair of ships and we'll go viking. We'll raid a fat Wessex monastery and there's the tribute."

"And even if you do submit," I ignored his idea, "and make a treaty, the Saxons will break it as soon as they think it's safe to invade you."

He nodded. "But I'll still have time to kill Sköll first."

"Unless I reach him before you."

He half smiled at that. "What happens if I refuse to submit?"

"The Saxons will get braver and braver. They'll provoke you with cattle raids, they'll keep small armies on the border, they'll tax your trade more heavily, their ships will capture your merchant ships, and in the end they'll invade."

"So either way we lose?"

"Not if we build up our strength."

He offered a mirthless laugh to that. "And how do I do that?"

"We beat Sköll," I said firmly, "and we bind Cumbraland to Northumbria. We force all those Norse bastards to swear loyalty to you. We make an army of *úlfhéðnar*. We unite the Northmen and put the fear of the gods into the Saxons."

"I like that idea," Sigtryggr said quietly. If I had known the truth of what I had just said I might have kept silent. Or perhaps not. Wyrd bið ful āræd. But at least Sigtryggr saw some hope in those words. He traced a finger around his crown, thinking. "And we can't subdue Cumbraland unless we're at peace with Edward."

I nodded reluctantly. "Yes, lord King, we can't fight both at once."

He stood. "Then let's go and grovel to the sick bastard."

And so we climbed the hill. We would grovel.

We passed Saint Ælfthryth's church where we had cornered the two fugitives. The night's rain had washed the blood from the street, and the town reeve's men had removed the bodies. A bell was tolling from the hilltop, presumably to summon the Witan, but the steep track leading up to the high church and the palace was being guarded by spearmen who barred us from climbing the hill while a procession of horsemen passed by. There were fifty or sixty riders, all in mail, all with helmets, all carrying spears, and all going toward the palace, and at their center was a small cart drawn by a pair of heavy horses. The cart, little more than a farm wagon, had been draped with dark blue cloth and furnished with cushions on which sat two women and a priest. One woman was old, the other young and long-faced with a close-fitting bonnet that hid most of her dark hair. She was richly dressed in somber gray and black, looked sad, and wore a large silver cross at her breast. The cart lurched alarmingly on the rough road, and the young woman clutched one of the side rails to steady herself. "Who's that?" Sigtryggr asked me.

"I don't know," I said, which was true, yet the long, sad face was somehow familiar. She glanced at me and seemed to recognize me, then quickly looked away as the cart lurched again. She appeared to be holding back tears. The older woman had just put an arm around the younger's shoulders, while the priest was murmuring to her, presumably trying to comfort her.

"Damn, but she's ugly," Sigtryggr said. "She looks like a horse."

"She's cold and unhappy," I said.

"So she looks like a cold and miserable horse."

We followed the cart and its escort up the hill, through the arch where our swords were taken from us, and so to the great hall where smoke from damp firewood swirled among the high rafters. The tables had been stacked to one side and the benches had been arranged in a half circle around the big hearth to face the platform, where five high-backed chairs were draped with deep scarlet cloths. Close to a hundred men had already arrived and were sitting as near to the fire as they could, though a few were standing and talking quietly. They looked at us as we entered, recognized us, and started whispering. To most of these men we were the strangest of creatures; pagans, the dwellers of their bad dreams come to life.

"Where do we sit?" Sigtryggr asked.

"We don't," I said, "not yet." The nobles of Edward's three kingdoms would occupy the benches, and to let Sigtryggr sit with the ealdormen, bishops, and abbots would be to diminish his status. I assumed the platform was for royalty and, though Sigtryggr was undoubtedly royal, I did not want him to take one of the chairs and then be publicly ordered to leave it. He had attended a Witan before, at Huntandun, where he had sat on the dais with Edward, but on that occasion he had been a guest of Æthelflaed, and she had possessed a courtesy her brother lacked. If Edward wanted the King of Northumbria in a place of honor he would extend the invitation, and if not, then it was better that we should stand apart at the rear of the hall. "You know what you're to say?" I asked him.

"Of course I know. You've told me ten times. Twenty times." He was nervous and irritable, and I could not blame him. He was being treated with disdain, humiliated by Saxons. More men were arriving in the hall, and I saw how they looked at Sigtryggr with both curiosity and amusement. They had spent their whole existence in an unending war between the Christians and the pagans, and now the last pagan king was standing like a supplicant at the back of the king's hall.

I saw Brunulf Torkelson, a West Saxon whose life I had saved, enter through the great doors and, leaving Sigtryggr flanked by Finan and the enormous Svart, I crossed to Brunulf's side. He was carrying a spear and shield because he was one of the royal guards who would either line the hall's sides or else stand in front of the platform. He greeted me warmly. "I heard you were here, lord, and hoped to meet you." He hesitated, then frowned. "And I heard about your daughter, lord. I am sorry."

"Fate is a bitch," I said, then fell silent as Æthelhelm the Younger strode through the doors followed by a retinue of a dozen men. He looked at me, seemed startled, and abruptly swerved to avoid passing near me. He wore the red cloak of his household troops, though his cloak had a fine collar of fur and was clasped with gold. He strode to the front of the hall, and men who had taken benches there hurriedly moved to let him sit. "Do you know Grimbald?" I asked Brunulf.

"I know three men with that name," he said.

"A follower of Æthelhelm," I added.

He turned and looked into the hall. "There," he said, nodding toward the benches that Æthelhelm had taken. "The man wearing a fox-fur cap."

I looked. "The one with the flattened nose?"

"That's him," Brunulf said. "You heard his men got into a drunken brawl last night? Five of them died."

"Who were they fighting?"

Brunulf looked at me suspiciously, but with a half-smile. "You mean you don't know, lord?"

"Me?" I asked. "Fight? Whatever makes you think I'd be part of a drunken street brawl? I'm an ealdorman of Northumbria, I'm respectable."

"Of course you are, lord."

I left him by the door and pushed my way through the growing crowd to the front of the hall. Æthelhelm saw me coming and turned to have an intense conversation with the stern-looking priest who sat beside him. Grimbald, sitting just a few paces away, began to stand, then realized he could not escape me, and sat again. I stopped right in front of him and just looked down at him, saying nothing. He gazed at my belt buckle, a wolf's head cast in bronze. All around us men fell silent. I saw Grimbald tremble, so I smiled, bent down, and whispered in his ear, "You're a dead man."

He did not move, just sat. I turned to Æthelhelm and smiled at him too. "Some time," I said, "you really must visit Bebbanburg and meet your nephew. He's a fine little boy. You know how I look forward to welcoming you."

Æthelhelm could not ignore me. He stood. He was a good-looking man, maybe thirty years old, with a narrow face and haughty eyes. A servant must have shaved him that morning because there were two small razor nicks on his chin. There was gold at his neck, on his red cloak, and on his fingers. He took a step toward me, evidently eager for a confrontation, but just then a horn announced the arrival of King Edward, and the seated men in the great hall stood, snatched off their caps, and bowed toward the platform. The blaring horn forced Æthelhelm to turn away from me and bow, though his bow was little more than a cursory nod. I neither bowed nor nodded, but just turned and walked back to Sigtryggr. "I just made someone wet himself," I said.

Sigtryggr ignored the boast. "Is that a king?" he asked derisively. He was looking at the platform.

I looked too and was shocked. I had seen Edward the previous night, but he had been slumped on the table, his body cloaked, and his face half hidden, but now, in the sunlight coming through the large eastern windows, I could see him far more clearly. He had become fat, he limped, his dark hair was lank and gray under the emerald-encrusted crown, his beard was gray, and his once handsome face was lined and blotched. He could not live long, I thought, and when he died, the cockfight for the crown would begin.

I had thought the five chairs would be for Edward, his wife Eadgifu, and his eldest son Ælfweard, with one of the others to be offered to Sigtryggr, but I was wrong. Queen Eadgifu and Prince Ælfweard were indeed to sit at either side of the king, but the two outer chairs were reserved for the archbishops, who followed the royal family onto the platform, both men swathed in richly embroidered robes. I did not know the new Archbishop of Contwaraburg, Athelm, a West Saxon who had a lean, ascetic face and a beard long enough to hide the pectoral cross on his breast. He looked sternly into the hall before taking his seat, while Hrothweard of Eoferwic smiled at the assembly, then waited for Eadgifu to take her seat before sitting himself. "They brought their sorcerers," Sigtryggr grumbled.

"They always do." I looked around the hall, searching for Æthelstan, but to my surprise he was nowhere to be seen. I assumed he reckoned his father would not welcome him and so had stayed away. I leaned close to Sigtryggr. "Grimbald is on the front bench," I whispered, "to the right of the hearth, he has a flattened nose and a fox-fur cap." Sigtryggr just nodded.

The day's business began, as it always did at a Witan, with a prayer and then a sermon. Athelm preached, and I wandered into the courtyard rather than listen to his tedious harangue. Sigtryggr, Svart, and Finan joined me, and we sat on the edge of a stone horse trough and I stopped a passing servant and demanded ale. Sigtryggr was apprehensive and sometimes paced the courtyard, watched by the royal guards who were posted all about the courtyard's edge. We must have waited for at least an hour before a nervous steward came into the sunlight and bowed to Sigtryggr. "Lord King, your presence is requested."

Sigtryggr rammed his crown over his unruly fair hair. "Shall we go?" he asked.

"Home?" Svart suggested.

"Into the hall," Sigtryggr said grimly, and went to learn his fate. We followed and stood at the back of the hall as Sigtryggr, now escorted by two guards, walked through the benches, around the hearth, and took his place in front of the platform. Now, I thought, we would learn just what humiliation the Saxons would demand of him.

Hrothweard, Archbishop of York, had been deputed to tell Sigtryggr of Wessex's terms, and that, at least, showed some tact on Edward's part. Hrothweard knew Sigtryggr well, and the two men respected and liked each other. Sigtryggr ruled in a city that had far more Christians than pagans, and he had ever followed Hrothweard's advice on how to curb antagonisms between the two, while the archbishop sternly demanded of his clergy that they did not preach hate against their fellow Northumbrians. Now Hrothweard smiled at Sigtryggr. "It is good to see you here, lord King," he said. He spoke in Danish, which surprised me.

A monk, one of two sitting at a table at the side of the platform where they were busily writing what I supposed was a record of the Witan's deliberations, interpreted for the benefit of the hall. "Louder!" a man called from the benches, and the monk repeated his translation, and then, almost immediately, Æthelhelm stood.

"I have a protest, lord King," Æthelhelm said loudly.

Hrothweard, about to start reading from a parchment, paused. Edward, who looked thoroughly disgruntled with the proceedings, frowned at his richest nobleman. "You wish to speak, lord?" he asked.

"I wish to speak, lord King," Æthelhelm said.

Edward paused, then nodded. "We shall hear you, lord," he said.

Æthelhelm turned to face the hall. "I do not believe, lord King," he spoke silkily, "that Uhtred of Bebbanburg was summoned to this assembly." He turned back to Edward. "I demand he be removed."

Æthelhelm's supporters, and that was at least half of the Witan, murmured their support, and the murmur grew louder until Edward held up a hand. Sigtryggr spoke some English, but not well, and he looked bemused by the protest. Edward scowled at me. "You were not summoned, Lord Uhtred," he said, plainly siding with his most powerful noble.

I had anticipated and was ready for the challenge. I could not say that Æthelstan had invited me because invitations to the Witan are issued by the king, not by his sons, so instead, respectfully, I claimed to have come as a witness.

"A witness?" Edward seemed perplexed by the word.

"As a witness for a petitioner, lord King," I said, "and witnesses have always been allowed to attend Witans since at least your father's time."

"We have enough business today without hearing any petitions," Æthelhelm snarled.

"I believe that is for the king to decide," Archbishop Hrothweard intervened before Æthelhelm's supporters could make any noise. "I am sure my lord of Contwaraburg would agree with me?"

Athelm looked startled, tugged at his beard, then nodded. "The king may allow whoever he wishes to attend," he muttered, and Eadgifu, looking resplendent in a gown of pale yellow silk, leaned and whispered in her husband's ear.

Edward looked annoyed, but waved a hand toward me. "You may remain, Lord Uhtred," he said, "but only as a witness. You can say nothing of other matters."

I bowed, Æthelhelm sat, and Hrothweard looked down at Sigtryggr, and, in English now, read out the list of demands that Edward was making for a lasting treaty of peace between the Saxon kingdoms and Northumbria. The monk translated each demand, and Sigtryggr stood, tall and straight, suffering.

The demands were mostly what we had expected. Svart, next to me, growled as they were revealed, but I could not share his indignation. The West Saxons, I knew, had no intention of keeping to the treaty. It bought them time, no more, and when they were ready they would tear up the parchment and send their warriors north. And if the West Saxons could ignore the terms, so could Sigtryggr.

The treaty, Hrothweard declared, would usher in an era of lasting peace between the kingdoms. Swords, he declared grandly, would be beaten into plowshares. Svart spat when that was translated. To bring that peace, the archbishop continued, it was necessary for Sigtryggr to acknowledge Edward as his overlord, to swear loyalty to him, and, in reparation for the damages done by Northumbrian outlaws who had preyed on honest Christian folk in Mercia, silver weighing three thousand pounds was to be paid into King Edward's treasury at Wintanceaster before the Feast of Pentecost. There was an intake of breath at that vast sum, but Hrothweard was not finished. He spoke gently, knowing how his words must gall Sigtryggr, but the demands were anything but gentle. Sigtryggr must swear he would do all in his power to prevent cattle raids and, if any such raids took place, the King of Northumbria undertook to pay the full value of the stolen livestock to King Edward's treasury and as much again to the folk whose cattle were stolen. Northumbrian merchants trading in Wessex, Mercia, or East Anglia were to pay a new tax, but no such levy was to be imposed on subjects of King Edward who traded in Northumbria. King Edward's troops could march through Northumbria without impedance. King Sigtryggr must agree to protect the lives and property of all Christian folk living in Northumbria. When he read that last demand Hrothweard had the decency to lower the document and smile at Sigtryggr, "As I know you already do, lord King."

There was a sharp gasp of surprise from the Witan at those last words and one or two men looked ready to protest, but Hrothweard held up a hand to quell the unrest. "Further," he read, "you are to allow Christian missionaries free passage and protection within the borders of your realm."

I was tempted to ask whether Wessex would allow men and women to travel its roads preaching the worship of Thor and Odin, but I had the sense to keep quiet. Sigtryggr was likewise silent, even though the terms being imposed on him were brutal, humiliating, and not negotiable.

"And finally," Hrothweard frowned slightly as he came to the end of the document, "we cannot rely upon the word of a pagan king, for it is well known in this kingdom and in all Christian kingdoms that pagans treat solemn promises with disdain, swearing their oaths on false gods and breaking such oaths with impunity." I doubted Hrothweard had written the words, but Athelm of Contwaraburg was looking mightily pleased with himself. Edward just looked bored. "To make certain that Sigtryggr of Northumbria keeps to the terms of this treaty," Hrothweard continued, "it is required that he undergo baptism this day and accept our Christian God in full faith as the one God, the only God, and the true God, and must understand that by that acceptance he places his soul in jeopardy of hell's eternal torments if he break so much as one sentence of this treaty. He agrees moreover that he will extirpate the worship of false gods and of foul idols from all his lands."

Finan nudged me. "He means you," he muttered.

Hrothweard waited as the monk translated his last

words, then looked sympathetically at Sigtryggr. "Do you accept the terms, lord King?" he asked.

Sigtryggr paused long enough for the hall to become restless. Edward, surprised by Sigtryggr's silence, sat up straighter. Like everyone else in the hall he had expected Sigtryggr to meekly agree to whatever was demanded. "Do you accept the terms, lord King?" Hrothweard asked again.

Sigtryggr answered directly to Edward, though his words needed to be interpreted by the monk. "You say, lord King, that you cannot trust the oath of a pagan?"

"That is true," Hrothweard answered for Edward.

"Yet it is the Christians who have broken their pledges," Sigtryggr said forcefully.

Uproar followed the translation of those words. Hrothweard called for silence, but it was Edward's frown and upraised hand that finally stilled the hall. "How have Christians broken their pledges?" he asked suspiciously.

"Was I not promised safe conduct if I agreed to attend this Witan?" Sigtryggr demanded.

There was an uncomfortable shuffling in the hall. Men started murmuring, but Archbishop Hrothweard raised his voice. "You were indeed so promised, lord King," he said loudly, silencing the protests.

"Then how can I trust your words," Sigtryggr was looking directly at Edward now, and repeating the words we had agreed, "when only last night your men made an attack on my life?" The monk translated, and there was a roar of indignation from the hall's crowded benches, mainly, I thought, from those men who looked to Æthelhelm for leadership. "I accuse Grimbald!" Sigtryggr had to shout to make himself heard. He waited for the noise to subside, then pointed at Grimbald, "I accuse Grimbald," he said again. "I accuse him of breaking the king's peace, of attempting to murder me, of bad faith." He looked back to Edward. "Give me justice in this matter, lord King, and I will accept all your terms. That is my petition in which I bring Lord Uhtred of Bebbanburg as my witness."

There was renewed uproar, of course, but every man in the hall knew of the bodies discovered in the street of the metalworkers, knew there had been a fight by Saint Ælfthryth's church, and knew that Grimbald's men had taken a beating. Some few, those who were the closest allies of Æthelhelm, must also have known that no one had demanded Sigtryggr's death, that the men had been sent to kill me instead, but that was hardly a defense for Grimbald, who, summoned to answer the accusation, stammered that his men had acted on their own, that he knew nothing of the night's events, and that he was not responsible for what drunken men did in the middle of an ale-steeped night. "Two men returned to me," Grimbald said desperately, "and I will punish them, lord King."

"Yet they confessed they acted on your orders," Sigtryggr pressed his advantage, "and in witness of their confession I bring Lord Uhtred—"

The mention of my name was sufficient to start another commotion, loud enough to startle the sparrows perched on the rafters, who flew about in panic. Beneath them men were standing and shouting, most of them, it seemed to me, supporting Grimbald's claim that he knew nothing of the nighttime brawl, but some, more than a few, shouted that I should be allowed to speak.

Edward again held up a hand for silence, while Archbishop Hrothweard thumped his silver-topped crozier on the platform's boards. "Lord Uhtred," Hrothweard called down the length of the hall when at last he could be heard, "are King Sigtryggr's words true?"

A few men started to protest, but were hushed by others who wanted to hear me. "They are true," I said to Hrothweard, "but you would expect me to say that. However, I am willing to bring the priest of Saint Ælfthryth's church to this assembly. He too heard the men say they were sent by Grimbald." Bringing the priest to the Witan was a risk, of course. The man might lie, and, even if he spoke the truth, he could not testify that the men were sent to kill Sigtryggr. I had thought to keep one of the two men we had captured and threaten him with dire pain if he did not tell the truth, but again the truth would not reveal a plot against Sigtryggr, and the man would most likely deny any plot at all, knowing his dishonesty would be rewarded by Grimbald and by Æthelhelm. Yet by offering a Christian priest as a witness I knew I had thwarted Grimbald's lies so long as the priest was not fetched from the lower town, and that, I thought, was most unlikely, because King Edward and the two archbishops wanted this tedious Witan over and done. The men in the hall simply assumed the priest would support Sigtryggr's account and so would not need to be summoned, and that assumption proved to be true.

There was an anxious silence from Æthelhelm's supporters as Hrothweard stooped to speak with Edward, who could hardly hide his impatience. Archbishop Athelm leaned across the moonfaced Ælfweard to add yet more advice, and Edward, who looked ever more unhappy, finally nodded.

Edward pointed at Grimbald. "I offered King Sigtryggr safe passage," the king said, his voice sullen, "and by breaking my peace you have forfeited your life." There was a gasp at that. Grimbald, still standing, opened his mouth as if to speak, found he had no words, and looked at Æthelhelm, who ostentatiously turned his back on the doomed man.

"Lord!" Grimbald at last found his voice, but by then two royal guards had taken his arms and he was being escorted from the hall. Æthelhelm did not turn to watch. Everyone present, the king included, knew Grimbald must have acted on Æthelhelm's orders, yet Æthelhelm did nothing to save Grimbald's life. The king could have saved him, but Edward wanted to see Sigtryggr on his knees, he wanted the peace treaty, he was greedy for the treaty's silver, and one Saxon life was a small price to pay for that triumph. Men muttered bitterly as Grimbald left, while Æthelhelm just stared bleakly into the flames of the hearth.

That one Saxon life was our sole victory of the day. I thought Sigtryggr's ordeal was over, all but for the misery of being baptized, yet when Grimbald was gone to his death Edward struggled to his feet and held out a hand for silence. He looked tired and ill, and I wondered what had happened to the young man I had known, and thought how swiftly he had decayed into this heavy, sullen graybeard. "It is our pleasure," he said tonelessly, "to seal this treaty by marriage, to bind Northumbria to our royal house with bonds of blood."

He stopped abruptly, evidently out of words, and just sat. And I could do nothing but stare at him in amazement. Marriage? No one had spoken of marriage, and the ashes of Sigtryggr's queen, my daughter, were scarce cold, yet Edward was offering a bride?

Then there was a stir at the door, spearmen marched in, and behind them came Æthelstan, and on his arm was the girl we had seen on the cart. I recognized her then. She was Eadgyth, Æthelstan's twin, whom I had last known as a child. She walked with a straight back, head held high, but her pale face was a mask of misery. Sigtryggr was wrong, I thought. She was not ugly. Her long face, like Æthelstan's, was strong, and her eyes piercing, but her unhappiness and the grim set of her thin lips made her look plain. Æthelstan stopped with his sister a few paces short of the rearmost bench, evidently waiting for a summons.

"It is our joy," Hrothweard spoke again to Sigtryggr, "and in the knowledge of your queen's sad death, to offer you as a bride the Lady Eadgyth, the beloved daughter of Edward, *Anglorum Saxonum Rex.*"

And with that, Æthelstan walked Eadgyth forward through the benches of watching men who, I think, were as surprised as I was. Eadgyth was to be a peace cow, a bride to seal a treaty, and I saw Sigtryggr's shock as he began to understand what was happening to him, but I doubted he understood the implied insult in this offer of a West Saxon bride. Edward was giving him his eldest daughter, but she was a daughter whom most men in Wessex considered illegitimate. Hrothweard had acknowledged her as Edward's child, he had even called her beloved, which was stretching the meaning of love, but he had deliberately not called her a princess. And she was old for marriage too, very old, at least in her middle twenties, a bastard royal, an unwanted girl, an inconvenience, and she had been fetched from whatever nunnery had presumably sheltered her, to marry a Northumbrian king whom everyone in the hall knew must eventually be slaughtered by Saxon swords. No wonder so many men smirked and even laughed as Eadgyth walked toward her doom.

But Eadgyth would become a queen, Sigtryggr would swear fealty, the priests would baptize him before they harnessed him to his peace cow, and Northumbria was humbled.

And all Northumbria had to show for the treaty was an unwanted woman and Grimbald's bald head that was impaled on a spear-blade and displayed in the palace courtyard.

And Edward had his peace treaty.

Sigtryggr was baptized that afternoon and married two hours later. Both ceremonies took place in Tamweorthin's high church so that as many folk as possible could see his humiliation. Æthelflaed had built the church, and I remember grousing to her that she would have been better off spending the silver on spears and shields, an argument I inevitably lost, and now, under a clear spring sky, the big church was packed to watch Sigtryggr. He was dressed in a white penitent's robe and ordered to climb into a great barrel filled with water from the River Tame, though Archbishop Hrothweard, who insisted on conducting the baptism, added water from a small jar. "This water," he declared, "was brought all the way from the River Jordan, the same river in which our Lord was baptized." I wondered how much he had paid for the stoppered jar, which, I suspected, had been filled from some monastery's scum-covered fish pond. Sigtryggr, who had taken the precaution of giving me his hammer amulet for safekeeping, looked bemused throughout the ceremony and good-naturedly allowed his head to be pushed under water as a choir chanted and as Hrothweard prayed. Afterward he was presented with a silver cross, which he dutifully hung about his neck.

He was still wearing the cross when he married

Eadgyth, though now he also wore his crown and a dark scarlet robe trimmed with fur, which was a gift from Prince Æthelstan. After the wedding, Sigtryggr and his bride were conducted to a chamber in the palace and that was the last I saw of him that day.

Next morning I sent to the far steading where my men had waited, and by midday we were all on the road north. Sigtryggr took back his hammer and ostentatiously hung it about his neck. The silver cross was nowhere to be seen. "I trust you had a good night, lord King?" I asked him mischievously.

"I slept badly," he grunted.

"Badly?"

"The miserable bitch was in tears all night."

"Tears of joy, I'm sure."

Sigtryggr scowled at me. "She's still a virgin."

"Still?"

"Still."

I stopped teasing him. "I knew her when she was a child," I said, "and she was clever then, and I'm sure she's clever still. She'll give you good counsel."

He growled at that. "Damn her counsel, I'd rather she gave me a dowry."

"There's no dowry?"

"She said I'd been given the best dowry of all, the gift of eternal life. Pious bitch."

The pious bitch was mounted on a white gelding, a present from her twin brother. She looked uncomfortable even though her maid had padded the saddle with a thick woolen cloth. She was flanked by two priests. One, Father Eadsig, was her confessor. He was a small, worried-looking young man who kept glancing nervously at the warriors who surrounded him, while the other, Father Amandus, was a Danish convert who had been appointed as Sigtryggr's chaplain, a job that could have explained his scowling face.

I let Tintreg slow, then spurred him between Eadgyth and her confessor. "My lady," I greeted her.

She offered me a sad smile. "Lord Uhtred."

"It's been many years, my lady," I said, ignoring Father Amandus's disapproving look. "You used to play on my estate in Fagranforda." Fagranforda had been my largest Mercian estate, now in the hands of the leprous Bishop Wulfheard who was said to be close to death, which was bad news for the brothels of Hereford.

"I remember Fagranforda," Eadgyth said, "you were always kind to us there. Does Father Cuthbert still live?"

"He does, my lady, though he's blind and old now. But still hale. He'll be glad to meet you again if you should come to Bebbanburg."

"Who is Father Cuthbert?" the Danish priest asked suspiciously.

"He is the priest at Bebbanburg," I answered levelly. "Half my men are Christians, and they need a priest." I saw the surprise on Father Amandus's face, but he said nothing. "He's also the man who married Queen Eadgyth's parents," I went on, "and has been forced to shelter from his enemies ever since."

Father Amandus gave me a sharp look. He plainly knew the rumor that Æthelstan and Eadgyth were bastards. "Enemies?" he asked.

"Enemies, lord," I corrected him and waited.

"Lord," he said reluctantly.

"If Æthelstan is the eldest legitimate son," I said, "then he has the best claim to succeed his father. Other men would prefer Ælfweard, and those men would also prefer it if Father Cuthbert were dead. They want no living witnesses to Prince Æthelstan's legitimacy."

"And who would you prefer?" Father Amandus asked, then remembered to add, "lord."

"Ælfweard," I said.

"You want Ælfweard?" He sounded surprised.

"Ælfweard," I said, "is a miserable earsling. His name ought to be Ælfturd, but if it comes to war between Wessex and Northumbria, which it will, I would rather face an army led by the earsling than an army led by Prince Æthelstan."

Eadgyth frowned. She was wearing a close-fitting hood, which gave her the appearance of a nun. "You would fight against my brother?" she asked sternly.

"Only if he invades my country," I said, "and your country too now, my lady."

She stared ahead at Sigtryggr. "I suppose it is," she said distantly.

We rode in silence for a while. Two swans beat overhead, going west, and I wondered what that omen meant. Eadgyth's eyes glittered with unshed tears. "He's a good man, my lady," I said quietly.

"Is he?"

"I doubt he wanted to marry any more than you did. He's confused and angry."

"Angry?" she asked. "Why—" then she stopped abruptly and made the sign of the cross. "Of course. Forgive me. I am sorry about Stiorra, Lord Uhtred," she looked at me and a tear ran down her cheek. "I should have spoken earlier. She was always kind to me as a child."

I did not want to talk about Stiorra, so changed the subject. "When did you learn you were to marry Sigtryggr?"

She seemed startled by the sudden question, then

looked indignant. "It was just last week!" she said and, for the first time since I had greeted her, she showed some animation. "I had no warning! They came to the convent, summoned me from prayers, took me to Lundene, gave me clothes, and hurried me north." She told me more of that week, and I half listened and half tried to comprehend why Edward had been in such haste. "They never asked whether it was what I wanted," Eadgyth finished bitterly.

"You're a woman," I said drily, "why would they ask you?"

She gave me a look that might have stunned an ox, then gave a mirthless laugh. "You would have asked, wouldn't you?"

"Probably, but I've never known how to handle women," I answered her, still drily. "Did your father say why he wanted you to marry King Sigtryggr?"

"To make peace," she said bleakly.

"And there will be peace," I said, "of sorts. Sigtryggr will not break the treaty, he won't attack south, but the Saxons will come north."

"King Edward will not break his word," Father Amandus said sternly, and again remembered to add, "lord."

"Maybe not," I said, "but do you think his successor will be bound by the treaty?" Neither had an answer to that. "The ambition of Wessex, my lady, is to make one kingdom of all the folk who speak English."

"Amen," Father Eadsig said. I ignored him.

"And you, my lady, are now queen of the last country that speaks English and is not ruled by your father."

"Then why marry me to Sigtryggr?"

"To lull us, to make us feel safe. You fatten the goose before you kill it."

The Danish priest growled at that, but had the sense to say nothing, and just then Rorik rode up from the rear of our long column, bringing Beadwulf and Wynflæd with him. I had told him to fetch the squirrel, but Brother Beadwulf had evidently decided to come too. I stretched back and caught hold of Wynflæd's bridle and drew her mare up between me and Eadgyth. "This, my lady, is Wynflæd. She is a Christian, a Saxon, and I would urge you to take her into your service. She's a good girl."

Eadgyth half smiled at the squirrel. "Of course."

I let go of Wynflæd's horse so that she fell behind again. "Thank you, my lady," I said to Eadgyth. "You're going to discover, my lady, that Eoferwic is mostly a Christian city."

"Mostly," Father Amandus said snidely.

Eadgyth nodded. "Archbishop Hrothweard told me the same. He seems a good man."

"A very good man," I said, "and so is your husband. He looks formidable, I know, but he's a kind man."

"I pray so, Lord Uhtred."

"Kindness," Father Amandus said, "is no substitute for godliness. King Sigtryggr must learn to love the faith." A pause. "Lord."

"King Sigtryggr," I told him sternly, "has no time to learn anything. He's going to war."

"War!" He sounded shocked.

"There is a man we have to kill."

Eadgyth was a peace cow, and she was discovering that the rivalry of nations is difficult. Religion, because of the hatreds it engenders, is difficult. Families, because of the spite they encourage, are difficult. Eadgyth, Edward, Eadgifu, Æthelstan, Ælfweard, and Æthelhelm made a tangle of love, loyalties, and hate, mostly hate, and that was difficult. The only thing that was simple was war.

And Sigtryggr and I were going to war.

War is not easy. Simple, usually, but never easy. Dealing with Edward's ambitions was like groping for eels in the dark, and I wondered if even he knew who he really wanted to succeed him. Or perhaps he did not care, because to think of the succession was to contemplate his own death, and none of us enjoy that prospect. As a young man Edward had shown promise, but wine, ale, and women had proved more appealing than the dull business of government, and he had grown fat, lazy, and sickly. In some ways, though, he had been a success, achieving what his more celebrated father had failed to. Edward had waged a campaign that had brought all of East Anglia under West Saxon rule, while his sister's death had given him the chance to include Mercia in his kingdom, though Mercia was still unsure whether that was a blessing or a curse. During Edward's reign much of his father's dream had come true; the dream of a united Englaland, and that dream told me that the treaty we had just agreed was not worth a sparrow's fart. The West Saxons, for it was the West Saxons who were creating Englaland, would never abandon their ambition to swallow Northumbria. That was simple, and being simple, it would mean war.

"Not necessarily," Æthelstan had told me on the night after his sister's wedding.

I scoffed at that. "You think we'll just surrender Northumbria?"

"You have a Saxon queen now."

"And my grandson," I had pointed out, "is Sigtryggr's heir."

He had frowned at that truth. We had met in the palace, in a small room adjoining the royal chapel. He had asked me to come, even sending men to escort me through Tamweorthin's streets in case Æthelhelm made another attempt on my life. I had gone reluctantly. Eadgifu had already tried to recruit my support for her infant sons, and I suspected Æthelstan also wanted my loyalty, so I had greeted him with surly words. "If you wanted me at the Witan so you could receive my oath," I had told him, "you won't get it."

"Sit, lord," he had said patiently. "There's wine."

I had sat, and he had then stood and paced the small room. We were alone. He fingered the cross about his neck, gazed at a leather wall-hanging that showed sinners tumbling to hell's fires, and finally turned to me. "Should I be King of Wessex?"

"Of course," I had answered without hesitation.

"So you'll support me?"

"No."

"Why not?"

"Because I'd rather fight Ælfweard."

He had grimaced at that, then paced the room again. "My father will leave me in Ceaster."

"Good."

"Why is that good?"

"It's harder for Æthelhelm to kill you there."

"I can't shelter behind walls forever."

"You won't," I said.

"No?"

"When your father dies," I had suggested, "you ride south with the men of Mercia and you claim the West Saxon throne."

"And fight Æthelhelm's forces?"

"If you need to, yes."

"I will," he had said forcefully, "and you won't help me?"

"I'm a Northumbrian. I'm your enemy."

He half smiled. "How can you be my enemy? Your queen is my sister."

"True," I conceded the point.

"Besides, you're my friend." He had stopped by a table on which stood a plain wooden cross flanked by candles. He reached out and touched the cross. "I do want an oath from you," he said. He had not looked at me as he spoke, but gazed at the cross. He had waited for my response, but I said nothing, and my obstinate silence made him turn to me. "Swear on whatever god you believe in," he had said, "that you will do all that you can to kill Ealdorman Æthelhelm. Do that, and I will swear you an oath."

I had stared at him in surprise. His face, so strong and hard, was shadowed, but his eyes glittered with a trace of reflected candlelight. "You would give me an oath?" I asked.

He was clutching his cross, perhaps to convince me of his earnestness. "I asked you to come here so I could swear you an oath. An oath that promises that I will never fight against you, and that I will never invade Northumbria."

I hesitated, looking for whatever trap that promised oath concealed. Oaths bind us and are not to be taken lightly. "You can kill Æthelhelm yourself," I said.

"If I can," he said, "I will, but he's your enemy too."

"And by taking your oath," I had said, "you promise not to invade Northumbria?"

"Not while you live."

"But you'd fight my son?" I asked. "Or my grand-son?"

"They must make their own agreements with me," he had said stiffly, meaning that Northumbria would be invaded when I died, and that, I thought ruefully, could not be many years away. On the other hand, if Æthelstan did become king, then the oath he promised would give Sigtryggr and me time to build up North-umbria's strength.

"What happens if your father orders you to invade Northumbria while I'm alive?" I had asked him.

"Then I will refuse. I will become a lay brother in a monastery if I need to. If I swear the oath to you then I shall keep it."

He would too, I thought. I had watched the nearest candle gutter, its smoke curling toward the ceiling. "I can't kill Æthelhelm while your father's alive," I said, "that would be cause for war." Then another thought occurred to me, and I looked at him sharply. "Are you asking me to kill him just to keep your conscience clear?"

He had shaken his head. "I'm offering you what you want, lord. Æthelhelm has tried to kill both of us, so let's be allies in his death."

"I thought you Christians prefer to settle your arguments without killing."

That had made him frown. "Do you think I pursue his death lightly? So long as he lives there cannot be peace in Wessex. If I succeed to the throne he will rebel against me. He wants his nephew on the throne, and he will stop at nothing to achieve that."

"Or he wants the throne for himself," I said.

"There are some who believe that, yes," he had answered guardedly.

"And by killing him," I said, "I make you king."

He had bridled at that, suspecting I was accusing him of an unworthy ambition. "Do you think I haven't prayed about that fate?" he asked sternly. "That I haven't struggled with my conscience? That I haven't spoken with Archbishop Athelm?" And that was interesting, I had thought. It suggested that the new Archbishop of Contwaraburg was opposed to Æthelhelm, or was at least a supporter of Æthelstan. "Kingship is a burden," Æthelstan had continued, and I had seen he was entirely serious, "and I am convinced I am best capable of bearing that burden. God burdens me! You may not believe it, lord, but I constantly pray Christ's prayer from Gethsemane; to let the cup pass from me! But Christ has not seen fit to spare me, so I must drain the cup, however bitter."

"When your grandfather was dying," I said, "he told me the crown of Wessex was a crown of thorns."

"If it's worth anything," Æthelstan had said forcibly, "it must be a crown of thorns."

"You'd be a good king," I said grudgingly.

"And I will be a king who will not fight against you."

I might not trust Edward, but I trusted Æthelstan. He was like his grandfather, King Alfred, a man of his word. If he said he would not fight against me, he would not. "Do we tell anyone of this pact?" I had asked.

"I think it best if we keep it between ourselves, lord," he had said, "and perhaps our closest advisers." He had hesitated. "Can I ask what Eadgifu wanted of you?"

"My support."

He had shuddered. "She's ambitious," he made it

sound unpleasant, "and of course she has the king's ear."

"More than his ear."

"And you told her what, lord?"

"I told her nothing. I just looked at her tits and listened to her."

He had grimaced at that. "Nothing?"

"She was too clever to ask me for anything because she knew what I'd say. That whole conversation was merely a show to convince Æthelhelm that I was her ally."

"She's a clever woman," he said quietly.

"But her eldest son is too young to become king," I said.

"But half the West Saxons claim I'm a bastard," he said, "and the other half knows that Ælfweard is unfit to be a ruler, so perhaps her infant son would be a safer choice." He glanced at the wooden cross. "Maybe he's the right choice?"

"He's too young. Besides, you're the eldest son. The throne should be yours."

He nodded. "I feel unworthy," he said softly, "but my prayers have convinced me that I would be a better king than Ælfweard." He made the sign of the cross. "May God forgive my pride in saying that."

"There's nothing to forgive," I said harshly.

"Ælfweard must not inherit the throne," he said, still speaking softly. "He is rotten with corruption!"

"Men say that of me too, lord Prince," I said, "they call me priest-killer, pagan, and worse, but you still want my oath."

He had been silent for a moment, with his eyes lowered and his hands clasped almost as if in prayer, then he had looked at me. "I trust you, lord. The Lady Æthelflaed, before she died, told me to trust you, to put my faith in you as she had done. So yes, lord, if I am to fulfill my God's commands then I want your oath, and you may swear it on any god you please."

So I gave it to him. I knelt, took the oath, and he knelt and gave me his oath, and I thought that by giving him a promise and in turn receiving his promise that we had shaped the future together. And though it is true that we have both kept the promises we made that night, the future still made itself. Wyrd bið ful āræd.

What I don't understand," Sigtryggr asked as we rode home, "is why they went to all that trouble? Why not simply invade now?"

"Because they're squabbling like stoats in a sack," I

said. "Edward wants to invade, but he needs the support of Æthelhelm. If he doesn't have Æthelhelm's troops, then his army is cut in half."

"Why doesn't Æthelhelm support him?"

"Because Æthelhelm wants to lead the invasion himself," I guessed, "and end up owning most of Northumbria. Edward doesn't want that. He wants Northumbria for himself."

"Why doesn't he just kill the bastard?"

"Because Æthelhelm is powerful. Attacking Æthelhelm means civil war. And Æthelhelm won't support Edward till Edward declares Ælfweard as the next king."

Sigtryggr snorted. "Easy then, just make the declaration!"

"But anyone of sense in Wessex and Mercia knows that Ælfweard is a piece of shit. If Edward names Ælfweard as his heir then he could provoke another rebellion. The Mercians want Æthelstan, probably. The sensible West Saxons want anyone except Ælfweard, but not Æthelstan. They might side with Eadgifu, I don't know."

"Why not just support Æthelstan? He's the eldest son!"

"Because their goddamned priests preach that Æthelstan is a bastard. And he's spent most of his life in

Mercia, which means that most West Saxons don't know him and don't know if they'll prosper under his rule. The fervent Christians support him, of course, at least those who don't believe he's a bastard, but most of the bishops and abbots are in Æthelhelm's pay, so they want Ælfweard. Eadgifu doesn't want either, because she thinks her son ought to be king, and I don't doubt she's recruiting followers by spreading her legs. It's a royal mess."

"So my queen is a bastard?"

"She's not," I said firmly.

"But they say she is?"

"The church says so."

"So why marry her to me?"

"Because they think you're stupid enough to believe that a bastard royal is a pledge of their sincerity. And because it confuses the Scots."

"Them too? How?"

"Because making Eadgyth your queen," I suggested, "tells the Scots that you're allied with her father, and that might make the hairy bastards think twice before they try to take Northumbria as their own. The West Saxons don't want you to lose half of Northumbria before they take it all for themselves."

"Even so," he said, "Eadgyth's not much of a prize, is she?"

"She's a good woman," I said firmly, "and I like her."

He laughed at that, then spurred on. I did like Eadgyth. She had her twin brother's good sense and her own gentle demeanor. Her marriage had come as a complete surprise to her. She had resigned herself to a life of prayer as a virtual prisoner in a convent, then just six days before the Witan, she had been plucked from the cloister, given cast-off clothes that had belonged to Edward's previous wife, and brought north to Tamweorthin. The speed with which Edward had made that decision was impressive, and I wondered why, then decided that the marriage was not really intended as a gesture to Sigtryggr. My daughter's death had offered Edward, or more probably his closest advisers, an unexpected opportunity to give Æthelhelm a subtle warning. Edward, by acknowledging Eadgyth as his child and by making her a queen, was suggesting he might make her twin brother into a king, and that threatened the future of Ælfweard, Æthelhelm's nephew. Yet Edward had also made sure that Ælfweard alone sat in a place of honor at the Witan, and so had preserved Æthelhelm's hopes. The West Saxon court, I reflected, was a wasp's nest, and I had secretly added my own sting to that royal mess.

And so we rode north, going to war.

PART THREE

Fortress of the Eagles

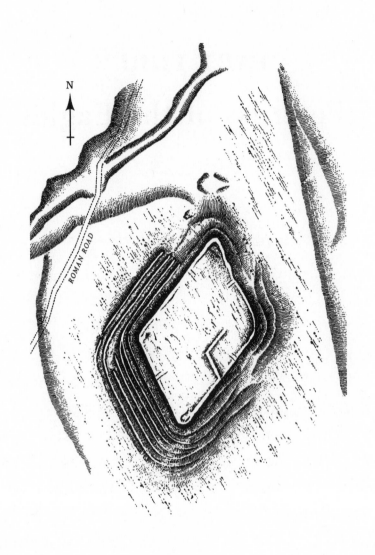

Nine

At Bebbanburg the sea kept up its ceaseless beat and the wind brought the smell of salt with the sea birds' cries. I had been away too long.

And at Bebbanburg I had to listen to the sympathy folk felt for Stiorra and the anger they harbored against her killers, and all I could do was promise revenge.

Taking revenge was another matter. Sköll, I knew, was somewhere in Cumbraland. That was all I knew. Whether he was on the coast or in the hills, I did not know. Brother Beadwulf, who had stayed in Eoferwic with the squirrel, had told me that Sköll had captured a silver mine in the hills, but when I had pressed him for more he confessed he knew almost nothing. "I heard men speak of him, lord, that's all. He lived far to the north of Arnborg's hall, I know that much."

"And he has a silver mine?"

"I heard men say that, lord."

I had heard rumors of a silver mine in Cumbraland, but such tales were common, and the mines elusive. My father had once become excited at the report of a gold mine in the hills, and for weeks he talked of the wealth we would have and the coins he would strike, but his search parties found nothing. It was far easier to risk the dragons and the ghosts by tearing apart the burial mounds of the ancient people, though usually the graves yielded nothing but cheap pottery and dry bones.

I had shared the rumor of a silver mine with Sigtryggr, and knew he had men crossing the hills to search for both silver and Sköll. I too sent out warbands, usually a score of men who were told to avoid a fight with Sköll's followers. "I just need to know where he lives," I insisted to them, "discover that and then come home."

Sigtryggr's first instinct, like mine, had been to assemble an army and ride westward without delay, but sense had made us both pause. Lindcolne, like Eoferwic and Bebbanburg, had to be garrisoned, as did the lesser fortresses of Northumbria. Wessex might have signed a peace treaty, but if we stripped our garrisons of our best troops then the temptation might have been too great, and I did not trust Edward to pass up such an opportunity. Besides, the Scots were also eyeing our land, and the strong garrisons in the northern forts helped to dissuade them from invasion. If we left adequate men in the fortresses then we could only lead some three hundred and fifty household warriors to Cumbraland, and that strength, such as it was, would be whittled down if we were to wander from settlement to settlement, fighting skirmishes and with no aim but to find our enemy, who would be watching us and ambushing us. I had persuaded Sigtryggr that our best course was to discover the wolf's lair and then march straight there and crush him, but that meant finding an enemy who was evidently well hidden.

The largest war-band that I dispatched west was led by my son, who took forty-three warriors to follow the great wall that the Romans had built across Britain. The old stone-built forts of the wall had attracted settlers, and I reckoned it was worth inquiring of them if they had news of Sköll. "But if you find him," I warned my son, "do not pick a fight."

"You want me to run away?"

"If my elder brother had run away," I told him, "he'd be the Lord of Bebbanburg now, not me. Sometimes the cleverest thing to do in war is to run."

And so I waited, and, while I waited, I had one unpleasant duty; to talk with Ælswyth, my son's wife.

She was Æthelhelm the Younger's sister, and had accompanied her father when he was my prisoner in Bebbanburg, and, while she was staying at her father's side through his final illness, she had become pregnant.

I could not blame my son. Ælswyth was a fragile, delicate, and beautiful girl with hair like fairy gold, skin pale as milk, and a face that could drive a man crazed with desire. "She's a goddamned elf," Finan had decided when he first saw her, and my fear was that the elf would prove too delicate for childbirth, but she had survived her firstborn and now carried a second child. The wise women in the village and among my men's wives declared that she was healthy, though to make certain they burned mandrake root, powdered the ashes that they mixed with cow's milk, then smeared the paste on her belly. She was a Christian, of course, but when I gave her a necklace from which hung a little golden cat, one of the symbols of Freya who protected women in childbirth, she wore it. She was wearing it on the day that my son led his war-band south and west and, when he was gone from sight, I walked with her on Bebbanburg's seaward ramparts. It was a blustery day and the sea was flecked with restless white, the breakers roared on the sand beneath us, and the wind lifted strands of her fair hair as we walked. "I love this place," she said.

"Do you?"

"Of course, lord."

"Your home in Wessex was surely more comfortable?"

"Oh yes, lord," she said brightly, "but I feel free here, lord." She offered me a smile that could have dimmed the sun. She had been thirteen when she came to Bebbanburg and, before my son ruined her father's plans, had been reckoned as one of the most desirable brides in all the Saxon lands. Her father's immense wealth and power would have ensured a dowry of royal proportions, and kings from across the sea had sent emissaries to her father's hall, and those emissaries had carried back reports of her beauty. Her father had guarded her carefully because he planned to marry her to a man who would increase his power. He had intended that Ælswyth would be the bride of a great lord, or even a king's wife, to be hung with jewels and crowned with gold, yet such had been his hatred of me that he had been prepared to offer her to my cousin to ensure that I never regained Bebbanburg, and, better still, died in the attempt. Instead my cousin was dead, Æthelhelm the Older was in his grave, and his prized daughter was walking the ramparts of Bebbanburg in a woolen dress, a sealskin cloak, and wearing a pagan amulet.

"You know," I said carefully, "that I met your brother in Tamweorthin?"

"Yes, lord."

"We hardly spoke."

"You told me, lord," she said meekly.

"What I didn't tell you," I added brutally, "is that he tried to kill me." She was, I thought, too young to know how to respond, and merely uttered an elfin squeak of either surprise or shock. We walked on. "And I have to tell you," I continued, "that I have made an oath."

"An oath, lord?"

"To kill your brother."

She again made the small noise, then turned and stared at the great gray waters where the whitecaps rippled to the horizon. There were no ships in sight, just wind-shredded waves that broke in bright spray against the Farnea Islands. I looked down at her face, expecting to see tears in her blue eyes, but instead she was half smiling. "My brothers," she said, still gazing at the sea, "were never kind to me, lord, and Æthelhelm was always the cruelest."

"Cruel?"

"He's much older than I am," she said, "much older! And he didn't like me."

"Did he beat you?"

"Not badly, not often, but he was spiteful. Mother once gave me a necklace of jet. It was beautiful, and Æthelhelm took it. He took whatever he wanted and if I cried he would slap me, but only slap." She shook her head. "He gave the necklace to one of the kitchen slaves."

"Who doubtless earned it on her back," I said.

She looked up at me, surprised, then laughed. "She did," she said, "and nine months later she gave birth to a little girl, but the baby died." She instinctively put a hand on the golden cat, then put her arm through mine. "When I was eight my father gave me a pony, and I called him Stifearh because he looked like a fat little pig." She laughed, remembering her pony. "And the first time I tried to ride Stifearh my brother put thistles under the saddle. He thought it was funny! And of course poor Stifearh bucked and I was thrown. I broke my leg!"

"Didn't your father punish him?"

"He laughed too." She looked up at me earnestly. "Father wasn't always unkind. He could be generous."

I drew her on, walking north on the high fighting platform. "So will you be angry with me if I kill your brother?" I asked.

"He's your enemy, lord, I know that." She hesitated, then frowned. "But I'm your daughter now," she added fiercely, "so I'll pray for you."

It seemed that telling my daughter-in-law that I had sworn to slaughter her brother was not so difficult after all, but finding Sköll was proving more than difficult. For a start he must have known we were searching for him because two of my search parties had been pursued and one man killed, and none of the scouts returned with any useful news. A messenger came from Eoferwic to tell me that Sigtryggr's men were being equally unsuccessful. "It's as if Sköll is a ghost, lord," the messenger told me. "Everyone has heard of him, no one knows where he is."

"Or they're too frightened to speak," I suggested.

"King Sigtryggr believes the sorcerer can hide Sköll's home, lord. That he can wrap it in cloud."

I touched my hammer and feared for my son. We were not just fighting Sköll, and he was formidable enough, but his sorcerer too. I had told Uhtred the Younger to be back within ten days, but two weeks passed and still he had not returned. Ælswyth spent hours praying in Bebbanburg's small chapel, while Finan, more usefully, led thirty men south and west, seeking news in every settlement, but folk had heard nothing of any fight in the far hills. "He'll come back," Eadith assured me. She had found me on Bebbanburg's landward rampart, gazing into the hills.

"He can be headstrong," I said.

"Like you," she responded with a smile and put her arm through mine. "He'll come back, I promise."

"You see the future?" I asked skeptically.

"You tell me to trust my instinct," she said, "and I tell you he'll be back."

Eadith had once been my enemy and now was my wife. She was a clever woman, skilled in the intricate dance of ambitious men, the steps of which she had learned as the mistress of Æthelred, Æthelflaed's husband, who had been the ruler of Mercia and another enemy of mine. I had told Eadith of my pact with Æthelstan, and she had approved. "He'll be the next king," she said.

"Æthelhelm will fight to prevent that."

"He will, but the men of Mercia will fight for Æthelstan." And that, I thought, was probably true. Edward, when he had inherited the throne, had been embarrassed by the brand of bastardy that was attached to his eldest son, and so had sent the boy Æthelstan into Mercia to be raised by Æthelflaed, which is how I had become his protector. Æthelstan might be a West Saxon by birth, but to most Mercians he was one of their own. "And you say Archbishop Athelm is opposed to Æthelhelm?" Eadith asked.

"I think he is."

"Then the church will support Æthelstan," she said.

"Not the churchmen who take Æthelhelm's bribes. Besides, the church has no warriors."

"But most warriors fear for their souls, so they listen to the church."

"And the moment I'm dead," I said bleakly, "the church will encourage Æthelstan to invade Northumbria."

She smiled. "Then it's a good thing that your son is a Christian."

"Damn him," I said, touching the hammer. "If he's even alive."

Eadith touched the cross at her breast. "He is alive," she said, "I know it."

She was right, my son was alive, and lucky that he was. He had left with forty-three men and returned with just twenty-seven, and six of those were wounded. They came through Bebbanburg's Skull Gate looking like beaten men, which they were. My son could barely meet my eyes. "We were ambushed," he said bitterly.

It had been a carefully designed ambush. My son had almost reached the far end of the great Roman wall, and as he went he had inquired at every steading and settlement for news of *úlfhéðnar* or for rumors about Sköll, and he learned nothing until he reached the settlement beneath the largest fort of the long wall, a fort built above the River Irthinam. We called that fort Spura, because its walls stood on a commanding hill spur, and the settlement was built beneath it on the Irthinam's southern bank. "A man told us he knew where Sköll lived," my son explained, "he said Sköll had captured his two daughters and he claimed he'd followed the raiders south afterward."

"And you believed him?" I asked. "A villager daring to follow *úlfhéðnar*?"

"The other men said the same, lord," Redbad put in. Redbad was a Frisian and devoted to my son. "Two of them had lost their daughters too."

"Who were these men?" I asked. "Danes? Norse? Saxon?"

"Saxon," my son answered miserably, knowing how thin his tale now sounded. "They said they held land from the monks at Cair Ligualid."

Cair Ligualid was at the far end of the great wall. I had been there often enough and had wondered whether the coming of so many Norse to the coast of Cumbraland had meant the destruction of the monastery and the town surrounding it. Nothing my son could tell me provided an answer to that, though the Saxons who had misled him had claimed that their families had taken shelter behind the monastery's high walls.

"So how many men were in this settlement?"

"Six," my son said.

"And they knew where Sköll lived?"

"They said he lived at Heahburh."

"Heahburh?" I had never heard of such a place. The name meant "high fort," and that could have been a description of any one of the hundreds of ancient hill forts that crowned Britain's heights.

"They couldn't describe just where it was," my son said, "but offered to take us there."

"And they were certain Sköll wasn't there," Redbad said, "they said he'd gone south, lord, to fight off raiders."

"I thought that sounded likely," my son went on, "because Sigtryggr has men in southern Cumbraland."

"He does," I said.

"Only Sköll hadn't gone south," my son said unhappily.

Sköll had been waiting on either side of a steep valley, his men concealed behind both crests, and, when my son's horsemen were at the valley's center, the *úlfhéðnar* had attacked. They swarmed down both slopes, gray-cloaked men in gray mail on gray horses, and my son's smaller troop stood no chance. He flinched as he described the scene. "You didn't think," I asked bitterly, "to have scouts on the high ground?"

"I believed the men who led us," he said, "and they said Sköll and most of his men were gone south."

"They were convincing, lord," Redbad added loyally.

"And I reckoned any scouts we sent to the hill crests would be seen by the men he'd left to garrison Heahburh," my son went on, "and I wanted to approach unseen."

"And the men who led you," I asked, "were Sköll's men?"

My son nodded. "They turned uphill to join the attackers."

In some ways I could understand why my son had been deceived. If the men who had betrayed him had been Danes or Norsemen he would have been far more cautious, but he had assumed that Saxon Christians would be his allies. Yet Sköll had clearly suborned the six men, a reminder that the leader of the *úlfhéðnar* was a subtle man. Rumor said he hated the Christians and took a delight in killing priests, but he evidently knew how to seduce and use them too.

My son had only escaped because Sköll had attacked a moment too late. The *úlfhéðnar* had ridden recklessly down the valley's slopes, but instead of striking the head of my son's column, the horsemen had severed it in half. The men at the rear had stood no chance, but my son and those who survived with him had spurred away. They had been pursued, of course, and two more were lost in that wild chase, but Bebbanburg's horses were good, and my son had come home.

He had come home defeated, and I knew that bitter feeling of failure, made even more dreadful by the need to tell women and children that their husband and father was dead. And I could taste my son's shame, that he had been so easily deceived, that he had decided, foolishly, to ride unfamiliar land without scouts, that he had then been humiliated by an enemy, and, maybe worst of all, that he had lost the confidence of my warriors.

Christians like to dream of the perfect world, a place where there is no fighting, where sword-blades are hammered into plowshares, and where the lion, whatever that is, sleeps with the lamb. It is a dream. There has always been war and there will always be war. So long as one man wants another man's wife, or another man's land, or another man's cattle, or another man's silver, so long will there be war. And so long as one priest preaches that his god is the only god or the better god there will be war. King Alfred, a man who loved peace because peace encouraged prayer, education, and prosperity, nevertheless wanted to conquer the land held by the Danes and wipe out the worship of the old gods. He would have done that by persuasion if he could, but what could persuade the Danes to surrender their land, their rulers, and their religion? Only the sword, and so the peace-loving Alfred beat his plowshares into swords, raised armies, and set about his Christian duty of converting his enemies.

And so long as there is war there will be warlords. Leaders. What makes a man follow a leader? Success. A warrior wants victory, he wants silver, he wants land, and he looks to his lord for all those things. My son was not a bad warrior, indeed I was proud of him and when I die he will hold Bebbanburg just as his son will hold it, but to hold the fortress he needs men who have confidence in him. Men who will follow him in the expectation of victory. One defeat at Sköll's hand would not destroy his reputation, but now he needed a victory to show my men that he was a leader who could give them the land, silver, and cattle they craved.

The easy way to give him some success was to send him north into the Scottish lands in search of plunder, but with Sköll threatening Northumbria, the last thing I wanted was to stir the Scots to anger. One enemy at a time is prudent. Besides, I reflected, there would soon be fighting enough, and Uhtred the Younger would have his opportunity.

And then, I thought, if leadership is about success, how had Sköll survived? He had lost his lands in Ireland and had retreated eastward across the sea. He had led his men across Northumbria, pierced the gate of Eoferwic, and there been repulsed. He had pursued me south toward Mameceaster, and then had refused battle, preferring to retreat. None of it suggested success. He had managed to capture some cattle and slaves, but his setbacks were far greater than his gains, yet all I knew of him suggested that his power grew. The Northmen were famous for deserting an unsuccessful leader, their loyalty dissolving with a warlord's defeats, yet Sköll's reputation grew. Men feared him and they feared his *úlfhéðnar*, but fear had little force against failure, and Sköll had failed. Yet his men did not desert him, indeed even more men were swearing allegiance to him. "It's his damned sorcerer," Finan said.

That was surely the answer. That Snorri was so feared that even Sköll's failures could not hurt men's faith in his ultimate success. Sköll possessed a sorcerer who could spy the future through blind eyes and use those empty sockets to kill men at a distance. I feared him! Men talked of Grayfang, Sköll's sword, but his real weapon was Snorri, and it was the sorcerer's reputation that persuaded ever more men to fly Sköll's flag of the snarling wolf from their hall roofs, that brought ships of men from Ireland and from the western isles of Scotland to give Sköll their oaths. His power grew, and each report made me regret that we had not ridden sooner. Folk said Sköll led five hundred warriors, a week later it was seven hundred, and neither Sigtryggr nor I knew the truth, any more than we knew where to find Sköll. "Heahburh," I said in frustration, "maybe there's no such place as Heahburh!"

Yet Sigtryggr's scouts had heard the same name. It seemed Heahburh existed, but where? I began to fear the rumors that Sköll's formidable sorcerer did indeed possess the mysterious power to conceal his fortress, and then, when I was close to despairing that we would ever solve the mystery, it was unraveled in the most unexpected way. It happened on a day when a letter was brought to Bebbanburg. The letter was from Æthelstan in Ceaster and was sent to Sigtryggr who, in turn, sent it on to me, carried by the priest who had brought the letter from Mercia.

That priest was Father Swithred, Æthelstan's confessor, who was escorted by six Mercian warriors and accompanied by a younger priest who seemed terrified of Swithred's disapproving eyes and sour tongue. "We have been dispatched," Swithred told me haughtily, "to make certain King Sigtryggr is keeping to the terms agreed at Tamweorthin. We were also charged with delivering this letter to the king." He handed me the letter, but gave me no chance to read it. "Under the treaty," he went on, "King Sigtryggr promised to protect the Christians in his realm."

"He did," I confirmed.

"Yet King Sköll has slaughtered every missionary in Cumbraland," he said indignantly.

"King Sköll?" I asked, stressing the "king."

"So he now styles himself."

"So he now styles himself, lord," I said pointedly, waited until he had said the word, then unfolded the letter. Æthelstan had written that he had received disturbing news from the land south of the Ribbel, "which land," he had written, "is ours to govern on behalf of our father, King Edward, and into which territory have come Christian folk fleeing the vile persecution of the heathen who calls himself King Sköll. This same Sköll has sent troops into our land below the Ribbel and done great harm to our folk, to their livestock and to their homes. Worse, to the great sadness of all Christians, the brethren we have sent to be a light to the gentiles have been foully put to martyrdom." The letter went on to point out that it was Northumbria's responsibility to stop Sköll, "and if you should be wayward in that duty our good King Edward will send forces into your land to punish the malefactor."

"Sköll has really killed your missionaries?" I asked Swithred. I talked to him in the sunlight outside the great hall. I had sent his escort and the nervous young priest to find food and ale.

"He has martyred them," Swithred said in disgust.

"Strange," I said, "because some Christian Saxons have allied with him."

"The devil stalks the land," Swithred said, "and works his mischief."

I read the letter again. It was formal and cold, which suggested to me it was not Æthelstan's work, even though it bore his seal and signature, but had probably been written by a priest. "Did you write this?" I asked Swithred.

"To the prince's orders, yes."

"And a copy was sent to King Edward?"

"Of course." I waited until at last, reluctantly, "Lord."

The letter, I thought, was really intended for Edward, assuring him of Æthelstan's loyalty, but nevertheless it confirmed that Sköll was getting stronger, and it also hinted that Sköll's savagery might give the Saxons reason to declare that the treaty had been broken and so provide them with an excuse to invade Cumbraland, and, if that invasion happened, Northumbria would never again rule the western part of its own land. By conquest it would become a part of Saxon Englaland.

"I trust you will extirpate this heathen," Father Swithred said when I had finished reading, then added, again reluctantly, "lord."

"I am sworn to kill him," I said curtly. I did not need a Saxon priest to tell me my duty.

"You say that and you do nothing!" Swithred retorted, and then his eyes opened in amazement as a gangly man climbed the steps to the rock platform in front of Bebbanburg's great hall where we talked.

The approaching man had white hair that hung to his waist and an aged face that was alight with enthusiasm, but what had astonished Father Swithred were the man's clothes, for he was dressed in a cassock, a chasuble, a pallium, and a miter, and he carried a bishop's crozier in his left hand, while on his right he wore a heavy silver ring studded with amber. He seemed excited to see Father Swithred, and, ignoring me, held his right hand toward the tall priest. "Kiss it!" he ordered. "Kiss it, man!" Father Swithred was so taken aback and, perhaps, so overwhelmed by the stranger's radiant garments, that he half bowed and dutifully kissed the bishop's ring. "Have you come from Rome?" the long-haired man demanded sternly.

"No," Swithred stammered, still confused.

"You're not from Rome!" The newcomer was outraged.

"From Ceaster."

"What earthly or heavenly use is Ceaster! The papal throne is in Rome, you benighted fool, you goat-dropping, you spawn of Beelzebub! The keys of the fisherman shall be mine. God has decreed it!"

Father Swithred, hearing the man speaking English with a Danish accent, was recovering his wits. He stepped back, frowning. There were enough Danes who had become Christians, but none, so far as I knew, had yet been made into a bishop. "Who are you?" Swithred demanded.

"I am he who will govern Christ's kingdom on earth! I am the Lord's anointed!"

"Father Swithred," I intervened, "meet Bishop Ieremias."

Swithred's reaction was all I could have wished for. He took another backward step, sketched the sign of the cross toward Ieremias, and looked furious. "You heretic!" he spat. "You disciple of Satan!"

"Bishop Ieremias," I rubbed salt into Swithred's wounded pride, "is my tenant on Lindisfarena. You owe me rent, bishop."

"The Lord will provide," Ieremias said airily.

"You said that six months ago, and the Lord still hasn't provided."

"I will remind Him," Ieremias said. In truth I never expected any rent from Ieremias, and I was not at all sure that Lindisfarena was mine to let anyway. It was church land, the home of Saint Cuthbert's great monastery that had been ransacked and burned by the Danes a generation before. The church had yet to reoccupy

the island, which, by tradition, fell under the protection
of Bebbanburg and, much to the fury of most churchmen, I had allowed Ieremias and his followers to settle
in the ruins of the old monastic house. Their fury, I
suspected, was because Ieremias was about as good a
Christian as I was.

His real name was Dagfinnr Gundarson, but Jarl
Dagfinnr the Dane had turned himself into Ieremias,
a self-appointed bishop. He had served Ragnar the
Younger, whose father had raised me, and one morning
Dagfinnr had appeared naked in Dunholm's great hall
and announced that he was now the son of the Christian
god and had adopted the name Ieremias and demanded
that Ragnar, a pagan, should worship him. Brida, Ragnar's woman and a hater of all Christians, insisted that
Dagfinnr should be put to death, but Ragnar had been
amused and let Ieremias live. The bishop was mad, of
course, but even the moon-touched can make some
sense, and Ieremias had thrived. He had owned a ship
that he renamed *Guds Moder* and used it to fish, and
his success attracted a following of landless men and
women whom he called his flock. "I have brought you
a message from God, lord," he now said, waving the
angry Swithred to one side and explaining his visit to
me, "but first I must tell you, with great joy, that the

flock has been diligent and made salt, which you may buy from us."

"I already have salt, bishop."

"He's no bishop!" Swithred hissed.

"May the devil fart in your mouth," Ieremias said loftily, "and worms shit in your soup." He turned back to me. "My salt is no common salt, lord. It is blessed by our Redeemer. It is our Savior's salt." He smiled triumphantly. "If you buy it, lord," he added slyly, "I will have silver to give you as rent!"

I sometimes thought he was not mad at all, and, like Ragnar, I was amused by him. "I gave you silver last week," I reminded him, "for the herring and salmon."

"I gave those coins to the poor, lord, as the Lamb of God commanded me."

"You being the poor?" I asked.

"The Son of Man hath nowhere to lay His head," Ieremias said mysteriously, then turned on Swithred, who was looking appalled. "Are you married?"

"I am not," Swithred said stiffly.

"I find a wife's breasts make a fine pillow," Ieremias said brightly. "Our Lord should have married. He'd have slept better."

"Heretic," Swithred spat.

"May maggots crawl up your arse," Ieremias said,

then turned to me, and for a moment I thought he was going to ask me about Eadith's breasts, but it seemed he had other matters on his mind. "You have heard of Sköll the Norseman, lord?"

I was startled by the question. "Of course I have."

"The heathen tyrant who calls himself a king," Ieremias said scornfully. He had changed to his native Danish, presumably because he did not want Swithred to follow the conversation. "He is an enemy of God, lord. Have you met him?"

"I have."

"And you live! God be praised!"

"How do you know of Sköll?"

He gave me a puzzled look. "How do I know? Lord, you do speak to your servants, don't you?"

"Of course I do."

"Well, I am God's servant."

"And he talks to you?"

"Of course he does! And at great length." He glanced at Father Swithred as if to make sure the priest was not understanding what we said. "God brings me tidings, lord, but there are times," he had lowered his voice, "when I wish He would speak less. I'm not married to Him!"

"So you've heard stories of Sköll," I said, trying to move the conversation on. I doubted Ieremias's god had whispered the news to him, but lurid tales of Sköll's cruelty were spreading across Northumbria and could easily have reached Lindisfarena.

"The heathen has come from his high place," Ieremias intoned, "and it is the Lord's will that you smite him. That is God's message for you, lord, that you smite him!" He hitched up his mud-stained cassock to reveal a pouch hanging from the belt of his breeches. He fished in the pouch and brought out a stone about the size of a walnut, which he offered to me. "This, lord, will assist in the smiting."

"A pebble?" I asked.

"That, lord," he said in an awed tone, "is the very same sling-stone with which David slew Goliath!"

I took the stone, which looked exactly like a million others on Lindisfarena's beaches. I knew Ieremias collected relics, all of them worthless, but all, in his mind, were real and sacred. "Are you sure you want me to carry this?" I asked.

"God commanded me to give it to you, lord, to grant you great smiting. That stone is a very holy and very precious object and will give you the power to overcome all enemies." He made the sign of the cross, and Father Swithred hissed disapproval. "Turds spew from your tongue," Ieremias spoke English again, glaring at Swithred.

I thought back to something Ieremias had said a moment before. "You mentioned a high place."

"The heathen is exalted," Ieremias said, "and must be brought low."

"You know Sköll lives in a high place?" I asked carefully, never quite sure whether Ieremias was listening to me, let alone telling me the truth.

"Very high, lord! His place of refuge touches the sky and lies above the pit of silver."

I stared at him. "You know where it is?"

"Of course I know!" He suddenly sounded entirely sane. "Do you remember Jarl Halfdan the Mad?"

I shook my head. "Should I?"

"He lost his wits, poor man, and led an assault on Dunholm. Jarl Ragnar killed him, of course, and then we all went north and laid his home waste. That was before God called me to His service." Ieremias used one end of his intricately embroidered pallium to blow his nose, making Father Swithred flinch. "Halfdan the Mad's fort is a very nasty place, lord! The Romans built it."

"Where is it?"

"Lord, Lord, Lord," Ieremias said, evidently calling on his god to help him remember. "You know the road from Jorvik to Cair Ligualid?"

"I know it."

"About an angel's flight from Cair Ligualid another Roman road goes north into the fells. It climbs, lord. If you follow that road you'll find Halfdan's fort. It's lost in the hills, very far and very high."

"Heahburh," I said.

"It is high!" Ieremias said. "And the higher you climb the nearer you come to God. I was thinking of building a tower, lord."

"How far is an angel's flight?" I asked.

"A very high tower, lord, to make it more convenient for God to speak with me."

"Angel's flight," I reminded him.

"Oh! Just a half-day's walk, lord." His face lit up as he remembered something. "Halfdan's fortress lies above the headwaters of the South Tine. Follow that river's valley and you must come to where you can smite him, but pray, lord, pray! Halfdan's fort is formidable! A wall, banks, and ditches, but I shall beseech God that he grants you good smiting. The Lord of Hosts is with you, you cannot fail to smite mightily!"

"But how can you be certain that Heahburh is Halfdan's fort?" I asked, praying that the answer would not be that his god had told him.

"I can't be certain," Ieremias said, sounding perfectly sane, "but all the reports say that Sköll lives above the pit of silver. Where else can it be?"

Some instinct told me that Ieremias's recollection of Ragnar the Younger's raid was the truth, which meant that Heahburh lay not too far south of the great wall, and not too distant from the place where my son had been ambushed. "The pit of silver?" I asked him.

Ieremias looked at me as though I were the mad one, then understanding dawned. "There were lead mines there, lord."

"And silver is smelted from lead," I said.

"From the darkness cometh light," Ieremias said happily, "and silver must be given to the poor, lord." He looked pointedly at the sling-stone I was still holding. "That is a very valuable relic, lord. King David himself handled it!"

Meaning he wanted silver, and, because he had told me what I needed to know, I gave him coins. He sniffed them, looked happy, then turned to the sea. "The tide is rising, lord. May I rest my head here tonight?"

"Did you bring your own pillow?" I asked.

He offered me a sly smile. "She is below, lord," he said, pointing down into the lower fortress.

Ieremias would be unable to get home that evening because at high tide the causeway to Lindisfarena was under water and the mad bishop was often sane enough to visit Bebbanburg just as a flooding tide would prevent him from riding home and just in time to share the garrison's supper, which, I suspected, was a lot better than anything his followers cooked. "And maybe we could have a morsel to eat?" he added.

"You will be welcome," I told him, and so he was, because I reckoned he had told me where I could find Sköll.

Not that I could do anything about it, at least not immediately, because the next day Sköll came to us.

He came without anyone telling us of his presence, and that was disturbing. If a Scottish war-band came hunting for slaves or cattle we would hear about it from the folk who fled. Some would go to their hiding places in the woods or hills, but others would run or ride to warn neighbors and so the news would spread until it reached Bebbanburg, but Sköll simply arrived without any warning. He must have led his men straight across the hills, not stopping to plunder or burn, just spurring on his horses so that he appeared on the hill above the village before anyone could reach us with news of his coming. He came not long after dawn on a mellow spring day, and the rising sun glinted from the mail, helmets, and spear-blades of his gray-cloaked horsemen. "They must have ridden half the night," Finan said.

"All night even," I said. It had been a cloudless night and the moon was full.

A horn was sounding from the great hall, summoning Bebbanburg's garrison to the ramparts. Villagers were running from their houses, driving pigs, goats, cattle, dogs, sheep, and children along the narrow neck of land that led to Bebbanburg's Skull Gate. Sköll could surely see them, but he sent none of his warriors down the hill to stop their flight. I shouted at my son to ready men who could ride out to protect the fugitives if Sköll attacked, but the Norseman stayed on the higher ground and just watched us.

"Two hundred and fifty men," Finan said dourly.

"So far," I answered, because more men were joining Sköll even as we watched. I had fewer than sixty men in the fortress. Most of my household warriors were at their steadings, and though they would learn soon enough of Sköll's arrival and would know to assemble south of the fortress, I could not expect to see them until midday at the earliest and even then I would have fewer men than Sköll.

But Sköll too had his problems. I suspected he had never been to Bebbanburg before, and, though he had doubtless heard of its strength, he was now seeing the fortress in all its grim glory. I doubted he had any ships on Northumbria's eastern coast, so the only way to attack us was along the narrow neck of land that led to the massive defenses of the Skull Gate, and if he some-

how managed to capture that outer bastion he still had
the Inner Gate and its mighty wall to overcome. So far
as I could see he had brought no ladders, so in truth he
stood no chance of capturing the fortress because even
his fabled *úlfhéðnar* could not overcome Bebbanburg's
defenses without some means of scaling the ramparts.
Unless, of course, his sorcerer had the power to defeat us.

And was that possible? I touched my hammer. I could
fight men, but I could not fight the gods, and surely, I
thought, Sköll must have known of Bebbanburg's leg-
endary strength before coming to the fortress, so what
gave him the confidence to come so boldly? "Oh, dear
Christ!" Finan interrupted my thoughts. He was staring at the far hill.

His eyes were keener than mine. "What is it?" I
asked.

"Prisoners, lord."

It was my turn to swear. I could see the prisoners
now, four men wearing nothing but long shirts, their
hands tied, their bodies draped over packhorses like
sacks of grain. "My son's men," I said quietly.

"Like as not."

By now there were almost three hundred men on
the far hill, and Sköll had raised his standard, the flag
of the snarling wolf. I could see him clearly, his white

cloak bright in the early sunshine. He was waiting, knowing we watched him, and ignoring the fugitives panicked from the village who had almost all reached the fortress. He was gloating, I thought. He had not come to capture a fortress, but to show how little he feared us.

And when he did approach he came slowly, his whole line of men riding sedately downhill and threading its way between the houses that lined the harbor. I thought men would dismount to plunder the abandoned village, but instead they all followed Sköll onto the narrow neck of land. The prisoners came with them. "Can you see who they are?" I asked Finan.

"Not yet."

The approaching warriors stopped at the causeway's narrowest point, where Sköll dismounted. He handed his helmet to one of his followers and then, accompanied by just one man, walked toward the Skull Gate. He stopped after a few paces, drew his great sword, Grayfang, and rammed it into the sand, then spread his arms wide to show he came to talk, not to fight. He walked on another few paces, then stopped and waited. His companion was Snorri.

I had only seen Snorri at a distance, now I could see him clearly, and he was far more frightening than Sköll. He was as tall as Sköll, but where Sköll was broad and heavily built, the sorcerer was thin as a wraith, his gray and white striped robe hanging loose from his shoulders like a shroud. His eye sockets were red scars in a bony face that was framed by a long tangle of white hair that hung past his white beard that was plaited into three ropes. He was led by a small white dog on a leash. He carried the leash in his right hand, while in his left was a wolf skull. I touched my hammer and saw Finan clutch at his cross.

The Christians have priests, whom I am pleased to call sorcerers because it annoys them, but Christians condemn sorcery. They believe their nailed god could walk on water, heal the sick, and summon devils from the mad, but they claim those feats are not magic, and spit on those of us who understand that the world can never be explained, that magic belongs to the spirit realm, and that some men and women are given the ability to understand the inexplicable. Those folk are the sorcerers and sorceresses, and we revere them even as we fear them. They are not priests, our religion needs no men or women to tell us how to behave, but we do care about the will of the gods, and some folk are better than others at divining that will. Our sorcerers are often blind, like the man waiting for us outside the Skull Gate, because the blind can often see farther into the shadows where the restless spirits live. Ravn,

Ragnar the Fearless's father, had been a blind sorcerer, though he preferred to say he was a skald, what we would call a scop, or shaper, a man who makes poems. "I am a skald," Ravn told me on our first meeting, "a weaver of dreams, a man who makes glory from nothing and dazzles you with its making." He had laughed at his own immodesty, but in truth he was much more than a man who made songs. I learned in my childhood to understand that Ravn the Skald, though blind, could see things we others could not. He could glimpse the spirit world, he could see truth in dreams, and discern the future in smoke.

And now Sköll's fearsome sorcerer was at my gate.

The two men waited. It had taken me some moments to leave the upper ramparts, go through the Inner Gate, and so to the Skull Gate. Sköll had only the one companion, so I just took Finan, who muttered a prayer and fingered his cross as we left the gate and walked toward the waiting pair. The sorcerer had let go of the leash, and the small dog just sat quietly at his feet as his master clutched the wolf skull in both hands and muttered under his breath. Finan, a Christian, was not supposed to believe in a sorcerer's skills, but Finan was no fool. Like most Christians he understood that there was a power in the shadows, and he feared it. I feared it too.

"Uhtred of Bebbanburg," Sköll greeted me.

"Sköll of Niflheim," I responded.

He laughed at that insult. "This is Snorri Wargson," he said, indicating the muttering sorcerer. "He is Fenrir's beloved."

I had an impulse to touch the hammer around my neck, but managed to resist. Fenrir is a monstrous wolf, son of a god, who lies bound and fettered because even the gods fear him. In the last days, when chaos engulfs the world, Fenrir will free himself and the slaughter he makes will drench the heavens in blood, but until then he howls in his bonds, and Snorri, as if knowing my thoughts, put his head back and howled at the sky. The dog did not move.

"And this is Finan," I said, "an Irishman who has lost count of the widows he has made among the *úlfhéðnar*."

"You will both die at my hands," Sköll said calmly, which only made Snorri howl a second time. "Snorri has seen your deaths," Sköll added.

"And I have seen yours," I answered. He was younger than I remembered. His face was deeply lined and there was gray in his fair beard, but even so I reckoned he was not yet forty. He was a man in his prime, and a formidable man at that. "The last time we met," I said, "you ran from me. My men call you Sköll the Frightened."

"And yet I come to meet you without a sword," he said, "and you carry one. Who is frightened now?"

"You're wasting my time. Say what you have to say, then run away again."

Sköll fingered the empty throat of Grayfang's scabbard. "When I came to Northumbria," he said, "I asked men who ruled in this land. They did not say Sigtryggr, they named you."

"They were wrong," I said.

"Uhtred of Bebbanburg," Sköll said grandly, "whom everyone fears. They told me of you! They told me of a man who wins battles, who soaks the land with his enemy's blood, who is the warlord of Britain! Even I began to fear you!"

"You should," Finan said.

"I took counsel," Sköll ignored Finan. "I, Sköll of Northumbria, took counsel of my fears! Suppose the great Uhtred was in Jorvik when I attacked the city? How could I win? Would my wolf banner hang as a trophy in Uhtred's great hall? If I am to be king in Northumbria then I must rule on both sides of the hills, and Uhtred rules on the eastern side! And my friend Arnborg persuaded me you could be tricked, that you could be sent to," he paused, "what was the name of the place?"

"Ceaster," I said.

"To Ceaster, yes! I planned to trap you on the way,

overwhelm you, but you took a different road. You escaped me."

"The gods love me," I said, and touched the hammer to fend off any offense I might give the gods with that bald claim, then thought it was not true. The gods had cursed me.

"I would have begun my conquest of Northumbria with your death," Sköll said. "I would have drunk my victory from your skull, but it was your daughter I killed instead."

I felt a pulse of fury and managed to suppress it. "And her forces drove you from Jorvik," I retorted. "What a conqueror you are, to be defeated by a woman!"

"I took much plunder, many cattle, slaves." He shrugged. "A kingdom is not conquered easily, if it were easy it would not be worth conquering. But conquer it I will. Snorri has seen it. He has seen that I will be king in Northumbria!"

"The only part of Northumbria you will rule is called your grave," I said.

"And you stand in my way," Sköll went on as though I had not spoken. "But I have met you now, Uhtred of Bebbanburg," he said, "I have seen you for what you are, an old man! A graybeard who cannot protect his own daughter, an old man who fled from me! You went south, desperate to escape me. You ran!"

"Only after I defeated your son."

At our first meeting that comment had roused Sköll to immediate fury, but this time he just shrugged as though he did not care. "He still lives, but he is wounded here." He tapped his head. "He cannot speak. He might as well be dead. I regret that, but I have other sons." He even smiled at me as he said those words. "So I took one of yours, you took one of mine. We are equal, yes?"

My father told me that when an enemy talks it is because he dares not fight. Sköll, I admit, was surprising me. He was staying calm and speaking reasonably and that meant he was less impetuous than I had thought, but self-control does not win kingdoms. He had come to Bebbanburg with a purpose. So far the village had not been plundered, and no pyres of smoke smeared the western sky, which meant no halls had been burned and no farms put to the fire. He might call me old, but the very fact that he was talking told me he still feared me, and the fact that he had not burned any of my tenants' steadings, nor ransacked the village suggested that his purpose was not to fight me. He had been waiting for my answer, but I had said nothing. "We are equal, yes?" he asked again.

"We shall be equal," I said, "when I kill you."

Sköll shook his head, as if he was disappointed in me.

"No," he said, "you won't. Snorri has seen your future. Shall he reveal it to you?" Again I did not answer and Sköll turned to his sorcerer. "Tell them, Snorri."

"At the fortress of the eagles," Snorri said dully, and the small dog, hearing his master's voice, whined. "Three kings will fight." Snorri abruptly stopped speaking. His vacant eye sockets had been facing the harbor as if what he said was irrelevant to us, which only made his strangely bored tone even more unsettling.

"Three kings," Sköll prompted him.

"Two with crowns and one without," Snorri said. He stroked the wolf skull. "And two kings will die."

"And what of me?" Sköll demanded, though in a respectful tone.

"The *úlfhéðnar* will make great slaughter," the sorcerer intoned, "the blood of their enemies will flow like streams in spate. The ravens will gorge on flesh till they vomit, the wolves will rend the carcasses, the widows will wear ashes in their hair, and King Sköll will rule." He shuddered suddenly, then bent as if in agony. "All this I have seen, lord King."

"And Uhtred of Bebbanburg," Sköll laid a hand on Snorri's thin shoulder and spoke in a surprisingly gentle tone, "what of him?"

Snorri suddenly moaned as if uttering prophecy hurt him. He had spoken distantly till now, but Sköll's question roused his voice to an agonizing screech. "He is the king without a crown," he pointed a wavering finger toward me, "and the Dane and the Saxon will join forces, and Uhtred will be betrayed. He will die by the sword, his fortress will fall, and his descendants will eat the dung of humility." Snorri crouched, moaning, and I heard him mutter, "No more, lord King, no more. Please, lord King, no more." The small dog licked his face as Snorri groped for the rope leash.

I felt a shiver in my spine and said nothing. I had heard prophecies before, and some had come true and some had yet to come true and some seemed false, though translating the words of sorcerers always demanded skill. As often as not they spoke in riddles and any question about their meaning was usually answered by more riddles.

"Did Snorri foretell that you'd conquer Jorvik?" Finan surprised me by asking.

"He did," Sköll surprised me even more by admitting it.

"So he was wrong," Finan sneered.

"I was wrong," Sköll said. "I asked the wrong question. I only asked him if I would capture the city, I did not ask how often I would need to try." He still had his hand on the crouching sorcerer's shoulder. "Now

be brave," he said to Snorri, "and tell Uhtred of Bebbanburg how he might escape the fate of the Norns."

Snorri raised his face so I was looking straight into
those ravaged eye sockets. "He must sacrifice, lord
King. The gods demand his best horse, his best hound,
his best warrior. There must be sword, blood, and fire,
a sacrifice."

There was a moment's silence. The wind whipped
the dune grass and lifted Snorri's long hair. "And?"
Sköll asked gently.

"And he must stay inside his ramparts," Snorri said.

"And if he won't sacrifice or stay?" Sköll asked, and
the only reply was a cackling laugh from Snorri and
another whine from the small dog. Sköll stepped back.
"I came to tell you all this, Uhtred of Bebbanburg," he
said. "If you fight me, you die. The Norns have decided and the shears are ready to cut your life thread.
Leave me alone and you live, fight me and you die." He
turned as if to walk away, but something caught his eye
and he turned back to stare past me. I saw a shadow
cross his face and I looked back to see that Ieremias, his
long white hair blowing in the wind, had come from
the Skull Gate and was watching us. He was wearing
his bishop's robes, and in the sunlight he looked as sorcerous as Snorri. "Who is that?" Sköll asked.

Ieremias suddenly began capering, I had no idea why. He danced, turned, and lifted the bishop's crozier high, and the rising sun flashed a bright reflection from the silver crook. "I see no one," I said. "Do you see anyone, Finan?"

Finan turned, looked, and shrugged. "Only spearmen on the wall."

"Your sorcerer!" Sköll insisted.

Ieremias had stopped capering and now raised both arms to the heavens. I assumed he was praying. "My sorcerer died a year ago," I said.

"His ghost appears though," Finan added.

"But only to doomed men," I finished.

Sköll touched his hammer. "You don't frighten me," he snarled, though the expression on his face said otherwise. "Snorri," he snapped, "come."

The small dog nudged Snorri to his feet and both men walked back toward the waiting horsemen.

"What of my men?" I shouted after Sköll. "Your prisoners?"

"You can have them," he called without turning. "I captured twelve of your men. The other eight I killed."

He plucked Grayfang from the sand, turned, and pointed the blade toward me. "When I am king in Jorvik you will come to swear me loyalty. Till that day, Uhtred of Bebbanburg, farewell." He slammed the long blade into its scabbard, mounted his gray horse, and rode away.

The gods like sacrifice. If we give them something precious it tells them that we hold them in awe, that we fear their power, and that we are grateful to them. A generous sacrifice will gain their favor, while an inadequate offering will bring down their enmity.

Sköll had come to Bebbanburg, and, instead of fighting, he had offered me prophecy and a truce. He had released the four prisoners unharmed, then left as he had come, quickly and without violence. And he and his sorcerer had unsettled me, which was why they had come.

"So, you must sacrifice?" Finan asked me that evening. We were walking on Bebbanburg's long sand, the endless sea roaring to our left, the looming ramparts gaunt above us. The sun had not yet set, but we were in the fort's deep shadow, which stretched far across the restless waters.

"Damn sacrifice," I said, and touched the hammer.

"You don't believe the sorcerer?"

"Do you?"

Finan paused as a great breaker crashed on the shore. The white foam ran fast up the sand, and I thought that if the foam reaches me I would be damned, but it stopped a hand's breadth from my foot, and then the water sucked back. "I have known sorcerers tell truth," Finan said cautiously, "and known them lie through their teeth. But this one?" He left the question hanging.

"He was convincing," I said.

Finan nodded. "He was. Until the end."

"The end?"

"He forgot to say you must stay inside the ramparts. Sköll had to remind him." He kicked some bladder-wrack and frowned. "I think Snorri was saying what Sköll wanted him to say, what they had practiced saying."

"Perhaps," I said. I was not so sure.

"And what they practiced saying," Finan went on, "would persuade you not to fight him. He might call you old, lord, but he fears you still."

"Perhaps," I said again.

"He fears you, lord!" Finan insisted. "Why else release the prisoners? Because he fears you. He doesn't want you as an enemy."

"He killed my daughter. He knows that makes him my enemy."

"But Snorri has convinced him he shouldn't fight you! He didn't come to frighten us, he came to persuade you from fighting."

I wanted to believe that, but how could I know if it

was true? I looked for an omen, but only saw the first stars showing above the shadowed sea. "You forget," I said, "that the gods have cursed me."

"Damn your gods," Finan said savagely.

"And when the gods talk," I went on as though he had not spoken, "we must listen."

"Then listen to Ieremias," Finan said, still angry, "he and God talk to each other morning, noon, and night."

I turned and looked at him. "You're right," I said. Ieremias did speak with a god. That god was not my god, but I am not such a fool as to believe that the Christian god has no power. He does. He is a god! He has power, as do all the gods, but alone among the gods of Britain the Christian god insisted that he was the only god! He was like a mad jarl in his hall who refused to believe there were other halls where other jarls lived, yet for all his madness the Christian god had ordered the mad bishop to give me a stone.

I felt in my pouch and brought out the sling-stone, which was little more than a large pebble. I rolled it in the palm of my hand and thought that if I carried the stone then the Christian god would reward me with victory. That was Ieremias's promise. Yet surely, I thought, my own gods would be furious if I were to rely on the gift and on the promise of a god who hated them, who denied their existence, yet did all he could to destroy them. A curse, I realized, was a test, and the Christian promise of victory was a temptation to abandon my own gods. Two sorcerers had spoken to me; one promised victory, the other defeat, and I would defy them both to amuse the gods.

And so I turned to the sea, to the fort-shadowed, wind-stirred, white-flecked sea, and I drew back my arm. "This is for Odin," I shouted, "and for Thor," and then I hurled the stone as far as I could. It flew above the waters and vanished into the curling foam of a breaking wave. I paused, staring at the ever-shifting sea, then looked at Finan. "We're going to Heahburh," I said. The sorcerer be damned. We would fight.

Ten

We gathered at Heagostealdes, a large village just south of the great wall. The settlement lay on the Roman road that came north from Eoferwic, threaded the Roman wall, and ended at Berewic, the most northerly burh in Northumbria and a part of Bebbanburg's estates. I was forced to keep warriors in Berewic to help the men of the settlement defend the earth and timber walls against the Scots who insisted it was in their land, but that springtime I left only five men, and those were old or half-crippled, because I would take as many warriors as I could to meet Sköll. I left another eighteen men, helped by the fishermen of the village, to guard Bebbanburg. That was a perilously small garrison, but enough to defend the Skull Gate. Merchants traveling south from Scotland had told me King Constantin was in the north of his country, skirmishing with the Norse who had settled there, and none spoke of men gathering for war near the southern border. King Constantin was doubtless watching Sköll, looking for an opportunity to take advantage of Northumbria's quarrels, and he would have liked nothing more than to capture Berewic or Bebbanburg while I was gone, but by the time he heard I had stripped the fortresses of their usual garrisons I expected the war against Sköll to be over.

It had taken long hard days to prepare; days of sharpening swords, cleaning and repairing mail, binding willow-board shields with iron, honing arrowheads, and riveting spear-blades to ash shafts. The smithy made new war axes and fixed the heavy blades to extralong hafts. The women of Bebbanburg baked bread and oatcakes, we packed boxes with hard cheese, smoked fish, dried mutton, and bacon, all from the stores left over from a frugal winter. We made ladders because, as far as Ieremias could remember, the old Roman walls still protected the fort. "They're not high, lord," he told me, "they're not like the walls of Jericho! No higher than a man. You could take small horns?"

"Small horns?"

"The ramparts of Jericho required large horns, lord,

but the walls of Halfdan the Mad's fort will fall to lesser instruments."

I preferred to rely on ladders instead. We repaired saddles, wove seal-hide ropes for the packhorses, and brewed ale. We made two new wolf's head banners and one day I had found Hanna, Berg's young Saxon wife, busily embroidering a different banner, which showed an eagle with spread wings. She had used a large piece of pale linen onto which the eagle, cut from black cloth, showed bold. "I hate sewing, lord," she greeted me.

"You're doing a good job," I said. I liked Hanna. "Where did you get the black cloth?"

"It's one of Father Cuthbert's cassocks," she said. "He won't miss it. He's blind. Can't count your cassocks if you're blind."

"And why," I asked, "are we making an eagle flag? We fight under the sign of the wolf's head."

"Better ask Berg," Hanna said, grinning. "I just do what I'm told."

"You have changed then," I said, and went to find Berg, who was practicing with one of the long-hafted axes.

"It's clumsy, lord," he said, hefting the long weapon, and he was right. The ax blade, with its deep beard, was heavy, and the whole weapon, with its sturdy ash shaft, was as long as a spear. "It needs two hands," he went on, "so I can't hold a shield while I use it."

"And it might just save your life. Tell me about eagles."

"Eagles?"

"A flag."

He looked sheepish. "It was my father's flag, lord. The banner of Skallagrimmr." He paused, plainly hoping that was explanation enough, but when I said nothing he reluctantly continued. "And we're going to fight against my people, the Norse."

"We are."

"And I would like them to know that the family of Skallagrimmr is their enemy, lord. It will frighten them!"

I hid a smile. "It will?"

"Lord," he spoke earnestly, "my father was a great warrior, a famous warrior! My brothers are great warriors. Sköll knows this!"

"You're a great warrior," I told him, pleasing him. "Is your father still alive?"

"He went to sea, lord, and never returned. I think the goddess took him for her own," he touched his hammer. "But I hear my brothers still live. And Egil and Thorolf are *úlfhéðnar*! When Sköll's people see the banner of the eagle, lord, they will know fear!"

"Then you'd better carry the banner," I said. I was fond of Berg, whose life I had saved on the Welsh beach and who had rewarded me with utter loyalty ever since. "Why didn't you stay with your brothers?" I asked him.

"Egil said it was not their task to teach a boy how to fight. So they sent me viking with another jarl."

"Who led you to a slaughter on a foreign beach."

He smiled. "Fate was good to me, lord."

I did more than prepare weapons and pack supplies. I sent more strong patrols west into the hills searching for news. Those patrols brought back reports that Sköll had retreated into the higher ground, presumably to Heahburh, though I would not let any of my men go close to where we thought that fortress stood.

Sköll knew we were searching for him and would be preparing for war, just as I was. He might hope that he had persuaded me to refuse battle, but even if I had taken his advice he would still have had to face an angry Sigtryggr, whose troops, I knew, were scouring southern Cumbraland. "Sigtryggr needs to leave troops south of Heahburh," I had told Eadith on the night before we rode to Heagostealdes.

"Why?"

I gazed up at the smoke that drifted into our sleeping chamber from the great hall and tried to see an omen in its shifting shapes. I saw nothing. Earlier that day I had watched a cat stalking a mouse and knew that if the mouse died then Sköll would die, but the mouse had escaped. "Heahburh," I said, "is a strong fort, but it's evidently high in the hills and far from anywhere." Sköll's sorcerer had called it the fortress of the eagles, and eagles nested in remote high places. "We think Sköll's staying in his fortress," I explained. "None of our scouts have seen his troops moving, but if I was Sköll? I'd cross the hills and attack Eoferwic."

"Why?" she asked again.

"Because Eoferwic is where the merchants are. It's where the money is."

"And money is power," she said.

"And money is power," I agreed, "and the land about Eoferwic is rich, and that means taxes and rents, and the money from taxes and rents becomes swords, spears, axes, and shields. And Sköll's fastest road to Eoferwic is to go south."

"And you think he'll do that?"

"I fear he'll do that," I said.

Knowing what the enemy is doing or planning is always the hardest thing in war. Sigtryggr's messengers reported that the Norse steadings around the Ribbel estuary had been stripped of men, and that, so far as they could determine, all those men had gone north to wherever Sköll was gathering his army. Sköll's lunge to Eoferwic at winter's end had been his declaration of war, and it had very nearly succeeded. His ride to Bebbanburg had been an attempt to persuade me to sit that war out because he knew that the coming battle would decide who ruled in Northumbria, but where would that battle be? If I had been Sköll I would have crossed the hills and brought the war to the richer eastern side of Northumbria, forcing us to pursue him and fight him in a place of his choosing, and that was why Sigtryggr was compelled to guard the routes that led south across the hills. We planned to approach Heahburh from the east, but feared Sköll might escape southward before we brought him to battle, and also feared that the forces guarding those southern routes would prove too weak to delay him while we struggled to catch up. Those fears kept me awake at nights, but all the reports seemed to confirm Sköll was staying in the high hills where his fortress stood, and where he was inviting us, daring us even, to assault him.

"What if he reaches Eoferwic?" Eadith asked.

"He'll capture it," I said bleakly.

"There'll be a garrison? And the men of the town?"

"A small garrison," I said, "and yes, the men of the town will help. But if you have *úlfhéðnar* climbing ladders you don't want silversmiths and leather-workers waiting for them. You want warriors."

"And what if he comes here?" Eadith asked.

"You don't do what my daughter did," I said grimly. "You hold the Skull Gate and wait for us to return."

I led one hundred and eighty-four men to Heagoste-aldes, and with them went thirty of my tenants who were skilled hunters with their bows, and over ninety boys and servants. Our packhorses were heavy with shields, spears, food, and ale. Sihtric of Dunholm, who held that great fortress in my name, brought sixty-two men. Sigtryggr arrived with a hundred and forty-three household warriors, while his jarls, those men who held estates and owed Sigtryggr allegiance, brought another one hundred and four. That was far fewer than Sig-tryggr had hoped. "So we have close to five hundred men," he said gloomily on the night we gathered in the village. "I expected more. But those bastards in the south," he left the sentence unfinished, but I knew he was talking of those Danes on Northumbria's southern border who had made their peace with Christian Mer-cia. "We're not fighting Mercia, but they still wouldn't send men. Bastards."

"And we can't punish them," I said, "because they're under Edward's protection."

"Then I had to give Boldar Gunnarson ninety men," Sigtryggr added gloomily, "and he needs double that number."

Boldar was one of his commanders, an older man of sense and caution, who was leading the troops who were guarding the roads leading to Eoferwic in southern Cumbraland. "Boldar will let us know if he's in trouble," I said, "and five hundred men should be enough to take Heahburh."

"You know that?"

"No." I shrugged. "But Sköll will be lucky to have five hundred, so it should be enough."

"Rumor says he has more than five hundred."

"Rumor always exaggerates the enemy," I said, and hoped I was right.

"And he has the *úlfhéðnar*."

"And I have this," I showed him the jar that Brother Beadwulf had made for me so many weeks before. The jar's wide top was stoppered with a plug of wood and sealed with wax.

"What is it?"

"An ointment that turns a man into an *úlfheðinn*. Henbane."

"Pig poison!" He hefted the jar. "How many men will this serve?"

"I don't know. A dozen?"

"I tried it once," he said ruefully, "and I was sick for a week." He put the jar on the table, then stood and walked to the tavern door. It was nighttime and the street outside was lit by flaming torches. He leaned on the doorjamb, staring into the night. "There are times," he said, "when I wish you'd never made me king."

"I know."

"I could have gone viking," he said.

"Maybe that's what we should do," I suggested. "Let Sköll be king, and you and I will live at Bebbanburg and keep a fleet. Think of all the new monasteries in Wessex! Great buildings stuffed with silver! We'll be richer than kings!"

He laughed. He knew I was not serious. "I paid a skald to look into the future," he said suddenly and softly.

I felt a shiver. "What did he say?"

"It was a woman."

I touched Thor's hammer. "And she said?"

"She gave me back my silver." He still spoke softly and I felt the shiver again. "She said the future was a mist and she could not see through it, but I think she did see and dared not tell me." He turned to me. "Finan said you met Sköll's sorcerer?"

"We did, but he spoke nonsense," I said dismissively. "He just said what Sköll wanted him to say."

"He talked of kings dying?"

Finan, I thought, should have kept silent. "He talked

nonsense," I said forcibly, "he babbled about eagles and a king without a crown." I had to steel myself not to touch the hammer as I spoke. Snorri had said three kings would go to the high place, and two would die. Sköll was one of the kings, Sigtryggr the second, and I was the third, the king without a crown. And two of us must die. Yet none of that made sense. Snorri had said that the Dane and the Saxon would betray me, and what had that to do with a war against the Norse? "It was nothing but nonsense," I insisted.

Sigtryggr came back to the table and sat. "Why did Sköll go to meet you?"

I frowned, wondering if Sigtryggr suspected me of disloyalty. "To persuade me not to fight him, of course."

"Yes, but why? He knows he killed your daughter. What made him think you might give up a chance of revenge?"

I suddenly understood what he was saying, and the realization struck me with the same force that the curse had made all those weeks before. I stared at Sigtryggr. "Because . . ." I began, then dared not say the words in case even speaking them made them untrue.

"Because," Sigtryggr spoke the words for me, "his sorcerer foretold that you would kill him."

"No," I said, but without conviction.

"Why else try to dissuade you?" he asked, then paused, but I said nothing. I gazed into the tavern's fire where a log spat. "I can't think why else he went to you," Sigtryggr said.

"We can't know the future," I said. "But I hope you're right."

"Stiorra would have cast the runesticks," he said wistfully. "She always said she could tell the future from the sticks."

"And Stiorra," I said, "is why we must kill Sköll."

He nodded. "I know."

As ever, a mention of my daughter tore at my heart. I wanted to talk of something else, anything else. "How's Queen Eadgyth?" I asked.

"Still pious," he said curtly.

"Like her brother and her grandfather."

"She doesn't cry as much as she did. She endures me," he said wryly, "and she even nags me!"

"Nags you?"

"She says I should wash more often. And you were right. She's clever."

"So you like her," I said, amused.

"I feel sorry for her. She's married to an unwashed king in a dying kingdom."

"Now you're the one talking nonsense," I said.

But I feared he spoke the truth. Wyrd bið ful āræd.

———

I could not sleep that night in Heagostealdes, and for a time I walked the small streets wondering if Sigtryggr was right in thinking that Sköll had only ridden to Bebbanburg because he feared his own sorcerer's prophecy. I wanted to believe that and searched for an omen, but found none.

There was a monastery in Heagostealdes, a surprisingly lavish building, and I heard singing as I neared it. The monastery's outer gate was open and I walked to the big church from which candlelight leaked through a high arched doorway. I stood under the arch and saw that at least a hundred warriors were inside, kneeling on the flagstones with their heads bowed as they listened to the chanting of monks. Some went on their knees to the altar and kissed the white cloth, and I knew they were preparing themselves for death.

"You can go in," an amused voice spoke behind me.

I turned and saw it was Father Swithred, the priest who had brought the message from Æthelhelm and who had ridden this far with us. In the morning he would carry on south to Mercia, while we struck westward.

"I like listening," I said.

"It is a beautiful sound," he agreed.

I nodded at the candlelit nave. "You know who those men are?"

"Warriors of Northumbria?"

"Half are mine," I said, "and the other half? Some of them follow Jarl Sihtric, others are sworn to King Sigtryggr."

"You want me to be impressed, lord," he said drily, and for once he did not leave a pause before saying "lord."

"Do I?"

"That Christians follow you, a pagan."

I shrugged. "They do."

"But what choice do you have?" Swithred asked. "If you refused to let Christians serve, then your armies would be weaker. They would be too weak. You keep your power, lord, because of Christians. You need Christian help." He paused, wanting me to say something, but I kept silent. "Your son is in there, yes?" he asked, nodding at the kneeling men.

"Probably."

"So one day, lord, Bebbanburg will be Christian too."

"But my son," I said angrily, "will still employ pagans."

"Not if he's a good son of the church, lord."

Swithred had never liked me and he had succeeded in nettling me. I touched the hammer at my breast. "None of us knows the future," I said curtly, and thought of three kings in the place of the eagle.

"But we do, lord," Swithred said softly.

"We do?"

"We Christians know what is to come. Christ will return in His glory, the great horn of heaven will sound, the dead will rise, and the Kingdom of God will rule on earth. Of that much we can be certain."

"Or the sun will turn dark, the warriors of Valhalla will fight for the gods, and the world will fall into chaos," I said. "Tell me something useful, priest, like what will happen three or four days from now."

"Three days, lord?"

"We're two days from Sköll's stronghold," I said, "so three or four days from now those warriors," I nodded into the church, "will probably be fighting for their lives."

Swithred watched as the worshippers stood. The chanting had stopped and an elderly monk was standing in front of the altar, presumably to preach. "In three or four days, lord," Swithred spoke low, "your men will fight to defeat a pagan tyrant. God will be on their side, and if God is with you, how can you lose?"

"Have you ever assaulted a fortress?" I asked, but did not give him time to answer. "It's the most brutal kind of fighting there is, worse even than a shield wall." I touched my hammer again. "Go tell King Edward that our men will die to keep the promises we made him at Tamweorthin."

"Ten days ago," Swithred still spoke quietly, "the king fell from his horse while hunting."

I had thought that this meeting with Father Swithred had been an accident, but those last words told me he had wanted to find me. He had brought me the formal letter complaining of Sköll's raids south of the Ribbel, but I now understood he had also brought a second message, one that could not be written down, and one that he had waited to deliver. "I'm surprised the king still hunts," I said, "he looked an ill man to me."

"King Edward loves to hunt," Swithred said.

"Women or deer?" I asked.

"Both," he said sharply, surprising me with his honesty. "He fell from his horse," he continued his tale, "and broke two ribs."

"Ribs mend," I said, "it's painful, though." The elderly monk had begun preaching, but his voice was weak so I could not hear him, not that I wanted to, but the men in the church shuffled closer to listen, making it even less likely that anyone could overhear our conversation. One of the four tall candles on the altar had begun to gutter, spewing a tangle of dark smoke. If it goes out before the service ends, I thought, then we will fail. The flame must stay lit, I convinced myself, to prove that Sigtryggr was right in thinking that Snorri had foreseen Sköll's death. If the candle went out, then Sigtryggr was wrong, we would fail, and Sköll would defeat us. I hated myself for such impulsive thoughts, for seeking an omen about life and death in the ordinary incidents of life, but how else could the gods talk to us without a sorcerer? I could not take my eyes from the struggling flame. "Have you ever broken a rib? I asked Swithred.

He ignored the question. He had more important things to say. "The king is not well," he said, "he has fevers. His flesh is bloated and his urine black."

"Because he fell from his horse?"

"The accident has made his health worse. Much worse."

"How long does he have?" I asked brutally.

"Who knows? A year, lord? Two years? A week?" Swithred did not seem offended by my question, nor particularly saddened at these forecasts of his king's death. "We pray he recovers, of course."

"Of course," I said with the same amount of sincerity that Swithred had used. The candle's smoke thickened.

"The king," Swithred went on, speaking even lower

now, "is being carried to Wintanceaster." The candle flickered, but stayed alight. "He commanded Prince Æthelstan to remain in Tamweorthin."

"As ruler of Mercia?" I asked.

"As the king's loyal deputy," Swithred said, and he was now speaking so low that I could hardly hear him. "The prince prays for his father daily."

Prays what, I wondered. That Edward would die? Æthelstan, I had come to realize, had an ambition as keen as any sword edge. "A son should pray for his father," I said.

Swithred ignored those dutiful words. "And the prince," he continued in a voice that was scarce more than a whisper, "further prays that you will go south if you hear the news of King Edward's death."

Those last words made me turn to him. So he knew of my oath to Æthelstan? We had agreed to keep that pact secret, but Swithred, who was one of Æthelstan's confessors and who now gazed innocently into the abbey church, must have known what his words meant. "So Prince Æthelstan," I said snidely, "needs pagan help?"

"If the pagan advances God's kingdom on earth, yes." He paused, still gazing into the church. "If a tree must be cut down, lord," he added, "the husbandman will use whatever ax is the sharpest."

I almost smiled at that. The husbandman was Æth-elstan, the tree was Æthelhelm, and I was the ax. "And what of you?" I asked.

"Me, lord?" Swithred turned to me with a puzzled look.

"You admitted to me that you send reports to King Edward. Have you reported that Prince Æthelstan wants me to go south at Edward's death?" I did not explain that going south meant killing Ealdorman Æthel-helm. I did not need to.

"I have not told the king any such news," Swithred said, "nor will I."

I frowned at him. "You've made your dislike of pagans very plain," I said, "so how can you possibly approve of the prince's request?"

"Approve?" Swithred asked in a very bland voice. "I do not know why the prince should seek such an assurance, lord," he said, lying through his teeth, "I am merely the messenger."

"Then tell Prince Æthelstan," I said, "that I will keep my word."

"Thank you, lord," he said, and, for the first time since he had met me, he sounded civil.

I looked back into the church. The candle had guttered out.

Then forth went the host, mighty in battle
Spearmen in armor, following their lords,
The host of the Northmen, eager were their blades.
King Sigtryggr led them, strong in resolve . . .

That is how a poet, a young priest from Eoferwic, began his description of our leaving Heagostealdes, which only proves that you can never trust a poet. He made it sound as if we rode out in good order, but in truth it was a shambles. Sigtryggr might have been strong in resolve, but he was also irritated and impatient, as packhorses were reloaded, ropes broke, men sheltered from a drizzling rain by waiting in the taverns where they demanded more ale, two of his jarls got into a fight over a missing horse and their followers turned it into a brawl that left two men dead and six wounded, and it was almost midday by the time the host went forth. Sigtryggr's men were the vanguard, while mine brought up the rear, following the vast herd of packhorses. But, despite the weather and the delays, the mighty host of the Northmen was at last moving. With two women.

There were probably many more women, there usually are, but these two made no attempt to conceal themselves among the boys and servants, instead they rode on gray horses and wore mud-spattered white robes. They were both young, perhaps about sixteen or seventeen years old, and wore their hair long and unbound like unmarried girls. "Dear Christ above," Finan said when he saw them.

They were led by a third extraordinary figure, Ieremias, dressed in his bishop's finery, who galloped recklessly alongside my column waving frantically. "Lord, lord, lord," he greeted me happily as he tried to curb his horse. "Whoa, Beelzebub. Whoa!" He finally brought the horse under control and smiled at me. "I have brought the angels, lord."

"Angels," I said flatly.

"Elwina and Sunniva, lord," Ieremias said, gesturing at the two girls and plainly believing he had solved whatever problems I might have. "They are angels, lord," he insisted, sensing my disbelief.

"They look like women to me," I said. Good-looking women too, which suggested the angels could cause trouble among my men.

"You must look with the eyes of faith," Ieremias chided me. "I could not let you ride against Sköll without the help of angels. God commanded me! He told me that even the stone of David will not give you victory without my angels." He paused, frowning. "You do still have the stone, lord?"

"Of course I do," I lied.

"Then we shall smite mightily," he said smugly.

"I also have something from a pagan sorcerer," I said to tease him.

He stared at me in horror. "You have . . ." he paused and made the sign of the cross. "What do you have?"

"A jar of ointment that turns men into wolves."

"No, lord, no! It is the devil's unguent! You must give it to me!"

"My servant has it," I said carelessly. In truth I was not quite sure why I had brought the jar and certainly had no intention of trying the ointment, but I had still been reluctant to discard it.

"I will protect you from Satan's wiles, lord," Ieremias said, "and my angels will stand guard over you."

I thought of sending him back to Lindisfarena, but on a chill spring day of drizzle his arrival, or at least the appearance of his two angels, had brought smiles to my men's faces. "Just keep your women safe," I said, "I don't want trouble."

"Lord," he remonstrated, "there can be no trouble. Elwina and Sunniva are heavenly beings! And in heaven there is no marriage."

"I wasn't talking about marriage."

"We shall all be chaste in heaven, lord!"

"Chaste?" I asked. "And you call that heaven?" I gave him no time to answer. "Take your women, make sure they stay chaste, and ride with the baggage."

"We shall pray for you, lord," Ieremias said, then beckoned his bedraggled angels to follow as he spurred ahead to join the servants and packhorses.

"What does he want?" my son asked.

"He's bringing us angelic help."

"We need it," he said, and so we did because we were making slow progress. The larger an army, I have found, the slower it moves as men try to keep to the tracks or stay on firmer ground, and so the column stretches, and, at any obstacle, it tangles itself, stops, and so stretches even further as the front of the column moves ahead. We were following the southern bank of the Lower Tine and the first few miles were easy enough as we rode through river meadows and past burned-out steadings, but low clouds misted the hilltops, which meant Sigtryggr's scouts were forced to ride on the lower slopes. Our disordered column would have made easy meat if Sköll had horsemen on those hills, but the day passed without sight of an enemy.

The clouds lifted in the late afternoon and with them went the steady drizzle that had been soaking us. My son rode with me most of the way and frowned as we passed yet another farm that was nothing but blackened ruin. "Sköll's work?" he suggested.

"More likely the Scots. Sköll needs all the food a farmer can grow."

"We're south of the wall?" he asked.

"We are." I knew what he was thinking, that if we garrisoned the old Roman wall and its forts we would keep Scottish cattle-raiders well away from most of Northumbria's farmlands, but, as I told him, we would need an army twenty times the size of this one just to man the forts. "Besides," I went on, "if we garrison the wall it becomes our frontier and we give Constantin all the land north of it, including Bebbanburg. He'd like that."

The Tine has two headwaters and we were keeping to the southern branch. The Upper Tine twisted through the hills to the borderlands with Scotland and its valley offered an easy route to the pastures of Northumbria. But at least the Scots weren't making trouble for us, at least not yet. They had problems of their own with the Norsemen who had settled their western coast, and that thought made me wonder about Sköll's ambitions. He would not recognize any frontier between Northumbria and Scotland, and he would surely find allies among the Scottish Norse, and even among the Irish who had settled in Strath Clota. Did he dream of a whole new northern kingdom that stretched to the wild cliffs of the far north? "Maybe we should ally with the Scots," I said to my son.

"Good God!" He stared at me, thinking I had gone as mad as Ieremias. "Make an alliance with the Scots?"

"We have the same enemies."

"The Norse, yes, but who else?"

"The Ænglisc, of course."

Now he really did think I was crazed. "But we are the Ænglisc!" he protested.

The Ænglisc! I think that was the first time I ever called the Saxons of Britain by that strange name. Now, of course, we all say we are Ænglisc, but it still seems weird to me. The Ænglisc of Englaland! That was King Alfred's dream, to make a new nation out of old kingdoms. "We're not Ænglisc," I growled, "we're Northumbrians." And so we were, which meant that we were the smallest kingdom of all those that had been settled by the Angles and the Saxons. I was not being serious about an alliance with the Scots, of course; the only alliance they would ever offer Northumbria would be conquest and subjugation. I suppose that if Sköll had not killed my daughter it would have made sense to reach an agreement with Cumbraland's Norsemen, and perhaps, I thought, with Sköll dead, many of his men might swear allegiance to Sigtryggr, and Northumbria would then possess enough strength to fight off the Ænglisc to the south and the Scots to the north. If Sigtryggr even survived the next few days, and that fear prompted me to touch my hammer. "We're Northumbrians," I said again to my son, "and we're something else. We're the lords of Bebbanburg."

He looked at me strangely, sensing that I was no longer speaking lightly. "We are," he agreed uncertainly, troubled by my tone.

"So one or two days from now," I went on, "when we fight, one of us must live."

He touched the cross at his breast. "I hope both of us live, Father."

I ignored that pious hope. "We have to keep Bebbanburg," I told him, "and your son won't be of age until he's much older, so you have to keep the fortress for him."

"Or you can," he muttered.

"Don't be a fool!" I snarled. "I can't live that long!" I touched the hammer again. "Bebbanburg has been in our family for almost three hundred years, and it should still belong to us when the world ends." I thought of Snorri's prophecy, that the Dane and the Saxon would unite against me, that I would die by the sword, that Bebbanburg would be lost, and my children's children would eat the dung of humility. I pushed that memory away, telling myself that Snorri had deliberately been trying to frighten me with riddles. "You have to survive this fight," I said harshly.

"You want me to hold back from fighting?" my son asked bitterly. He still felt the keen shame of losing so many men to Sköll's ambush and the need to prove himself all over again.

"Yes," I said harshly. "You hold back. If I die, you must live. If we lose this fight, you have to escape, and you have to live long enough to see your son become the Lord of Bebbanburg."

I have fought many battles. I have stood in shield walls and heard the sound of axes biting willow boards, I have heard men howling, heard them screaming, I have heard the butcher's sound of blades cleaving flesh, the heart-wrenching sound of grown men weeping for their mothers' comfort. I have heard the grating breath of the dying and the lament of the living, and in all those fights I have fought for one thing above all others. To take and to keep Bebbanburg.

So my son must live.

Hard were the foemen, hungry their swords.
And stout their ramparts, they offered death
To any man brave enough. Then stood Sigtryggr,
Bold in strife, and called on the Measurer . . .

"The measurer?" I asked the poet.

"The Measurer is the Lord God," he said. He was an inky-fingered young priest named Father Selwyn, a West Saxon who served Hrothweard, the archbishop of Eoferwic. "He measures our lives, lord."

"I thought the Norns did that," I said, and he looked at me blankly, "and besides," I went on, "Sigtryggr called on Odin for help."

"It's a poem, lord," he said weakly.

"Were you there?"

"No, lord."

"Who told you to write the poem?" I asked.

"The archbishop, lord."

Hrothweard of course wanted to spread the idea that Sigtryggr's baptism had converted a pagan into a Christian. That was not dishonesty, even if it was untrue, but rather Hrothweard's passionate hatred of warfare. Despite the treacherous Scots he still believed that no two Christian nations would ever go to war with each other, and so wanted to convince the Saxon south, and probably himself too, that Sigtryggr led a Christian nation. The archbishop ordered the poem to be copied by monks and sent south to be read aloud in halls and churches, though I suspect most copies were used to wipe arses or light fires.

We lit no fires that night, which we spent in an upland valley close to the river. We put sentries on the higher ground, and deep in that cold night Finan and I climbed to join one group of men who crouched in the lee of a boulder and gazed westward. The low clouds had lifted and far to the west I could see one star through a rent in the night sky, and beneath it a flicker in the darkness, the dim glitter of firelight on a far-off hilltop. "That must be the fort," Finan said quietly. No other lights were visible. No fire burned in a hearth to leak flamelight past a shuttered window. The earth was as dark as it must have been when it was first made between the realms of fire and ice. I shivered.

And next day it was our turn to lead the column. We were still following the river, but now the Tine had shrunk to a size that could be easily crossed in places and so I had to put scouts on both flanks, north as well as south. I sent Eadric and Oswi to explore far ahead, trusting their ability to stay hidden. Eadric, the older man, had a poacher's ability to slide through country unseen, while Oswi had a natural cunning. He had been my servant once, and before that an orphan making a living by theft in the streets of Lundene. He had been caught trying to steal from my storeroom and brought to me for a whipping, but I had liked him, and he had served me ever since. Those two, the older man and the younger, would disappear into the hills, but closer to us I had two large and very visible bands of men, one on the southern skyline and the other high above the river's northern bank. Both bands numbered thirty men. I called them scouts, but I hoped both were large enough to deal with any attack that might come from Sköll's scouts. He must have men searching for us, I thought, but as the morning passed we saw no sign of them.

We still made slow progress. I might have scouts on either side, but I feared a sudden attack like that which had severed my son's troops, and so I insisted that the column close up and stay closed up, and that meant we could only move as fast as the slowest person on foot. The river slowed us even more because it was in spate, foaming around dead trees that had been carried downstream, and flooding its banks. In one place, where we were forced to ride around a churning flood, I saw Ieremias up to his knees in the rushing water. He had ridden to the head of the column, assuring me that was the best place where his god could warn him of danger, and something had caught his eye in the river. "What are you doing?" I called to him.

"The ram of Abraham, lord! The ram of Abraham!" he called excitedly, bending to his task.

I had no idea what he meant, nor how the ram of Abraham, whatever that was, had reached the Northumbrian hills, but nor did I want to ask for fear of a long and complicated answer. "And where are your angels?" I asked him instead.

"Safe, lord, safe! Still chaste!" He tugged at the tangled birch that half blocked the river, and I saw he was struggling to pull something from the gaunt branches. It proved to be a dead sheep, its fleece reduced to a sodden gray bundle and its body just bones. He managed to wrench free the skull that had a fine pair of curled horns. He held it up triumphantly. "See, lord? The heathen will be humbled! They shall be smitten!"

"By a dead ram?"

"Oh, thou of little faith!" He staggered in the fierce rush of water. "Didn't Sköll's sorcerer have a skull in his hands, lord? When he visited you?"

"A wolf skull."

"Then we need a skull! A Christian skull! Behold," he held up the ram's skull. "The ram of Abraham!"

He was still buffeted by the current's force as he tried to reach the river's edge so I reached down from the saddle, offered a hand, and helped him and his precious skull up onto the bank. "Stay out of trouble, bishop," I said, "your flock needs you."

"My flock are on their knees, lord, praying mightily for us."

By late morning I was beginning to fear that we

needed those prayers. I had joined the scouts on the crest of the southern hill and could see a smear of smoke in the west, but no enemy horsemen. The smoke, which seemed to come from a distant valley, betrayed a settlement, but if it was Heahburh then why did the smoke come from a valley? And we would surely have seen Sköll's men by now. Had they gone south? Were they even now pushing Sigtryggr's men out of their path and advancing on Eoferwic?

Then, at midday, we had word at last. Sköll and his army were waiting for us.

Eadric and Oswi brought the news. "They're at their fort, lord," Eadric said, "and it's a bastard."

"And we're on the wrong side of it," Oswi added gloomily.

I ignored Oswi's words for the moment. "How many?" I asked Eadric.

He shrugged. "Hard to tell, lord, most of them are inside the walls. Maybe two hundred outside? We couldn't get close, we had to watch the bastards from across the valley." He explained that the Tine was joined by a stream a couple of miles ahead. "The fort," he said, "is across the stream's valley."

"And it's steep," Oswi added.

"Is that why we're on the wrong side?"

"It'll be hard to attack from the valley this side,"

Oswi said, "but to the west there's a hill that overlooks the fort."

That sounded strange. Given a choice, no one would build a fort beneath a hill instead of on the summit, but the Romans were not fools, so if Oswi was right there had to be a reason. I looked at Eadric, who nodded confirmation of Oswi's news. "And it's a good-sized hummock, lord. Get on top of that, and the bastards will have a job to drive us away."

"They won't try," Sigtryggr said. He had joined us on the heights as soon as he saw the scouts returning, "we have to defeat them, which means we have to assault the fort. They won't attack us, they want us to attack them."

"The walls?" I asked Eadric.

"Big enough, lord. They're not like Ceaster or Bebbanburg, but you'll need the ladders." Like Oswi, he sounded gloomy.

"There were men outside, you said?"

"Scouring out ditches, lord."

"Odin help us," Sigtryggr said unhappily.

I pointed at the distant smear of smoke. "Is that Heahburh?"

Eadric shook his head. "That smoke's well to the south of the fort, lord, and closer to us."

"Lead smelting?" Finan suggested.

"Whatever it is," Sigtryggr said, "it can wait till we've taken the fort." He looked at me for agreement, and I nodded. "So let's look at the damn place," he finished.

We took sixty men, half Sigtryggr's and half mine, and, led by Eadric, spurred up into the hills. It seemed strange to be riding across the fells toward an enemy who was making no attempt to stop us. We had scouts ahead of us, but those riders saw nothing threatening. The fort, I thought, even if it was overlooked by a hill, had to be formidable if Sköll was content to let us approach it unchallenged, and the country we rode invited such an ambush because, though the rolling hills were bare, they were cut by steep valleys where streams, dark from the peat bogs, had worn down their beds as they tumbled to the Tine. It was a hard country, bleak and high, and perhaps the only reason the Romans had built their fort here was to protect the pits where their slaves had dug for lead and the furnaces where they had smelted the silver from the ore. There had to be a road, I thought, how else could the Romans carry away their ingots? And where, I wondered, had those ingots gone? All the way to distant Rome? And I thought of British lead and British silver being dragged across a whole world, through Frankia and whatever countries lay beyond.

I had met men who had journeyed to Rome, and they had told me the road was long and hard, it crossed mountains, only to end at a ruined city where wild dogs roamed and where great pillars and towering arches stood amidst the weeds. King Alfred had made the journey twice, both times to meet the Pope, and the king had told me how guards had been hired at the foot of the mountains to protect the travelers from the savages who lived in the high places. But the journey, he had told me, was worth the hardships and the dangers. "The city must have been glorious once," Alfred had recounted, "a wonder! But it was brought low by sin." As so often, he had been in a melancholy mood, regretting a fallen world. "We must make a new Rome," he had said, and I had imagined trying to build a great city from clay, wattles, timber, and thatch, but knew, as Alfred himself knew, that the world of glory was gone and we were sinking into a darkness of smoke, fire, savagery, and blood.

"Lord," Eadric startled me from my thoughts. "There, lord."

And I looked across the valley to see Heahburh. At last.

Then did Uhtred, hoary in winters,
Summon his men, eager for battle-slaughter,

Their swords keen-edged, their shields bound tight,
They prayed to the Measurer . . .

"There's that measurer again," I accused Father Selwyn.

"It's a poem, lord," he said weakly.

"And tell me," I spoke threateningly, "what does 'hoary in winters' mean?"

"That you're an experienced warrior, lord," he said promptly, he had obviously expected the question.

"Old, you mean."

"Experienced, lord, and your beard . . ." his voice faltered.

"Go on."

"Your beard is white, lord," he said, blushing, then paused. "Well, gray, lord." Another pause. "Grayish, lord?" he tried. "In places?"

"And my men," I went on, "were not eager for battle-slaughter."

"It's a poem, lord."

"My men were terrified," I told him. "They were frightened. I'd rather fight through the pits of hell than attack Heahburh again. It was a ghastly place."

It was, too. I first saw Heahburh from the hill across the southern valley, and, seeing it, I cursed the Romans. They had built the fort on a wide spur of land that jutted out from the heights to dominate the Tine's valley. We were a long way distant, perhaps a mile, but as we climbed the hill I saw more and more of the defenses, and understood why Sköll had chosen to wait for us rather than carry the war across the hills.

The fort, which had stone walls with stubby towers at each corner, was built across the spur's long crest. I reckoned the two longer walls were some one hundred and fifty paces each, the two shorter maybe a hundred. Those walls had decayed over the years, but Sköll, or maybe Halfdan the Mad who had once occupied Heahburh, had heightened and reinforced the broken places with stout timber barricades. There were buildings roofed with turf inside the fort and the ruins of smaller buildings just outside. Off to the west, where the long hill rose above the fort, I could see pits where, presumably, lead had been mined.

That rising ground to the fort's west was the obvious place from which to attack. The land between that higher ground and the fort was level, meaning attackers would not have to struggle uphill to reach the walls, but the Romans, or perhaps others who came after them, had seen the danger, and in front of the fort's western side there were rows of ditches and banks that wrapped around the northern and southern ramparts. They were the ditches that Eadric had watched being deepened. Finan, staring down at the place, made the sign of the cross. "That's a bastard," he said mildly.

Sigtryggr leaned on his saddle's pommel and just stared as a cloud shadow slid across the distant fort. He sighed, and I knew what he was thinking, that too many men must die in this high place. "If I was Sköll," he said, "I'd put a shield wall on those ditches."

"He doesn't need to," I said. "He can just let us stumble across the ditches and hurl spears at us."

"I can't see too well from here," Finan said, "but it looks as if the entrance behind the ditches is blocked off." There were four entrances, one on each of the fort's walls. There were well-worn paths from three of those gates, but outside the fourth gate, which faced the widest stretch of ditches and banks, the grass showed no wear.

"Maybe we just leave the bastard where he is," Sigtryggr said morosely.

"And do what?" I asked.

"He must have farms, his lead mines. Destroy them, force him to come out and fight for them."

I looked northward to the valley of the Tine and guessed most of Sköll's steadings were in the valley's depths. "And if he refuses to fight?" I asked.

Sigtryggr did not answer. Sköll wanted us to attack him, which was reason enough not to make an assault on his fortress. Our wisest course was to withdraw, but that gave him a victory he needed, a victory that might attract even more men to his banner of the wolf. And as we retreated he would follow us, eventually forcing us to turn and face him. "If we go south," Sigtryggr suggested, "we could combine with Boldar's men."

None of us said anything. None of us wanted to retreat, but nor did we want to carry our spears against that formidable fortress. "It will have to be fast," Sigtryggr said.

"The journey south?" Svart spoke for the first time.

"The assault," Sigtryggr said. "There'll be precious little water on that hill," he nodded to the land to the west of the hill, "and no shelter. We'll have to reach that hill, form the wall, and attack."

"There are horses in the fort," Finan said.

"Why wouldn't there be?" Sigtryggr asked irritably.

"We make a shield wall, lord King, and the bastard could release horsemen onto our flanks."

Sigtryggr grunted, plainly unhappy at Finan's words, but unable to deny their truth. "What choice do we have?" he asked. He was plainly reluctant to abandon an assault. We had marched so long, we had Sköll in front of us, and to retreat was to gamble on finding a friendlier battlefield.

"The Lord of Hosts is with you! You cannot fail!"

a voice called from lower down the slope, and I turned to see Ieremias spurring his horse Beelzebub to join us. Sigtryggr, who had less patience than I for the mad bishop, groaned. Ieremias was holding a stout staff on which he had managed to tie the ram's skull that, as he joined us, he pointed toward the fort. "The far corner, lords," he said, "that is where the heathen can best be smitten."

Sigtryggr looked annoyed, Svart was puzzled, but Finan knew that Ieremias had moments of sense. "The far corner?"

"Ragnar assaulted from there!" Ieremias was pointing the ram's skull at the northernmost corner of the fort, "and by God's grace we smote Halfdan the Mad."

"How many men did Halfdan lead?" I asked.

"A host, lord, a host," Ieremias said. Plainly he did not know.

"There's a host and a half down there," I pointed out.

"The Lord of Hosts is with you, how can you lose?"

"Easily," Sigtryggr snarled, but I could see he was still reluctant to abandon an attack on the fort. He twisted in his saddle to look at me. "Ragnar?" he asked.

"Knew what he was doing," I answered. "He was good."

He turned to stare at the fort again. We could not see the ground beyond the northern corner because the land there dropped away, which meant it would be an uphill attack from ground we had not yet seen. "We can't do it tomorrow," Sigtryggr said, "we need to scout it first." He paused, wanting someone to agree with his suggestion, but none of us spoke. "And if it looks impossible," he finished, "we'll march away."

"And if it's possible?" Svart asked.

"We attack," Sigtryggr said.

Which meant the Measurer, or rather the Norns, or perhaps both, would be measuring.

Eleven

War cries were loud. Ravens and eagles
Were eager for corpse-meat, the earth trembled.
Men let fly their spears, file sharpened,
Bows were loosed, shields hard blade-struck,
Bitter was the onslaught . . .

"Onslaught," I said quietly.

Father Selwyn looked at me anxiously. "Is that the wrong word, lord?" he asked.

I had not realized I had spoken aloud. "It's the right word," I assured the poet, "but I don't remember any eagles."

"Could there have been eagles, lord?"

"In those hills? I suppose so, yes. Their sorcerer called it the fortress of the eagles, so I suppose there must have been eagles." I paused, then added, "And of course there was Berg's banner."

"Berg's banner, lord?"

"You didn't hear about that?"

"No, lord."

"It showed an eagle," I said, smiling, then fell silent.

"Lord?" the young priest prompted me.

"It doesn't matter," I said, "think about eyes and lips instead."

"Eyes and what, lord?" he thought he had mis-heard me.

"Eyes and lips," I repeated. "They're the first things the ravens eat. Eagles too, probably. They perch on the helmet rim and begin with the eyeballs, then tear off the lips. After that they rip up the cheeks. Have you ever eaten cod cheeks?"

"Cod cheeks?"

"They're delicious. Fishermen usually toss the cod heads, but when I was a boy we used to scoop out the cheek-meat. Ravens seem to like the taste of our cheeks, unless of course you've laid the man's skull open with an ax, then they feast on the brains first."

Father Selwyn had a boyish face and fair hair that fell across his eyes. He frowned. "I'm not sure I can put those things in a poem, lord," he said faintly.

"And after the ravens," I went on, "the dogs come.

Dogs, foxes, and wolves. They like corpse-meat too, but they start feeding lower down the corpse, usually . . ."

"So really, lord," Father Selwyn dared interrupt me, "the word onslaught can stay?"

"It's the right word," I said again, "and bitter is right too."

War is bitter. The poets give battle a splendor, extolling the brave and exulting in victory, and bravery is worth their praise. Victory too, I suppose, but the poems, chanted in mead halls at night, give boys and young men their ambition to be warriors. Reputation! It is the one thing that outlives us. Men die, women die, all die, but reputation lives on like the echo of a song, and men crave reputation, as they crave the heavy arm rings that mark a warrior's victories. We revel in reputation and I am as guilty as the next man, proud that when men speak of me they tell how I slew Ubba Lothbrokson, cut down Svein of the White Horse, killed Cnut Longsword, and defeated Ragnall the Sea King. But reputation does not remember the ravens tearing a man's face, the weeping of men dying, or the weariness of victory. There is almost nothing harder than leading men to battle knowing that some will die, that young men we have trained to fight and come to love as comrades will whimper like infants. "It is better to talk," Hrothweard, the archbishop, often told me, "than to kill," but how does one talk to a man like Sköll, who craved reputation and claimed a kingdom and was willing that any number of young men should die to sate his appetite?

I remember the ravens. They kept us company next day as we struggled to reach the place from where we could launch our onslaught. The ravens were big and glossy-black, raucous and hungry, and they seemed to know what feast we were preparing, and those preparations took all day as we left the Tine valley and crossed a high saddle of the hills to the southeast of Heahburh. Once across the saddle we dropped to another valley where a stream ran fast. Sköll must have watched us, but such was the skill of his scouts that we saw none of them, though once in a while a raven would fly from a boulder, and I suspected the bird had been disturbed, but when my own scouts climbed the heights they saw no one. Perhaps Sköll sent no scouts. He must have guessed we would attack from the high ground to the west and were hiding in the valley beyond. We would stay in the valley through the night, and our horses would stay there when we attacked at dawn. Sigtryggr sent twenty men down to the Tine with orders to light fires once night fell. I doubted Sköll would be fooled by the glow in the darkness into thinking we were camped there, but Sigtryggr wanted to put a small nagging doubt into his mind.

I had a thousand nagging doubts. At dusk, just as the rain started, Sigtryggr, Finan, Sihtric, Svart, and I climbed to the hilltop with a dozen men to protect us. We lay on the coarse damp grass and stared down at the fort. The southern corner with its low tower faced us, and in front of the western wall I counted seven banked ditches. "He'll expect us to attack there," Sigtryggr said. "Across the ditches. It's the easiest approach."

"Which is why there are ditches," I said.

"And your mad bishop thinks we should assault the northern corner?"

"So do I," I said. From our new vantage point I could see there was a ditch at that far corner, but it looked shallow, and beyond the ditch was a rough patch of land before the ground fell sharply away to a stream. There was a tower at that northern corner. I supposed it had once been made of stone, but now was a timber platform with a wall around its summit. A flag hung limp and damp from a pole on the tower.

"We should do what he expects," Sigtryggr said, "and attack from the hill. And maybe that will pull men away from the northern corner. Then we make a surprise assault from the north."

I was not sure how we were to spring that surprise.

The defenders on the wall and the corner tower would be above us and could watch our movements. "That might work," I said dubiously, "but he has plenty of men." I could see my comment had annoyed Sigtryggr. He wanted to attack and was in no mood to hear of difficulties; he knew them anyway, and the persistent rain, that was being blown by an east wind and was hard enough to obscure our view of the fort, only added a new problem. "The bowstrings will be sloppy," I added.

"Bugger the bowstrings," Sigtryggr snarled, but he knew I was right. In rain the bowstrings became slack. I had brought the archers to harass the men on the ramparts, and wet bowstrings would make the arrow strikes feeble. Even a dry and taut cord would not give a hunting arrow enough force to pierce a shield, and it was a rare strike that drove through mail, but a hail of arrows forced men to keep their faces down beneath their shield rims.

"So what do we do, lord?" Svart asked.

"Dawn, tomorrow," Sigtryggr sounded anything but enthusiastic. "We'll attack across the ditches," he had stressed the "we," meaning that his own household warriors would make that attack. "But we don't push it too hard. We're trying to make them think that's our main assault. You," he had edged back from the skyline and was looking at Sihtric who had brought sixty-two warriors from Dunholm, "you'll be on our right. You and your men are there to stop them outflanking us with horsemen, and you, Father-in-law," he looked at me, "will be on the left, doing the same thing."

"Stopping horsemen?"

"And slowly getting closer to the northern corner." He paused, as if expecting me to say something, but I just nodded. "And when you think the moment's right," he went on.

"We attack." I finished the phrase for him.

"You attack the northern corner." He sounded anything but confident, and I knew he was tempted to withdraw, to leave Sköll in his fortress and march south in hope of finding a better place to fight. "Damn the rain," he said, as he slid back from the skyline.

The rain not only enfeebled bowstrings, it made sword hilts slippery, it made shields heavier, it seeped beneath our mail so we were chilled and the leather liners chafed. It was the same for the enemy, of course, but that night our enemy was in shelter, with fires, listening to the rain pelt on the roof. They slept while we suffered and prayed.

"Prayed, lord?" the poet-priest asked me eagerly.

"We were horribly vulnerable there," I explained. "We were in a deep valley, and Sköll could have led his men out and attacked us from the heights. He didn't. He left us alone." I paused, remembering. "It was a risk, but the Norse don't like fighting at night. They never have."

"But you prayed," Father Selwyn insisted.

I saw what he was suggesting. "Of course we prayed," I said, "but to Freyr, not to your god."

"Ah," he reddened. "Freyr?"

"He's the god of weather," I explained, "the son of Njörðr, the sea-god. Doesn't your religion have a god of weather?"

"There is only the one god, lord," he was too nervous to see I was teasing him. "One god, lord, to govern everything."

"No wonder it rains so much, but Freyr answered our prayers."

"He did, lord?"

"The rain stopped overnight and the wind went into the south."

"South, lord?" He understood that the rain ending was good news, but could not see the significance of the wind backing.

"What happens when a warmer wind blows over wet land?" I asked.

He gazed at me for a heartbeat. "Fog, lord?"

Fog. The dawn brought a dense fog that shrouded

the hills, and it was in that fog that men hefted the shields that had served as pillows, loosened swords in damp scabbards, drank ale, and stamped warmth into wet feet. We marched before sunrise, or at least we moved away from the place we had spent the night, filing up and around the hill, seeing nothing that was farther than twenty or thirty paces away. We startled a deer that bounded away down the slope, and I tried to find the omen in that sudden flight.

Fog, thicker than any smoke in the hall, wrapped about us and we hoped it deadened the sounds we made because, though we had ordered our troops to be silent, the gray light was filled with scabbards banging on shields, footfalls, the curses of men tripping, and the tearing of grass and heather. Yet the gods loved us that morning because somehow we did not get lost on the hill. Eadric, with his poacher's skill, led us, but it took time, so much time, to make the short journey uphill. At first we followed the remnants of a Roman road, but as we neared the fort we turned left, making for the gentler slope above Sköll's ramparts. I had hoped, like Sigtryggr, to make the assault in the half darkness, but the sun was glowing through the eastern fog by the time we were in place. Shapes shifted in the fog, the fog itself drifted, and I had a glimpse of a wall and of spearmen lining the rampart. Our silence had been wasted, because the enemy was awake and ready for us. They would have woken anyway as Sigtryggr and Svart began shouting at their men to make a shield wall, and the enemy, hearing the orders, began to bellow insults. An arrow flew from the fortress to bury itself in the turf, well short of any man.

"Bebbanburg!" I shouted, not as a challenge, but to rally my men. Finan and my son echoed the shout, and slowly my warriors appeared from the fog.

"Shield wall!" Finan bellowed. "Here!" He was standing to the left of Sigtryggr's men, who were still making their own wall as stragglers came from the wind-stirred fog.

"Move! Move! Move!" my son was yelling. Some of Sigtryggr's warriors joined my men by mistake and there was confusion as they left to find their own ranks. The fog was thinning. I had climbed a small hummock to see over the shambles of our half-formed shield wall and could see helmeted men watching us from Heahburh's wall. They were watching and jeering, telling us we were all doomed men.

Rorik brought my standard. "Plant it here, boy," I told him, "and—"

"Stay out of the fight, lord?" he interrupted me.

"Stay out of the fight," I said, helping him thrust the banner's staff into the hummock's turf. "And if it all goes wrong," I added, "you run like the wind." Why did I tell him that? I think even at that moment as the fog thickened again and as Sköll's men jeered us I knew we had made the wrong choice. We should have fought Sköll anywhere except at this high place where he had wanted us to fight him.

"End of the wall here! Here!" That was Berg. Somehow he had managed to bring his precious eagle flag as well as a shield and a spear, and he rammed the flag's staff into the turf to mark the northernmost end of our shield wall. "Line up on me!" he shouted. "Here!" He spread his banner to make himself more visible. "Here!" He was facing us, and a sudden shift in the fog revealed Sköll's men beyond him, beyond him and near to him, much too near, men who had left the fort to attack us before our shield wall was formed, gray-helmeted men with snarling wolves on their shields, warriors who came howling from the gray fog.

And Berg had not even drawn his sword.

Then was the clashing of shields. The sea-wolves came,
Furious to the fight. The spear often pierced
The life-house of the doomed . . . They stood fast,
Warriors in combat, warriors falling
Weary with wounds. The dead fell on the earth.

I read Father Selwyn's lines and flinched as I remembered that sudden attack from the morning fog. "I suppose we did stand fast," I told the poet, "eventually."

"Eventually, lord?"

"They surprised us," I said, "in that fog we were supposed to surprise them, but they surprised us. We weren't ready. What saved us was that Sköll didn't send enough men. I don't think there were more than sixty. He should have sent two hundred."

"And they were, what is the word, lord? *Úlf—*"

"*Úlfhéðnar,*" I said, "but no, these men weren't crazed, but you're right, they came furious to the fight."

Sköll's men might not have been crazed by henbane, but they still came like wolves, howling, they came to kill, and in that first moment I lost eight men. I blame myself. If you lead men and women then your success is their success, but the failures are all yours. All mine.

I remember the leaping enemy, mouths open, shields held to one side so they could stab with spear or sword. Cerdic, big and loyal, but always slow, was the first of my men to die. He had been going to join Berg and I saw him turn in surprise, he did not even have time to resist and a Norseman's spear went clear through his body, so hard was that opening thrust. I saw the mail at Cerdic's back bulge, then the spearhead tore through and a second Norseman

slashed his sword across Cerdic's face and the blood
was bright in that gray morning. The enemy was yelling, triumphant. Wulfmaer, another Saxon, was behind Cerdic. He had been one of my cousin's warriors
who had sworn his loyalty to me and I watched him
die. He had time to raise his spear, level it, even begin
to charge against the mass of men hurling themselves
toward us, but he was jarred back by a spear thrust
to his shield, he half turned, lunged his own weapon,
and a Norseman's sword knocked it aside and another
man drove an ax down through Wulfmaer's helmet
and split his skull like a log.

I ran forward, Serpent-Breath drawn, then Finan
slammed into me from my right, stopping me. "To
me! To me!" he shouted. The gods only know how fast
he must have moved because only a moment before he
had been yards away from me. "To me! Shields!" He
knocked his shield against mine. "Raise it!" he snarled
at me. I confess I was in a daze, appalled by the sudden onslaught. Someone, it turned out to be Beornoth,
stood to my left. Sköll's Norsemen were twenty paces
away. Berg had vanished. Kettil, another of my Norsemen, had been following Wulfmaer, probably teasing
him, now he whirled, sword drawn, and bellowed defiance. A Norseman charged him, spear leveled, Kettil
danced clear, slashed once and the enemy reeled away,

blood streaming from his face. "Come back!" Finan shouted, and Kettil tried, but two men trapped him, drove him a pace backward, Kettil lunged forward, his sword pierced a man's belly and was trapped there and I shouted in futile anger as another warrior's sword ripped across Kettil's throat. Kettil had been a fine swordsman, a man who loved embroidered clothes, a vain man, but one whose jests could fill a hall with laughter. More men were joining our shield wall, I could hear the clatter of willow boards touching as we made the wall, but ahead of us men were still dying. Godric, who had been my servant, was pinned to the earth by a spear through the belly. He screamed like a child. Eadwold, surly and slow, tried to run, and was tripped by a spear. He screamed too. Thurstan, a devout Christian, who would earnestly tell me my soul was in danger, killed a Norseman with a massive spear thrust and was still thrusting and shouting as two swords sent his soul to heaven. He had a wife in Bebbanburg and a son in Eoferwic who was studying to become a priest. Then Cenwulf, a reliable man, honest and patient, had his belly opened by an ax. He moaned as he fell, trying desperately to cling to his sword as his guts spilled and he collapsed onto the blood-soaked turf. He was a Christian too, but like so many others he wanted to die with his weapon in his hand.

The poet-priest was right; *wæl feol on eorþan*, the dead fell on the earth.

All that happened in a moment. The dead men had been going to join Berg and were caught by the Norsemen who came streaming across the corner of the ditches. So my warriors died, but their deaths slowed the attackers for an instant, just long enough for the rest of my men to make the crude shield wall, but what really saved us was Svart charging in from the right at the head of Sigtryggr's men.

Then was the clashing of shields.

Svart came like an *úlfheðinn*, maddened with battle-rage, a huge man, his beard hung with bones, and with a great war ax in both hands. At least a score of men were with him, their shields clashed against Sköll's shields, it was Norseman fighting Norseman in a fury of blades. "Forward!" I shouted and my shield wall went into the fight. There were men beside me, men behind me, men screaming, as much from fear as defiance. But we were a shield wall, as were Svart's men, and Sköll's men had attacked in a frenzy that left them scattered. Their battle-rage was singing in their heads, they were slaughtering, they could not be beaten, except by a shield wall, and we struck them hard. Spears lunged. Svart had killed two men before my shield wall hit the Norsemen, but we added two more dead, both pierced by spears, and I saw a black-bearded man bellowing at Sköll's men to make a wall. More of my men were coming, more of Sigtryggr's were joining Svart. Beornoth, beside me, rammed his spear at the black-bearded man, who fended it off with his shield. I saw a new scar of wood slash across the snarling wolf daubed on the man's shield, he lunged with his own spear, aiming at Beornoth who, in turn, caught the blade on his shield and I stepped forward and rammed Serpent-Breath at the big beard and felt her point cut into his throat. He half fell backward, held up by the men behind, and Finan cut at the man next to him, slicing Soul-Stealer into his mail-clad shoulder. A hammering of shields to my left and I saw my son had extended our wall, was leading new men into the fight, and then we could go no further. The Norse had made their wall, our heavy shields crashed together, and we heaved against each other.

Serpent-Breath was the wrong weapon for this fight. Her blade was too long for the deadly embrace of shield walls. I dropped her and drew Wasp-Sting, my short seax, and slid her between my shield and Finan's. She struck wood, I pushed on my enemy's shield. Above the iron rim my enemy had fair hair, a dirty pox-scarred face, gritted teeth, a slit up the side of one nostril, and a short beard. He was young enough to be my son, he was shouting his hatred at me. A spear came from behind me, over my shoulder, and sliced open his cheek. Blood started fast, his shield faltered, and I skewered Wasp-Sting again, this time feeling her strike and pierce mail. The hatred on the young man's face turned to surprise, then fear. Something struck my helmet, and for a heartbeat I was dazed. I did not see the blow, nor knew whether it was a spear or a sword that gave it, but the blow forced me back and Wasp-Sting slid free. I pushed forward again, shield high, and kept pushing, kept stabbing. Svart, disdaining to use a shield, was roaring to my right, swinging his massive ax to drive Sköll's men back. The young man opposite me was shouting again, every bellow bubbling blood from his sliced cheek. Our shields grated together and I spat a challenge as I felt Wasp-Sting bite again, and this time she sank deep into the flesh beneath the mail and I twisted her, tried to rip her upward, and felt an enemy's sword pushing at my waist, then that pressure suddenly vanished. A horn had sounded from the ramparts and it must have been some kind of signal because the men opposing us went backward, then turned and ran back along the ditches toward one of the fort's three remaining entrances. The fourth, which faced Sigtryggr's men across the western ditches, had been blocked with thick timbers.

The fog was almost gone, leaving slow tendrils that

writhed above the bloody turf. Heavy spears were thrown from the ramparts and one hammered into my shield, weighing it down. I stepped away from the men hurling the spears and wrenched the blade free from the willow board. I picked up Serpent-Breath. Neither my men nor Svart's had followed the retreating Norsemen. I saw that the young man with the wounded cheek had gone with them, but he was limping and staggering. I wiped Wasp-Sting on the hem of my cloak and looked at Finan. "I'm sorry."

"Sorry, lord?"

"I was slow. You weren't. I'm sorry."

"They were quick, lord, they were quick."

"Maybe Sköll's right. I'm getting old."

The Norse in the fort were jeering us. "Welcome to Sköllholm," they shouted.

I looked at our dead. "Did Wulfmaer have children?" I asked and should have known the answer.

"Two," Finan said. "The oldest was that little redheaded bastard who pushed his sister into the cesspit."

"You're bleeding."

He looked at his shield arm. One of his arm rings was almost severed, the mail sleeve beneath was ripped, and blood was seeping through a rent in the leather liner. "I think I killed the bugger who did that." He flexed his fingers. "No real damage, lord."

It is strange how there is sometimes a sudden calm in a battle, not that it was quiet, because Sköll's men were still shouting and banging sword-blades against their shields, but for a moment neither side was trying to kill the other. We had made a long shield wall that straddled Heahburh's high spur, but were making no attempt to advance, while the enemy was content to wait behind their ramparts. I counted seven dead from my men and four from Svart's troop. Seven Norsemen had joined them in death, and Berg was missing.

Berg, whom I loved like a son. Berg, so eager to please and so fearsome in battle. Berg, whom I had saved from death and who had proved so loyal a companion. He had been at the left-hand end of our line when I last saw him, and I walked there to ask if anyone had seen him. "He went down the hill, lord," Redbad told me.

"He escaped?"

Redbad, a Frisian, shrugged. "Lost sight of him, lord. Bastards were on us."

I walked a few more paces to gaze down into the next valley where another fast stream tumbled on its stony bed. The valley was empty. Berg and his precious eagle flag were both gone. I supposed Sköll's men had taken the banner as a trophy, but had they taken Berg too?

My son had the same fear. "You think he's a prisoner?"

"I hope not," I said, then wished I had not expressed the hope. Better to be a prisoner, I supposed, than dead, but any prisoner of Sköll's might expect a foul death. I had seen enemies carve a screaming man to a slow death as a taunt to his watching comrades, and Sköll was more than capable of the same cruelty.

"Maybe he joined Sigtryggr's men, lord?" Redbad suggested.

"He wouldn't do that. He's one of us."

"I can look, lord?"

"If you want." Though I knew he would not find Berg. If, somehow, the young Norseman had survived the sudden assault from the fog he would have sought me out. I touched the hammer at my breast and prayed that he lived.

Sigtryggr was shouting at his men, telling them to hoist their shields, to keep the wall straight, to carry their swords and spears to the enemy's ramparts. A score of boys had carried the unwieldy ladders up the hill, and men in Sigtryggr's second rank now hefted the ladders. "We can win!" Sigtryggr shouted. "We will win!" He paused to let his men answer the shout, but the response was poor. He called again, assuring them of victory, but the battle's opening had gone Sköll's way, and our men were uncertain. None wanted to go forward to where Sköll's jeering men were confident behind their wall.

Battles rarely begin with a sudden blood-letting. Insults come first. Men stand and watch the enemy, they listen to the taunts of the enemy and the shouts of their leaders and they summon the courage that is needed before a fight. But this battle had begun abruptly with Sköll's assault from the fog, and it had left our troops cold, damp, and dispirited. Had the sorcerer cursed us? In truth none of us had truly wanted to attack the fort, but Sigtryggr desperately wanted this campaign over. He wanted Sköll, who was claiming Northumbria's throne, dead. Perhaps we should have withdrawn, gone south, waited for Sköll to follow, and then fought a battle in open land. Instead we were locked in a deadly embrace with a grim fort, and it was too late to withdraw. If we retreated we would be pursued by Sköll's triumphant and vengeful men, by warriors on horses who would harry us down the hill like a pack of wolves savaging sheep.

The poet-priest frowned when I told him that. "Why didn't you have horses, lord? I thought the leaders were always mounted in battle."

"Not always."

"But you could have taken your horses?"

"It would have been difficult," I said, "the path up from the valley was steep, and there was no space on Heahburh's spur for a mass of horsemen, but yes, we could. We thought about it, and Sigtryggr and I discussed it the night before, and we decided no horses."

Father Selwyn frowned. "But don't you see better from horseback?"

"We do," I explained patiently, "but we knew it would be a hard fight, maybe a desperate fight, and if we had taken our horses then our men would think we were ready to flee if the worst happened. By staying on foot, like them, we ran the same risks, and they knew it. That's why."

"So then you attacked the fort?"

"Only after we'd shared the last of the ale. We'd brought it all to the hilltop. But then? Yes, we attacked."

Sigtryggr and Svart led that attack. They took their shield wall forward and the spears began coming as soon as they reached the outer ditch. Very few arrows, I noticed, it was mostly heavy spears that were being hurled from the ramparts. I could hear the blades thumping into shields. Sigtryggr's rearmost ranks were throwing spears back, not really in hope of killing any of the defenders, but trying to force them to shelter behind their shields.

Cuthwulf, a hunter from Bebbanburg who led my

archers, came to join me. "Should we be using the bows, lord?" He was a sinewy, sun-darkened man, whose limp did not prevent him from being the most deadly of my hunters.

"How many arrows do you have?"

Cuthwulf spat. "Not enough, lord. Fifty apiece?"

I winced. "Save them." I jerked my head northward. "You see that far corner?" It looked a long way off. "Use the arrows when we attack there. Not until then." I glanced up and saw a watery sun showing through the lifting fog. "That'll give your bowstrings time to dry out."

"I kept them under my hat," Cuthwulf said, "so they're dry enough, but God save you, lord."

My shield wall overlapped the fort so that we could look north down its long side toward the Tine valley. The lower part of the wall was made of stone, but over the years men had removed the upper courses to build barn or hall foundations, and the upper part was made of coarse thick timbers. There were plenty of defenders on that long wall, too many, but I had promised Sigtryggr to do my best to draw men from the rampart he was assaulting and it was time to keep that promise. Sigtryggr's men were crossing the ditches, assailed by spears, trying to protect themselves with shields made even more unwieldy by the spears lodged in the willow boards. I could hear Svart shouting them forward. It was a struggle. The ditches were deep and the banks between the ditches were steep and slippery. Two of Sköll's men were in the short tower at the fort's corner and were hurling spears that were being handed up to them from inside the fort. "Cuthwulf," I called him back. "You can kill those two bastards."

Cuthwulf selected an arrow, notched it on the string, took a deep breath, drew his short bow, held his breath, and loosed. The closest man on the tower was about to hurl a spear and the arrow struck him on the helmet. He jerked back, turned, and the second arrow pierced his nose. He sank down, clutching the wound. The other man ducked behind the parapet, and Cuthwulf grunted. "I meant to kill them both."

"You did well," I said, then saw that Sigtryggr's wall had crossed five of the seven ditches. Time to go, I thought. I had never felt so little enthusiasm for a battle, even the thought of revenging Stiorra's death left me cold. It was the curse, I thought, and I remembered Snorri's prophecy of the two kings dying, and I drew Serpent-Breath, tried to forget the curse, and shouted at my men to follow.

And on that hill of death we went to the ramparts.

Now they go forth, birds screeching,
The gray wolf howls, the shield-wood clashes,
Shield answers shaft. Wake now, my warriors,
Grasp shields, be strong in valor,
Fight your way forward!

"I never told them to be strong in valor," I said. "There's no point in saying something like that. You can't make a man brave by shouting at him."

"It's a—" the young priest began.

"—a poem," I said, "I know." I smiled. I liked Father Selwyn. "Bravery is overcoming fear," I said, "and I don't know how you do that. Duty helps a little, experience, of course, and not letting down your comrades helps a lot, but really bravery is a kind of madness."

"Madness, lord?"

"It seems as if you're watching yourself. You can't believe what you're doing. You know you might die, but you keep doing it. Battle madness. It's what the *úlfhéðnar* have, but they use henbane or ale or mushrooms to fill them with the madness, but we all have some of it. If we didn't we'd simply give in to the fear."

He frowned. "Are you saying," he hesitated, not sure if he should speak what was on his mind, "are you saying you were frightened, lord?"

"Of course I was frightened," I admitted. "I was terrified! We were fighting the wrong battle in the wrong place. Sköll had planned it well. He let us come. He didn't interfere with us as we approached. He wanted us to come to his walls and to be slaughtered in his ditches, and like fools we did just what he wanted. I knew we would lose."

"You knew—" he began to ask.

"But we still had to fight," I interrupted him. "We couldn't retreat, not without being pursued and harried and killed, so we had to try to win. That's fate. But yes, I knew we would lose. We'd made a mistake and we were doomed, but there's only one way out of a mess like that. You have to fight your way through it."

We went forward, and, as I told Father Selwyn, I felt doomed. We were advancing down the side of the fort, which meant that once we had crossed the place where the ditches and banks turned around the tower, we were walking along the ridges, not across them, which made our advance quicker. We went in a rush and I remember being surprised that it suddenly seemed so easy. Spears came from our right, but they rattled or thumped on our shields, and then we turned, crossed two ditches, and closed on the wall. Then it stopped being easy. "Axes!" I shouted.

I had given our biggest and strongest men the long-hafted axes with their broad blades and deep lower beards. Each shaft was as long as a spear, which made the weapons clumsy, but my men had learned how they were to be used. My front rank stood with me under the ramparts and the Norse hammered our raised shields with spears and axes. The wall was not much higher than a man, which meant the defenders were close and their blows heavy. I felt my shield splintering as the ax blades crashed into the boards. The Norse had seen us coming, had seen the gold around my neck, the arm rings glittering, and the silver on my helmet. They knew I was a lord and they wanted the reputation of killing me. I could not fight back. To lower the shield so that I could lunge up with Serpent-Breath's long blade would expose me to the defenders, which meant our duty, the front rank's duty, was to stand in the sloppy mud of the ditch and keep those defenders busy by making ourselves into easy targets.

And behind us the big men with the strangely long axes struck. Those men, like Gerbruht and Folcbald, both Frisians, let the axes fall over the defenders and then hauled back, using the long spiked beard of the blade to gaff the enemy like fish. The heavy blows on my shield ended as the first ax blows landed, I heard a shout from above, then blood splashed on my splintered shield and some dripped through a split in the wood. There was another bellow from above me, and a Norseman came tumbling over the rampart to fall at my feet. Vidarr Leifson, beside me, stabbed down with his short seax, the man jerked like a landed fish and then died. I remember the man dying, and then little more. My axes were working, at least until Sköll's men learned to hack at the long shafts with their own axes, but every man we killed or wounded on the wall was immediately replaced by another, and it was one of those newcomers who hurled down a great block of stone that shattered my weakened shield and struck the left side of my helmet.

I showed the battered helmet to the poet. "See the gash?"

Father Selwyn fingered the metal that had split where the stone had crushed the helmet. "That must have hurt, lord."

I laughed. "I had a headache for days after, but at the time? It didn't hurt, I was knocked unconscious."

Father Selwyn ran an ink-stained finger across the scar that disfigured the silver wolf that crested the helmet. "You never had it repaired, lord?"

"It's a reminder of my stupidity," I said, making the young man smile. "And I have other helmets."

"Were you attacking the northern tower when it happened?"

"We hadn't got that far. The idea was to draw men away from that corner."

Like almost everything else that day, the plan to weaken the northern corner by attacking the southwestern angle of the fort did not work. Sköll had crammed a small army into Heahburh, and he had no need to weaken any part of his ramparts. All he had to do was let us make futile attacks on his walls until we finally abandoned the assaults, and then pursue us to destruction. That had been his plan ever since he had withdrawn from Bebbanburg, and, like fools, we obliged him.

My attack on the northern stretch of the wall failed. We lost another seven men, Sköll lost two men. We had sixteen wounded, including myself, and Sköll had maybe a half-dozen injured at the most. I did not see our retreat from the wall and its ditches, I was unconscious. I had been struck by the lump of stone that splintered my shield and split my helmet. I fell, and Finan later told me how Gerbruht and Eadric seized my arms, rescued Serpent-Breath, and dragged me back. A spear struck my left thigh while they hauled me over the banks. The blade cut deep, but I was unaware of it. Finan tried to keep the men at the wall, tried to gaff yet another Norseman and haul him down to the inner ditch, but when my men saw me being pulled back to the safer ground beyond the ditches they lost heart. They retreated with me, pursued by Norse jeers and thrown spears.

At first, as I recovered, the only thing I was aware of was the triumphant shouts of a victorious enemy. They bellowed their insults, blew horns, and clattered swords against shields as they invited us back to the ramparts. Sigtryggr's bigger assault, like mine, had also been driven back, and Sköll's men were mocking us. "I never even planted one ladder," Sigtryggr told me later. "There were too many of the bastards."

The next thing I remember is the sharp pain as Vidarr pulled off my damaged helmet. "Christ, be careful!" Finan snarled at him as blood flowed from my scalp. He poured water on my head. "Lord? Lord?"

I must have mumbled something because I remember Vidarr's surprised words. "He's alive!"

"Take more than a bloody rock to kill him," Finan said. "Bandage his head. You, girl! Come here!"

"Girl?" I muttered, but no one heard me.

Elwina, one of Ieremias's angels, was evidently on the hilltop. "Tear a strip off your gown," Finan ordered her, "and tie up his head."

"I'm all right," I said, and tried to sit up.

"Stay!" Finan snarled at me as though I was one of his dogs. "Bind it tight, girl."

"She shouldn't be here," I said, or tried to say. I was gazing up at a clearing sky, though the left side of my sight was darkened. I flinched, suddenly aware of the pain in my skull. "Where's my sword?" I asked in panic.

"Safe in her scabbard, lord," Finan said, "now lie down and let the girl bandage you."

"I want to see," I said, and struggled up, hauling on Elwina's arm. She was surprisingly strong and managed to pull me into a sitting position. My sight was blurred, still dark on the one side, but I saw Ieremias had come with his angels.

The mad bishop was in his embroidered robes, still carrying his crozier on which he had tied the ram's skull. He crouched in front of me and stared at me with his intense dark eyes. "The stone, lord," he hissed, "we need the stone!"

"Bugger off, bishop," Finan snarled.

"What's happening?" I asked.

"You got a tap on the head," Finan elbowed Ieremias aside.

"The stone!" Ieremias insisted. "Give me the stone or we lose!"

"He'll give you the stone when he's ready," Finan said, having no idea what he was talking about. "Bind it tight, girl."

"I need a helmet," I said.

"The stone!" Ieremias called again.

"Bishop," Finan said angrily, "unless you want your two angels to spend the next month flat on their backs pleasuring Norsemen you'd better go. Take them back to the horses, then go back home."

"I'm needed here," Ieremias said indignantly.

My son pushed the bishop further away and stooped to me. "Father?"

"I'm all right," I said.

"He's not," Finan insisted.

"I need a helmet."

"Your day's done, lord," Finan said.

"A helmet!"

"Stay still, lord," Elwina said. She finished bandaging my skull. "Does it hurt, lord?"

"Of course it bloody hurts," Finan said, "now bandage his thigh."

"Sigtryggr says we should attack again," my son said.

Finan used a knife to cut open my breeches. "Bind it tight, girl."

"We have to help Sigtryggr," I said.

"You're doing nothing more, lord," Finan said.

"I've done nothing yet," I said bitterly, and moaned as pain stabbed through my skull.

I do not know how much time had passed. As I sat, half stunned, trying to clear my sight, it seemed as if we had only just arrived and the fight had been as brief as it was disastrous, but the fog had cleared, the sky was blue and the sun high. Horns were sounding from Sigtryggr's ranks, men were cheering, Svart, huge and fearsome, was calling them back to the fight. "We have to help them," my son said.

"Stay with your father," Finan said. "I'll lead this one."

"Finan," I called, and the effort provoked another lance of pain in my head.

"Lord?"

"Be careful!"

He laughed at that. "Lord," he was talking to my son, "if your father can walk, get him downhill to the horses."

"We're not running away," I insisted.

"I'll come with you—" my son began speaking to Finan.

"You stay!" Finan ordered him sharply. "And get your father to the horses. You, girl, help him."

I waited for Finan to leave, tried to stand, and fell back, dizzy. "We stay here," I growled, and so I just watched the second assault on Sköll's fortress and it fared no better than the first. We had made such a mess of this fight. We had been impetuous, unwilling to wait, trusting to fate to see us across the ditches and over the wall, and fate had spat in our faces. The defenders were throwing more blocks of masonry pulled from the Roman ruins, and each was heavy enough to crush a skull. Finan, evidently abandoning our plan to attack the northern corner, had ordered Cuthwulf and his archers to harass the men defending the wall we had assaulted before, but most of the arrows were wasted on shields. I could see snarling-wolf shields stuck with a score of arrows, and behind them the Norsemen hurled down stones or thrust with spears. Finan even managed to get one ladder against the wall, but before he or anyone could climb it, a man leaned down and swept it aside with an ax. Gerbruht seized the man's arm and hauled him over the ramparts, and I saw my men's spears rising and falling in vengeance, but that was their one small victory.

Sköll's men gained a far greater triumph. Sigtryggr, filled with a battle-fury born of desperation, had collected spears thrown from the ramparts and had twenty of his men hurling the weapons back at the defenders. I watched, impressed by the number of missiles his men were raining on the wall, and, as the defenders crouched beneath their shields, Sigtryggr led a rush of men across the ditches. They carried two ladders that they rammed against the wall. A brave Norseman leaned down to throw one ladder aside and succeeded before a spear raked into his shoulder. The ladder fell, but Sigtryggr was already mounting the second ladder when Svart unceremoniously threw him off the lower rungs and climbed himself. He swung his huge ax one-handed, driving back two defenders. I could hear Svart bellowing, hear Sigtryggr yelling at his men to put the first ladder back, saw the spears still flying at the ramparts, and Svart was almost at the short ladder's top, flailing his ax. He was a huge man, terrifying, and the defending Norsemen were backing away from that massive blade as Svart climbed another rung, was almost over the wall, and then the ladder's rung snapped. He jarred down, almost fell, and had to reach out with his ax to steady himself and a Norse defender darted forward and rammed a spear at Svart's neck. The defender was immediately struck by a thrown spear and fell out of sight, but not before his long blade had pierced Svart's throat. I could see the sudden blood. Somehow Svart stayed upright, swaying. He tried to lift the ax, but another defender, screaming defiance, swung a sword that bit into the bleeding wound, and Svart, a warrior of a hundred victories, fell back into the ditch.

The death of Svart gave the defenders new confidence and drained Sigtryggr's men of their defiance. I did not know it, but Sigtryggr had also been wounded. A spear had bitten into his shoulder. His men pulled him back, and Finan, seeing the retreat of that larger group, called an end to his own futile attack. Sköll's men were laughing again, cheering, calling us cowards, inviting us to surrender and telling us they would enjoy our women and enslave our children. Sköll himself came to the wall, the first time I had seen him that day, and he stood, massive in his white fur cloak that he wore above his shining mail. His helmet, I saw, was ringed with a circlet of gold, his sign of kingship. He mocked us. "Have you had enough? You want to come to my wall again? You'll be welcome! If you try harder maybe I'll have to wake some of my other warriors." One of Sigtryggr's men threw a spear and Sköll took one contemptuous sideways step so that the weapon flew past him. "You have to do better than that!" he called. He was searching the hundreds of men gathered on the far side of the ditches. "Is Sigtryggr Ivarson here?" No one answered, and Sköll laughed, still searching among his enemies. Then he saw me, sitting off to one side. He pointed. "The old man's here! Are you hurt, old man?"

"Get me up," I growled, and my son gave me his arm and I forced myself up. I swayed, my head hurt, but I stayed on my feet.

"Don't die, Lord Uhtred!" Sköll shouted. "I want to kill you myself. I will add your head and your banner to the trophies in my hall." His ramparts were crowded. His men were grinning and laughing. We were beaten, and Sköll knew it. "But don't go away yet!" he called. "Stay an hour or so and I'll wake up my *úlfhéðnar.*" He laughed again, then went from the parapet.

And I knew it could only get worse. The *úlfhéðnar* would be unleashed to crown Sköll's victory. And two kings would die.

Twelve

Many a carcass they left to be carrion,
Left for the white-tail'd eagle to tear it, and
Left for the horny-nibb'd raven to rend it, and
Gave to the scavenging war-hawk to gorge it, and
That gray beast, the wolf . . .

I had to smile. "Horny-nibbed raven?"

"You think it should be horny-beaked, lord?" Father Selwyn asked anxiously.

"You're the poet," I said, "not me." I remembered the ravens flying up from the Tine valley, hosts of black wings in a dread morning, coming to the feast we were preparing for them. "But I didn't see any wolves," I told the young priest, "except of course for the *úlfhéðnar.*"

"So Sköll," he said, "sent his *úlf*—" he paused, uncertain of the word again.

"His *úlfhéðnar*."

"His *úlfhéðnar* to fight you, lord?"

I nodded. "We didn't think he would, at least not while we were so close to his walls."

"Why not, lord?"

"He had us beaten! We had a choice. Either we assaulted again and more of our men would die, or else we ran away. That would be the time for Sköll to let loose his savages. When he said he'd wake up his *úlfhéðnar* we thought he was just trying to frighten us. Trying to persuade us to give up and retreat down the hill." I closed my eyes, imagining. "Can you understand what would have happened?" I asked the poet. "Broken men, wounded men, defeated men, stumbling down a steep hillside pursued by the wolf-fighters. Our men would have panicked. It would have been a slaughter."

We almost gave Sköll the chance to inflict that slaughter. I was standing unsteadily, my sword arm around my son's shoulders, and still dazed when Sigtryggr came to find me. He walked slowly, there was blood on his left shoulder where his mail had been torn open, and his shield arm was hanging limp. He frowned when he saw me. "You're hurt," he said. I was wearing a dead man's helmet that had blood on its rim.

"So are you, lord King."

"Spear-thrust," he said dismissively.

"You can still hold a shield?"

He shook his head, then turned to look at the fort. "It's a bastard," he said quietly, and I knew that was an admission of failure.

"It is," I agreed.

He paused. "Svart's dead."

"I know, I saw."

Sigtryggr's one good eye gleamed. "He was a good man. The best."

"He was."

"He died holding his ax."

"So we'll meet in Valhalla."

"We will," he said, "and maybe sooner than we want." He offered me a skin. "There's no ale left, so it's water." He watched me drink. "So what do we do?"

I winced as a pain seared through my skull. "Try again?"

"The northern corner? As your madman suggested?"

"If you bring your men around to this side," I suggested, "I can take mine to the northern corner."

"Not many arrows left," my son muttered.

Sigtryggr looked at the bodies we had left in the ditch. He grimaced. A Norseman, to taunt us, was standing on the rampart pissing on our dead. "The bastard," Sigtryggr said quietly. Behind us, on the rising ground, our wounded were lying in pain. A boy, one of those who had helped carry the ladders up to the fort, was weeping over his dying father. Sigtryggr flinched, then looked back to the ramparts. "He has too many men," he said, "and he hasn't moved anyone from that far corner." Which meant our efforts to persuade Sköll to weaken the north to reinforce the west had failed.

"We can't leave," I said, "they'll cut us down like sheep."

"They will," he agreed, "but we might have to."

"No," I said as forcefully as I could, "we have to attack."

Sigtryggr tried to move his shield arm and flinched at the pain. "And if another attack fails?" he asked.

"It mustn't fail," I said, "because if it does we're doomed."

Sigtryggr appeared not to hear those words, which were, I admit, little more than dutiful. I might sound defiant, but at that moment both of us knew we were doomed. He had turned to look back the way we had come in the morning's fog, a fog that had utterly vanished. "I'm thinking," he said, "that if we make a shield wall across the track then we can send away the men we want to save. Like your son."

"No—" my son began.

"Quiet!" Sigtryggr snarled at him and turned back to me. "We make one long shield wall, and that should hold up their pursuit long enough."

"You should leave too," I said.

He scoffed at that suggestion. "I've failed. I can't run away and leave my men to die." He looked again at the fort. "I'll send a dozen good men to take my children to Bebbanburg. Your son can protect them there."

"He will," I said. I remember the chill wind blowing across the spur as I realized that this was the place where my life thread would be severed. Two kings must die, and I, the king without a crown, was one of them. I touched the hammer and thought how I had let down my daughter. I had come for revenge and I was failing. I could see my men gazing at me, wanting me to lead them to a surprise victory. They had an absurd faith in me. "We've been at the arse end of fate before," I had heard Eadric telling Immar Hergildson, the young man I had saved from hanging at Mameceaster, "and he always gets us out. Don't worry, lad, we have Lord Uhtred. We'll win!"

Except I knew of no way to win. We had been fools to assault the fort, and now we must take the bitter consequences. Sigtryggr knew it too. "So we make the shield wall?" he asked bleakly.

"If Sköll sees men slipping away," I pointed out,

"he'll send horsemen after them. They'll ride around our shield wall and kill the men we send away."

Sigtryggr knew I was right, but knew, as I did, that we could do nothing about that threat. "We must try," was all he could say.

And then the gate opened.

We were standing on the rising ground to the west of the ramparts and could look down the fort's long side toward the northern corner that Ieremias had encouraged us to assault. Two-thirds of the way down that wall was one of Heahburh's three remaining gates, and it swung open.

For a moment no one appeared there. We just stared, waiting, then there was an unearthly scream, and Snorri, the sorcerer, appeared on the earthen causeway that crossed the ditches. Sigtryggr and I both touched our hammers, while Finan and my son clutched at their crosses. Heahburh's hill spur went silent after the scream because blind Snorri's appearance had ended the jeering from the ramparts, and the defenders just watched as the sorcerer was guided across the ditches by his small white dog, then as he stopped and faced us. Snorri seemed to be gazing at us, while his small dog wagged its stubby tail. I remember that. It seemed so unnatural in that place of death, a little dog's tail wagging. "Who is that?" one of Sigtryggr's men asked.

"His galdre," my son answered quietly.

"His sorcerer," I translated the Saxon word.

Sigtryggr touched the hammer again, then clutched it as Snorri slowly raised his wolf skull and pointed the muzzle toward us. I could see his mouth moving, and I supposed he was cursing us, though he was too far away for us to hear the curse. A man shouted from the ramparts and was silenced by his companions. Sköll's men wanted to hear the curses that the dreaded Snorri cast on us. "They say he can kill with a curse?" Sigtryggr asked.

"If he can kill with a curse," I said, "why does Sköll need warriors?" Sigtryggr did not answer, but just kept holding his hammer as the small dog led Snorri closer to us. The sorcerer stopped a long spear's throw away. "Sköll's trying to frighten us," I said. He was succeeding too, and I could see him watching and smiling from the long rampart. Snorri began howling, and in between the shrieks and howls he hurled more curses. He was in earshot now, and he cursed us by land, by the sky, by the earth, he cursed us by fire, by water, by air, he gave our bodies to the Corpse-Ripper of Niflheim, he promised us an eternity of pain from Hel the goddess of the rotting dead, and he raised the skull and his sightless eyes to the heavens and called on Thor to strike us and on Odin to blight us.

Sköll laughed with every phrase of the curse. He was in his great white cloak, pointing at us, talking to the men around him. He cupped his hands and shouted, "You're all doomed! Snorri will kill you with his next curse!"

"They're just words," I shouted, but I could see that my men, even the Christians among them, were troubled by Snorri. They knew the gods controlled our fate and knew that a sorcerer was closer to the gods than other men or women, and they had all heard the dread rumor that Sköll's sorcerer could kill men at a distance, just by curses. "They're just words!" I called again, even louder. "Just nonsense!" But I saw men making the sign of the cross or touching their hammers. Some began to edge away, and I knew our men trembled on the verge of a panicked flight. They could fight against men, but not against the gods. The Norse on the ramparts were jeering us again as Snorri seemed to take a deep breath ready to launch his most powerful sorcery.

Then Ieremias leaped out in front of us. My immediate impulse was to pull him back, but Finan put a hand on my arm. "Let him be, lord, let him be."

Ieremias turned and hissed at me. "Have the stone ready, lord!" He looked back at Snorri, raised his arms, and screamed like a soul in torment.

There was another silence after that scream. Sköll's

men were plainly surprised to see that we had a sorcerer too, and they went quiet, not in fear, but rather anticipating a battle of sorcerers, both of them old, both white-haired and skinny, and both calling on the mysterious power of their god or gods. But Snorri, who had evidently expected no rival sorcerer and who was astonished by Ieremias's scream, was momentarily speechless. Ieremias, meanwhile, appeared to be dancing. He was turning and leaping, singing in a high, crooning voice. There were no words, just the strange keening sound as the fool in his bishop's clothing danced and twisted and capered toward Snorri.

"He's drunk!" Sigtryggr said.

"No," I answered, "he's used the ointment."

"Ointment?"

"The henbane. He thinks he's flying."

Ieremias suddenly crouched, then sprang up, arms wide. "Thou turd of Satan!" he shouted, pointing at Snorri, then he loped toward the Norse sorcerer with his dirty bishop's robes trailing in the grass. He stopped some twenty paces short of Snorri and lifted his crozier on which the ram's skull was still perched. "I curse you!" he called in his native Danish, a language very close to the Norse tongue. "By the power of Abraham's ram I curse your head, I curse your hairs, I curse your eyes."

"He doesn't have any eyes, you fool," I muttered.

"I curse your face, I curse your nose, I curse your serpent's tongue, I curse your teeth, I curse your neck, I curse your hands, I curse your belly, I curse your prick, I curse your arse!" He paused for breath. His words were slurred, but clear enough to every man in both armies. "I curse every part of your foul being from the hairs of your head to the soles of your feet. I curse your loathsome soul and consign it to the deepest pits of hell. I doom you to be torn apart by Lucifer's hounds, I condemn you to the torture of Satan's endless flames, to the perpetual agonies of eternity."

Snorri screamed back, calling on the frost-giants of Niflheim to tear his rival from limb to limb with their dread axes of ice. "Let the gods hear his screams!" Snorri shouted as he raised his empty eyes to the sky. "He is pus from the arse of the Corpse-Ripper, so let him be destroyed. I call on you, Odin! I call on you, All-Father! Kill him now! Kill him!" He held his wolf skull toward Ieremias, and for a heartbeat I held my breath, thinking to see the mad bishop fall.

He did not fall. "I live! I live! I live!" Ieremias called triumphantly. He was capering again, the ram's skull teetering on the crook of his crozier. He went closer, much closer to Snorri, still screaming. "May worms gnaw your bowels and swine feed on your flesh! May cockroaches shit on your tongue! I curse you in the name of the Father, I doom you in the name of the Son, and I banish you from the living by the power of the Holy Ghost!" And on the last word he jerked his crozier fast forward, swinging it down from high above his head until it pointed toward Snorri. I think the gesture was simply meant to point the ram's skull at Snorri, but such was the force of the swing that the horned skull flew from the crozier's tip and struck the pagan sorcerer on his breast. The blind Snorri staggered back, more surprised than hurt, and as he staggered he let go of the rope leash, and the little dog, yapping happily, ran to Ieremias, who seemed just as amazed as his rival. "I win!" he called, unable to hide his astonishment, "God wins! The heathen is smitten!"

And Ieremias had indeed won. Snorri had been driven backward, and instead of responding with a curse of his own he was stooping and groping for his dog, but the dog had deserted Snorri and run to the mad bishop, who was cackling in triumph, and it was the dog's treachery that seemed to anger the watching Norsemen. They knew they were victorious that day, but Ieremias's triumph over Snorri was an insult to their pride, and suddenly the gate opened again and a stream of warriors came across the causeway while others leaped down from the wall, and almost every one of those warriors wore the gray wolf skin cape of the *úlfhéðnar*.

"Shield wall!" I shouted, and pain seared through my head. "Shield wall, now!"

Ieremias might have been half-crazed by the henbane ointment, but he retained enough sense to flee when he saw the enemy warriors coming for him. He ran toward us with the small dog scampering beside him. "The stone of David, lord," he panted as he got nearer, "throw the stone now! For the living Christ's sake, throw the stone!"

I kicked the soil and a scrap of stone, probably a chip from a block of Roman masonry, skidded away from my toe. I bent, picked it up, tried to ignore the stabbing pain in my head, and hurled the stone toward the enemy.

Ieremias shouted as I threw the stone. "We will win! We will win!" He pushed his way between the shields of my front rank to find a safety that I feared was merely temporary. He stooped, picked up the small dog, and beamed at me. "You believed me, lord! The stone of David is cast! We will win!"

But the *úlfhéðnar* were coming to kill us.

Then carry your willow-shields
Before you, and ring-mail coats too,

And shining helmets into the crowd of foes.
Slaughter their leaders with bright swords,
Their fated leaders. For your foes
Are doomed to die, and you shall have fame.
Glory in battle!

"I didn't say anything like that!" I told the poet.

"Well, lord—"

"It's a poem, I know."

"So what did you say to your men, lord?"

"Probably something like kill the bastards. Or keep the shields tight. You make speeches like that one," I tapped the parchment, "before a battle, not during it, but Sköll didn't give us time for speeches."

Father Selwyn frowned. "Ieremias," he said uncertainly. He knew the mad bishop was a heretic and he was uncomfortable talking about him. "Had he used the henbane, lord?"

"He stole it from my servant, and yes, he smeared it on his chest. He was shaking when he reached us, shivering and babbling. He collapsed behind us." I smiled, remembering the small dog licking the mad bishop's pale face. "I'm not sure the poor man even knew what he'd just done."

The priest frowned. "He'd provoked an attack by the *úlfhéðnar!*" he said disapprovingly.

"He had, yes."

"Did Sköll come with his *úlfhéðnar*?"

"No, he stayed on the wall and watched."

"How many wolf-warriors were there, lord?"

"Not many, sixty or seventy. There wasn't time to count them, we just had to fight them."

Later, much later, I learned that Sköll had been keeping his *úlfhéðnar* for the battle's end, saving their savagery for the slaughterous pursuit as we retreated, but Snorri's defeat had enraged them, and men who are under the influence of a sorcerer's potion are incapable of obeying orders. They are like hounds smelling blood, they just want to fight, and so the *úlfhéðnar* had simply charged through the open gate. No one ordered that charge, Sköll probably did not want it, but he was evidently content to let his crazed warriors make their headlong assault, knowing that even if his *úlfhéðnar* went down to a bloody defeat that would not change the battle's outcome.

"But surely he didn't want to lose them?" Father Selwyn asked me, puzzled.

"You can't control the *úlfhéðnar*," I tried to explain. "It's as if they're drunk. They believe they can fly. They believe they're invulnerable, and, believe me, such men can do an astonishing amount of killing before you put them down. They're usually the youngest hotheads, men who want reputation, men who want to boast in the mead hall of their exploits. Sköll probably didn't want to lose them, but it would only add to his reputation if they panicked us. I remember looking at him as they charged, and he was laughing."

Sköll was laughing, and his men, up on the walls, were cheering. This was a spectacle, a crazed charge by drugged warriors, a revenge for Snorri's defeat. Not every man who came toward us was an *úlfheðinn*, some other young men had joined the madness. There were probably about a hundred warriors altogether, most of them in the gray cloaks, though some were bare-chested, and many of them came without either shields or helmets. They believed they could not be harmed because the henbane had given them the courage of the insane.

And we made the shield wall.

Which meant it was discipline against madness.

Rorik had brought me a dead man's shield and I tried to stand in the front rank, but Finan unceremoniously pushed me to the third rank. "You're not recovered, lord." He did the same to Sigtryggr, who was unable to hold a shield, then turned to look at the approaching men. "Shields up!" he shouted. "And use spears!"

The charging men screamed. I had an impression of wild faces, unbound hair, mouths open, fierce eyes, long swords, and then the leading men leaped at us. Was it because they believed they could fly? They leaped as if to jump over the front rank and were met by spears. I saw a savage-faced man screaming at us, jumping at the men in front of me, and Beornoth just lifted his spear and impaled the Norseman. The man, still screaming as blood appeared in his mouth, slid down the long shaft to be met by a sword cut that ended the scream abruptly. Another *úlfheðinn*, wielding an ax, beat down two of our front rank, screamed his triumph, and waded into the second rank where three men hacked him to death with swords and axes. He was not the only man to break the wall, but those crazed warriors who threw themselves at our shields had no one to support them. Sheer impetuosity split our shield wall in places, but the wall closed up relentlessly. Then it went forward. Finan was bellowing the order, "Forward! Forward!" And still the *úlfhéðnar* came, slamming into us, screeching and flailing, and still we went forward, step by step, slipping on blood-slicked grass. A bare-chested man hurled an ax at our wall and the big blade split a shield in two and the man followed with no weapon but his hands, clawing at Beornoth whose shield was splintered, and my son killed him with a vicious upward thrust of his seax. "Close up!" Finan shouted. "Close up! Keep going!" Men stepped over the blood-laced bodies of the dead, and still the wolf-warriors fought. It usually took two men to defeat each, one man to take the attack of ax, sword, or spear on his shield, and the other to kill. Some of our men seemed infected by the madness of the *úlfhéðnar*. I saw Redbad break out of the front rank and slam an ax down on a charging man, splitting his skull in a mist of blood and brains. My son hauled Redbad back, the shields touched, and the wall went forward again. Immar Hergildson, who I had taken care to keep in the rearward rank because he was not as well trained as most of my men, had somehow worked his way to the front and was screaming defiance. I saw him slice down with his sword, saw him kill a second man, and saw the battle-joy on his young face. Sigtryggr's men who had been facing the ramparts where Svart had died were running to join us now. We were advancing down the long wall between the western and northern towers, driving back the survivors of the mad brave charge.

Not all the enemy were mad and some lost their bravery. They saw their companions die, they smelled the blood and shit of dying men, they saw the grim wall of shields coming, a wall glinting with spears and swords. The right-hand end of that wall was being assailed by

spears thrown from the ramparts, and I shouted for
Cuthwulf. "Use your arrows on them!" I called, pointing at the men throwing the spears.

"All of the arrows, lord?"

"All of them!" I had realized that we had no chance
of overcoming the fort's walls. There were too many
defenders. Even if the northern corner was easier to
approach, we would still face a rampart packed with
warriors. We would have to be content with this small
victory over Sköll's vaunted *úlfhéðnar*, though once
they were killed it would be our turn to face the slaugh-
terers.

Our shield wall advanced inexorably, step by slow
step, to drive Sköll's men back, and Sköll, it seemed,
decided enough was enough because a horn sounded
urgently from the ramparts, a signal to recall the surviving *úlfhéðnar*. Most of the wolf-warriors ignored it,
too crazed to abandon the fight and too crazed to obey
an order, and so they kept trying to break our wall,
kept stabbing and screaming, and the screams turned
to cries of agony as they were cut down. But some few
turned to retreat, and most of the young men who had
joined the charge of the *úlfhéðnar* also obeyed the summons. They ran back to the gate.

And it was closed.

Men beat on the gate. It did not open. Maybe half

the men who had charged us were now bunched at the entrance, screaming at its defenders to let them in. My son saw the opportunity before anyone else and shouted, "Kill them! Kill them!" He broke out of the shield wall, and, followed by his closest companions, charged at the gate.

The mad bravery of the *úlfhéðnar* can turn to terrified panic in a heartbeat. Men who a moment before had thought themselves unbeatable were suddenly turned into sobbing, desperate fugitives. They beat at the gate, they screamed for it to be opened, they screamed even more when my battle-maddened men began their slaughter on the causeway that crossed the ditches. I was hurrying after them, all of us were going toward that gate, and I looked above the arch to the fighting platform where I expected to see Sköll's men hurling spears into our ranks.

And instead I saw the eagle.

And men fighting.

Almighty God
Lord and ruler, gave them wondrous aid.
The valiant heroes with their precious swords
Then hacked a bloody passage through
The host of foemen; they split the shields,
Cut through their shield wall.

"Almighty God?" I asked.

"The archbishop asked for the poem, lord," Father Selwyn said very primly, "and I don't think he'd be pleased if I gave the credit to Odin."

I grunted. "I suppose not. But you don't even mention the eagle!"

"I do, lord!" he protested, then leafed back through the pages. "There, the white-tailed eagle—"

"Not the bird," I said, "the flag! The spread eagle! Berg's banner!"

"Was that important, lord?"

"Of course it's important! Didn't you even talk to Berg? Or to his brothers?"

"No, lord."

"The flag was flying over the shut gate," I said, "and all three brothers were there. You should talk to the oldest, he's a poet."

"Is he, lord?" The young priest sounded distant, as if he did not like hearing about a rival poet.

"He's called Egil," I said. "He's a skald and a fighter and something of a sorcerer too. He's a remarkable man."

"He certainly sounds so, lord," the priest said, still distant. "You say the flag was over the gate?"

"Berg was waving it."

The gods do play with us, and, like children, they

love surprising us. I could almost hear their delighted laughter when I saw Berg desperately waving his precious flag. I had no idea what it meant at that moment, for a heartbeat I even thought he had joined Sköll's forces, but then saw that the men around Berg, those men high on the platform above the gate, were throwing spears at the lower ramparts. They were throwing spears at Sköll's men, not at us, and at that moment I knew the curse was lifted. The pain in my head and the ache in my thigh did not matter because Berg's banner, the spread-eagle banner of the Skallagrimmr family, was flying over Heahburh.

When Berg had vanished at the battle's opening the banner had disappeared with him, and I had feared he was dead or a captive, but the truth was much stranger. The gods loved Berg, which made it odd to remember that when I had saved him from death on a Welsh beach I had promised King Hywel I would let the Christians try to convert him. I had kept that promise, but Berg had never succumbed to their persuasion, and ever since the gods had rewarded him. Berg was lucky.

And never more so than on that day at Heahburh. He had thought he was dead when the first surprise attack came from the fog and he was almost overwhelmed by Sköll's men. "I knew I couldn't reach you, lord," he told me after the battle, "so I ran down into the valley.

I was going to keep running, but heard my name being called."

"It was your brother?"

"Both brothers, lord!" Berg had two elder brothers, Egil and Thorolf, who, on the death of their father, had sent their younger brother to sail with a viking crew so he could learn the business of raiding, an education that had ended on the beach where I had discovered him. The older brothers, in the meantime, made farms on Snæland, that raw island of ice and fire in the stormy waters of the northern ocean, and it was there that they heard stories of a new Norse kingdom being carved from the coastal lands of western Britain. And so, leaving their families in Snæland, they had sailed with two ships and seventy-two men. "They only arrived a fortnight ago, lord," Berg told me.

"They want to settle here?"

"Sköll promised them wealth and land. So if they find good land? Yes, lord, I think they might bring their women too."

I was not surprised. I had been to Snæland, and life there was hard, the winters were cruel, and rich enemies were few, which meant plunder was scarce, and so the Skallagrimmrson brothers were restless, bored, eager for the sea and for new lands. Sköll had beckoned, they had come, and at Heahburh they had found their younger brother. "And you persuaded them they were fighting for the wrong side?"

"Yes, lord," Berg said, "but I think what really persuaded them was Snorri's defeat. Egil said that was a sign from the gods." He hesitated, plainly about to add something, then decided it was best left unsaid.

I guessed what he was reluctant to say. "And you promised your brothers I'd give them land and wealth if they fought for me?"

He had blushed. "I just said you were generous, lord."

Egil Skallagrimmrson's men had been charged with defending the northern section of the wall, from the gate to the tower, and they had let the *úlfhéðnar* loose by opening the gate after Snorri's defeat. "If the wolf-men defeat your Lord Uhtred," Egil had told Berg, "we will know what the gods want." And it had become clear that the gods did not want the *úlfhéðnar* to win, and so Egil had shut the gate and kept it barred as my son's men hacked and speared their way through the survivors of the crazed charge. Sköll realized too late what was happening, but as soon as he understood that Egil's men had turned on him he began the fight I had seen on the ramparts. And while Egil fought off Sköll's men, Thorolf Skallagrimmrson opened the gate to mine.

We were inside Heahburh. My son was first. His

men pulled away the bodies that blocked the gate, then helped to haul the great gates open before bursting into the fortress. We followed, climbing over the *úlfhéðnar* corpses that were strewn on the causeway, then going into the narrow lanes between the Roman barracks. I could hear women screaming, children crying, dogs barking, and horses whinnying. The barracks still mostly had stone walls, though the walls were much patched with timber and all were now roofed with turf rather than tiles. Some were being used as stables, others were sleeping quarters, one was a storehouse of grain, another was heaped with silver ingots, and we now fought past all the buildings and through some, though Sigtryggr, his left arm lamed, and I with my blurred sight and wounded leg could not keep up with the younger men who were surging through the alleys and screaming like fiends as they cut down an enemy who had never expected us to pierce their defenses. I found one of Sköll's men dying in a doorway, his guts spilled onto horse dung. "Lord, lord," he called to me, and I saw that his sword, a cheap blade, had fallen from his hand. I edged it nearer him with my foot and his hand closed around the hilt. "Thank you, lord," he said. Oswi, coming behind me, slashed his sword across the man's throat.

"He was dying," I said.

"That's seven, lord," Oswi had not heard me, and would not have cared if he had. He ran past me, eager for his eighth victim.

"Lay down your weapons!" Sigtryggr shouted, and some of his men took up the shout. Berg's brothers and their Snælanders had stayed by the gate, anxious not to be mistaken for Sköll's men by our vengeful warriors. Discipline had let our men defeat the *úlfhéðnar*, but that order now vanished in a horror of slaying. Our men filled the alleys with rivers of blood. I smelled the stink of gore. I saw men hacking at corpses, screaming as if they were themselves *úlfhéðnar*. I called on them to make shield walls, to defend themselves against a desperate, panicking enemy, but they were men who had expected to die, and they took revenge for that despair by killing in a fury.

Most of Sköll's warriors were still on the fighting platforms of the ramparts, above the slaughter in the fort, but even those men began to surrender. Berg, who was known to my men, had left his brothers and was shouting at the enemy to drop their shields and swords, and Sigtryggr was calling the same encouragement. Some men leaped from the walls onto the outer ditches, but Sihtric of Dunholm, whose men had been on the far left of our shield wall during the failed assaults, had stayed outside the fort, and those defenders who tried to escape were either killed by the men of Dunholm or else meekly gave up their weapons.

I remember my father saying that nothing is certain in battle except death, which makes battle resemble life itself. Be ready for surprises, my father had preached. Be ready for the spear thrust that comes under the shield, be ready for the ax blade that hooks over the shield's rim, be ready for everything, he liked to say, and you will still be surprised. I had been surprised by Berg's survival, by the unexpected help of the Snæ-landers, and now I was surprised by the speed with which Sköll's vaunted army collapsed. The fighting died suddenly, as if men were exhausted by the slaughter. The killing-fury of my men was sudden and vicious, but then they began to realize they had won and that to go on killing was to risk being killed themselves. Sköll's men laid down their shields when they sensed the fury was past, and men from both sides greeted each other. Many of Sigtryggr's warriors and a good few of mine were Norsemen, and, like Berg, were finding men among the enemy that they had known years or months in the past. I saw Vidarr Leifson embrace a bloodied enemy who, moments before, had been trying to kill him.

Only Sköll, his sorcerer, and his closest household warriors were left, and most of those men, some of them wearing the gray cloak of the *úlfhéðnar*, showed little desire to fight. They had lost and they knew it. I knew Sköll himself would not give up, but the only remaining thing worth fighting for was to make Snorri's prophecy come true; that two kings must die. Sköll might have lost this day, but he could still retrieve some pride and make a reputation out of the disaster.

And so he came to find us. To find us and to kill us.

Sigtryggr had joined me at the center of the fort where an open space made a wide square in front of the largest building, which I assumed had been the Roman commander's quarters. He had grinned at me. "How's the leg?"

"Stiffening. Your arm?"

"Numb." He turned and frowned as men started to shout. The sound grew louder, and it could only mean that Sköll was coming and that to the Norse this was more than a contest, it was an entertainment.

Finan led his men into the square and frowned when he heard the shouting. "They're drunk," he said.

"Probably." Sigtryggr watched the alley opposite us. More and more men were coming from its shadows to line the edges of the open space. "He's coming for a fight, isn't he?"

"He is," I said.

"And you let me fight him," Finan insisted.

"No," Sigtryggr said.

"Your shield arm, lord King—"

"I fight with a sword," Sigtryggr interrupted him, "not a shield."

"Stiorra!" I said, and they both looked at me. "For my daughter's sake, he's mine."

"No, lord!" Finan said, and just then men parted on the far side of the square and Sköll appeared with Snorri. The blind sorcerer was plucking at Sköll's arm, talking low and insistently. Sköll seemed to be listening, but then saw us, stopped, and put a hand over Snorri's mouth to silence him. He stared at us for a moment, and then, very slowly and very deliberately, he drew his great sword, Grayfang.

The excited shouts died. Sköll, aware that every man watched him, stepped into the center of the square. He wore his great white fur cloak over unscarred mail. His helmet shone, ringed with the gold of the kingship he claimed and crested with a wolf's tail. He held Grayfang in his right hand, and with his left he guided Snorri so that the two of them stood at the center of the circle of men. He looked at Sigtryggr, then at me. "Who do I give the sword to?" he asked.

We were all so surprised by the offer to surrender that, for a heartbeat, no one answered. Then I found my voice. "To King Sigtryggr," I said, "of course."

"Lord King," Snorri said, pawing at Sköll's arm, "lord King!" The sorcerer's eye sockets were shadows.

"Quiet, my friend," Sköll said, patting Snorri's shoulder. The sorcerer was shaking slightly. He wore long, grubby white robes. He had lost his wolf's skull and seemed bereft without his small dog. "All will be well," Sköll told him, then looked at Sigtryggr. "I have one thing I must do before I give you the sword."

"One thing?" Sigtryggr asked, puzzled.

"Just one," Sköll said, and with that he took one pace away from Snorri, turned quickly, and struck with Grayfang. Snorri had no warning. One moment he stood, frightened, then Sköll's blade slashed across his throat with sudden savagery. Sköll kept the sword moving, driving it and pulling it back to saw Snorri's gullet, and he opened the sorcerer's neck to the spine. Snorri's long white hair and plaited beard turned red. He made no noise, he just fell, crumpled, a mess of blood, hair, and robes. An astonished gasp went up from the men watching. For a moment Snorri's body twitched as his blood soaked into the earth, and then he was still. "He failed," Sköll said. "What use is a sorcerer who fails?"

"Give me your sword," Sigtryggr said coldly.

Sköll, who seemed to be the calmest man in Heahburh, nodded. "Of course," he said. He took Grayfang into his left hand, holding her by the blade just beneath the hilt, and walked toward Sigtryggr. And I could see the treachery. He was right-handed, yet he held the sword with his left, leaving the hilt free and his right hand empty. A drop of blood fell from Grayfang's tip as he walked toward us. He was smiling. "You won," he said to Sigtryggr, who took one pace forward to accept his enemy's sword.

And Sköll snatched the hilt with his right hand and swept Grayfang in a mighty back-handed slash that should have broken Sigtryggr's one good arm, except that the instant I saw Sköll's hand take Grayfang's hilt I stepped forward and shoved Sigtryggr hard so that he fell to his left, and I kept moving so that my borrowed shield crashed into Sköll and drove him back so forcefully that he tripped, and suddenly both he and Sigtryggr were on the ground.

And I drew Serpent-Breath, her long blade hissing as she came from the scabbard's throat. "He's mine!" I shouted, because both my son and Finan had started forward, and Sigtryggr, recovering from his surprise, was climbing to his feet. I stepped forward, ignoring the pain in my left leg, and I kicked Sköll's booted foot. "You're mine," I said.

"Stupid old man," he snarled. He was still on the ground, but tried to swing Grayfang at me, but only hammered her into my shield's iron rim. "You want to die here?" he asked.

"You will die here," I said, and stepped away from him, letting him stand.

And I remember thinking that maybe Sköll was right; that this was stupid. I had dozens of young sword-skilled warriors who were faster and maybe stronger. Finan was old too, but he was still one of the most feared fighters in Britain. But I was Uhtred of Bebbanburg, and I had reputation, and the vanity of reputation made me want to kill Sköll. And I would kill him for Stiorra's sake. For my daughter, and the memory of her face gave me an anger that overcame the stupidity. It was a cold anger, underlaid with fear. Sköll was formidable, and, as he scrambled to his feet with the bloodstained Grayfang in his hand, he looked confident. "Keep your shield, old man," he sneered.

He had no shield. I let mine hang at my side, exposing my body, and stepped backward, away from him, as if I feared him. I exaggerated my limp. My mail coat was torn, and the bloody bandage around my left thigh showed, and I wanted Sköll to see it. I kept Serpent-Breath low.

"Your daughter screamed when she died," Sköll said. He was circling to his right, my left.

"I hear your son drools now," I said. I had heard no news of the son whose skull I had broken, but it seemed I touched a raw place in Sköll because he looked furious for a heartbeat and took three quick paces toward me. I did not move, reckoning his steps were a feint, and he went back again, but still moving to my left. I turned, deliberately wincing when my weight was on my left leg. My vision on that side was still blurred, but it was clearing. "Can your son speak?" I asked. "Or does he just make noises like a pig farting?"

Sköll said nothing, but I could see my words were hurting him. I could also see him trying to calm himself, trying to plan an attack that would devastate me. "Can your son control his bowels?" I asked. "Or does he spew shit like a drunken goat?"

"Bastard," was all he said, and he sprang at me, sword swinging from my left, and I simply stood and let the shield hang on my left and Serpent-Breath on my right, and because his swing had been aimed at my left leg and my shield now protected it, the blow was wasted. Gray-fang crashed hard against the shield's iron boss, but did no damage. The blow had been struck in anger, which made it futile, and Sköll knew it. He tried to disengage the sword from my shield by stepping backward, but I moved with him, then feinted myself by bringing Serpent-Breath up, and he twisted away from the threat, going back fast, and I laughed at him.

"When are you going to begin to fight?" I asked. Men at the edges of the square echoed my laughter, and that mockery galled Sköll, who came at me fast and angry, again swinging from my left, and the years of sword practice took control of me so that I did not need to think, but just parried with my shield or else with Serpent-Breath as he hacked again and again. I did not try to counterattack, but just defended, trying to judge his skill. I fought with the sword every day, matching myself against the best of my warriors, and Sköll, although he was fast and he was strong, was not nearly as fine a swordsman as Finan or Berg. He stepped back after six or seven massive blows. "Was that your best?" I asked him.

"You're a coward," he spat, "who fights with a shield against a man who has none."

"You told me to keep it!" I said. "But I don't need it." I let go of the handgrip so that the heavy shield fell from my arm onto the ground. "Is that better?"

Instead of answering, he attacked again, and again on my left, though both blows were easy enough to parry, then he attempted a lunge, quick and low, which I only just avoided by stepping to my right. Grayfang's blade slid by my waist, I heard it scrape on my mail's rings, and he jerked the blade up as if to sever my left arm, but there was not enough force in his outstretched arm and my mail stopped his blade. I turned away from the blow and stepped a pace back. "If you want the shield," I said, "pick it up. It's yours."

He took two paces back. He was breathing hard, watching me from beneath the gold-edged rim of his helmet. I had been judging his skill and he had been judging mine, though he must have realized that I had not yet made one offensive stroke. The watching men had begun to cheer as we fought, and they were cheering me, even some of the men who had been fighting for Sköll were joining those cheers. He was feared, not loved, and his terrifying sorcerer was dead, and Sköll himself would soon be dead. He knew it. Even if he killed me, his life would not be spared. The best he could hope for was a quick death and a reputation as the man who overcame Uhtred of Bebbanburg.

We were four or five paces apart as Sköll caught his breath. His attacks had driven me close to the southern side of the open space so I walked back to the square's center, again exaggerating my limp. He followed me, eyes narrowed, both hands on Grayfang's hilt, and I saw him glance at my leg. The watching crowd had fallen silent, but one man, an *úlfheðinn* judging by his gray cloak, called out for Sköll to kill me. "Slaughter the old bastard, lord!" he shouted.

"Lord King!" Sköll corrected him, and my men began jeering.

"Lord King!" they shouted mockingly. "Lord King!"

And I took one pace forward, lifting Serpent-Breath, and Sköll came for me. He roared a great challenge, a wolf-howl of defiance, and he put all his strength into a swinging cut that should have struck my left side, and I watched his eyes, saw them glance at my waist, and I guessed the massive swing was a feint, and, suddenly, with a quickness I had not seen in him before, he turned the sword in his hands so it was not coming in a wild hacking cut, but was a lunge to my right that would force me onto my weak left leg if I wanted to avoid it, and it did force me onto my left leg, but I had seen the feint, my leg was not as weak as Sköll believed, and I lunged in turn.

Sköll's lunge missed. Mine pierced his mail at his bottom rib. I felt Serpent-Breath break the links of his armor, felt her burst through the leather beneath, felt her grate on and then break the bone, and then I twisted her as she went deeper, and Sköll's face was already grimacing, he was trying to wrench his body away from the pain, and I kept Serpent-Breath twisting and turning, ripping flesh and bone, and then I barged

him with my right shoulder and he went down. I let go
of Serpent-Breath and let her fall with him. Sköll tried
to bring Grayfang back in a cut, but I stepped on his
right arm, then stamped my left foot on his face. He
was shuddering, and Serpent-Breath, still buried in his
body, quivered.

"Greet the Norns," I told him, "and give them my
thanks." Then I tugged Serpent-Breath free and Sköll
whimpered in pain, shuddered, and blood welled up
through the rent in his mail. I held the sword's bloody
tip at Sköll's throat. "Lord King!" I called to Sigtryggr.

"Lord Uhtred?"

"You want to kill the bastard who killed your wife?"

I heard Sigtryggr draw his sword. Sköll was staring
up at me, weakening. His eyes widened as Sigtryggr
lifted his blade. "Wait," I told Sigtryggr, then leaned
down and prised Grayfang out of Sköll's grasp. I threw
it toward Finan. "That," I said, "is for my daughter."

"No!" Sköll cried. "Please, no! Give me my sword!"

And Sigtryggr struck.

And so Sköll went to Niflheim where he is a feast for
the Corpse-Ripper.

Stiorra was avenged.

I think of my daughter every day. I have watched her
children grow and wept that she would not see them

become a man and a woman. I tell them of their mother and sometimes tears still glint in my eyes when I speak of her. The waves roll on Bebbanburg's long beach and the wind comes across the wild waters and I know she is somewhere in the afterlife. Not in Niflheim, nor in the Christian heaven, but somewhere. Ieremias tells me there is a blessed place for good pagans, a vale of soft grass and clear streams. "She's happy there, lord," he tells me, and I try to tell myself that he is not mad and that he speaks the truth. He goes nowhere without his small white dog that he calls Scarioðe, "Like Judas, lord, who betrayed his master."

I have added Sköll's flensed skull and Snorri's wolf skull to the masonry niches in Bebbanburg's Skull Gate. The skulls gaze blindly southward to where Northumbria's enemies will gather. The Norse still live in Cumbraland, but have sworn oaths to Sigtryggr. He is king of all Northumbria, but Egil Skallagrimmrson, whom I have come to treasure as a companion, tells me the Norse cannot be trusted. "Can I trust you then?" I asked him.

"Of course not!"

"But I do."

"That, lord, is because you are a fool. But I am a poet, and poets love fools."

I gave Egil and his brother good land north of Bebbanburg. They gave me their oaths because, Egil said, I had saved the life of his youngest brother. "We shall keep our oaths, lord," he promised me as we rode home from Heahburh. "Not that I care about Berg, of course. He's so ugly!"

I had laughed. Berg was a good-looking boy, while Egil was extraordinarily ugly, yet women seemed attracted to him like flies to blood, and soon there will be babies born in Bebbanburg with ears like bat wings and chins like ship prows.

And still the waves roll in and the wind blows, and one day, I know, a horseman will ride up the coast road and he will bring me news from far away, of the death of a king, and of an oath to be kept.

Wyrd bið ful āræd.

Historical Note

There was unrest in Mercia following Æthelflaed's death, though the siege of Chester (Ceaster) is fictional. Æthelflaed had wanted her daughter, Ælfwynn, to succeed her, but Æthelflaed's brother, King Edward of Wessex, swiftly placed Ælfwynn in a West Saxon convent and took the Mercian throne for himself. By then he had put aside his second wife (if we believe that he had a brief first marriage to Æthelstan's mother) and married Eadgifu, who gave him yet more sons, and thus, eventually, more possible claimants to his throne.

Æthelstan did have a twin sister, Eadgyth, and she did marry Sigtryggr. I confess to some regret for killing off the fictional Stiorra, but her death was necessary to bring Eadgyth into her proper place as Queen of Northumbria. That country, still independent, was troubled by Norse settlers on the western coast. Sköll is fictional, Ingilmundr and the brothers Egil and Thorolf Skallagrimmrson are not. "Heahburh" is Whitley Castle in Northumberland, and the battle I describe there is wholly fictional. Whitley Castle (sometimes known as Epiacum) is the highest fort built in Britain by the Romans and lies north of Alston just off the A689 close to Kirkhaugh (or you can reach it by following the wonderfully named hiking path Isaac's Tea Trail). All that remains of the fort are the earth walls and the extraordinary array of ditches that the Romans dug to protect the ramparts. All Roman forts were built to a pattern, it's sometimes called the "playing-card" design because the regulation shape of Roman forts was that of a playing-card, but to fit Whitley Castle to its high spur of land the Romans squeezed the playing-card into a lozenge shape, another feature that, with the outlying ditches, makes Whitley Castle unique. The fort was doubtless built to protect the lead and silver works among the adjacent hills.

The poetry fragments in Chapter Ten are my own, but try to imitate the form of Old English verse, while those in Chapters Eleven and Twelve are very free translations of existing poems. The first in Chapter Eleven ("War cries were loud") and second ("There was the clashing of shields") are from "The Battle of Maldon," a poem describing a Saxon defeat at the hands of the Vikings in AD 991, some seventy years after the fictional battle in the novel. The third ("Now they go forth") is probably earlier and is a conflation of two brief passages from the *Finnsburh Fragment*, which, as the name suggests, is all that remains of a much longer poem. The surviving fragment is only known now by copies of a seventeenth-century copy, also now lost, which describes a fight at a besieged hall. The first in Chapter Twelve ("Many a carcass they left to be carrion") is from a very short poem about the Battle of Brunanburh, which is quoted in the Anglo-Saxon Chronicle for the year AD 937. Rather than attempt a translation, I adapted Alfred Lord Tennyson's version, which he published in 1880 in *Ballads and Other Poems*. The second ("Then carry your willow shields") and third ("Almighty God, Lord and Ruler") are from a poem called "Judith" that tells the ancient story found in the extracanonical *Book of Judith*, which describes how the eponymous heroine beheads the Assyrian general Holofernes. The poem is probably from the ninth century, and, though the setting might be Israel, the battle descriptions (and much else) are thoroughly Anglo-Saxon.

Snorri's prophecy about the Dane and the Saxon joining forces will eventually come true, though not till

AD 1016, long past Uhtred's lifetime. The story of how the family lost Bebbanburg is wonderfully told in Richard Fletcher's book *Bloodfeud: Murder and Revenge in Anglo-Saxon England* (Oxford University Press, 2004). In Chapter Six I mention Father Oda, a Danish priest, and say he became a bishop. That is not a novelist's fancy. Oda's parents were Danes who, it is thought, came to Britain in the service of Ubba and then settled in East Anglia. Oda was converted to Christianity, became a priest, and was appointed Bishop of Ramsbury in the 920s. His story did not end there, he was consecrated Archbishop of Canterbury in AD 941, the first Dane to head the church in England.

The young Oda was probably a priest in Æthelhelm the Elder's household, but in time became a supporter of Æthelstan, whose chief rival for Edward's throne was indeed Ælfweard, whose mother was a daughter of Æthelhelm the Elder. The rivalry between Ælfweard and Æthelstan must wait for another novel. King Edward of Wessex, who claimed the title *Anglorum Saxonum Rex* and who is usually known as Edward the Elder, is overshadowed by his father and by his successor, but it is worth noting that Edward did much to unite the territories that would become England. He inherited Wessex from his father, conquered Danish-ruled East Anglia, and then annexed Mercia on the death of his sister Æthelflaed. That left only Northumbria. It is also worth noting that the unification of England was a West Saxon project, that it moved from the south to the north, and that whoever inherited the throne of Wessex would inevitably inherit the ambition for unification that had burned so fiercely in King Alfred.

War of the Wolf is set in the early 920s. Uhtred, though born a Saxon (his mother was a Saxon, his father an Angle, though for fictional purposes I usually conflate the two), thinks of himself as Northumbrian. He is surprised by the word Ænglisc, English, but that word will come to have real meaning during his long lifetime. Englaland, England, does not yet exist, but its birth, in blood, slaughter, and horror, is close. But that too is a story for another novel.

About the Author

B ERNARD CORNWELL is the author of over fifty novels, including the acclaimed *New York Times* bestselling Saxon Tales, which serve as the basis for the hit Netflix series *The Last Kingdom*. He lives with his wife on Cape Cod and in Charleston, South Carolina.

THE NEW LUXURY IN READING

We hope you enjoyed reading
our new, comfortable print size and found it
an experience you would like to repeat.

Well – you're in luck!

HarperLuxe offers the finest in fiction and
nonfiction books in this same larger print size and
paperback format. Light and easy to read, HarperLuxe
paperbacks are for book lovers who want to see
what they are reading without the strain.

For a full listing of titles and
new releases to come, please visit our website:

www.HarperLuxe.com